70001768171 9

Also by Peter Newman

The Deathless
The Ruthless

The Vagrant
The Malice
The Seven

Short Stories

The Hammer and the Goat
The Vagrant and the City

The Boundless

PETER NEWMAN

Harper*Voyager*
An imprint of HarperCollins*Publishers* Ltd
1 London Bridge Street
London SE1 9GF

www.harpercollins.co.uk

HarperCollins*Publishers*
1st Floor, Watermarque Building, Ringsend Road
Dublin 4, Ireland

First published by HarperCollins*Publishers* 2020
This paperback edition 2021
1

A catalogue record for this book is available from the British Library

ISBN: 978-0-00-822911-5

Typeset in Sabon LT Std by Palimpsest Book Production Limited,
Falkirk, Stirlingshire
Printed and bound in the UK by CPI Group (UK) Ltd, Croydon CR0 4YY

To Phil
For not letting go

CHAPTER ONE

Beneath Lord Rochant's floating castle was a great chasm in the earth. It was said that it had no end. From it, tendrils of misty essence rose, sometimes in thick belches, sometimes in finger-thin strands, but constant. Every castle of the Deathless was built above a crack in the earth such as this one, for only in these places was the updraught of essence strong enough to hold them in place in the sky.

In the past, a few people had tried exploring them, along with a couple of unfortunates who had fallen in by accident. None returned. And so, for a thousand years, all sensible souls gave the chasm a wide berth.

Lady Pari Tanzanite could be said to be many things, but sensible was not one of them.

She and her brother, Lord Arkav Tanzanite, dived down together, like twin stars in their glowing armour. Though it protected them and provided light to see, it also presented a problem: The tanzanite plates had been fitted to their bodies and given fine, curving wings designed to catch the currents and ride them. The armour wanted to fly, not fall. In fact, it was a common trick of the Deathless to use the strong currents around their castles to gain height for a hunt.

To compensate for this, both Pari and Arkav each held onto a length of chain that had been wrapped several times around a heavy chunk of stone. Unlike the tanzanite, the stone did not interact with the otherworldly currents, it fell as surely as if they weren't there, dragged down by gravity.

The stone had been provided by the Bringers of Endless Order, who had their own reasons for supporting the venture. Their theory had been sound, the stone more than heavy enough to pull Pari and Arkav along with it.

What they hadn't considered was how it might feel to inhabit the fragile flesh being acted upon by two opposing forces.

Pari had a good mind to educate the Bringers if they got back.

When, thought Pari. *When we get back. Oh yes, then I'll tell those masked fools a thing or two.*

Luckily her armour mitigated the worst of the aches in her arm. It was not so much that she didn't feel it, more that she was above the petty demands of her current body, able to note them but not be enslaved by them. Of more concern was the strain being placed on her wings. She turned her head to look at them, then at Arkav's. Though both sets trembled in a way she hadn't seen before, they seemed to be holding. She made a mental note to buy something extravagant for their Gardener-smiths if they made it back.

When we make it back. Stay optimistic, Pari!

The bravado had been easy when she'd been standing on the chasm's edge. Exalted in her armour, emboldened by it, she had decided that she would be strong for her brother. A petty part of her had enjoyed showing off to the Bringers as well. It was rare to see the mysterious figures outside of the context of rebirth, and informative too. When not united by the rules of ritual, they were as divided and flawed as everyone else.

Now though, reality was sinking in.

At some point, several lifecycles ago, Arkav's soul had journeyed where they were heading, as all their souls did when between lives. Somewhere down there, in that unknown oblivion, a demon had snared him and bitten off a piece of his soul, leaving a hole behind. And though most of Arkav continued to be reborn, life after life, there had been something missing since then. An absence that had become a kind of abscess, festering and damaging him from within.

They were going to get that piece of his soul back, to restore her brother to the brilliant, smiling man he'd once been. Either that, or die in the attempt.

And they could die here. Not just these bodies either. If their souls fell too far from the world, it was even possible that their Godpieces would not be able to bring them back. It was also possible that the demons waiting down below could steal their souls or tear them to shreds or . . .

Pari rolled her eyes. She was damned if she was going to let any of those things happen.

The walls of the chasm were smooth, pale grey and mostly featureless. It disguised how fast they were moving, and created the lie that, perhaps, they weren't really moving at all. She was grateful for the odd crack as it flashed past, as it provided evidence of their progress.

With effort, she looked back over her shoulder, and was

shocked to find she could no longer see the sky. There was only a distant blackness above, pinpricked by tiny points of golden light.

'Watch for our lights,' the lead Bringer had said. *'There will be seven, no more, no less. Only they will guide you home.'*

She'd been mustering her courage at the time and had taken their words at face value. But now she thought about it, there was some subtext here she wished she'd explored. Were the Bringers suggesting there might be other lights down in the depths? Tricks to lure the unwary? And if so, how did they know? Supposedly nobody had ever come back.

No, thought Pari. *The Bringers didn't say that. They said the last attempt to retrieve a piece of soul from the demons and rejoin it had failed. That isn't the same thing. I'll bet somebody did come back, and I'd also bet that the Bringers know more than they've told us.*

On they went, faster and faster, deeper and deeper, with no end to the chasm in sight. There were changes though. The colours of the essence strands were richer here, and she fancied that she could see the remains of shapes, as if, below them, someone were making fine pieces of essence art that slowly distorted as they rose.

Another realization: The chasm walls were getting further apart. She'd been worried about the opposite, of getting stuck or crushed or smashed to pieces if the chasm narrowed. But this was alarming in its own way. As the walls receded, so too did her sense of scale, of space.

They were falling through the mists now. It reminded her of flying through low clouds, except the ones here were more vividly coloured – purples and greens and yellows, rather than greys and whites – and that they seemed to slide round each other rather than mix together.

She looked across to Arkav, worried about how he would be faring, but her brother's face was turned away from her, his expression hidden behind the crystal helmet. He'd noticed something she hadn't: A silvery thread of essence, bright but small, travelling in the same direction as them.

What is that? she thought and as if in answer heard her brother say in wonder:

'It's a soul.'

It too was getting easier to see with the naked eye.

A soul? A human soul? A shiver went through her. *Is it aware of us? When did it die? Has it been falling alongside us since the start, invisible?*

The walls had gone from sight, and she didn't risk looking up again, for fear that even the dark above would be gone, and the Bringer's lights with them.

And things felt . . . different. Her instincts told her this, but she couldn't rationalize them at first. They were still moving just as fast, the rock punching a hole through the essence clouds as they plunged after it. But there, just visible through the mists, was a . . .

Pari had no idea what it was.

She wanted to say it was a wall but it was too thin to be a wall, and shadowy things were visible through it, thrashing about. She wanted to say it was a window, but its surface was in motion. She wanted it to be something fixed, solid, but she knew, deep down, that it wasn't.

It's like the surface of a lake. It's like the outer skin of a bubble. It's . . . And some old part of her soul knew exactly what it was because she'd been here before, many times, between lives.

It's a gateway.

And we're coming towards it awfully fast . . .

Pari wondered what would happen if they hit it. Would it catch them? Would they break on its surface or go through? She had no way of knowing what the right thing to do was. They were in uncharted territory. However, there were really only two options: Keep hold of the chain or let it go.

The Bringers had said that Arkav's presence would draw out the demon with the stolen piece of his soul, and so far, they had seen no demons. Given that neither of them was about to go back empty handed, that meant there was little to do but grip the chain tightly, and hope.

In the last seconds before impact, she thought she could hear something, hard to make out over the rushing of the wind in her ears, but definitely there: Voices speaking from the other side. Their whisperings were muffled by the gateway but not entirely blocked. Pari had just enough time to feel curious and then she was bracing herself.

The stone passed through the surface of the gateway without even a ripple. The chain just as smoothly. A second later Pari's gauntlet made contact. It felt as if she'd struck a flag being held at each corner by a group of servants. It formed around her fist like a second skin, then her arm, her shoulder, the surface of the gateway continuing to give, bending around her and Arkav, smothering, stretching, thinning. Tight.

There was a flash of light, followed by a tearing that she felt as much as heard, and then they were through.

Much of their momentum had been stolen by the gateway,

leaving them to drift on the other side. The stone no longer pulled at her arm, rather, it hung horizontally from the end of the chain, aimless. No currents of essence moved them here, no gravity. There were no colourful clouds. Nothing at all. She was neither flying nor falling, but floating, in a place without up or down, without rules.

Though her arm was a little stiff, she was otherwise unharmed. Arkav was still next to her, a blue-violet glow in the shape of a man. She raised her hand to him and gave a little wave.

There was the slightest bit of resistance in the air and, when she squinted, she could make out some weak essence vapours. Not enough to fly with, but perhaps enough to navigate in some way. They boiled away at her touch, giving her a shimmering aura.

She saw the same thing around Arkav when he waved back but his attention wasn't on her, it was on the gateway. Following his gaze, she realized that after they'd come through, the gateway had snapped back to its original shape, wobbling back and forth as it slowly shrugged off the violence of their arrival, settling. She couldn't see any cracks or tears. Whatever hole they'd made to come through had been sealed tight.

The silvery soul slipped through to join them. Though the gateway did not react visibly, she heard a noise, like the ringing of a large, dolorous bell.

On their side of the gateway, dark shapes clustered around the point of entry. She found them hard to classify. Like clouds crossed with Snakekin, crossed with Spiderkin, crossed with shadows. They varied in size. The smallest no larger than her leg, the biggest several times her size. As she looked around, she saw more of them, more than she could count. They fell upon the little piece of silver, snaring it, ripping it, fighting over the scraps.

Slivers of light slipped down many throats, each one squirming, alive with anguish. There was a last moment of fractured agony. Then it was gone.

Pari's heart wrenched at the sight.

The poor bastard didn't have a chance.

As soon as the creatures had finished devouring every last wisp, they began to gather around the edges of the light cast by her and her brother's armour. Their close proximity both repulsed and intrigued her.

And I know I've seen them before. Many times. And they've seen me . . .

They were the source of the whispers she used to hear between lives. On this side of the gateway they were louder but remained hard to make out. The creatures all spoke at once, muddying each other's words.

Nevertheless, they were using words. Normal, recognizable words. And after a while she could see that on their dark hides, there were many slits. Some like flapping gills, others like embryonic lips, struggling to open. For now, none of the creatures were coming closer. Most simply hung there, watching, while others circled the perimeter of her aura, as if looking for a way in.

She motioned for Arkav to let go of the chain. There was no need to say anything, her brother had always been able to read her intent. When he'd done so, she gently wound her chain around her arm, making a loop from hand to elbow as she winched in the stone. It came back easily, lighter than a kite.

Meanwhile, more of the creatures gathered, their whispering growing in intensity.

'Arkav, do you feel anything? Do you think your soul is being held by one of these . . .' she gestured to the dark shapes all around them. 'Demons?'

He shook his head. 'Not close by, but I do feel a tugging in my chest.'

'Which way is it tugging you?'

'I don't know.'

She experimentally opened her hand and waved it from left to right in front of her, like a paddle. There was resistance again, less than if she'd run it through a pool of water, but enough to make her body turn a little.

'Having fun?' asked Arkav.

'Of course. I always love going to new places.' She pulled her hand back again, and was gratified to find herself rotating to her original position. 'It would be slow-going, but I think we could swim through this place if we had to.'

He held up a hand for quiet. She soon realized why. The whisperings had ceased, and the creatures had stopped circling. The only movement, a rippling of fissures on their skin. They hadn't been prowling around her as she'd first thought, they had been filling in the gaps, arranging themselves around them to form an imperfect bubble of flesh, with her and Arkav in the middle. She had the horrible sense that something bad was about to happen.

Arkav must have felt the same because he'd shifted into a battle-ready stance. He wasn't armed. Priyamvada, High Lord of the Tanzanite, had forbidden him weapons until his condition had improved. Admittedly, when she'd given the order, she'd been sending Arkav on a diplomatic mission, rather than a dangerous foray into the unknown.

Pari readied the great chunk of stone, unsure whether to use it as a shield or to throw it at any creatures that got too close.

'It's coming,' said Arkav.

He didn't need to elaborate. She was very good at reading him too. *He means the missing piece of his soul is coming. And that means that whatever has it is coming too.*

Surrounded as they were by a writhing sphere of shadow-skinned monstrosities, they couldn't see anything approaching. Pari opted for cautious readiness, she and Arkav gathered for action, but neither of them moved. The creatures seemed to be taking the same approach.

Unified in tension, they all waited.

She felt it in her stomach first. As if she'd ingested some great and heavy meal that was sitting uncomfortably within. Then she noted the thin vapours around her shifting. It was slow, very slow, but she was moving. Not just her either, but Arkav too, and the living sphere of monsters, all of them were travelling at exactly the same speed, drawn along by some invisible force.

'Pari, I feel like we're in a trap.'

She adopted her sweetest, most sarcastic voice. 'Really? Such insight, brother. Whatever revelations will you come up with next?'

'We need to take control of the situation.'

'Can you be any more specific?'

'. . . No. I just . . . I need to get out of here! Now!'

And by that he means I need to do something brilliant.

She decided to experiment with the stone first. She threw

it towards the demons directly in front of her, keeping hold of one end of the chain so that she could pull it back if need be. Just as it had with the gateway, the stone passed through them without resistance. The demons neither moved nor reacted to the stone.

She let go of the chain, and that too passed through them and out of sight.

Fine. Let's try something else.

With a single stroke of her arms, she swam forwards, closing the gap between her and the demons. She'd noticed that they'd left a uniform space around her and Arkav, and wanted to see what would happen if she changed it. As the light of her aura intensified, she saw the bodies of the nearest demons begin to smoke. They writhed and wriggled, like a Purefish that had been pulled from a river, but they did not break formation.

Interesting. Our armour is poison to these demons just as it is to the ones in the Wild above.

She uncoiled the whip at her side and flicked it out so that the barb of sharpened tanzanite on the end would make contact. After many lifecycles' practice, her aim was perfect and the barb embedded in the demon's hide.

This time there was a reaction.

At the point of contact, she saw a section of the demon simply evaporate. Lines of light scorched outward from the initial wound, searing across its body, dividing it into separate chunks that burned and burned until there was nothing left. Beyond it she saw another piece of living dark, another demon, settling in to fill the gap.

She also heard whispers, quieter than before, but she was very close now and able to pick up the odd word.

'. . . *Fixed* . . .'

'. . . *Pain* . . .'

'. . . *Prisoners* . . .'

'Arkav,' she said. 'Come closer.'

He paddled awkwardly to her side. 'What is it?'

'Listen. Can you hear them?'

He edged still closer, and she saw the demons squirm even more. Time passed and Arkav said nothing. She knew he was attending to the demons and she dearly wished for his insight. However, she also knew they were still moving.

'Arkav?'

'I think something else is holding them here against their will.'

'I heard them say prisoners before. Do you think they're talking about themselves?'

'No. That's not right . . . I think that's how they refer to us.'

She looked at the nearest demon. 'I am Lady Pari, child of the Tanzanite Everlasting. If you can understand me, say something.'

'. . . *Burning* . . .'

'Sorry about that. If you let us out, we'll stop burning you.'

'. . . *Fixed* . . .'

Arkav shook his head. 'They can't let us out. They don't have a choice.'

'Don't make me feel sorry for these demons, Arkav. Things are bad enough as it is.'

His head jerked down and to the left. 'We're too late. It's here.'

* * *

Vasinidra had ordered the hunt but the castle was eerily quiet. No drums played. The castle did not sing. It was a liminal time, caught between mourning the death of the old High Lord and celebrating the rise of the new one: Him. Yesterday he had been Vasin, a lord of the Sapphire Deathless. Now he was head of the house, with a new name to go with his new title: High Lord Vasinidra Sapphire. Nobody knew quite how to behave, nor how to act on a hunting day without the ancient traditions to guide them. For all that, Vasinidra felt oddly calm. Usually, he was a bundle of nerves on the morning of a hunt, the anticipation growing until the release of flight and action. Today was different. He was different.

Long ago, the village of Sorn had made a sacrifice and it had gone unanswered. Because of that, many had died or been dragged into the Wild, and the Scuttling Corpseman roamed their land unchecked.

So many things to set right: Mother. The threat of the Scuttling Corpseman. Aiding House Ruby before it crumbles. Clearing up the mess Yadavendra left behind. What to do about the false Lord Rochant? For that matter, what to do about the real one when he emerges again? And do I truly trust Gada or Yadva to support me?

He paused for a moment. Without the drums, it was hard to know when he should leave. Then, his face split into a grin and he laughed aloud.

Whatever time I choose will be the right one. They will all keep pace with me now.

He was just about to go when he heard a familiar voice singing for entrance; his brother, Gada. Vasinidra waved him inside, and noted Gada was dressed as he was, in tight silks that would fit under their armour. His hair was pulled into a topknot, making the long face seem even longer.

'I won't keep you, High Lord. I merely wished to offer my congratulations again, and speak privately on a matter close to both our hearts.'

It was odd seeing Gada be so deferent but Vasinidra could not bring himself to direct his brother to do otherwise. This was one perk he would happily get used to. 'Thank you for your support, though in future, if you could act before Yadva hits me, I'd appreciate it.'

Gada's eyebrow twitched but his face remained solemn. 'Does it hurt badly?'

He nodded, remembering the violence that had preceded his promotion. His stomach ached where she'd struck, his neck felt tender, and with the pain came a memory, of being lifted off the floor by Yadavendra, his predecessor. His uncle.

'I suspect the bruises will follow me to my next lifecycle.'

'Ah.'

'What was this other matter?'

'Mother, of course. How is she?'

'The years have been hard on her, but she endures. She's in Sorn. After we've dealt with the Corpseman, I'm going to bring her home.'

'Might I counsel you to wait. Her return will be even more controversial than your new name, and you have only just taken power.'

'She's suffered long enough, brother.'

'Oh, I don't mean that she should linger in the Wild. I'm just counselling that we bring her in quietly. That way we can choose the best time to break the news to the others.'

'That would be a different kind of torture. She is innocent, and I will make that clear to the house.'

In times past, he knew Gada would argue, but he simply nodded. 'You know that I stand with you.'

'I know and am grateful. Now, are you ready?'

'Yes.' He turned to go, then stopped by the door. 'I am proud of you.' He cleared his throat. 'In the past I may not have treated you with the proper respect. That is, I have not always done right by you. I may even have given up on you for a while. For once, I'm happy to be proven wrong.'

Vasinidra crossed the room and embraced Gada. 'I'm going to need cautious heads to advise me in the years ahead. And sometimes I'll need someone to hit Yadva with a giant stick.' He patted Gada on the back. 'I'm glad I have you, brother.'

The weak smile came back, but it didn't irritate Vasinidra as much as normal.

'Is it time to hunt, my High Lord?'

'Yes, Lord Gada, it is time to hunt.'

Satyendra scowled as he wound his way into the depths of Lord Rochant's floating castle. He'd woken that day with a headache. Or the equivalent of a hangover. Or perhaps both combined. The headache part had come from having his skull smashed against the hard floor of the throne room by that monstrous beast, Yadva. The hangover part was more of a come-down, the low that inevitably followed a great high.

When Yadavendra, the High Lord of the Sapphire and great thorn in Satyendra's side, had been disgraced in front of the house, he had felt the man's shame and fear. Literally felt it. Felt it and tasted it and drunk it down until it had filled him up. For a brief ecstatic time, he had been strong, powerful, quick. The best that he could be. That power had enabled him to stand toe to toe with the strongest of the Sapphire Deathless and hold his own. Nevertheless, raw strength was not enough when faced with multiple lifetimes of experience, as Lady Yadva had taught him most painfully.

The worst of his injury had already healed. But, as his fractured skull had slowly popped back into shape, it had weakened him. Whatever power he had stolen from Yadavendra had been used up to save his own life.

He was hungry now, and grumpy. And he knew just what to do to feel better again.

Down he went, below the level of the castle's walls, into the areas excavated from the great slab of rock it sat upon. No sunslight could reach down here, and for that he was grateful. Where everyone else drew comfort from the three suns, he found them unpleasant. Much better to be in the shade somewhere, preferably without the endless chatter and babble of others.

Veins of the purest sapphire cut through the rock in places, shedding a soft blue light. It was said that the crystals on the outside absorbed the energy of the suns over the day and then fed it throughout the structure, providing heat and light within. Perhaps that was why Satyendra didn't like them much either.

It wasn't just the sight of the glowing crystal, it was the sound as well. The castle talked. Constantly. Oh, everyone knew that on hunting days or times of great celebration, the castle would sing in response to the music of its people. But what most people did not know was that it was always making some noise or another. Sighing to itself, humming, communing in some way with the essence below and the suns above.

Satyendra knew.

And he hated it. The sound grated in his ears and set his teeth on edge. Though the light was lesser here, there was nothing to distract him from the castle's whisperings. He wondered if the castle was aware in some way. Sometimes it felt like it was watching him, and that it disapproved.

On he went, to a little pocket of rocky chambers that sat in a space between the veins; dull, grey, and lifeless. Perfect.

Some of the chambers were used to store food that needed to be kept cool. Others were used as cells, dark places to hold those who had fallen out of favour. Satyendra made his way towards one of these.

He saw a guard in House Sapphire livery coming the opposite way. She had a lantern in one hand. A pitiful little shard of blue on the end of a chain. When she came to a stop, it swung towards him, making him grimace as the light washed over his face.

'My lord,' she said, saluting. 'Have you come to see the prisoner?'

He nodded. Lord Rochant was known to be a man of few words, though he was also known to be possessed of surpassing eloquence when the need arose. Satyendra found it much easier to fake the former.

'I've just brought him some food,' added the guard. 'If I may, my lord, he's very sorry about what he did.'

Satyendra kept his face a passive mask. 'How do you know this?'

'He told me so. Begged for a chance to make it up to you.'

'I thought he was gagged.'

'Well, he is, my lord. I have to take it off to feed him.'

He paused for a moment. The guard was getting nervous, just enough to make his blood stir and take the edge off his headache. He knew it was wrong to treat her this way, and he knew his hunger could take him to dark places, but he was too weak to resist. *I'll draw it out just a little,* he told himself. *An appetiser to keep me going*. 'Do you recall my orders?'

'Yes, my lord.'

'Recite them to me.'

She swallowed hard. 'You said . . . to bring Pik here and . . . bind his mouth.' When he didn't say anything, she continued, 'And that you'd deal with him after the celebration of your rebirth had ended.'

He nodded again, sharp. 'And what else did I say?'

'My lord?'

'It's a simple question: What else did I say?'

He watched her frantically try to recall. Her embarrassment was like the first smells of a cooked dinner, the shred of fear bubbling beneath a sneaky taste of the sauce before the food was served. After a few painfully delicious moments she shook her head. 'I'm sorry, my lord. I don't remember.'

'I said that we were to forget that he existed.' She nodded hurriedly as if to say: *Of course! That was it! It was on the tip of my tongue!* 'If he tries to talk when you feed him, we must withhold his food. He has betrayed us. I do not want to hear what he feels or what he thinks. I do not even want to hear his name. Do you understand?'

'Yes, my lord. I'm sorry, my lord. It won't happen again.'

'Go to the entrance to this corridor and wait there until I return. See to it that I am not disturbed for any reason. Dismissed.'

She moved past him, then hesitated. 'You have no lantern, my lord. Would you care for mine?'

'Keep it. I have lived in this castle for many lifecycles and know it as I know myself.'

The awe in her eyes was pleasant in a very different way, and he savoured it as she marched out of sight. The truth was he knew the castle well because he had worked hard in his short life to do so.

It's better like this, he thought. *Fitting. To meet him in the dark where we both belong.*

Satyendra waited for the guard's footsteps to become distant echoes, and went inside. The cell was really a stunted hole with a door attached to one end. There was just enough room for one person and a bowl for their waste.

The prisoner, Pik, a teenager three years his junior, was still wearing yesterday's clothes and the stink of sweat was pungent. His wrists were bound and fixed to the wall, and his mouth was gagged. Satyendra could well imagine Pik's stupid face. Often worried. Sometimes smug. Always dominated by that ridiculous nose.

He had seen that face many times in the courtyard when they had trained together. Like him, Pik had been an apprentice hunter. He had also been a spy for his mother and had betrayed his secrets to her. He owed Pik a horrible revenge, but first he would get some sustenance from him.

'Now,' he began. 'What are we going to do with you?'

There was muffled sound as Pik tried to respond through the gag. Satyendra ignored it. 'Usually, a traitor would be cast out. Either sent back to the road-born in disgrace or into the Wild to die.'

The mere mention of the Wild was enough to set Pik's heart racing. His chains clanked in time with the trembling of his limbs. As the sweet fear rose into the air, Satyendra inhaled deeply.

Ah, yes, that's more like it.

'I cannot send you back to the road-born. They are my people and I love them too much to insert a nasty little Wormkin like you into their lives.'

His headache from earlier was completely gone now. The lethargy with it. He could feel his mood lifting, his body filling with energy, his bones starting to wake.

It was tempting to do something truly horrible, like stab Pik or pull out some of his hair. The emotions he could stir! But he held off. Such crude methods would provide a hearty meal but he wanted something more nuanced, something closer to what he'd enjoyed from Yadavendra. He also held off to make sure he still could. The desire to hurt, physically hurt, pulled at him like a master tugging on a leash. Deep down, he was as scared by it as he was thrilled.

'I have, however, decided to be merciful and spare you the Wild.'

A sudden spurt of hope mixed in with the boy's fear. The new emotion did not dampen the old one, it heightened it, like a hint of sweetness in a sharp drink, enhancing both flavours.

Better. I'm getting closer to it. Now to build him up just a little more before the twist.

Pik was holding his breath.

'Even you don't deserve that.'

The breath was let go in an explosive mumble of gratitude. Probably some kind of thanks or obeisance.

'No,' he continued, 'you lack the spine for it. The Wild would finish someone like you too quickly for it to be a true punishment.'

He felt a fresh surge of panic smother the hope, mixing with it and the older despair, making layers, giving texture. His mouth began to water.

'Tonight, when the suns have set—'

A song outside the door interrupted him. Immediately, the mood shifted, the perfect tension becoming something not quite so perfect. He ground his teeth in frustration, and also fear. What if he'd been overheard by one of the older staff, or worse, one of the many Deathless currently in residence? They would find his behaviour suspicious, out of keeping with the real Deathless he was impersonating.

'My lord?'

It was the guard's voice. As soon as he recognized it, his fear flipped into frustration. *Can she not follow one simple instruction!*

He opened the door and stepped out so abruptly that she nearly dropped her lantern. 'What did I say? What did I say just moments ago?' He was aware he was doing a poor job of imitating Lord Rochant's legendary patience but couldn't stop himself. 'Was I not clear enough? Should I have the Cutter-crafters carve it into your forehead?'

'I—No, my lord, you were most clear. But Win came down to see me himself. You've been summoned by High Lord Vasinidra.'

'And it couldn't wait for a few minutes?'

She looked appalled, then said in a voice high with tension,

'He said you were to go now, my lord. It's not my place to say but . . . it sounded urgent.'

The rushing in his blood calmed, allowing sanity to return. *Even Lord Rochant cannot be seen to disrespect his High Lord. Especially him. Why was I cursed to be descended from the loyal, clever one?*

He shut the door behind him.

'Very well. I will go to him directly. Keep the prisoner gagged until my return.'

He turned away before she could respond.

As he made his way back towards the light, he decided that the day had still got off to a good start. He felt strong, energized. Even the brief encounter with Pik had done much to rejuvenate him. Yes, his moment had been spoiled but, perhaps, it was for the best. *How far would I have gone if she hadn't interrupted? Better that I keep away from Pik, for my own sake. Yes. It's better this way, for both of us.*

But even as he thought this he knew that, sooner or later, he would return.

CHAPTER TWO

The Wild closed in around Chandni. Silhouettes of trees and Birdkin blurred together to become a single creature: A darkness formed of compound eyes and feathers, leaves and branches, all focused on her. And somewhere ahead, a figure waited. Taller than a person should be, as tall as a Deathless exalted in armour. She couldn't see them any more, not truly, but their outline remained etched in her mind, a black line on a black canvas. It too was made of many things, of wings and hearts that beat together, pulsing in time with each drop of blood that ran from her forearm to fall from her deadened fingertips.

She had cut her arm on purpose. Three cuts for the three times she'd dealt with the Wild. One would have been enough to see her exiled but, for her child and her lord and the future of House Sapphire, Chandni had sold her honour again and again. Now her duty had been fulfilled. Lord Rochant's soul had taken residence in her son's body – *My poor, sweet, Satyendra!* – taken control of his castle once more. She was no longer an Honoured Mother, no longer required to run the castle, no longer needed. All that was left was for her to account for her sins.

Though she was afraid, she held her head up high, like a true Sapphire. That was how she had lived and it was how she intended to die. With dignity.

It felt as if she had been walking forever. Surely she should have reached the demon by now? Was it toying with her? Perhaps it wanted to crush her spirit before consuming it. Well, if that was the case, Chandni would happily disappoint.

For I will neither bend nor break.

She could no longer hear Glider's barking. The Dogkin had been left behind some time ago, along with Varg, and she prayed they were both safe. Her loyal friends had opted to come with her, even knowing she sought death. Even knowing it could mean their own.

I do not deserve their love, she thought, but it warmed her all the same.

Drip, went her blood, as it splashed on the earth and the roots. *Drip*, went her blood, into the gullet of something hopping alongside, invisible. *Drip*, went her blood.

Thud, answered the heart of the thing before her. Right before her now.

Too close!

She walked smack into it, was caught by long rustling limbs, wrapped in a cocoon of feathers. Darkness within darkness.

Thud-thud-thud-thud, went her heart, beating crazily against her chest. She was afraid. Terrified! But she would not show it. Not to this thing. It would have her life and nothing more.

Thud, went its heart, its chest warm against hers.

The Birdkin above and around them opened their beaks wide, and a voice, richer than she'd expected, issued from them: 'Be hushed, Iron Purebird. Be hushed and be welcome once more.'

Though she had been in the Wild before and met many terrible things, she was certain this had not been one of them. And yet, it did seem . . . familiar in some way. 'I think you may have mistaken me for someone else. I . . . My name is Hon-Chandni. I was once—' she shook her head and felt feather tips brush her cheek. 'It doesn't matter what I was.' She dug deep and summoned all her courage. The words she had to say were hard enough without being in the embrace of some kind of bird demon. Nevertheless, she managed them: 'I have come here to die. Will you help me?'

There was a pause, then a chorus of squawks, then:

'No.'

She blinked in surprise. 'What?'

'I may take your life as my own, but I will not end it.'

A thought occurred to her then. *I am here because I have traded with the Wild before. This is not some mindless beast here to kill me. It is a power of the Wild come to make a pact.* She suddenly realized there was much more than death to fear. 'If we are to negotiate for my life, what will you give me in return?'

'Whatever you desire.'

A chill ran down her spine. If it were just her alone, she would refute the demon. Thoughts of Varg and Glider ran through her mind. They had given so much to her, and she wouldn't allow them to suffer. *So easily do I consider a fourth deal.*

'Firstly,' she said, somehow keeping her voice even, 'and this is not part of the deal, I would have your name.'

'Yes,' it replied. 'You bear my mark, you have my favour, why not my name as well?' It was strange having this conversation. Though its words sounded all around her, like a chorus, she felt that the demon was right in front of her, that whatever it had for eyes were only inches away from hers. 'I am Murderkind, a Prince of this place, and we have dealt before, you and I. It was I who listened when you called out to the Wild. I who accepted your gift of blood and bone. And it was I who saw your child safe and strong. From babe to man.'

'That cannot be true,' she retorted, irritation suppressing her fear. 'I took my Satyendra with me when I left here and raised him myself, in a place beyond your power.'

'You speak true.' The Birdkin all paused to laugh. She wasn't sure if they were laughing or Murderkind was, but the laughter was unpleasant and aimed at her. 'Though your heart is deceived.' She felt it shift slightly, as if puffing out its chest. 'I raised your child. Here. In my domain. Raised and re-named, guided and armed, held and healed. All as promised.'

It was lying. It had to be lying. *Then why do I believe it?*

'You believe because your blood is in my beak and our hearts press too close for lies to slip between them.'

How does it know what I'm thinking?

The Birdkin all laughed again.

'You believe because you know the thing you took from the Wild was not truly yours.'

A memory came to her then, of the day Lord Vasin had brought her home in his carriage. As soon as they'd got onto the Godroad, Satyendra had started to scream. His skin had lost its colour, had bubbled, and his face . . . by the Thrice Blessed Suns, his other face! *All these years, I'd thought he'd been cursed by the Wild. But no. I gave my love to a . . . a thing?*

'A demon. A Whisper's echo.'

'But Lord Rochant has been reborn into it! What will become of him?'

'Again, your heart is deceived. The one you call Rochant, who is known to me as Bane-friend, is already in a man's body.'

'Wait, you're telling me that Lord Rochant does not dwell in the body of my son? That he has not just undergone a rebirthing in his castle?' The ramifications of this whirled through her mind. 'So the man who sent me to my death is not my Deathless Lord. And the boy I've given the best years of my life to is not my son.' She shook her head. 'He's not even human!'

It was her turn to laugh. She laughed and laughed, the sound bursting from her indecorously, which only caused her to laugh more. After a while, the Birdkin joined in. *They get it,* she thought.

Suddenly, the Birdkin stopped laughing, and her skin felt cold.

'This matters not,' said Murderkind, 'it is not the question that must be answered. Tell me, Iron Purebird, what is your desire?'

'I barely know any more. To . . . to make something good out of this mess and for my life to mean something. I want to keep my son, my real son, safe. And I want to help Varg find happiness. I want to redeem my soul.'

She felt herself being pulled deeper into an embrace. The scent of Murderkind was in her nose, musky and earthy, its feathers pressing on her lips. 'Be hushed, be hushed. Listen. How is it you cannot hear your own heart? Its tune clashes with your words, painfully.'

'What do you mean?'

'You want your son. You want to see him and hold him. You want to know what he has become.'

'Yes,' she whispered.

'You want Varg, as your mate and companion.'

Her cheeks blazed, but she did not deny it.

'You do not think of your house. You think of yourself.'

She nodded into its chest.

'You are angry.'

She nodded again.

'And you desire revenge.'

There were tears on her cheeks now. She rubbed them away on the demon's feathers.

Around her, wings rustled and Birdkin shrieked. Though she couldn't feel it, she was aware that her arm was still bleeding, the blood leeching slowly from her.

Murderkind rested its head against hers. 'Yes,' it said. 'We have an accord. Be angry. Be passionate. Be vengeful. And then, in return, your blood will be mine. Your body, mine. Your soul and all else within your flesh, mine.'

Chandni didn't say anything. She wanted to refuse, but she knew there was no point. Her heart had already said yes.

I am in a room, thought Sa-at.

In a castle.

In the sky.

Since his arrival in the dead of night, Sa-at had been through several rooms of different sizes and shapes. There was the kitchen where they'd arrived. Which was a lovely hot room full of wonderful smells. A stairwell, or as he thought of it, a twisting pile of rocks stacked most strangely upon each other. Several corridors, which were very long rooms that did not seem to be for anything at all, and lastly, the old cook's quarters.

This was smaller and colder than the kitchen. There was no food here and it smelled musty. In fact, the room was worse than the kitchen in every conceivable way Sa-at could think of. Despite this, it kept the wind out and them hidden from their enemies.

The cook, Roh, had left them here some hours ago to prepare breakfast for the inhabitants of the castle. There were many people here to celebrate the fake Lord Rochant's arrival. More than Sa-at could count. More than he could even imagine counting. Hunters, traders, servants, guests – including other Sapphire Deathless. It made his toes wriggle with excitement. All his life, he'd wished to know more people, and now it seemed that he would get that wish. Rochant had promised that, after they had got his castle back for him, he would introduce Sa-at to them all.

But there was much to do before that could happen. Sa-at didn't fully understand what, but he knew enough to know that it would be dangerous. He also knew that there would be bloodshed. Normally this would upset him but he was still too angry to be upset. The people who he would have to fight had killed his father and his cousins, robbed him of the chance even to get to know them. They had stolen

Rochant's name and castle, and done terrible things to the man's body. Sa-at remembered finding Rochant, half-starved, half-dead, and shuddered.

Despite Sa-at's best efforts, Rochant was still too thin, his frail body swaddled in thick layers of clothing and buried under several blankets. As if sensing his thoughts, the man turned his head towards Sa-at. The second of the suns, Vexation, was rising outside the window, giving Rochant a red tinged smile.

'Good morning.'

'Hello,' replied Sa-at.

'Have you been awake long?'

'Yes.'

'It's hard to sleep when your mind is full.' Rochant glanced at Tal, who was curled up next to Sa-at, snoring peacefully. He gave another smile.

Sa-at returned it. 'How does he sleep so much?'

'Rest will be a precious commodity for us. In his own way, Tal is wise.'

'What's going to happen now?'

'I'm going to think, Tal is going to sleep, and you're going to be quiet and enjoy the sunsrise.'

At first, Sa-at was frustrated. He didn't want to be quiet. He wanted to ask questions. So many questions! But when he went to the window and looked out, they blew away like petals in a breeze. He'd never been so close to the sky before. Instead of being above him, it was all around him. And the three suns were huge. Even Wrath's Tear, which was just coming up after Vexation, seemed to have grown. The walls of the castle glimmered wherever the sapphire veins peeked through, and when he rested his hands on the windowsill, he felt the stone thrum softly against his fingers.

He watched as the three suns rose together, the two red ones chasing the golden one higher and higher. Gradually he became aware that the castle was becoming noisy with the sound of people. Morning greetings, the bustle of many feet, it was all just out of view. Sa-at pressed his face against the glass but was unable to see anything below the tent tops that packed the main courtyard. These too were interesting.

It is called a tent.

It is made of hide.

A tent is a room made of hide.

Time passed. The initial buzz of people waking settled into a quiet hum of industry. Sa-at marvelled at all the different voices and wished he could make out what they were saying. More questions began to bubble in the back of his brain.

The snoring behind him became a snuffle, and then a yawn, and he turned back to see Tal stretching. The boy was taller than him, with pale skin and a noticeable lack of earlobes. Every time he saw them he was reminded of the day he'd saved Tal's life and Crowflies had eaten them.

Crowflies! He thought with a pang of panic. *I will come back for you. I will.* But that did not shake the memory of the Birdkin's distress nor the feeling of guilt.

Tal came over to stand next to him. 'You all right?'

'I'm sad.'

The boy put a finger to his lips. 'Ssh. Lord Rochant is still asleep.'

Sa-at glanced over. Though his eyes were closed, Rochant was most definitely not asleep. He could tell. He didn't contradict Tal though. Somehow it would feel like a betrayal of his secret understanding with Rochant. Instead he said, 'I'm thinking about Crowflies.'

'Ah.' Tal pulled a face. He'd never really liked Crowflies very much. 'How's your hand?'

'Okay.'

'Can I see?'

'Okay.' He held out his right hand and turned it over. In the centre of his palm there was a circle of raised white skin, completely smooth. Yesterday, a piece of a demon had been there, but when he'd stepped foot onto the Godroad, it had burned all traces of it from him.

It was already hard to remember how much it had hurt. The pain had been so intense it had become unreal in his mind, like a dream.

Tal frowned at the injury. 'Well . . . it doesn't look any worse.'

'You do.'

'What?'

'Look worse.'

'Oh, I'm tired. And my shoulders ache. And my arms. Well, all of me aches.'

'But you slept for aaages.'

'Doesn't feel like it.'

Rochant spoke quietly, but they both heard him clearly. 'Tal. Make sure my hood is covering my tattoo, then both of you hide.'

'Yes, my lord,' replied Tal, rushing forward. Each Deathless bore golden tattoos bearing their legend, and each set were unique, relating to their previous lives and deaths of note.

'Why hide?' asked Sa-at.

'Because Roh will be back soon, and she may not be alone.'

They had barely carried out his commands when the door opened and Roh stepped inside. She was brawny and old and slow, her brown skin full of wrinkles, her remaining teeth yellowed by time. But there was something about her that was not slow. Like Rochant, she often seemed to be one thing while really being another.

She carried a fragrant sack in one hand, and a heavy bottle in the other, knocking the door closed with her bottom. 'And how are we this morning, my good lord?'

'I'm well, thank you, Roh. What news?'

'Oh, lots of news. Lots of comings and goings. Everyone's always busy. Busy, busy.' She came over to his bedside, setting the bottle down. 'I'll tell you all about it as soon as you've had something to eat.' He looked as if he might protest but she kept talking, the pause so brief Sa-at wasn't sure if he'd imagined it. 'We need to get some flesh on those bones and some muscle under that skin.'

'Is that supposed to be some sort of joke, Roh?' He glanced down at himself. 'What use are muscles to me now?'

The old woman chuckled. 'Ah, well, that's one of me bits of news.' She took a steaming bowl from the sack and spooned out a portion. 'I'll tell you just as soon as you've had some of my Kinmix stew.'

Rochant's expression gave nothing away, but he opened his mouth and allowed himself to be fed.

Sa-at was confused. When he'd found Rochant, his torturers had taken away the use of his arms and legs. Poor Tal had carried him from down in the Wild, all the way up the mountainside, and up, through a secret gap in the walls to get here.

It seemed to take an age for Rochant to finish the stew. Roh attended him patiently as he chewed, always ready with the next spoonful. When they were done, she handed the half-full bowl to him and Tal, who set to emptying it with gusto.

'Bad news first,' said Roh. 'Honoured Mother Chandni's gone. I thought it was odd when she didn't come to see me yesterday. She always comes, same time every morning. As reliable as death, that one. Always comes when I ask, too. And be sure that I asked for her, made one of my lads send the message. Wanted to warn her about the imposter, I did.' Roh shook her head. 'But she'd already gone. Just walked out, so I'm told. No carriage, no bags. Like she was taking a stroll. Didn't tell a soul she was going neither.' Roh shook her head again. 'Not one soul. That's not like her. Normally she does it all proper,' she waggled a finger at Rochant, 'just like you. Oh, that imposter's behind it. I know it in my bones. He's weeding out the loyal ones. And old Roh will be next.'

'That's a shame,' said Rochant, and both he and Roh looked at Sa-at.

'What? Why are you staring like that?'

'I was hoping to be able to introduce you,' Rochant replied. 'To keep my promise.'

When Sa-at continued to look confused, Roh came over and put a gnarled hand on his shoulder. 'She's your mother, boy. One of the good ones.'

'My . . . mother?'

'I can see her in you, clear as day.' She glanced back to Rochant and tapped the side of her head. 'Takes after his father though.'

A look passed between them and Sa-at realized that they too, had some kind of secret understanding. This made him feel odd inside.

Chandni.

My mother's name is Chandni.

He'd never had a mother before. Never thought too much about it. But now he knew that he'd lost her, he suddenly wanted to see her. *Does she want to see me? Does she even know about me?* The absence felt keener because it had been hidden so long.

Rochant closed his eyes again. 'You said you had other news?'

'Oh yes, there's good as well as bad. Ever since the night of the attack, when Honoured Mother Chandni was poisoned, I been thinking about it. I kept some of that poison and tested it. Nasty stuff, it is. Severs the connection between body and soul. Might be a rebirth would see you right as rain.'

'I wondered this myself. Nidra told me that it wouldn't and I believe her. My soul no longer remembers its connection to my limbs. That will still be true even if I return a thousand times.'

'What if you could be made to remember? I helped Chandni where I could. Slowed the poison, stopped it. Couldn't cure it though. But she's just a woman with one life. Not like you. Her only memories are in her head.'

'Did you give some of your memories to the Corpseman?' asked Sa-at. 'Do we need to go and get them back?'

The mention of the demon's name had an immediate impact on the room. Tal looked nervous, as usual, and Roh's face folded in a most unhappy way.

Rochant's remained calm. 'I did not.'

'The poison comes from the Wild,' snapped Roh. 'Last thing we need is to get involved with them. Where did you grow up, boy? In a bush?'

'No, in a tree.'

'A tree!' She turned back to her master. 'I can't make head nor tail of this one.'

'Not now, Roh,' said Rochant softly. 'Tell me what you have in mind.'

For a moment, the unhappiness remained on her face along with a healthy dose of suspicion, but then it fell away to be replaced with a look of cunning. 'Your armour, my lord. It will remember you as you were. I'll bet my last teeth on it.'

'I feared that was your answer. It's no longer an option. They'll have remade it to fit the imposter.'

'So they did, my ever-quick lord. So they did. But I kept your old set in secret. Tucked it away for safekeeping the very night they stole you from us. Everyone was so busy trying to protect your line, they didn't even think about your armour. And by the time they did, it was too late.

'I'll need help to get it, mind. A couple of pairs of strong hands and quiet feet to sneak it back here.'

Sa-at and Tal suddenly found themselves the centre of attention.

'Go with Roh, both of you,' said Rochant. 'Do exactly as she says.'

Tal bowed and moved to the door.

'But,' said Sa-at. 'What about my mother?'

'I'll answer your questions about her when you come back,' replied Rochant.

'But, what if she's in danger? Roh said the imposter monster had got her.'

'No, an imposter isn't a monster. It's a way to describe a person when he pretends to be someone they're not. And she didn't say he'd got her. She said the imposter sent Chandni away.'

'But where? We need to go there.'

'We don't know where. Sa-at, listen: The best way to help her is to help me. When I'm in power again, it will be a simple matter to send people to find her.'

'But what if she's in trouble?'

'All the more reason to go with Roh now.'

Sa-at's shoulders slumped. 'Okay.'

It made sense. Rochant always made sense. He'd made sense when he'd told Sa-at to leave Crowflies behind. He'd made sense when he'd got Sa-at to stay on the Godroad, even though it hurt and burned. Sa-at just wished that things making sense didn't always have to be so hard. And now that he knew about his mother, he couldn't keep her out of his mind, nor could he shake the conviction that she was in trouble.

Satyendra paused outside the door. Technically, as the lord of the castle, he did not have to sing for entrance. But the person inside knew he was not really the lord of anything and he didn't want to annoy them. Before he could make up his mind a servant appeared and ushered him inside.

After announcing him, they left. He listened as their footsteps retreated down the corridor, then turned to his host.

High Lord Vasinidra had been expertly dressed and made up so that the marks of yesterday's fight could not be seen.

However, Satyendra could sense the man's discomfort, and that sense drew his attention to where the injuries were: A bruised neck, an injured stomach, minor scrapes on the knees and hands.

He bowed. 'You summoned me, High Lord.'

Vasinidra beckoned him closer. 'I haven't had a chance to thank you for yesterday. You showed great courage.'

Despite himself, he smiled. He hadn't thought of it that way, but yes, he had been fearless.

'Few people would dare to face Lady Yadva alone,' Vasinidra continued. 'And you . . .' he shook his head in wonder. 'She's twice your size, for suns' sake!'

'I had to act for the good of the house,' lied Satyendra. In truth he'd been drunk on power and desperate to enjoy its use.

Vasinidra's eyes softened. 'I know how it feels to be on the receiving end of my cousin's anger. How are you? You look . . . much better than I expected.'

The brief feeling of pride evaporated. With Vasinidra, he didn't have to pretend to be Rochant, but he still had secrets. *I should be dead after what that monster did to me and the High Lord knows it. Fool! I must hide my nature, now more than ever.* He gave a tired smile. 'It is just an illusion, my High Lord.'

'I would advise you to drop it then. I hunt for the Corpseman today with my family. They will see you for an imposter the moment you take to the air.'

Satyendra nodded, secretly pleased. He'd been looking for an excuse to get out of the hunt and Vasinidra had just provided it. Being unable to fly wasn't the true problem; the sapphire plates actually burned his skin. To wear a whole suit of crystal armour would surely kill him. 'I will let my injuries show. Between that and my being recently reborn,' he noted Vasinidra's frown at the lie, 'nobody will think ill of me remaining here to recover.'

'That will have to serve us for now. When I return, we will discuss a more permanent solution.'

The offhand mention of his fate scared him and made him angry. 'Have I not proven my worth, High Lord?'

'You have. But no matter how useful you are, you are no Deathless. You cannot lead a hunt. You cannot protect our people. While you occupy Lord Rochant's place, we are all weakened.'

'You said that if I did as you asked, I need not fear.'

'I'm not going to kill you, Satyendra. But did you honestly think I'd let this mockery continue? The needs of the house,' a pained look crossed his face, along with a flash of worry, 'of all the houses, must come before yours.'

Bile rose up in Satyendra's throat. He'd been used. Betrayed. And now he was going to be cast aside. 'That's easy to say now you're in power.'

'It's easy to say because it's the truth.'

'I deserve better than this! Without me, you'd be serving under High Lord Yadva!'

Vasinidra sighed. 'I will find the best life I can for you but it will not be Rochant's. The sooner you make peace with that, the better. Now, the hunt must be set into motion. Have your people do what is necessary and be sure to keep things in good order here for our return.'

Vasinidra has no need of me. No one does. I am a misfit. Despite everything I've done, that hasn't changed. For a moment loneliness and desperation threatened to overwhelm him and he bowed low, as much to hide the expression on his face as to show respect. 'At once, my High Lord.'

Vasinidra stood in the Chrysalis Chamber, resplendent in his armour. He took his helmet from the Gardener-smiths, pressed a bloody thumb against the crystal to wake it, and pulled it on. He waited patiently as they threaded his long hair through the back. When they were finished, he straightened, towering over them on his Sky-legs.

As he twisted the other gauntlet into place, he felt the familiar rush of exaltation. He was more than a man now. Stronger. Faster. Superior.

'My compliments to you,' he said, 'it is no easy thing to dress so many Deathless in such a short time.'

The Gardener-smiths bowed low and smiled.

'Are my family prepared?'

The smiles vanished. 'All save Lord Rochant. Some of his plates have more growing to do. We did our best but the crystals cannot be rushed.'

She's afraid I'll be angry. He spread his hands to show he was not. 'Of course. As he is restored, so will his armour be. All things must happen in their proper time. Now, do you have my spear?'

The Gardener-smith handed it over. The silver shaft sat snugly in his hand and the sapphire tip glinted beautifully in the sunslight. He tested the weight. 'Perfect.'

'Hunt well and thorough, High Lord.'

The great glass walls slid aside to allow him onto the balcony. Three other Deathless were waiting there: Umed, Yadva, and Gada. Umed stood tall in his armour. Though his current body was old, it was held upright by the sapphire encasing it. Lord Umed was the oldest remaining member of House Sapphire, known for his quiet dignity, a good temper, and his sprightly dancing. Vasinidra's eyes automatically went to Umed's neck. Hidden beneath the gorget was a golden tattoo, marking the premature end of an old lifecycle, and the end of Umed's confidence in battle.

Yet still he is here to support me. I should honour that.

Even out of armour, Lady Yadva was impressive, with a thick neck and broad frame packed with muscle. In it, she was monstrous. To accommodate the bulk, her crystal wings stretched wide to either side of her before scything up towards the sky. She carried a spear in either hand, one made for throwing and the other heavier and more suited for stabbing, though she could throw that too if the mood took her. She was without doubt the most powerful warrior in the house, and it had pained her to bend the knee to him. He wondered how long he could count on her loyalty.

By contrast his brother, Gada, appeared long and delicate in his armour, like a stretched-out Flykin. He was stoic, methodical, brittle. A solid hunter but nothing more. They hadn't flown together in years, mostly because Gada couldn't stand to be outshone by his younger sibling.

Each had their problems but, for all their flaws, they were Sapphire and he knew each would give their best for the glory of the house.

The courtyard was packed with solemn faces. Four blocks of hunters stood in the centre surrounded by a crowd of staff, family, guests, and traders, all shuffling nervously. Without the noise of the drums and the song of the castle, there was nothing to guide them or focus their anxiety.

Again, Vasinidra was surprised by his own sense of calm.

He moved to the edge of the balcony and did not have to wait for the attention of the assembled to rest on him. As always, the words came easily. It was just a matter of saying what was in his heart.

'Many years ago, the village of Sorn called out to its Deathless for aid. We failed to answer and because of that, the village of Sorn was lost. It became a wound that House Sapphire has carried ever since.' He let his gaze sweep the crowd. 'It is time for us to cleanse that wound. As a mark of respect for the dead, we will go not in glory but in silence. We did not carry our people when they needed us, and so this hunt will go into the Wild without your voices behind our wings, alone, as they were.'

They watched Vasinidra make his way down from the balcony, followed by the other Deathless. And they watched as he and the hunters began to march towards the open drawbridge. He felt their eyes on his back as he accelerated into a bounding run. Sky-legs rasped on stone, stark in the silence, propelling them all out of the castle and into the waiting sky.

CHAPTER THREE

So, thought Pari. *The demon is here.*

'Good,' she said to Arkav. 'From what the Bringers said, we need to pull your soul free and then everything else should resolve itself.'

The demons making the living sphere around them continued to whisper. '. . . *Crushing* . . .'

'Yes. Pari, is it me or are the demons moving?'

She looked around. They were constantly moving. Shifting next to each other uncomfortably, especially the ones nearest to them.

'. . . *Burning* . . .'

But that wasn't what Arkav meant. More and more of the demons seemed to be reacting to the light of their armour. One or two of them caught light, causing the others to make hushed moans of pain. Even the ones furthest from them were suffering in a way they weren't before. It took her a few moments to realize the obvious.

Oh no.

The sphere was shrinking, like a giant living fist closing around them.

'But,' she said, 'this doesn't make any sense. They'll all be destroyed. Why do that?'

'I don't know,' replied Arkav. 'But I think whatever is behind them is here for me.'

He swam closer to Pari to put more space between himself and the demons. The sphere was already half the size it had been, and on fire in more than one place. More demons were flooding in behind.

'. . . *Cracking* . . .'

'Did you hear that?' Pari yelled. 'They said cracking. These things don't crack, they burn or boil.'

Arkav nodded. 'The demons aren't talking about themselves.'

'No, they're warning us. It means to crack our armour. Then there'll be nothing to stop it taking the rest of your soul.'

'. . . *Out* . . .'

'There!' she said. 'The demons are agreeing. If they crack our armour, the lights will go out. Or maybe they're saying we need to get out. I don't know. They're agreeing either way!'

'But to get free of here, we'll have to destroy them.'

He sounded far too sad about this for Pari's liking. 'If we don't fight now our auras will destroy all of them, and then they'll destroy us. Is that what you want?'

He paused for a moment.

'You have to think about that? Honestly!'

'No,' he said quietly. 'I just don't feel right about the—'

'We can talk about it later for as many lifecycles as you

like. For now though, dear brother, shut up and follow my lead.'

She flicked out her whip again, lodging it deep in a hapless demon, then held out her free hand to Arkav. He took it, and they clasped wrists. Then, she pulled on the whip.

In normal circumstances, that would yank the barb free, or pull her opponent close. Here, though, they weighed nothing, so they were propelled forward. As they moved closer, she swung Arkav towards the demons and he thrust out his legs in a two footed kick.

There was a bright flare of light as the demons were blown, flaming, away from them. She caught a glimpse of a way out. 'There! Before they close it again.'

He grabbed the nearest demons with his free hand, the touch of his gauntlet making them hiss in agony, and swung Pari towards the gap. Her head fit through cleanly, her shoulders less so, though this wasn't a problem for her as her wings sliced easily through everything in her way, and she was rewarded with a view of the space outside.

It was vast and shifting. Not empty like the sky but full of starless nebulae, parting and closing, giving glimpses of golden lights beyond. Lights that were arranged in circular formations, seven for each hoop. Hoops lined up at regular intervals to make tunnels. Tunnels stretching from one unknown to another, crisscrossing the sky like the veins of some unfathomable beast. And within them, not blood but darts of silver, too many to count, moving swiftly and safely.

Souls.

Pari gasped at the size and wonder of it.

There were many demons too, streams of them, swimming with purpose. Not towards the distant tunnels of light and their silver bounty. Towards her. They were looking to re-inforce the sphere. And behind them was another demon, bigger, like a great swollen cloud of nightmare.

This one was different from the others she'd seen. This one she knew. It was like some great fat Snakekin covered in bits of bloodless people. Mouths, ears, toes, all moving independently of the thing itself. Her eyes roamed across it until they saw a familiar face, faded and flush against the demon's skin.

Arkav's face.

'Pari!' it cried.

'I'm coming!'

She fought and kicked her way free of the sphere, dragging Arkav with her. The sphere smoked and burnt and then broke apart, the creatures that had made it up floating lifelessly away.

'Pari!' cried the face again.

Now free of the sphere, it was Arkav's turn to look at the demon.

A great many eyes studded its hide, of different shapes and colours. They all looked back at Arkav.

Arkav began to snarl, which Pari thought was most unlike him.

After that, things got messy.

Arkav started swim-dragging himself towards the big demon, which Pari dubbed Facestealer in her mind.

The smaller demons swam towards them at speed, whispering miserably as they did so.

Facestealer also came towards them but it moved slowly, content to let the others engage first.

If she did nothing, Arkav would be overwhelmed by the

lesser demons before he'd even get to Facestealer. But in this place, it was hard to move. There was nothing to push against. Normally, there were essence currents that could be played with, or physical things to launch from, even the voices of their people could sustain flight if they were in sufficient number.

That's it! At least, I hope it is.

She kicked out a couple of times to put herself directly behind Arkav. By the time she'd got into position, the lesser demons were starting to swarm around them both.

'. . . *Prisoners* . . .'

'. . . . *Burning* . . .'

'Listen!' she said. 'That thing may control your bodies, but it does not control your voices.'

'. . . *Crushing* . . .' They replied, joining tail to head to tail again, forming a hoop that rapidly drew tight around her legs.

'Join with me.' She turned her head towards Arkav and called out, half speaking, half singing. 'You can do this, brother! Go! Take back what is yours!'

'. . . *Take* . . .' whispered one of the demons.

'. . . *Fight* . . .' added another.

And then a third. '. . . *Free* . . .'

Suddenly all the demons were whispering. The words were different, but she saw a shift in Arkav's momentum. Meanwhile, the demons continued to attack them both, several starting to burn, their whispers reduced to senseless hissing. Pari swung her arms back and forth to stop any getting to her face. 'It's working. It's working! Hear us, Arkav: Take! Fight! Free! Take! Fight! Free!'

It seemed that as the bodies of the lesser demons joined to constrict them, so too did their voices.

'. . . TAKE . . . FIGHT . . . FREE . . .'

Now Arkav was moving. The demons attached to his arms weighed nothing, and their pained voices whispered directly to his wings.

Facestealer twitched and started to move backwards.

Too late, thought Pari. *He's got you.*

Arkav plunged into Facestealer like a diver into a midnight lake. The surface of the demon rippled and tore, and the many mouths on its surface opened in a silent chorus of screams.

Instantly, the lesser demons around Pari's legs broke formation, as did the ones that had been around Arkav's arms. As soon as they'd put a safe distance between themselves and the damaging aura of the tanzanite armour, they stopped, drifting slowly in the void. They kept whispering their support though. Pari swam forward until she was in the current and allowed it to carry her towards Facestealer.

She could see it writhing in pain, her brother a furious glow within it, thrashing his arms and legs. Pari lashed Facestealer's side with her whip, using it to swing past the demon so that her wing cut a gash along its flank. She allowed her momentum to carry her in a tight spiralling orbit, slicing a corkscrew wound around its body.

It lashed out at her, but she was too quick. It lashed out again, reacting rather than predicting, each time catching the space Pari had already left.

The tenebrous matter that made up its skin began to bubble, the gills opening too wide as Facestealer began to tear itself apart in an effort to disgorge Arkav.

There was no more slack in Pari's whip as she slammed into it. The impact of her armoured body was the last straw and Facestealer moaned from a score of mouths. She saw Arkav's hand reach up from inside it to claim the image of his face. Then she saw nothing but movement as the lesser demons descended, biting and snapping at Facestealer with shocking fury.

In seconds they had ripped Facestealer from her brother as if it were no more than a set of paper clothes. Then they began to fight over the other pieces.

Arkav floated amongst the carnage as if in a daydream. The perfect glow of his aura was marred by two cracks, one across his chest plate, the other on his right wing.

Pari's heart sank as she grabbed Arkav's arm. 'It's time to go.'

He looked at her, dazed, then joined in as she swam them awkwardly towards the gateway. It was slow going, especially as Arkav had one arm close to his chest, his fist loosely clenched. 'Stay with me,' she said.

He nodded, then looked over his shoulder. Following his gaze she saw they'd attracted followers. A shoal of demons were keeping pace behind them, whispering quietly. She had no idea what they were saying, nor if they were the same ones that had fought Facestealer.

She was too tired to care either way.

When they'd come through the gateway the first time, it had been at great speed. This time, they lacked the momentum to punch through and Pari had to tear a way open with her gauntleted hands. It was hard, awkward work. When it finally gave, she felt the powerful currents just in front of her. All she had to do was go forward a little and it would carry her all the way home. She gave Arkav a smile of triumph.

He wasn't smiling back.

But it seemed to her as if the demons were.

They dived for the hole, slamming into Arkav and Pari, heedless of the harm it caused them. A few started to burn, but the majority surged out, taking Pari along for the ride.

This far down the essence currents were pure and ferociously strong. They took hold of Pari's wings and threw her towards the distant sky.

She flipped and tumbled, tumbled and flipped, using her lifecycles of training to gradually right herself. Things continued to spin in her vision for a few moments as she desperately tried to locate the lights.

It was the demons that guided her. They were ascending even faster than she and Arkav were, their dark wriggling bodies stark against the paler clouds of essence.

Her instincts said to follow them, and she did, fighting the currents that wanted only to send her up, and up and up.

And then a circle of golden lights. *Seven. No more, no less.*

They reminded her of the other lights she'd seen below. Thousands of them, beyond her ability to count, but all arranged in circles of seven. All familiar. Pari had glimpsed a mystery and she knew it would haunt her until she'd solved it.

The space shrunk down around them, smooth walls replacing open air.

We are back in the chasm under Rochant's castle.

It occurred to her that the shoal of demons would escape into the world. Perhaps the Bringers would stop them. Perhaps the demons would feast on the Bringers.

Arkav continued alongside her. The crack in his wing seemed longer, the gap in the light there, wider. She reached down to take his hand but missed, grasping at empty air.

She tried again but this time their stretching fingers weren't even close.

I'm going faster than him. I'm leaving him behind.

'Arkav!' she shouted.

He looked up at her and nodded. There was peace in his eyes. And sadness. And farewell.

'Don't give up now, you idiot! We're almost home.'

He continued to look at her, until her vision blurred with tears. His lips moved but she couldn't hear him. She didn't need to. He loved her. He thanked her. He'd see her on the other side.

As his hand moved in a final wave, hers moved too, flicking her whip out. It snared his wrist, the barb looping around three times before catching tight. 'You're not getting away from me that easily!' she cried.

It was hard to tell, but she thought her brother laughed.

The demons surged ahead of her, blasting out from the chasm and into the sky. She could make out the Bringers of Endless Order standing around the lip, diamond-tipped wands held aloft to guide her home. They watched the demons too, but did nothing to intervene.

Why am I not surprised?

Onwards and upwards went the demons, towards Lord Rochant's floating castle. And suddenly they were rolling and twisting, contorting their bodies in a doomed attempt to change direction. Perhaps it was her imagination, but she thought she heard them screaming. Caught in the currents they were helpless to resist as their journey was taken to an abrupt and speedy end. Sharp jags of sapphire protruded from the great hunk of rock the castle was built on. They hummed with stored sunslight, like teeth, like rows of spears set before a charge.

One after another the demons were thrown onto those sharp points. One after another they burned.

Pari turned her attention to her own ascent. Angling her wings, she drifted towards the edge of the current and, as she and Arkav emerged from the chasm, they flew out into normal air, and began to glide down. Arkav landed first.

Safe! He is safe at last.

And she dropped lightly next to him.

'Well?' she asked. 'Did it work?'

'Yes,' he replied.

'Truly?'

'Yes! Truly. I . . .' He put a hand across his chest. 'The hole, the . . . absence. It's gone.'

She thought she'd be jubilant but she wasn't. Mostly, it just felt like relief coupled with a hint of wariness. 'Good. Because charming as you are, I don't think I can go through that again.'

He opened his arms. 'Let me hold you for a change.'

As they embraced, she shot a glare over his shoulder in the direction of the Bringers. *Don't get too comfortable. You're next.*

Chandni sat, cocooned in the dark, communing with Murderkind. It knew her questions as she did, and answered them without guile. Indeed, it had treated with her most fairly, but she could not fully relax.

There will be a catch or a trick. It is only a matter of time.

'You will find no trickery here, Iron Purebird,' replied the chorus of Birdkin. 'We need no deception for you are ours. On the second point you speak true. It *is* a matter of time, and you must be swift in your service. In times past your son was my eyes in places we could not go. He spied for me and mine, and what he saw was troubling. Many demons flocked to the Corpseman's banner, out of order, out of shape, upsetting the balance and flow that was. Such action demands response: You. You must be my voice in places I cannot speak, to ears that will not listen.'

'How can I speak to someone that will not listen?'

'Not to me, but only to me. For you, my Iron Purebird, they will make time, they will attend your every breath, and you will make them attend me.'

'Who are they?'

'Another Prince of the Wild, a peer, an adversary, a fellow victim of the Corpseman's plans. Bring them to me with warm eyes so we might bury our grievances in the Corpseman's flesh.'

'You wish to make an alliance with this other prince?'

The Birdkin cawed derisively, then spoke in one voice. 'We desire it not, and yet it must be done. Prince Kennelgrove is a trickster, a curse mother, a false-jointed thief. But even that is preferable to the strange destroyer, that is the Corpseman, this walking death that spreads itself among us like a sickness, unseen and unstoppable. Do this for me, Iron Purebird.'

Chandni could not see its face, but she felt for it in the dark, so she could look directly at Murderkind and reply. 'I dealt for the life I wanted first. A family. A home. The return of my son, time with my lover.'

'Do this first or there will be none of these things. The Corpseman cares little for your pacts or mine.'

'Very well. I will do this for you, but that does not mean I will run your errands every time you ask.'

'So be it.'

'Where can I find Prince Kennelgrove?'

'Those that hate you know the way. Your white-faced friend can take you to them.'

Before she could reply, cracks of light broke through the darkness, bright and brighter red, and gold that was brighter still. Chandni squeezed her eyes shut against the sudden intrusion. As Murderkind pulled away, she shivered, suddenly aware of the cold air rushing in.

In moments, it was gone, leaving the forest unusually quiet. The Birdkin had gone too, scattering, shrieking and, it seemed to Chandni, laughing. She now sat between the trees aware that above her, night was retreating, pulling back as the three suns rose.

A single Birdkin remained, black feathered, with a white beak and a thoughtful demeanour. It stood ten feet from her, regarding her with a compound eye.

'Hello,' she said.

The Birdkin circled her, walking slowly, one eye on her at all times. She sat up straighter and lifted her chin. 'Is there something you want?'

It came to a stop on her right side, twitching its head at an angle, and hopped forward.

Of course, thought Chandni. *The blood.*

Three times she'd cut herself, once for each of her crimes. The blood was still fresh on her right arm. Even in the day blood could draw out the demons of the Wild, and the suns were barely in the sky. The Birdkin looked at the wounds, then up at her in a quick gesture, then to the wounds, then back to her.

Chandni shivered. This creature was probably only the first of many.

'My blood is not yours to take,' she said as imperiously as she could. 'It belongs to Murderkind.'

The Birdkin gave her a knowing look.

'Did Murderkind send you to me?'

The Birdkin nodded and hopped forward again. She forced herself to appear calm as it examined the three cuts close up, each in turn. Then a second time, its beak hovering over each one for less than a heartbeat. On the third pass the beak flashed down, nipping the highest wound closed.

Chandni marvelled as she saw the torn flesh rejoined, the cut replaced by a clean white scar. 'Thank you,' she said as the Birdkin considered the second cut. 'My name is Chandni.'

It looked up at her sharply and she felt as she had as a girl when interrupting her mother's work. 'Cha-aan,' it replied in a tone that was equal parts greeting and admonishment.

The second wound was closed as swiftly as the first. The blood around the cut had vanished too and she wondered if that was the price of the healing or if the creature simply took pride in its work. *I hope it's the latter.*

She didn't mean to interrupt it again but the words slipped out. 'Do you have a name?'

The Birdkin gave her a glare and then dipped its head towards the last cut, opening its beak wide. A proboscis levered out from deep in its throat, plunging into her arm.

It should have hurt, but that part of Chandni's body no longer felt pain. No longer felt anything. And yet, for the first time in years, she had a tingle of sensation deep within her forearm. Another shiver took her body and as it did so a thought bloomed in her mind:

Crowflies.

When she looked at the Birdkin again, the third wound was closed and clean.

'Your name is Crowflies?'

It nodded its head.

'Thank you, Crowflies. Please pass on my thanks to your master.' She stood up carefully, swaying as a brief wave of dizziness passed through her. 'Now, if you'll excuse me, I ought to find my friends. They'll be worried.' This was easier said than done, though, given how lost she was.

Crowflies rose into the air with a flap of its wings and landed on a nearby branch.

'Cha-aan!'

'Yes?'

'Cha-aan!' it said again, holding her gaze. When she walked towards it, it flew away, further into the forest.

With no better options, Chandni did her best to keep up.

Sa-at found the castle bewildering. They seemed to be underground but he knew they were in the sky. How could you be under the earth and in the air at the same time? The tunnels under the castle twisted and turned constantly, and there were no stars, no suns, nothing to navigate against.

The uniformity of the walls also puzzled him. In the Wild every tree was different, every bush characterful. They stuck in the mind. He knew them even if they moved. But here, the personality had been smoothed off the stone. How was he to tell one from another?

He knew that somewhere above the suns shone brightly, but not a shred of their light penetrated this far down. The only illumination came from sapphires set into the walls at regular intervals. He touched each one as they passed. They were cool under his fingers, but not cold like the stone. In places natural veins of sapphire could be seen making glittering patterns. They weren't as bright as the crafted gemslights but he thought they looked nicer.

More than once he'd been distracted by his surroundings and almost lost sight of Roh. The old woman wasn't stopping for anything, forcing him and Tal to match her pace. She was making a strange noise as she walked, reminding Sa-at of much bigger beasts from the Wild. A sort of huffing, angry exhalation.

Like a big grumpy Bearkin.

The thought made Sa-at snort and the other two shot him a glare.

'Ssh!' said Tal.

They continued in silence, past several small doors set into the wall.

'What are they?' asked Sa-at.

'Cells,' replied Tal in hushed voice.

'What's a cell?'

'Ssh!'

Sa-at resolved to ask Rochant when they got back.

Eventually the tunnels became less uniform, the kind carved naturally rather than by hand. Sa-at preferred this, though Tal bumped his head on the irregular ceiling several times. There were no lights down here but Roh didn't slow.

'I don't like this,' he whispered to Tal.

'Me neither,' replied his friend.

Without either of them saying anything, they found each other's hands in the dark. Things felt a little better after that. They followed Roh's breathing through the darkness. The air became chill and Sa-at's other hand brushed against something that was not stone. It was hard, cold, and damp. It swung away from his touch, then swung back, nudging him, hard.

'It smells of death down here.'

'And so it should,' chuckled Roh. 'Have to store the meat somewhere.'

Sa-at stopped to think about that. He reached out again. Yes. It was dead flesh. A great carcass suspended from the ceiling. He soon found more of them, setting each in motion with a gentle push.

A growl sounded nearby. Tal squeezed Sa-at's hand. Sa-at squeezed back.

'W-what's that?' asked Tal.

'That's my boy,' replied Roh. 'Always tell the staff to take meat from the front, never from the back. But people are stupid. Oh yes, they are. Especially the young ones. Old age doesn't make you clever, but youth makes idiots of us all. So when one of my young idiots comes down here to get supplies, my lovely boy keeps them near the front.'

Sa-at wasn't sure if Roh was referring to her child or something else but he didn't ask. The old cook scared him.

Chains rattled in the dark and then there was the sound of padded feet on stone and a soft whump of impact.

'There you are!' said Roh, and Sa-at heard scratching, slurping, and a happy whine. 'Missed old Roh, didn't you, you soppy thing. You love old Roh, don't you? Yes, you do. You love her.' There were more slurping noises. 'I brought you something. Here you are. Not much mind; have to keep you hungry or you'll get soft. Can't have you being too friendly, can we?'

A wet mouth chomped industriously in the dark.

After a few satisfied grunts, they heard Roh's voice again. 'This way. Not far now.'

Another stumble in the dark, another turn, and they arrived.

Roh pulled on some fabric, the rustle echoing in the cold space, and suddenly there was light, soft and blue and beautiful. Sa-at gasped. He had never seen anything like it before. To his eyes it looked like a sleeping crystal giant. Its skin glowed like the gems on the castle walls, from fingertips to toes. But the thing that struck him most were the wings. Large and curling, like Crowflies' at full extension but shaped differently. There was no sign of the bone beneath or an ability to flex or flap or close. They just looked permanently, perfectly open.

Roh reached out and pinched Sa-at's arm, then she pinched Tal's.

'Ow!' said Sa-at.

'Ow!' said Tal.

'Shut your mouths and open your ears,' said Roh. Sa-at had thought his ears already open but decided he couldn't ask about it without making Roh angry. 'This armour is sacred. You handle it like you would the good Lord Rochant himself, gentle as a babe. I'll wrap each piece and give it to you to carry. You carry it by the cloth. Your grubby little hands never touch a single bit of crystal, do you hear?'

'Yes,' said Tal.

'Yes,' added Sa-at.

'Mmhn, I'll be checking every piece when we get there and I'd better not find any smeary fingerprints if you know what's good for you,' muttered Roh.

The armour weighed less than Sa-at expected, each piece sitting lightly in his hands. The problem was bulk. The wings were attached to the back plate and there was no way to reduce their size. Tal and Sa-at had to carry it between them.

They moved through the castle quietly, back through the cold room with the meat and Roh's 'boy'. Back through the rough tunnels. Back to where the walls became carved and adorned with lights. Roh went ahead to make sure nobody saw their cargo. When they did encounter someone, she chattered irritably with them before sending the unfortunate on their way, often with a sore ear or a new errand.

The last bit of the journey was the worst. In the more populated parts of the castle it was impossible to move completely unseen. And even though they kept their heads down, and even though nothing overt was said, Sa-at felt questioning eyes fall on him.

It's like being in the wrong part of the Wild as the suns go down. Trouble is already waiting for us.

They were nearly back to Roh's room when the old cook stopped and bowed her head. Tal and Sa-at copied her, letting their hoods fall forward.

'Shouldn't you be in the kitchens?' said a voice, young but imperious.

'Ah,' puffed Roh, 'the good Lord Rochant misses nothing . . . I've been looking for Honoured Mother Chandni . . . Been all over the castle and I can't find her anywhere. Most unlike her.'

Good Lord Rochant? Thought Sa-at. *This must be the imposter. My enemy.* He wanted to look very badly but he knew he should keep his head down. He bit his lip. Surely a little look wouldn't hurt?

'I have given her leave to travel and see her family, a reward for her long years of service.'

'Very kind of you, my lord. People don't forget that sort of kindness.'

Sa-at had the feeling that Roh was saying one thing and meaning another.

'If you have need of my seneschal, Win has taken the post. Take your concerns to him unless you feel the need to come to me directly.'

'No need to bother you, my lord. It's nothing.'

'You have run yourself half to death for nothing?'

'I mean it's nothing for a Deathless Lord to concern himself with. The little things are all the world to the likes of old Roh.'

Sa-at couldn't bear it any longer. He lifted his head a fraction so that he could see the man Roh was speaking to. He saw black and blue silks, an inner layer that was tied tight on the arms and legs, and then an outer layer that flowed around him to pool at his feet. The man was not tall and the silks made him seem bigger than he probably was. Sa-at was not fooled though.

Many animals in the Wild do that trick, and they do it much better.

But a glance at a pair of legs and a body was not enough. Sa-at tilted his head a little more and saw a brown face with short black hair. His own face, but with a golden tattoo across one temple, the lines like cracks in the surface of his skull, or lightning, forking down to the cheek. It was identical to the one on Rochant's cheek. He saw the man's eyes – *they are my eyes!* – half-lidded by a frown, and he gasped. They were staring right at him.

CHAPTER FOUR

Satyendra's eyes bored into the stranger's. They were wearing a servant's hood which was odd in itself as they were indoors. He noticed a long strand of hair spill from the hood. He had possessed hair like that once, as long and dark as his mother's. Until, that is, she had cut it away. Not long ago, his face had been clear of gold paint just like this one. He looked into those wide eyes and it was like looking into a mirror of the past.

From the moment he'd found Roh in the corridor, he'd known something was going on. A liar always knew another liar and he was a creature made of lies.

'I assume these staff are new,' he said to Roh, though his gaze did not leave the too familiar face.

'That's right, my good lord. Two of my kitchen lads.'

'I would have their names, and see them observe proper manners within my castle. Hoods are for outside, not in.'

'Oh, but they know the rules, my good lord, it's just that their hands are full.' She put a hand to her back and groaned, though Satyendra was not convinced by the display of discomfort. 'All this running about has worn these old bones hard. Might we be excused?'

He glanced to the guard at his side. 'Make sure she doesn't fall.' The guard nodded and took the cook's arm. He forced his attention to go to the other figure, wanting to save his mysterious twin till last. 'Let me get that for you,' he said, smiling as he threw back the young man's hood. A pale face was revealed. It was worn and tired, unremarkable save for the scars where his earlobes should be. There was a delightful amount of worry there, even for a servant meeting his lord for the first time, and yet Satyendra found it hard to absorb. Something was wrong. 'What's your name?'

'Tal, my lord.'

'You have the look of a road-born, Tal.'

'Y-yes, my lord. I was born and raised in Sagan.'

'And then raised to my castle, it seems. Who brought you into the kitchens?'

'I . . .'

Roh cleared her throat. 'It was Honoured Mother Chandni, my good lord, she did it as a favour.'

Lies. I've never seen this boy before and my mother didn't bring people in for favours. She brought in the best. But he kept his face civil. 'I see. Welcome, Tal. What happened to your ears?'

Tal's cheeks flushed scarlet and he looked at the floor. 'The Wil—'

'Fool tried to pierce them as a child,' interrupted Roh. 'Got infected.'

More lies. Not even good ones. He took a moment to take what he could of Tal's mounting terror, but it was as if something was muting it, interfering with his ability to feast. In fact, he himself felt uncomfortable. His armpits had become sweaty and he resisted the urge to scratch them. Lord Rochant would never be seen to scratch in public.

'Welcome to my castle, Tal of Sagan. Serve me truly and you shall have nothing to fear.' The fear and guilt were so clear on Tal's face it was embarrassing. *I'll keep this one in the cells when I'm done. Between him and Pik I'll not want for food.*

'And you?' he said, turning at last to the other one again. Their eyes met a second time and it was just as much a slap in the face as the first. Unlike Tal, he got no fear from this one. There was curiosity mixed with anger and determination. Nothing he could use. 'What's your name?'

Roh took a breath to answer for him but Satyendra's hand came up, silencing her. 'Let him speak for himself.'

'My name is Sa-at.'

'I've never heard a name like that before.' He reached out and pushed back Sa-at's hood. Beneath the cloak, he could see black feathers. Part of some garment that bore no resemblance to any of the castle fashions. And that face! His face. A perfect copy. 'We could be brothers,' he murmured. Then added: 'In body. You could be related to this body.'

Sa-at regarded him with similar fascination. 'You're like me.'

Conflicting feelings rose within Satyendra. He wanted to touch Sa-at, to see if he were real. *To see if I am real.* He wanted to rake that face with his hands and destroy it. He wanted to flee the intense scrutiny.

He realized that Sa-at wanted to reach out to him too, but couldn't as his hands were already full. And that brought his attention to another oddity. 'What are you carrying, exactly?'

Both Sa-at and Tal gave worried glances towards Roh. The old cook was leaning against the guard, her eyes half closed. 'Don't look at me. When your lord asks you what you are carrying, you show him.'

Sa-at was the first to move. He proffered one of the cloth parcels towards Satyendra, who took it. There was solidity beneath the fabric, along with an unpleasant feeling. A familiar, unpleasant feeling. The skin of his palms tingled unhappily.

I don't want what's in here. I want to give it back.

But at this point he had to open the parcel. To do anything else would appear strange. After all, he'd asked to see it. As the cloth fell away, he found himself looking into the empty eye holes of a helmet. Clearly it belonged to a Sapphire Deathless, but despite being of similar design it was not his helmet, that one was smaller. He'd just seen the other Sapphire Deathless arrayed in their armour before they'd left to hunt. None of their helmets matched what he held in his hands.

'What is this?' he murmured.

The burning sensation intensified, and he felt that strange shifting in his hands, as if the flesh were trying to get away from the crystal. He was just about to give the helmet back to Sa-at when he heard a gasp and a thud.

'By the thrice blessed suns!' he exclaimed, turning towards the guard. 'I told you to stop her from falling.'

But Roh had not fallen.

She was standing, very much alert, with the guard unconscious at her feet. In her hand was a long, thin needle that glinted as she dipped it into a pocket of her cloak.

'Guards!' he yelled.

Roh moved towards him. He should have been able to avoid her. But he was distracted by Sa-at's stare and the pain in his hands and the sluggish feeling brought on by contact with the crystal.

The needle went through two layers of fabric and into his shoulder. Immediately it started to tingle.

'Might want to get that seen to, my good lord,' said Roh.

He dropped the helmet and fell back against the wall, screaming for help. As more of his staff arrived, Roh and the other two fled down the corridor. 'Sound the alarm!' he shouted as he prepared to give chase. 'Gather every able-bodied guard you can and bring in Roh. She's a traitor!'

They stared at him, uncomprehending. A small voice in the back of his mind warned him that he was behaving in a most un-Rochant like manner. He ignored it. 'Now!'

As the servants rushed off to fulfil his orders he realized there was only one way to save himself. One thing to do. He set off after Roh while clutching at his shoulder. The skin around the tiny wound tingled, the sensation slowly spreading. He wondered what foul poison was in his veins. *Am I already dead?*

He continued on, faster, tears on his face, alone and in pain. And privately, he yearned for his mother.

Chandni followed Crowflies through the trees. It was quiet, almost tranquil, and she was reminded of the brief moments of joy she'd experienced here so long ago. *It's strange. For all the horror that time in my life brought, I had moments of true happiness too. Can I say that about any other time?*

She thought of her life in the castle. There had been a

background sense of satisfaction over her work and moments of quiet pride at her achievements, but it had always been weighed down with stress and fear. Even before her son had been replaced, her life had been one of duty, not pleasure. Before Varg, she'd never really wanted anything for herself. Never even considered it an option.

'Cha-aan,' said Crowflies. There was a note of warning in its voice. The Birdkin was not far ahead, it was looking into a small clearing where she could just make out Varg leaning against the white block of Glider's back.

They're alive!

She wanted to run to them but her courtly upbringing stopped her. She turned to the branch Crowflies was sitting on. 'Thank you for helping me. I'm afraid I don't have much to offer you in return for your kindness but you could have some of my hair for your nest if you'd like.'

Crowflies made a derisive noise.

'A piece of colourful thread from my clothes, then?' One look at the Birdkin's face told her this was no good either. 'I'm sorry. I've never had to deal with a creature as magnificent as you before. Is there anything you would like before I go?'

Crowflies looked up towards the sky. She looked up too but could see nothing unusual. She realized it had exposed the underside of its beak but there was nothing amiss as far as she could see. Then it dawned on her. 'Ohh, you'd like me to deal with an itch?'

There was a flash of movement, a lightning fast nod, and then it was looking up again.

'Of course.'

She gently scratched the space underneath its beak.

'Aaark,' it said. 'Aaaarhhh.'

After a moment, she saw its wings lower as the tension left its body.

'Well, I should be getting back to my friends now. Thank you again.'

But as she turned to go, Crowflies caught her sleeve in its beak.

'What is it?'

The Birdkin offered her the top of its head. She sighed. 'Very well, but then I really have to go.' She quickly scratched the top of its head and then waved goodbye. She expected Crowflies to leave but it remained on its branch, watching her with intensity.

Varg didn't notice her arrival. His head was buried in his knees. She could see the grey streaks in his hair and the tired slump of his shoulders. He seemed smaller than usual, like a shrivelled version of himself.

He was sitting against Glider, who most definitely had noticed her. She too, appeared tired. Both her blue human eye and the dark canine one were bloodshot. Though she remained curled around Varg, her head lifted slightly in Chandni's direction, and her tail began to thump softly on the earth.

Chandni put a finger to her lips and crept over to them, kneeling down.

'Hello, Varg.'

She heard a sniff, and then he very slowly looked up at her. 'Chand?'

'Yes.'

'I thought you . . . I thought I'd never see you again.' His eyes began to well with tears, then narrowed. 'Is it . . . really you?'

'It's really me, Varg.'

'Prove it.'

'Well, for one thing, Glider isn't growling at me.'

'Glider's been wrong before. And you went into the Wild to die. You were bleeding and they took you in. I've heard a lot of tales of folk being stolen by the Wild but I ain't never heard one where the Wild gives someone back.'

The reunion wasn't quite going as Chandni had imagined it. 'I'm right here, Varg.' She went to take his hand to prove how real she was but he flinched away from her into Glider, making the Dogkin grumble in protest. Chandni held up her hands.

'You need to prove you're really her and not just something that looks like her.'

She pulled back her sleeve. 'You see the three fresh cuts? I made them with your knife. You see the older ones? Made in the back of your wagon on the morning after we first met.' She pulled off her glove. See the missing nails? Taken by the Hunger Tree when it saved me from the poison. Do you believe me now?' He didn't reply, just stared at her, slack jawed. 'Oh, for fuck's sake, Varg, just kiss me!'

And then they were kissing, him pressing forward until the two of them tumbled together, him on top. They were fumbling kisses, desperate and messy, and punctuated with laughter. Varg's tears splashed on her cheeks and his beard tickled her lip and she didn't care.

She left her right arm encircling his body and used her left to explore beneath his clothes. Her fingers brushed through the hair on his chest and against the harder muscle beneath. Then down, to start loosening his belt. It was surprisingly difficult, one handed, especially as he was still intent on kissing her.

He paused when he realized what she was up to. 'You want to do this here? Are you sure?'

'Yes!' she replied, her voice louder than she'd intended. 'Help me.'

They undressed each other. In their rush, clothing got caught and tangled. Buttons were lost. Varg swore several times and Chandni laughed and joined in. Glider began barking and tried to get between them until they told her, loudly, to go away. No magic had changed the forest floor. It was just as rough and uncomfortable as it had ever been. But again, she didn't care. Mohit, her past lover, had been diligent and followed her instructions to the letter. Varg didn't need instructions, he just needed encouragement.

And she gave it in a voice her mother wouldn't have recognized.

Afterwards, when they had settled against each other, their breathing falling into mutual rhythm, he brushed the hair from her cheek and looked at her.

'What does this mean, Chand?'

'It means we can be together.'

'But how? The Wild don't give up fresh blood.'

'It didn't.' She put a finger on his lips to stop him from blurting more questions. 'A demon took some of my blood, and I made a deal. That means I get to be with you and to live the way I want.'

He gently pulled her hand away from his mouth. 'And what does it get?'

'It gets me.'

'Oh no. Oh shit.'

'But not today. Not for a long time. It has to give me what I want first. It's going to help me find my son, my real son. The Satyendra that sent me to my death isn't the baby I brought here with you all those years ago. Murderkind, that's the demon's name, will help me find him. But that's not all. I've bargained for a life with you, Varg. A good, long life. We can finally be together.' She looked down, suddenly shy. 'If you still want this.'

He lifted her hand to his lips. 'You know I do.'

'Are you sure? What about your duty to Lady Pari?'

'I've paid my debts there. I want my own life now. I want a family. Do you want a family?'

'You mean children?'

'Yeah.'

'If we can, then yes, and I want Satyendra to be part of this family too. And Glider.' She paused and looked around. 'Where is Glider?'

She saw the Dogkin had taken herself to the other side of the trees and had her back to them, though one floppy ear had pricked up at the mention of her name. 'Glider, come here!'

In seconds she had bounded over to eagerly accept a hug. Chandni gave herself a moment to enjoy being in such loving company, then looked up at the sunslit leaves. 'Before we can start building a life here, there's something I need to do for Prince Murderkind.'

Glider and Varg both raised their eyebrows. One barked and the other protested: 'I thought you said we'd get our time first before you were his. A good long time.'

'I did. And we will, but Murderkind is just asking for this one thing now. I think it's something only I can do.' When she'd been with Murderkind, heart to heart, she had felt no deception, and yet she felt odd defending the demon.

Varg shook his head. 'Well, what is it?'

'I need to find another Prince of the Wild called Kennelgrove and persuade him to ally with Murderkind against the Corpseman.'

'Sounds dangerous to me. And how are we supposed to find this Kennelgrove?' Glider barked so loudly that Varg had to raise his voice. 'I've never heard of him.'

'No,' she agreed, and then pointed at the Dogkin. 'But she has.'

Glider barked again, and as soon as they looked at her, she bounded off into the trees, pausing occasionally to howl, long and loud.

'Where are you going?' Varg shouted.

'Get dressed, we need to go after her.' Chandni started collecting her clothes and putting them on. She became aware of Varg's admiring gaze. 'Hurry up. I don't want to lose her.'

With a muttered curse, Varg tucked his enthusiasm back into his trousers.

It wasn't hard to know which way Glider had gone. They heard her howling not too far away. And then, they heard other howls, other Dogkin, at least half a dozen. The trees too, were murmuring uneasily. That feeling transferred itself to Chandni's stomach.

'I don't like the sound of that,' said Varg. 'We should get out of here while we can.'

'No,' said Chandni. 'Glider wouldn't abandon us.'

'That's exactly what she just bloody did!'

'I mean that she wouldn't abandon us if we needed her.'

'Think about it, Chand. If something's big enough to threaten old Glider, what use are we gonna be?'

She took his hand and started walking. 'Argue if you want, but we're going.'

'Fuck,' said Varg, but that was all he said, and they made their way towards the howling together.

The idea for Satyendra's salvation had come to him in a flash: his hunger. When he'd gorged himself on Yadavendra's shame he had become immeasurably stronger and that strength had allowed him to heal from terrible injuries overnight. If his body could reassemble a crumpled skull, then surely it could handle a little poison? All he had to do was feed before the effects kicked in.

It didn't take long to catch up. Sa-at and Tal were already slipping into Roh's room, but the old woman herself had lagged behind. As he crept closer, she stopped to lean against the wall. This was his chance. He blinked away tears and tried to soften his steps, keen to catch her unawares.

Meanwhile, the tingling numbness was spreading from the wound, not fast, but continuously, bringing with it a rising sense of panic. Perhaps that was why he rushed the approach, or perhaps Roh was more alert than she appeared to be. In either case, as he closed in on her, she turned to face him, that long needle in one hand, held between them. Poison glistened on its tip.

To a normal person, it would be a powerful deterrent, but Satyendra was not normal. He did not stop nor even slow, surging forward with hands outstretched. He barely felt the needle as Roh slipped it deep into his gut. What was more poison after all?

He grabbed her and tried to slam her against the wall, but she was surprisingly strong, and bigger than him. For a few seconds, they wrestled, equally determined, as the poison continued to spread. She gave him no fear, no pain, nothing he could feed on. In fact he felt nothing from the old cook save contempt.

In desperation he bit her cheek, sinking his teeth into the flesh, and pulling. This got a reaction, and he bit harder. In return, she let go of one of his hands and punched the needle where it protruded from his side.

That was her mistake.

For now he had her blood on his teeth, and her pain in his body, and he had a hand free. His hand grasped her face so fast that her skull was rebounding against the wall before she even registered contact.

Shock.

Pain.

Fear.

At last, he felt these things from her. He took her hand from the needle and crushed it in his own, powdering the bone. Then he removed the needle, and then, as the power and the hunger surged within, he got to work.

By the time the guards arrived, Roh was dead. Sensation had returned to his shoulder and stomach, and the tiny pinprick wounds had vanished. 'The traitors are hiding in there,' he said, pointing towards Roh's room. 'Bring them to me.'

The guards' salute was slow in coming. Most of them had grown up with the cook, as had their parents. She was almost as much a part of the castle as the walls.

'Now,' he added, through gritted teeth. The guards' attention drifted to his face. To the blood around his mouth.

He stood up, and to them, he seemed taller somehow. 'Is there a problem?'

'No, my lord,' they replied, though it was clearly a lie.

Satyendra followed them as they approached the door. The high still sang in his veins but he was troubled despite it. *I have killed an old woman. And I . . . enjoyed it. And it was easy.* He tried to tell himself that it was necessary for his own survival, and that he had never liked Roh anyway. It did nothing to assuage the guilt. In fact, as he thought about what he'd done the hunger within him stirred and a muscle he wasn't normally aware of flexed within his face, as if it wanted to open in a different way.

Pausing in horror, he brought his fingers up to either side of his nose. The skin there felt normal. He let them roam across his cheekbones and forehead but found nothing amiss.

Yes. This has been a warning. The hunger must be resisted before it becomes too much of me. He told himself that he wouldn't feed it again.

But as he got to the door he felt it stir again, tempting.

They flew along the Godroad in twos, the sunslight playing across their wings. Vasinidra was alongside Mia, his finest hunter and mother to his children. He already feared the day she'd be gone. She'd been a rock to him in this lifecycle and had become the yardstick against which others would be measured.

Behind them were his hunters, then the other Sapphire Deathless; Umed, Yadva, and Gada, each one backed by their own flight. He felt both joy and sadness considering them. Joy because the sight of his family flying together in the same direction gave him hope. Sadness because they were a wounded house, reduced forever from seven Deathless to six. Nothing he could do would ever change that.

When they reached the village of Sorn he banked to the right, knowing that the others would follow. Somewhere below, in that overgrown ghost place, was his mother, Nidra. It was a childish thing, but he stared at the buildings below as he passed over them, longing to see her. And longing for her to see him in his new station.

But if Nidra were down there, she gave no sign. Only a foolish exile would stand in the open, and Nidra was no fool.

Not long now, Mother.

Away from the Godroad, the essence currents were weaker, inconstant, and harder to navigate. Alone, he might be able to glide all the way to the hill Lady Pari Tanzanite had told him about. However, the others would never get that far.

He glanced back, waiting for the tell-tale wing dip of one of his family losing altitude. It wouldn't do to get separated in the Wild. As he suspected, Gada was the first to go. Before his brother began to drop noticeably, Vasin signalled for his flight to descend. There were no perfect landing spots, but he could see a long thin gap in the trees.

Good enough.

He and Mia flew down together, Sky-legs bringing them to a bouncing stop at the furthest edge of the opening. He turned to see how the rest of the house would fare. With so many landing at the same time in such a narrow space, everyone would be focused entirely on themselves. Such unguarded moments were rare and gave him useful insight into the state of his hunters.

Each flight kept formation, the hunters landing in an orderly fashion. *No other house can match our discipline,* he thought proudly. *If I didn't know better, I'd think Uncle*

Umed were still in a younger body, and even Gada, our worst flyer, managed admirably. There are no weak links for the Wild to exploit.

He raised his spear and every other spear came up together in reply. Pride for his people filled him. Without another word, he turned and bounded into the trees. Deathless and hunters fell in behind him, Sky-legs hitting the ground in time, making them sound like a single creature, a giant come to destroy its enemies.

The trees picked up the sound of their progress and sent it out in all directions, a warning for others. Not long after, he heard the howls of Dogkin and the shrieks of Birdkin. *No doubt the whole of the Wild knows we're here. Let us hope the Scuttling Corpseman still sleeps deeply.*

One moment they were running through the forest – and it seemed as if the trees leaned away from them to avoid being gored by their razor-edged wings – the next, he was in the open looking at a tall hill with near vertical sides.

Vasinidra didn't stop. He used his momentum to leap forward. His Sky-legs bent with the force of the landing, as did his knees, then both straightened together, propelling him into the sky.

He landed on the top of the hill. As Mia and the other hunters tried to catch up, he took in his surroundings. A lonely silver birch sprouted to one side, and there were various spiky bushes dotting the hilltop, but the dominant feature was a dome of amber. The peak of it rose a couple of feet above ground level, visible from here but not from below. The rest of the structure was tucked away beneath the surface.

Just as Lady Pari described it.

But as he moved closer, he saw that wasn't true for every detail. She had told him of an amber cocoon with the Corpseman just visible within. But there were no shadows lurking inside the structure. She'd not mentioned there being cracks in the surface either, dividing it into sections, nor the slight misalignment of those pieces.

As if someone had pushed it open from the inside and then put the pieces back . . . we're too late, he thought.

Lady Pari had told him that there were other things buried within the hill too. That bodies stolen from Sorn had been subjected to the whims of the Corpseman. Like the dome, their amber coffins had been cracked open and the earth had then been packed back into place.

He called his family to him while the hunters waited at the bottom of the hill.

'Where's our fight?' asked Yadva.

'Out there somewhere,' Vasinidra replied.

Umed sighed. 'The Wild looks after its own. It must have warned the Corpseman that we were coming.'

Vasinidra sighed as well. The Wild had done more than warn its own, it had hidden them. His hunters had found no tracks, no clues. It was as if the Corpseman and all its victims had vanished.

He heard Gada clear his throat. 'What would you have us do, High Lord?'

'I would hear your counsel before I make my decision.'

Yadva was the first to speak. 'Spread out in five of the seven directions. We still have hours of sunslight and the Corpseman can't be far away. Once one of us finds it, they signal the others.'

'While our Story-singers will lament if we return empty

handed,' said Umed. 'We risk losing more than just time if we linger too long.'

Gada pursed his lips. 'Even the Corpseman could not carry half a settlement's worth of people. Either it has allies to move them or they moved themselves.'

Typical Gada. He'd rather offer facts than risk conflict with the others.

Vasinidra was aware that his family were watching him. Aware that the flights of hunters were waiting for his decision. This was it. His first real test as High Lord.

Should he push on as Yadva wanted and risk weakening the house further? Follow Umed's advice and have his tenure as High Lord begin in failure? And what about his mother? How much longer could she last alone?

Vasinidra did not panic. He was in his armour, exalted and strong, and the answer was already there, obvious, just waiting to be seen.

He looked at them. 'I know where the Corpseman is.' Yadva punched her spears into the air with delight. 'It's gone to join the attack on House Ruby. Quiverhive has been sending demons at them for some time now, and I know it has been communicating with the Corpseman throughout, no doubt planning for this moment.'

Umed frowned. 'Forgive me, High Lord, but the Wild reacts, it doesn't plan.'

'It *didn't* react. It *didn't* plan. Now it does. The Corpseman has changed the way the Wild is and we have to change too.'

'Even if that is true, how can you be sure it has gone to the Ruby lands?'

'The attacks there have been building to something. This

is it. Besides, our lands have been quiet for years, while others have suffered. We can no longer afford to do nothing.' He clapped his uncle on the shoulder. 'Take our people to the Ruby High Lord's castle. Be ready to fight. I'll meet you there.'

'But,' Umed stammered, 'where are you going?'

He prepared to launch himself from the hill. With a combination of height and his peerless skill in the air, he was confident he could take flight from a single jump. 'To put right a very old wrong.'

CHAPTER FIVE

Sa-at and Tal stumbled into Roh's room. Roh herself had fallen behind. The last time Sa-at had seen her, she'd been leaning against the wall, the sweat gleaming on her face.

It reminded him of a Dogkin he'd seen in the Wild once. It had been in the throes of birthing a difficult pup and it had panted just like that. The Dogkin had died in the end. He wondered if Roh were about to die too.

'You have it?' asked Rochant. He was still propped against the wall where they'd left him, mostly obscured by a sheet.

'Yes, my lord,' said Tal.

'But?'

'But the imposter saw us. I don't think we've got long.'

'He looked like me,' said Sa-at. 'Why does he look like me?'

Rochant ignored him. 'You need to dress me in my armour immediately. Where's Roh?'

'Outside,' said Sa-at. 'She looks sick.'

There was no expression of concern on Rochant's face,

no flicker. He merely nodded. 'Then it's up to you two.'

'But, my lord!' Tal protested. 'What about the sacred rites? Shouldn't I get a Gardener-smith?'

'Consider this your apprenticeship,' answered Rochant coolly. 'Traditions are there to serve us, not the other way around. Now, unwrap the pieces and lay them out on the cloth. Try not to touch them with your bare hands.'

They did as instructed. It was hard not to handle the plates. The sapphire looked so smooth it demanded to be touched. Sa-at had enjoyed how smooth the crystal lights on the walls were and he suspected the armour would be similar.

As they attached the greaves to his shins, Rochant said, 'I need one of you to cut me and dab my blood on the armour.'

Sa-at looked up at him in surprise. 'Like making a pact in the Wild?'

Tal gasped.

'No,' replied Rochant and Tal visibly relaxed. 'It's very different.'

But Sa-at suspected Rochant was saying one thing and meaning another again. He took Tal's gathering knife and pricked Rochant's palm, catching the blood on the side of the blade before applying it to the greave.

They quickly fell into a rhythm with Tal attaching the plates and Sa-at daubing them with Rochant's blood. As Sa-at watched, the drops were absorbed into the crystal, leaving no stain behind.

It is like making a pact in the Wild!

'Listen,' said Rochant. And they did. People were coming,

and quickly. 'Sa-at, bar the door. Use anything you can find. Use your body if you have to.'

'But—'

As the shouts and running footsteps grew louder. Sa-at moved some of the heavier jars and boxes in front of the door and went back to Rochant. They attached his winged back plate, his chest plate, and the vambraces. Tal's hands shook constantly and he apologized every time he slipped or touched the armour or made some mistake that Sa-at did not understand.

'Open this door,' commanded a voice outside.

They ignored it and tried to put on Rochant's gauntlets. This was harder than the other pieces because his fingers kept catching rather than slotting inside.

A hammering fist accompanied the voice this time. 'In the name of Lord Rochant, open this door.'

Despite the situation, Sa-at saw Rochant's lips curl into a smile.

At last, Tal managed to put the helmet on and Sa-at dabbed some blood on it. There was a sudden change in the armour, as if it had been sleeping before but was now awake.

'Did it work, my lord?'

Rochant just stared at his feet, almost as if he were trying to peer through them.

It hasn't worked yet. Maybe we haven't done it properly. If Roh were here she'd know.

The hammering resumed, getting angrier.

'Come on,' he said to Tal, and ran to the door.

They arrived to see it shake in its frame, breaking the catch and scattering the boxes he'd placed there. Sa-at braced himself against the door and Tal did the same. It jolted against his back, hard enough to send him forward a pace. He threw himself back against it.

Three times they held the door, but on the fourth the guards managed to wedge something into the frame and then the door began to open very slowly, pushing Sa-at and Tal as it went.

'I'm sorry, my lord!' said Tal.

'It's all right,' said Rochant. He nodded to himself. 'Yes. All is well now.' He stood up. And it seemed to Sa-at that in that motion he grew, becoming not just taller, but bigger. The room was suddenly full of Rochant's presence, tinting the walls a dazzling blue.

With a final push from the outside, the door swung open, knocking both Tal and Sa-at to the floor.

Guards poured in but they drew to a halt beneath Rochant's gaze.

'M-my lord?' asked one, dropping his spear in surprise.

The others were already on their knees.

Rochant took a single step over them, seeming to fly rather than walk, twisting his wings to dive through the doorway.

Nobody else moved. The guards were so still, Sa-at wasn't even sure they were breathing. With some surprise, he realized he'd been holding his breath too. As if his body had been stunned by the proximity of the man and only now could he breathe again. Curiosity and excitement came back to him in a rush and he scrambled to his feet, leaped over the kneeling guards, and ran out of the room.

Rochant was in the corridor, crouching down by a crumpled Roh. One of her hands was twisted and tucked against her belly. The blood between her fingers glistened in the light of his armour.

A few whispered words were given, a secret goodbye, and then Rochant stood up. He summoned the guards from the room and looked at each one in turn. 'You have hurt one dear to me. Believe that her suffering will be visited upon you ten-fold.'

The man bowed his head.

Then another guard spoke up. 'Please, my lord. I don't understand. It was you that attacked her. You were out here, with us. I . . .'

'This was not done by my hand,' corrected Rochant. 'Come with me and I will show you exactly what you have been serving. Tal, help them tend to Roh. See that her remains are treated with the utmost dignity. Sa-at, come with me. You'll want to see this.'

Satyendra was running. He'd watched the guards opening the door and then he'd felt the light on the other side, flaring into life. Some part of him recognized the danger, even before he'd seen the blue tinge in the air. That part of him had taken hold of his body and used his stolen strength to move. Now he was halfway back to his chamber.

Gradually, his heart slowed and his thoughts became intelligible again. Whatever that light was, he hoped very much that his guards had dealt with it.

He returned to his room and cleaned the blood from his face, changing into fresh silks.

Now that he had calmed down, he realized that his last orders to the guards had been out of character. It was understandable, given the fact he'd been dying at the time, but it was not acceptable. His charade would have to be perfect if he was to keep his position.

And how am I going to deal with Vasinidra? As soon as he gets back, he'll be looking for a way to get rid of me. I'm not going to live out my days in some village somewhere, struggling for scraps. Not after everything I've gone through. But what choice do I have? The High Lord is too strong to face directly.

He is new to the role though and his hold on power is tenuous. Perhaps Yadva could be turned . . .

By now his guards should have reported back. He thought of the blue light in Roh's room and shuddered. She'd been up to something. It occurred to him that it was too quiet outside his room, and he stepped out to investigate.

The corridor was empty. He walked a little further and was alarmed to find the whole floor deserted. Given that they were hosting huge numbers of guests, this was especially odd.

It didn't take him long to work out that there was a gathering in the courtyard.

A bad feeling settled in the pit of his stomach. It seemed too soon for Vasinidra to have returned. *Unless something has gone wrong with the hunt. Please let it have gone wrong.*

He made sure his posture was straight, his step measured and his manner as much like Lord Rochant's as he could manage. Then, he stepped out into the mid-afternoon sunslight.

The courtyard was full. People lined the walls three rows deep. They made way for him though, parting so that he could see through to the large circle kept clear in the middle. Win, his seneschal was there and beckoned for Satyendra to join him.

As he moved into the space, he felt that something was wrong. 'What is all this?' he asked Win.

Win mumbled something. He made out the words 'my lord' at the end but that was it. The man wasn't meeting his eye. The man was afraid.

He's afraid of me.

Even as the hunger stirred, even as a part of him could not help but revel, another part began to panic. He moved closer to Win so that he could pitch his voice low. 'Look at me. Speak clearly, and answer my question: What is going on?'

'I . . .' Win began. His eyes flicked to Satyendra's for the barest moment but they flicked away again immediately. Satyendra felt the fear spike in that moment. It was as if Win was facing an executioner rather than his lord.

'I said look at me!'

Another flick to him and away. But not just away. Away and up.

A shadow passed over them. Normally, Satyendra liked shadows. They gave him a little respite from the burning light of the three suns. But this shadow brought no respite, stabbing at the skin on the back of his neck just as hatefully.

He looked round to see a Deathless landing barely five feet from where he stood. He'd not seen the man before but he recognized the armour. It looked like the set being grown for him. The set that Pik had modelled for him in secret. Except this set was larger. As he looked closer, he could see the man's face. Could see a golden tattoo that matched his own.

'You're . . .' He wanted to say the real Lord Rochant but didn't dare in such a public space.

The crystal helmet nodded.

'But . . . that's impossible.'

'I might say the same of you, Lord Rochant.' There was no malice there, the words delivered with only the slightest hint of irony.

Satyendra tried to think of a suitable reply. There had to be a way out of this. There had to be! Even if he drew from Win's fear he could not hope to stand up to a fully exalted Deathless. But Rochant hadn't attacked. That said something. Perhaps there was still time to salvage the situation.

For once, his quick mind failed him.

Rochant beckoned him to step forward.

Satyendra took one look at the armoured figure and shook his head. Close proximity to any sapphire was painful. Rochant's glowed with the strength of the suns and he knew it would burn.

There was no indication that Rochant was about to attack. One moment he was standing there like some great sapphire statue. The next he was flowing forward, a tidal wave of crystal crashing down on Satyendra, who turned and tried to run.

Fingers bored into the meat of his back as Rochant lifted him into the air one handed. Satyendra bucked like a Purefish on a hook but could not get free.

'How can it be that I return to my castle to find another with my name?' asked Rochant. 'How can it be that this creature bears the face of my Honoured Vessel?'

The pain was indescribable. Satyendra could feel the flesh puckering where Rochant's gauntlets touched it. He could feel that strange rippling sensation as if it wanted to peel itself off the bone to escape the searing crystal. It made him into an animal, a thing of pain alone. He screamed and wailed. He cried and wept. He changed.

'Behold,' said Rochant, ripping the silks away from his body. 'The Wild is cunning. It can wear our shapes, speak with the voices of our loved ones. But it will always reveal itself to be false.'

Satyendra saw the faces of the crowd. The way they leaned back. The horror. Several turned away, unable to look upon him. Through the pain, he managed a simple panicked thought:

What am I?

A bare arm swept across his vision. It was his arm, though he didn't recognize it. The brown skin had leeched to grey and then to nothing, showing bone and vein beneath. It was moving too, rippling like disturbed water.

What am I!

The pain was too much to bear. His mind fled from it, his vision tunnelling to a narrow point. The last thing he saw was his strange double, staring at him with an anger he recognized all too well.

What . . . am . . . I . . .?

But there was no answer to his question. Just hurt, hate and then, oblivion.

The immediate danger had passed but Pari didn't feel ready to come out of her armour just yet. She and Arkav were still with the Bringers of Endless Order. They had led the two of them away from the chasm beneath Lord Rochant's castle to a small cave tucked away from sight of the Godroad.

She had to duck and twist to fit her winged bulk through the entrance, but once inside there was plenty of room. One by one, the Bringers approached the shadows at the back of the cave and vanished. The last of the robed figures, the one that had been most eager to help Arkav, gestured for them to follow. She too was swallowed up by the darkness.

'I'll go first,' said Pari, her curiosity piqued. As she stepped forward, the light from her armour pushed back the shadows, revealing a moss-covered wall of natural rock. It seemed as if the Bringers had vanished.

She reached out to the wall and her fingers passed through, the surface no more substantial than a cloud.

'More tricks,' said Arkav. 'More lies.' He sounded angry. For the last few lifecycles his anger had been unpredictable and violent, and she readied herself for trouble.

But Arkav seemed to be in control.

Furious. But in control.

'I think it's rather fun, myself,' she said, and began to feel for a physical edge to the illusion. The actual entrance was wide enough for two people, or one Deathless, to walk comfortably side by side. She was pleasantly surprised to find it was higher than it looked too. 'Come on, time to get some answers.'

The path sloped downwards leading them through a circular tunnel. The walls were perfectly smooth. It reminded Pari of the chasm walls, except that these were flawless. Not a single crack or scratch marred their surface. She resisted the urge to make one herself.

They hadn't gone far when the tunnel brought them into a larger room. The Bringers blocked her view of most of it, but Pari saw curving walls behind them. These appeared equally perfect, but made of brass rather than stone. Some kind of slab dominated the middle of the space, not unlike the ones in the Rebirthing Chamber, save that this one did not sit above a pit, and it had a series of multi-jointed arms sprouting from the base. It was as if a brassy Spiderkin were on it's back underneath the slab, and the slab were its prey.

The Bringer that had talked with them before stepped forward. Pari could tell them apart now. This one was shorter than most of the others, and a little heavier on her feet.

'We will not be observed here.'

Pari wasn't convinced they'd have been observed beneath the castle either, but she kept that to herself. 'You seem awfully keen on hiding.'

The Bringer ignored her comment. 'We have many questions.'

'You have questions! Oh, my dear, I suspect I have at least as many as you, and mine are going to be much harder to answer, believe me.'

'No, Lady Pari,' the Bringer replied firmly. 'Our assistance was offered and taken. Lord Arkav Tanzanite has been restored. Now you will answer our questions.'

Pari could feel Arkav's anger rising next to her. She was fairly sure he wouldn't do anything rash. But not so sure that she wanted to take any risks. 'What do you want to know?'

'We wish to know what you saw.'

'We saw lots of things.' She started to tell them about their descent, and the strange living gateway they encountered. 'There was something else travelling down with us. I didn't see it at first but the deeper we went, the brighter it became.'

'It was a soul, wasn't it,' said Arkav. He had not phrased it as a question.

The Bringer paused then nodded. Some of the other Bringers shared a look at this. One shook their head, clearly frustrated.

Interesting.

'I'm sorry to say,' Pari continued, 'that when we passed beyond, the soul came with us. There were demons on the other side. They ripped that poor thing to shreds.'

'Continue,' said the Bringer. 'What else did you see?'

Before Pari could speak, Arkav put a hand on her arm. 'Look, Pari. Look at them!'

'I'm already looking at them.'

'Don't you see it?'

Pari frowned. She saw seven robed figures in black and white. All of them were masked and hard to read. She had the sense they were uneasy with the situation but other than that they seemed as inscrutable as ever. 'What exactly am I supposed to be seeing?'

'They're not surprised. They know what happens to souls that pass through.' He pointed an accusing finger at them. 'And they don't care.'

The Bringers did not acknowledge Arkav. Rather, they looked at Pari expectantly, waiting for her to continue. *They're not confirming or denying it but I suspect they care more than they let on. Silence is their tool. If I'm to learn more, I need to find a way to get them talking.*

'The thing that surprised me about the demons,' she said, 'was that they talked to us. They kept saying the word "prisoners". What do you think they meant by that?'

The Bringer looked away. 'We're all prisoners here.'

The other Bringers suddenly broke formation. One shouted for the lead Bringer to stop. Several looked openly worried, while several more just seemed to slump, as if they could no longer be bothered to mask their despair.

Pari could feel it now. She suspected Arkav had noticed some time ago. *They're desperate. They need us!*

She laughed, startling everyone in the room, which only made her laugh some more. Despite their air of misery, a part of Pari was excited. She felt she had several pieces of a puzzle that looked tantalizingly close to connecting to each other.

'I saw other souls down there,' she continued, 'travelling through tunnels that reminded me very much of the circles you make with your wands during the rebirthing ceremony. Are they coming from other castles?'

'No.' There was a pause. 'They are coming from other worlds.'

Pari sat with that for a moment. 'I see. Well, that's exciting. And these . . . tunnels the souls were travelling through, they keep them safe from the demons?'

'Yes.'

Arkav stepped forward. 'Why are there no tunnels here? Why are the souls of this place not protected?'

The Bringer sighed. 'A long time ago, before you or I were born, our people discovered essence, an element that is made of the things that essentially make us what we are. Our soul if you will. We also discovered ways to interact with essence, to move it, or in the case of your wings or the castles, to enable it to move us.

'Ultimately, we found a way to capture the soul, intact, from the body and implant it in another. From that day on we ceased to be bound by a single lifespan just as we ceased to be bound by the shapes that nature had given us.'

'What do you mean?' asked Pari.

'By combining special surgical techniques and essence manipulation we could alter the human form to suit our needs. But more than that, we found ways to cheat death in all but the most unfortunate cases.'

'This is fascinating, my dear, but I do hope you haven't forgotten my question.'

'I haven't. We believe that it used to be the case that when a person died, their soul would be broken up much like a body is after death. In the case of a body, it decays down into its component parts, feeding the soil and scavengers that are nearby. A consequence of our evolution was that we had cut off a source of nourishment for those that required essence to survive.'

'The demons,' added Pari.

'Yes. After a while, they sought us out in the places where we managed the soul transfer. Some even found a way through . . .' The Bringer closed her eyes. 'It was a dark time. We developed those tunnels you saw as a way to protect our people. We'd learned that while some types of essence were food to the demons, other kinds, those charged by the power of our three suns for example, was poison to them.

'This worked at first. But the light of the tunnels brought demons in such numbers that we knew it was only a matter of time before they would overwhelm our defences. To survive, we needed a better solution.

'It was clear that whatever deterrent we created, it would only stir the demons to new levels of desperation. The longer we starved them, the more dangerous they became. So, it was decided that in order for the many to enjoy immortality, a few would have to be,' she paused, glanced at Arkav and

Pari and then down at the floor, 'sacrificed. In order to satiate the demons.'

Pari held up a hand. 'Are you saying that the people under my care are being farmed as soul food?'

'Yes.'

'And how were we chosen for this great honour? Was there a competition? A vote? Did we lose a war?'

'No. No, it wasn't like that. Your world had already been corrupted. It was the obvious choice.'

'My world?' Pari raised her eyebrows. 'Not your world?'

'No. None of us were born here.'

'So . . . my people are the food. Arkav and I are the prisoners?' Her lips curled in distaste. 'Or the farmers? Which must make you and yours the jailers.'

'Pari,' said Arkav. 'She's hiding something, even now.'

'I'm sure she is. And none of this explains why they seem so worried.'

The Bringer seemed to brighten. 'This is actually very exciting.' When Pari blinked at her, she continued: 'What Lord Arkav is doing is reading my essence. Our eyes are adapted to do the same, but you seem to have developed the talent naturally.'

'Stop that,' said Pari. 'No flattery, just answers. What aren't you telling us?'

'When you were down there, did you see any other crystals? They would have been at least as big as you, long and sharp at one end, with light shining through their cores, like a ribbon through a bead.'

Pari shook her head and the Bringer sagged. 'Why are they so important?'

'They're our way home. We should have been replaced, but no one has come.'

'How late are your replacements?'

'Over two thousand years.' The Bringer sighed again, long and deep. 'Lady Pari, we are sick of this world.' The others nodded. 'Sick of this sky and its pale suns. Sick of the hungry Wild and the same rituals being played out over and over again. We cannot endure another millennia of this with only the faint hope that at some point we will be remembered.

'It is time for us to go home. Will you help us?'

CHAPTER SIX

It didn't take long for Vasinidra to reach the ruins of Sorn. Only days had passed since his last visit but it already looked different, the Wild reclaiming more of the buildings and pathways. It didn't bother him though. Once he'd taken his mother home, the demons were welcome to it.

He flew down, landing smoothly outside what had become her dwelling. Vines crawled up the walls, obscuring the wood completely in places. A couple of runners trailed over the path, inching their way towards the doorway and what he hoped was a Birdkin of some kind, was nesting in the roof.

Knowing his mother's penchant for traps and alarms, he stopped, checking the way ahead carefully before proceeding. But there were no wires, no secret holes, nothing to stop him approaching the house. He began to worry.

It was impossible to be subtle in a seven-foot-tall suit of glowing sapphire armour. She would know he was here, and yet she was not standing in the doorway.

Has something happened? Am I too late?

He tried to tell himself she was out hunting or patrolling the grounds but it didn't work. Instead, he started to picture the worst possibilities: his mother dead or taken by the Wild.

'Mother?' he called out.

When no answer came, he banged on the door once before tearing it from its frame and tossing it aside. 'Mother? It's me. Where are you?'

Someone snorted from within. It was not quite a laugh, nor was it quite a sound of disgust but somewhere between the two.

'Mother?'

He ducked and stepped inside. The blue light from his armour spilled ahead, illuminating a bundled figure by one wall. He saw a wizened face and a single hand clutching the blanket closed at her neck. It was Nidra but she seemed to have aged years in the few days he'd been away. *Am I too late? Is she dead?* But no, the rage still burned in her eyes, the expression on her face spiteful, hateful, and directed at him.

'Did I scare you, my sweet one? Was it hard to have to wait for me to speak?' she tutted. 'You have no idea what waiting is.'

'I'm sorry.'

'Apologies are worthless. I do not want them.'

He went down on one knee before her. 'I've done it, Mother. I'm High Lord of the Sapphire now. I've come to take you to the Bringers and restore you to your proper place.'

She studied him for a moment, her features rigid. 'Truly?'

'Truly.'

'Say it again.'

'As the new High Lord Sapphire, I am here to take you home, Lady Nidra.'

Tears fell from her eyes, vanishing into the folds of her crumpled face. She made no sound as she cried, though her body shook violently. He steadied her with his hands and, when she was done, lifted her gently into his arms. She weighed nothing to him. It was like carrying a bag of twigs.

He bounded out of Sagan towards the Godroad. The rest of the house were already on their way to the Ruby lands. But they would be going most of the way on foot. He would fly. First to Lord Rochant's floating castle and then to the home of the Ruby High Lord. A smile grew on his face as he imagined the challenge. He might even beat them there.

One leap took him up onto the Godroad, and he immediately felt the fizz of essence beneath his wings, making him feel light, energized. He started to run, eager to take to the sky once more.

'What are you doing?' snapped Nidra.

Her voice distracted him, making it harder to keep the right rhythm. 'Taking you home.'

'By flying? While carrying another person? Don't be a fool, Vasin.'

He slowed, stung by the rebuke, then started to accelerate again. 'I can do it.'

'And what happens if you drop me? This body is all I have. It's old and weak. It will break. Is that what you want?'

'No.'

'If you don't want me to die, you'll stop behaving like it's your first lifecycle. High Lords cannot afford to be so reckless.'

Vasinidra slowed to an easy jog, gliding a little after each step.

'Better,' muttered Nidra. 'Now, tell me what has happened. What state are the family in? Who is with you? Who is against you? And what has happened to Rochant? I want to know everything.'

'Yadavendra is gone. It was . . .' He struggled to find the right words. 'Horrible. I wish there had been some other way.' In the end, his uncle hadn't seemed like a person any more. That last sight of him outside his armour would haunt Vasinidra forever. Stripped of the illusion of power his armour gave, Yadavendra was revealed; lost, a burned-out shell, full of paranoia and bile and . . . he glanced down at the bundle in his arms, and the similarities struck him like a physical blow.

'There was no other way. My brother was mad. Now, what of the others?'

'I . . . You were right about Gada. Once he knew you were alive, he stood with me. Uncle Umed is with us too, as is Yadva. For the moment.'

'We will have to watch her.'

'Yes. I don't know where the real Rochant is, but his vessel underwent the ceremony and managed to fool the Bringers.'

'How?'

'I don't know. But once things are calmer, I'll have him quietly moved away and give Rochant's Godpiece to a new Deathless.'

'Yes, that will be a powerful tool to move the others. We will have to think carefully about who we add to the house.'

Mia, he thought. *I want it to be Mia.* But he kept the idea to himself. Better to wait and tell his mother after her restoration.

'House Ruby teeters on the brink of destruction. I've sent the others there with our hunters. I only hope they arrive before the Corpseman does.'

'It's not the Corpseman we need to fear. It's Rochant! He was the one who corrupted my brother. He's the real danger.'

'We have to look to the Rubies first. Their need is greater.'

'No, Vasin. That's what he wants. He's tricking you, don't you see? Distracting you with other things.'

'It's no trick. The Rubies are being slaughtered. Whatever Rochant is up to will have to keep until I'm back.'

'No. No! Listen to me, Vasin. Listen! Let the others deal with the Rubies. You have to see me attuned to Rochant's Godpiece so he can't be reborn. Then, you hunt him down and kill his body. Do this for me, Vasin. Do it for all of us.'

She took his nod as agreement and settled her head on his chest. Within a few minutes she was asleep. Even at rest, the lines of worry remained visible on her face. He wondered idly if they would follow her through to her next lifecycle. The Story-singers said that some wounds followed the Deathless through the ages. Perhaps these ones were too deep to heal.

He looked down at her and wondered if he'd been too late to save her after all. 'My name is Vasinidra now, Mother,' he whispered, then took to the sky.

The forest was calming by the time Chandni caught up with Glider. Whatever had stirred it up seemed to have gone away, or been killed, or met some other fate she'd rather not think about. She still had Varg's hand. It was warm and solid and a little bit rough.

Just like the rest of him.

Glider was not alone. She was sitting opposite a pack of Dogkin, all white furred, most of them five-legged. Like her, their eyes were mismatched. It seemed as if they were discussing something, though it was impossible to tell the subject matter. The last time Chandni had seem them, they'd been trying to kill her and only Glider's sacrifice had kept them safe until Lord Vasin arrived. She could still see the old burn scars where the Deathless had beaten them, and the kinks in their legs where the bones had not set straight.

They hadn't forgotten her either. As soon as the two of them came into sight, the pack's leader raised its head and snarled.

'Oh shit,' said Varg.

As the pack sprang to their feet, Glider did the same and the air was suddenly alive with low growls and the threat of violence.

Chandni assessed their situation quickly. *There's no way our Dogkin can hope to beat so many and we can't outrun them.*

'Glider,' she said in her sternest voice, 'stand down.'

The Dogkin turned to her with a puzzled whine.

'Stay there. It's fine.'

'It is?' Varg whispered.

'Yes,' she replied, squeezing his hand. 'But keep behind me.' She had an idea in mind, a dangerous one that she dared not think of too hard lest she run from it. *Be strong, Chandni. There is no place for doubt.*

The pack quickly spread out, blocking off their escape, while the leader loped towards them. She didn't seem interested in Glider or Varg; all her hatred was saved solely for Chandni.

She thought about their first meeting, years ago. They'd hated her then too. It wasn't hard for her to work out why.

'This is about Fiya, isn't it?'

The pack howled at the mention of the old woman's name. Chandni had killed Fiya to save her baby, offering the body to Murderkind as a sacrifice. Now, the pack wanted revenge. She wasn't sure what the connection between them and Fiya was, but it had clearly been powerful.

'You want to hurt me.' She nodded sadly and held out her right arm towards the leader. 'I know what it feels like when those you love are threatened or killed. I understand.'

Varg's chin brushed her shoulder as he spoke. 'What are you doing, Chand?'

The pack leader opened her jaws wide.

Chandni placed her hand in its mouth.

'Chand!' Varg pulled at her left arm but she snatched it free.

She didn't feel the teeth puncture her skin. There was no pain at all, not even a whisper of sensation. She heard the bones crunch though and knew that it was bad. *Don't think about it. You are a Sapphire. You do not break.*

The pack leader's glare shifted to surprise when Chandni didn't react. She was careful not to look at the blood – *my blood* – staining its muzzle. Instead, she met its eyes and said, 'I understand how you feel, but you should not have done that for I am not yours to hunt.' She pulled the black feather loose from her hair and turned her head to display it. 'See?'

The old Dogkin let go of her hand and sniffed at the feather, then recoiled as if stung.

'Murderkind,' she said, and the pack fell silent. She noted

the angry glares were gone, the mismatched eyes wide with fear. 'Murderkind,' she said again. This time the trees themselves fell quiet, as if the wind had died. Crowflies came and landed on her shoulder. It looked from her hand, to the Dogkin's bloody jaws and shook its head.

The pack were utterly still now, watching her with abject terror.

'All I need to do is say that name once more. And I will. Unless you agree to serve me for one year. That is the price of my mercy. Will you pay it?'

The pack exchanged glances and then looked to the leader, who howled once, long and loud, and then lowered her head.

'Good. Now, look at me.'

This close, she could see that, like Glider, the pack leader's human eye was clear while those of the other Dogkin were clouded.

The great white head regarded her and Chandni felt a sadness well up inside. 'Varg, do you remember that story Fiya told us about her ancestors?'

'What about your hand? It's a fucking mess.'

'Not now, Varg. The story, do you remember? I think it's important . . . I think . . . I . . .'

Everything fell out of focus for a moment, then came back.

'Chand!' said Varg.

'Cha-aan!' said Crowflies.

'I . . .' she looked down at her hand. Her eyes refused to work properly but she could tell it was the wrong shape and there seemed to be blood everywhere. 'Oh. On second thoughts, perhaps you should look at my hand now, Varg.'

Crowflies leapt from her shoulder as she fell.

Someone caught her. Probably Varg. She smiled at the idea

of being caught by Varg. *Such strong hands,* she thought, the smile fading from her face as she passed out.

Sa-at's mouth hung open. The figure dangling from Rochant's arm, the one that seconds ago had looked so much like him had changed. He'd watched the image of his own face deform, the features starting to melt, save for the eyes that darkened and rolled. Brown skin had paled and faded from view, becoming a window to the organs and bones beneath. But the bone structure was wrong. A vertical line ran down the skull from the forehead to the top of the jaw. When the imposter had still been conscious, it had looked like it was trying to open, to unfold in some way.

It was not a human skull.

There was a gasp from the crowd as Rochant threw the body down at his feet. He turned to the guards, who seemed just as stunned as everyone else. 'Take this creature and lock it beneath the castle.'

Seven stepped forward, laying their spears down in a row to make a kind of stretcher and then rolled the body onto it with the toes of their boots. Everyone watched in silence until it had been taken from sight.

'Attend me,' said Rochant, pulling off his helm and tucking it under his arm. 'Many of you have heard the story that I was attacked during my last lifecycle and that my family were killed. You will have heard that Honoured Mother Chandni saved the last of my descendants and brought him here though, as you have seen, it was no Sky-born baby she raised, and my blood does not flow in its veins.

'Many of you will have questions. Many will have fears. I too have questions.' He glanced in the direction the guards had gone. 'And I will get my answers. For now though, let me put some fears to rest.

'As you can see, the rumours of my assassination were,' he gave a slight smile, 'exaggerated. I am just as strong as I ever was. But there is much work to do. While I attend to matters of castle security, the gates will be kept closed. No one is to enter or leave until I am satisfied.' His expression softened but Sa-at was sure there was something hard lurking beneath it, just out of sight. 'Consider yourselves my guests for a little while longer. Before I go, I want to introduce you to my real Honoured Vessel.'

Rochant beckoned for someone to come forward.

After a moment, Sa-at realized that he was the one being gestured at. He went and stood by Rochant's side, blinking in the glare of the sunslight. Everyone was looking at him. He wasn't sure what to do, so he stayed very still as Rochant continued to speak.

'He has had a difficult life and a long journey to get here. But he is home now. Please, make him feel welcome. And remember: Much of this is new to him. Be generous when answering his questions, and do not trouble him with your own.' He leaned down towards Sa-at. 'I promised that one day you would get to meet people.' He gestured towards the crowd.

But Sa-at couldn't shake the images of his twin from his mind. 'What will happen to the demon?'

'You don't need to worry about that. I'll take care of it.'

'But why did it look like me and why—'

'I told you. Don't worry.' He gestured to the crowd again. 'Go on. They're waiting for you.'

Sa-at's frustration was replaced with astonishment as he

realized what Rochant was saying. 'All of them? They want to meet me?'

'Yes. There is no need to hide any more. Go forth, make friends. I will send for you later.'

And with that, he walked away, a gaggle of staff following in his wake.

Sa-at was alone.

The crowd looked at him.

He looked at the crowd.

The only other time he'd been the attention of so many people had been outside Sagan. He remembered their jeers and the pain as they'd thrown rocks at him. The memory made his hands shake and his throat draw tight.

He wanted to say something. He felt that he ought to say something but the words wouldn't come. They wouldn't even form in his mind.

Then, he caught sight of an older man with kind eyes. The man was smiling at him. He tried not to think about all the other people and just focused on the man.

Their eyes met and the man waved a hand in greeting.

He waved to the man and was surprised when a forest of hands waved back. There were many smiles now. The man approached and offered his hand. 'Welcome, Honoured Vessel,' he said. 'I am Kir.' He clasped Sa-at's wrist and, after a pause, Sa-at clasped his. He'd once seen the Gatherers greet each other this way. The man's grip was firm, reassuring.

What is an Honoured Vessel? It sounds very special. I will have to ask Rochant about that.

And then there were many people all around him, and hands squeezing his shoulders or taking his arm. The names came thick and fast until he gave up all hope of being able to remember them all.

Sa-at was so happy at the attention he thought he would pop.

I am here, he thought. *I am home and these people, all these people, are going to be my friends. Everything Rochant has promised is coming true.*

He looked around to see if Rochant was still there, and saw him on the far side of the courtyard talking to a man in servants' garb with three sapphire studs at his collar. The more Rochant talked, the more worried the man looked.

When they finished talking Rochant bounded over. Sa-at noticed that he was now carrying a long wooden spear with a sapphire tip. 'Come,' he said. 'We should get you inside.'

'Is something wrong? I'm making lots of new friends.'

Rochant steered him away from the crowd. 'They will still be there when we're done.'

Sa-at noted the speed at which they'd re-entered the castle. 'Is it very bad?'

'One of our enemies returns sooner than anticipated.'

'Something from the Wild?'

'No. A Deathless, like me.'

'Will you fight them?'

Rochant looked thoughtful. 'If I have to.'

It was strange. Rochant was talking of enemies and fights but he seemed so calm. 'What's an Honoured Vessel?'

'An Honoured Vessel is the chosen favourite of a Deathless. It is the duty of my people to teach them, help them, and keep them safe. You will be much loved here.'

Sa-at smiled. He liked the sound of that. 'Do I have to do anything?'

'Simply continue to observe and think. The rest will take care of itself.'

They'd walked to a part of the castle Sa-at hadn't seen before, turning several corners and ascending two flights of stairs. Then, they stopped. Rochant pressed against the wall and it opened.

'You've made a cave!'

'Yes, but one that is too small to accommodate my wings.'

'I'd fit.'

'Yes,' replied Rochant smoothly. 'Show me.'

Sa-at slid inside. 'It's dark.'

'Feel around at head height until you find a handle, then slide it to your left.'

Sa-at did as he was told, and was rewarded with the feel of cold air on his face. Leaning forward he could see outside towards the castle gates. The servant he'd seen earlier was standing outside and, to Sa-at's eye, appeared uncomfortable.

However, that was nothing compared to the spectacle of a second sapphire-armoured figure landing in front of them. 'Wow,' he whispered.

'You can see something?' asked Rochant.

'Yes.'

'Tell me.'

'Like a story?'

'Yes, like a story.'

And so Sa-at did, narrating what played out before him. 'There's a man in armour that looks like you. But his shoulders are more curly and his helmet's a different shape. Oh, and he has long hair like mine, but less tangly and more like water.'

'His name is Vasinidra.'

'That's a long name.'

'It is.'

'Why does he have such a long name?'

'Because he's important. The length of the name denotes his status.' Then Rochant quickly added, 'I will explain what status means later. What is he doing?'

'He's walking towards the gates. The old man you spoke to earlier is waiting for him.'

'Win, my seneschal. Is Vasinidra alone?'

'Yes.'

'Look closely at the bridge behind him. Is there anyone on it?'

'No.'

'Now look at the mountainside beyond the bridge. Are there people climbing it?'

'No.'

'Look a third time to be certain. Is he alone?'

'The only one I can see is Vaseendra but—'

'It's Vasinidra.'

Sa-at thought that's what he'd said. He tried again, breaking the unfamiliar word into parts. 'Vas-in-ee-draa has got something in his arms. It could be a sack. No, it's a . . . it's a person!'

'Describe them.'

Sa-at pressed his face against the stone to get a better view. He could see grey hair and a lolling head. 'She looks old. She might be dead but I don't think so.'

'She?'

'Yes. I saw her outside Sorn the day I found you. She was with the lady with the golden lips.'

'That is good, Sa-at. Her name is Nidra, she is Vasinidra's

mother. She will not be dead, trust me on that. You are looking at our true enemies.'

Sa-at found himself wondering about the demon in the courtyard again. 'I thought the one that looked like me was your enemy.'

'He was but a tool. Consider my spear. It is deadly only when guided by my hand. With my enemies, Nidra is that guiding hand. She controls her son and he controls House Sapphire. That means she has many, many tools at her disposal.'

'She has lots of spears?'

'Exactly.'

'More than you?'

'Far more.'

Sa-at frowned. 'What are you going to do?'

'What would you do in my position?'

It was hard to imagine being in Rochant's position. He was having a hard time reconciling the frail body he and Tal had dragged up the mountainside with the powerful form that stood behind him. *There are lots of things I don't understand.* He tried to remember the way Rochant had guided his thinking in the past. *Vasinidra is the enemy. He is powerful like Rochant is powerful. Nidra is more powerful because she controls Vasinidra. She has many spears but the spears aren't here.*

'They're not here!' he said out loud. 'The spears aren't here. Nidra is asleep and he is alone. You should get them now before their pack comes back.' He paused as a worrying thought struck him. 'Are you stronger than Vasinidra?'

'Not stronger, no. We are closely matched in strength.'

Sa-at thought back to how Rochant had advised him to

fight the last of the Red Brothers. 'How are you better than him?'

'I am more composed. I plan ahead even in battle. I have fought to get here whereas he was born in a place like this. He is bound by its rules as he knows no other way.' Rochant's voice changed slightly and Sa-at suspected he was doing that odd smile again. 'And he does not know I am here.'

'How is he better than you?'

Rochant's answer was immediate. 'He is better in the air. He is faster.'

'You need to get him on the ground.'

'Yes. Go back inside and keep out of sight until I call for you. Do not go anywhere near Vasinidra, do you understand?'

'Yes.'

'Good. Go quickly.'

Sa-at nodded. 'I will.'

He pulled the handle back, closing the hole, and then stepped outside. Rochant sealed the cave behind him and sprang towards the place where the walls met. He kicked between one wall and the other, rapidly gaining height, and Sa-at watched, amazed, as Rochant landed in a crouch on top of the battlements.

Then he remembered that he was supposed to be going quickly. He pulled up his hood, lowered his head, and ran.

Vasinidra stood at the gates to Lord Rochant's floating castle. Despite his mother's warnings he'd made good time. He only wished she'd been awake to appreciate it. As he strode forward he could see Win, the new seneschal, already waiting for him.

The man bore a harried expression that was most

unbecoming of his station. *A good seneschal should always appear calm. Even if there are visitors from other castles. Especially then.*

It didn't help that Rochant's previous seneschal, Honoured Mother Chandni, had been superb in the role. The comparison was doing Win no favours.

His mother was starting to wake but when he went to put her down she gave a slight shake of her head. Though her eyes were open, he realized that she remained limp in his arms. *Is she so exhausted she can't even lift her head? Or is this just a ruse to make our enemies underestimate her?*

'High Lord Vasinidra,' Win began, bowing deeply. 'Welcome back from the hunt. I see you have outpaced the others by some considerable margin.'

'The hunt is far from over. We fly to the aid of House Ruby. I am merely here to . . .' he paused. Something was wrong. Of all the Crystal Dynasties, House Sapphire was the most disciplined. Everything placed with care and precision, from the gemslights on the walls, to the walls themselves, to the guards placed on those walls.

He frowned. It was the middle of the day and the gates were closed. He could think of no reason why that would be. He returned his attention to Win. His mother did the same. Standing alone, the man looked more than just harried, he looked nervous. Like a prey caught in the hunter's jaws.

'Is everything in order?'

'Yes, High Lord.'

'Why are the gates closed?'

'Ah . . . Lord Rochant ordered it.'

His mother gave a slight tut as he asked: 'Why in the name of the Thrice Blessed Suns would he do that?'

Win glanced over his shoulder as if looking for support. 'I . . . that is, he thought that it would be safest given the . . . ah . . . situation.'

'You just said everything is in order.'

'It is, it is. Lord Rochant just wishes to keep it that way.'

This is what happens when I show leniency. The power has gone to Satyendra's head. I will have to deal with him. Soon. 'Where is your lord now?'

Win's expression grew pained. 'He is within, High Lord . . . reacclimatizing to his, ah, duties.'

'Your name is Win, yes?'

'Yes, High Lord.'

'And you have served the house loyally for many years?'

'Born and raised here, High Lord.'

'Then I can trust you?'

He straightened and met Vasinidra's eye. 'Of course.'

'Pick out some people that you trust and take this woman into the castle. Do it discreetly and see that she is well cared for. Then I want you to summon the Bringers of Endless Order. Tell them it is urgent. Tell them that they are to grant this woman's request as if it came directly from me. When they arrive, bring them to her. Do not let anyone else see her. Do not let anyone else visit her. That includes Lord Rochant.'

He could see that Win had questions but to the man's credit he didn't ask them.

'Carry out these orders above all others. If Lord Rochant doesn't like it, tell him I will explain everything when I return. Perform well in this task, Win, and House Sapphire will remember.'

Fail, he added silently, *and I will remember.*

Something of his thoughts must have communicated themselves through his expression as Win swallowed nervously. 'Yes, High Lord.'

He looked down to find his mother looking back through half-lidded eyes. 'You're leaving me here?'

'I have to.'

'You have to do nothing. You are High Lord. You are choosing to leave me.'

There was no arguing with that. 'Will you be all right?'

'I suppose you'll find out when you *choose* to return.'

He embraced her one more time and set her down, before easing her carefully into Win's care. The old man shouldered her weight with difficulty.

'High Lord,' said Win. 'Lord Rochant would be honoured if you would join him for lunch in the castle.'

It was tempting. Staying would give him time to settle his mother, perhaps even speak to the Bringers in person. He could set Satyendra straight on how to play his role better and stop him making any other foolish decisions. *And I could have something to eat.* The day had already been full of exertion and there was a lot of flying left to do. He decided he would stay long enough to ensure his mother was safe and his belly was full. But as soon as he took a step forward, the image of the empty hill came to mind. Hot on its heels was a memory of Lady Anuja Ruby's face, her gaze accusing as he'd left her beleaguered lands to come home.

He stopped.

The assembled might of House Sapphire was on its way there at this very moment, about to do battle with a very different Wild. With not one but two of the greatest demons and their minions. The idea of being anywhere but at their side was ridiculous.

'No,' he said, making Win turn back in surprise. 'We all have our duties. Win, I have made yours clear. My duties are clear too and they take me back to the hunt.'

Win nodded, seeming so relieved that he might cry. 'Hunt well and thorough, High Lord,' said Win.

Vasinidra nodded and started to run. There was a short stretch of rock before the edge which gave him enough momentum to leap out into the essence currents that flowed around the castle's base.

He looked one more time towards the gates before he plunged downwards and thought he saw something, a blue glimmer on the battlements, like the outline of a man. But when he blinked, it had gone.

CHAPTER SEVEN

The Bringers of Endless Order all watched Pari, waiting for her to answer their question: They wanted to go home, their home, in another world, and they needed her help. She wondered if those sparkling green eyes were able to see the thoughts running through her mind and rather hoped they couldn't.

She let the silence run long and awkward enough that even Arkav turned to look at her with an expression of impatience, then she said:

'Well, it seems to me that we have concluded our previous deal. You helped me restore my dear brother, and we brought back information about the place beyond the chasm. If you want my help a second time, I'd need to know what that would involve and what, exactly, would be my incentive for doing it.'

The Lead Bringer responded immediately. 'We want you to take us down to where the souls move safely from world to world. There we would abandon our bodies and return home.'

'That sounds so easy I really don't see why you need my help.'

'The distances are great, and our presence might attract the demons' attention. Your job would be to keep us safe while we make the transfer.'

'You're saying it could be dangerous and you need my protection?'

'Yes.'

'I see why you want me there. What I don't see is why I'd want to take the risk.'

'We would offer you, and Lord Arkav if he wished to assist, a choice. Either we could use our influence here to improve your fortunes, or, if you prefer, you could come with us.'

Pari looked at Arkav. He'd know she was tempted by the latter. Few things were as alluring as an unopened door in her opinion. She suspected he'd rather stay, however. 'I think my brother and I need a moment to discuss this in private.' She gave them all a smile. 'And after millennia of waiting, I'm sure a few more minutes won't hurt.'

The sourness of their silence suggested that perhaps it would.

'So be it. We look forward to hearing your answer.'

The Bringers moved back a respectful distance. Arkav watched them, then turned back to her, his face creased with concern. 'You realize they have shown us too much to let us say no.'

'Oh, Arkav, the issue has never been whether to say yes or no. We have more pressing matters. For example, how outrageous can we make our list of demands?'

He raised an eyebrow. 'You don't want to take the option where you go with them?'

'I might do. But I thought you'd want to take the option where we come back. I also thought that if we made the list, I could convince you that nothing on it is even half as exciting as exploring another world.'

'I'm not interested in making a list. I don't trust the Bringers to honour the agreement, and even if they did, I'm not sure we should make the deal.'

'Whyever not? This is our chance to go somewhere incredible or to change this world in a way that suits us. Think of the things we could make! The people we could annoy! The possibilities are endless.'

'No, Pari, think about what this will mean. If the Bringers leave, they aren't coming back. It will be the end of everything. The Deathless will stop returning, the hunts will fail, and the Wild will spread unchecked.'

'All the more reason to go. If the Bringers do get home, why will they care what happens to us? But if we go, Arkav. You and I. We care. We can make them send replacements.'

He looked at her, his expression somehow full of admiration and exasperation at the same time. 'How can you possibly know what we can or cannot do there?'

'I don't know them, but I know us. We'll find a way. I don't trust the Bringers either, which is precisely why I want to go with them. But before I do that, I want to make sure my lands are in order and my people are happy. I also want to show the newly restored you off to the High Lord so that she doesn't get any ideas about replacing us.'

'You're talking as if I've already agreed to the idea.'

She gave him a twinkling smile. 'But you have agreed. You just haven't realized it yet.'

When he rolled his eyes, she knew she'd won.

'I suppose you did just save my soul.'

'Exactly. The least you can do in return is help me save the world.'

'If I go with you, I'm not just going to get replacement Bringers. I want to learn how this all works. I can't help but feel this is wrong somehow.'

'Which bit?'

'All of it.'

She mused on this for a moment. 'Agreed. My only condition is that when you reach your conclusions you consult with me before you start the fires. If we're going to destroy everything, we should do it together.'

They clasped wrists.

The Bringers looked up as Pari approached them. 'We've decided to take you up on your offer.'

'Good,' replied the lead Bringer. 'Are you ready to start?'

'Now?' She laughed. 'That's delightful, but no. There's a few things to do first.'

The Bringer sounded as petulant as a child. 'What things?'

She ticked them off in her mind: *Collect our people and our carriage from Lord Rochant's castle, report Arkav's success to the High Lords and allay my own High Lord's concerns about me.*

'Just a few loose ends. Don't worry, as soon as our futures are secure, we'll get straight onto yours.'

Sa-at was sure the woman Win carried through the gate was the same one he'd seen outside Sorn but it was hard to believe. Before she'd seemed like a predator but now she was old and weak.

But Rochant was weak when I found him and he's strong now. Maybe she can be strong too when she wants.

The thought made him look at the woman – Nidra, he reminded himself – with fresh eyes. Beneath the layers of old musty clothing he saw the shape of the strange dagger she'd carried, the one that looked like a sharp bit of sky.

With a dull thud, the gates closed behind them.

He watched Win struggling to get Nidra across the courtyard and went over to help. Given how light Nidra was, the man seemed to be sweating an awful lot.

'Do you need to stop?'

'No,' replied Win sharply. 'I need to keep going. The fewer people that see this the better.'

Sa-at looked around. With all the traders and guests trapped within the castle, there were many bored faces, all with nothing to do but look at them. They were trying to hide their interest but Sa-at could see it as clear as the stars on a cloudless night. He could also see Rochant gliding down from the battlements.

He swept over their heads to land with his back to them.

'No,' hissed Nidra. 'No, no, no.'

Win's head drooped in defeat, which confused Sa-at. *He should be happy. Why isn't he happy?*

Rochant turned slowly, removing his helmet. He seemed as calm as ever. 'Nidra Un-Sapphire, welcome to my castle. Of course, as an exile, you know the penalty for returning to our lands.'

Nidra's eyes narrowed but she said nothing.

'You can let her go,' Rochant continued. 'Give her a little space. She's stronger than she looks.'

I knew it! thought Sa-at.

Win did as instructed and Nidra stood without support easily enough. Her eyes seemed to take everything in, including Sa-at. Something about that made him feel uncomfortable.

'Now,' said Rochant. 'You and I are going to have a talk about the future. Somewhere more private than this. Are you going to accompany me with dignity?'

As he talked, Sa-at saw Nidra's right hand inching towards the small of her back where the dagger was stowed.

'You haven't answered my question,' prompted Rochant.

'Answer one of mine and I will.'

'And if I do, will you come with me? Calmly.'

'Yes.'

'Then ask.'

Her fingers worked deftly to pull aside the fabric, revealing a simple wooden hilt. Sa-at was sure that her dagger was powerful. Perhaps it was even strong enough to pierce Rochant's armour.

'How are you restored?' she asked. 'I thought your body would never recover.'

'I thought the same. But then, like you, I'd only thought about what the poison could do to a person, not how it did it. Fortunately, others had devoted years to the question. I'll tell you all about it, but not here.'

Sa-at leaned forward, as quiet as he'd ever been, and slipped the dagger from Nidra's belt.

'I have another proposition,' said Nidra. 'A trade.'

He smiled that odd smile of his. 'That's what I've always admired about you. You never give up. I'll listen. But not here. Inside.'

'Very well,' she said, but as she stepped forward, she

pivoted on the ball of her foot and sprang towards Sa-at, her hand reaching for the dagger that was no longer there. Surprise registered on her face as she closed with him.

Sa-at sprang back on instinct, and her fingers cut the air where his chin had been. But she was still coming, faster than his mind could process. As he tried to back away, he stumbled, ducking an attack that was actually a feint as she struck the dagger out of his hand.

It spun in the air between them, going up, slowing, then starting to fall.

He reached for it.

Nidra reached for it.

Rochant caught it before either of them. With his free hand he snatched Nidra by the neck, and she dangled from his grasp like a cub being held in the jaws of its mother.

'Thank you, Win,' said Rochant smoothly. 'Thank you, Sa-at. That will be all. I will need some time alone with Nidra. We are not to be disturbed under any circumstances. I trust you can manage things for a few hours?'

'Y-yes, my lord,' said Win.

'What should I do?' asked Sa-at, but Rochant had already turned his back on them and leapt away. He repeated the question to Win but to his surprise the old seneschal didn't reply. He just put his head in his hands and started to sob.

Chandni woke up. Her head was pillowed on Glider's belly. A pack of Dogkin slept around them in curled mounds, like a circle of snowy hills. Crowflies was on a nearby branch staring at her with intensity, while Varg unwittingly did his best to match its stare with his own.

When her eyes met his, his beard curled around his mouth with delight. 'You're awake!'

She gave him a tired nod. 'Yes, and hungry.' As she spoke, Crowflies leapt from its branch and flapped off into the canopy.

'We'll have to go forage something,' said Varg. 'Be like the old days.'

'Yes, it will.' They shared a smile. 'Have our new friends been any trouble?'

'Nah, just sat there quiet as Mousekin. Went off to sleep not long after you did, and their ears are twitching now you've woken up. Reckon they're waiting for you to tell them what to do.' He scratched his chin. 'Reckon we all are.'

Chandni made the conscious effort to raise her right arm. It had been numb for so long now that she often forgot it was there until it knocked into something. Her mind no longer mapped it as part of the space she filled and so it took constant effort to remember. And, in truth, it was not hard to recall the crunching sound the pack leader's teeth had made as they had bitten down on her hand.

It was time to survey the damage. She brought her right hand up to eye level.

Suns! she thought, squeezing her eyes shut. She wasn't sure what she'd been expecting to see but this was worse.

Be strong, Chandni. Be strong. You are a Sapphire.

Slowly, deliberately, she opened her eyes again, forcing herself to face the situation.

The thing on the end of her wrist no longer looked like her hand. Her third finger was a crumpled twig, her little finger unrecognizable. Much of the hand itself had been crushed and distorted by the Dogkin's powerful jaws.

Teethmarks ran roughly across her skin, leaving scabby tracks.

She forced herself to look, to take it in and accept this new reality. The one good thing was that the wounds were already closed and cleanly sealed. *More of Crowflies' work, I think.* She made a mental note to thank the Birdkin when it returned. She was sure it would, if only to claim a reward for its assistance.

Her index finger and thumb still worked, as did her middle finger, though this was crooked now.

There is some functionality there. That's something. A wave of tears threatened to break but she held them back. *No, Chandni. You will not cry. Not here. The pack must see you as strong.*

She lowered her hand and did her best to ignore the naked sadness on Varg's face. 'I'll need to eat if I'm going to heal.'

'Then we'd better start foraging.' He got up and offered to help her stand. The assistance was unnecessary but she took it anyway, drawing comfort from Varg's close proximity. Glider and the other Dogkin got up too and began to pad after them.

With gold and red light still finding its way through the trees, and a big pack of Dogkin at their side, it felt almost pleasant to wander the Wild. No animals dared cross their path, and for the moment, the dangers of the forest either slept or chose to keep their distance.

Varg leaned in close so he could speak quietly. 'I gotta say, that was pretty clever how you tricked them Dogkin. How did you know that would work?'

'I didn't know, exactly. It just seemed logical given what I know about the Wild.'

'You didn't know? Fuck me! That was some gamble. But Chand . . .' his eyes flicked down to her maimed fingers.

She touched his arm and squeezed it. 'Given how much I stood to lose, my hand was a small price to pay.'

Tears glimmered in Varg's eyes. 'You could have lost everything.'

'But I didn't. There's no use holding onto what could have been. There's enough to worry about in the present.'

Varg stopped walking. 'You're just gonna pretend that this is normal?'

'Of course not! We are far from normal here. That's why I had to take decisive action. What else would you have me do?'

'I dunno. It's just that when we found you leaving the castle, you were ready to die. No, it was worse than that, you wanted to die. And me an' Glider weren't enough to keep you here. I begged you, Chand, and you didn't care. And then you give everything to a demon prince like it's nothing—'

'How can you say that?' interrupted Chandni, a sense of outrage building. 'I made that sacrifice so that I could be with you. I thought that's what you wanted.'

'It is. But I'm not sure it's what you want. Like, you tried to kill yourself, then you gave your soul to a demon, and then you put your hand in a wild Dogkin's mouth without even blinking. That's fucking crazy!' He searched her face as if looking for a sign. 'You say you want to have a life with me, but I see you like this and I'm not so sure. Do you want a life with me, Chand? Do you even want to live?'

'You know I do.'

'Cos from where I'm standing it looks like you still want to die or punish yourself or some other Sapphire bullshit.'

'No. I want to live and I want to protect those I love. I'll do anything, sacrifice anything if I have to.'

'I hear that. But maybe don't sacrifice it all, eh? Leave something for us to love.'

She managed a nod and they carried on walking for a while, the air between them awkward. A part of her was angry for him saying such things when she was doing everything she could. Another part of her felt the sting of his words too keenly to dismiss them completely.

After a while, Varg broke the silence. 'How come you only asked them Dogkin to serve you for a year and not, like, forever?'

'Because I wanted them to agree. A year seemed significant as a price but not so large that they'd risk Murderkind's wrath to oppose it.' She thought back to the stories Fiya had told them. 'And it felt right. I think that's important here.'

'Well, it seems to have worked so far, but I'm keeping Glider between me and the others just in case.'

They hadn't gone far when Crowflies returned.

'Cha-aan,' it said, and then flew off again. 'Cha-aan,' it repeated.

'I think it wants me to follow it.'

'Mmm,' Varg grumbled. 'Don't like that Birdkin.'

'I have to follow. It might be a summons from Murderkind.'

'I don't like the sound of that either.'

Crowflies led them through the trees, and then landed at a seemingly random spot, checked about itself and then tapped the ground with its beak. 'Cha-aan.'

She stopped and the Dogkin stopped behind her, sitting back on their haunches.

'What is it?'

It tapped the ground again, impatient.

Chandni looked at the spot but there was nothing of interest there, just dirt. She couldn't even see any Wormkin. 'I don't understand.'

Crowflies made a strange tutting sound in the back of its throat. It then hopped forward and prodded her foot with its beak before returning to its original position and tapping the ground again.

'I see,' she said, and stood there.

Crowflies looked at her, gave a satisfied nod and knocked three times on a nearby tree. It then looked up. Chandni did the same.

Long branches reached over her head and provided a modicum of shade. She saw pretty yellow-green leaves rustling as one of the branches shook. Then there was a soft pop and something was falling towards her. Her left hand came up on instinct and caught it.

In her hand was a plum, fat and round and purple. It took all her self control not to take a bite immediately. 'Oh, thank you, Crowflies. This is very kind of you.' She briefly rested her forehead against the bark of the tree. 'And thank you. This looks delicious.'

'It does,' agreed Varg. 'Hey, Birdkin. Can I have one as well?'

Crowflies cawed derisively, then shook its head.

'Shit.'

'Don't worry, Varg. We can share.' She tried the plum. It was sweet and ripe and the juices ran down her chin.

'That looks good.'

'Mmmm, oh it is. It's wonderful!' She took another bite.

'Can I have some now?'

She finished what was in her mouth. 'I just want a little more.'

'Right.'

Three bites and over half the plum later, she handed it over. She'd meant to share it equally but it had been too good. So good in fact, that she felt no guilt at all, and when Varg gave her a reproachful look, she couldn't help but laugh.

She realized that her hunger had gone completely and she felt alert. 'Glider, I need to find Prince Kennelgrove. Do you know where it is?'

Glider looked at Fiya and started to bark enthusiastically. Slowly the pack leader rose from her haunches and padded over. There was a look of deep sadness in her eyes, but she took Chandni's sleeve and gave it a gentle tug, then set off into the woods.

'What do you think that's about?' asked Varg, who was busy sucking the last of the plum's juices from the stone.

'I think she can help us. Come on.' And she took his hand, partly to lead him after the Dogkin, and partly because she wanted to.

Pari and Arkav made short work of the climb up the mountain but both came to a stop when they found the gates to Lord Rochant's castle closed.

'Well,' said Pari. 'This is unexpected.'

'What now?' asked Arkav.

'We knock, of course. I can't abide a closed door.'

They crossed the Bridge of Friends and Fools carefully, balancing the spring of their Sky-legs against the sudden swings in the wind. When they reached the other side, they both pounded on the wood with their gauntlets, naturally keeping time.

A guard's head appeared on the top of the battlements. 'Who goes there?'

'Lady Pari and Lord Arkav of the Tanzanite Everlasting. We demand entrance.' There was a brief pause and then she added, 'I suggest you either open the gates or find someone who has the authority to open them before my brother opens them for you. I'm afraid he has no patience today.'

'Really?' sighed Arkav. 'Why do I always have to pretend to be the angry one?'

'Because you do it so well, my dear.'

He started to pace and rant. Words like 'outrage' and 'consequences' sailed up into the air. The guard's head disappeared.

'That seems to have done the trick. You can stop now. Honestly, it seems like you can't cross a Sapphire threshold these days without some kind of nonsense.'

Arkav came to a stop beside her. 'Between us, we could probably force the gate.'

'What, and start the war we were sent here to prevent?'

'I'm sure you could talk them down afterwards.'

'I could, but why do I always have to be the one to—' She stopped. 'Ah, I see what you're doing. Very funny. But just once I'd like to do this without making a mess.'

He chuckled. 'I'm not sure I believe you.'

'Let's at least give them the chance to behave like a decent civilized house before we humiliate them.'

'Very well.'

She looked back at the gate and then at her gauntleted hands. 'Though it would be very satisfying to just break in . . .'

'I don't think we should.'

'Then why, my sweet yet taxing brother, did you suggest it in the first place?'

He assumed an expression of innocence. 'I was simply making an observation.'

Just as the temptation was getting too much to bear, the gates opened enough to admit an old man in a seneschal's uniform. He looked up at them – mounted, in their armour – obviously afraid. 'Lord Arkav, Lady Pari, welcome. I regret to—'

'Oh dear,' interrupted Pari. 'What has happened to Honoured Mother Chandni? I was rather fond of her.'

The question banished whatever it was the man had been about to say. Despite the day having plenty of life left in it, the man already appeared exhausted. 'She is quite well. She is just, ah, enjoying a rest after having . . . that is, after the rebirth of Lord Rochant.'

'I see. Well, in that case . . .' she paused, 'I'm sorry, I don't know your name.'

'It's Win, Lady Pari.'

'Win? What, the little Win who used to chase that boy around the courtyard for kisses and had the most adorable crush on Lord Rochant's cook?'

'Well,' he stammered, 'it is an honour to be remembered, though I don't recall having feelings for the cook.'

'Yes, you do,' said Arkav. 'You still do.'

Win met his eyes and his face fell. 'I apologize.'

'Think nothing of it and open the gates for us,' said Pari. 'And instruct our staff to prepare the carriage for departure.'

'I'm sorry but Lord Rochant has ordered the gates closed. None may enter or leave until he decrees otherwise.'

Pari gave him a patient smile, and Arkav chuckled.

'Forgive me,' said Win, 'but my lord was most serious when he gave the edict.'

'I'm sure he was. You Sapphire are the masters of being serious. However, we did not come here as visitors nor guests. We did not even come here as Tanzanite Deathless.' She waited to see if he'd understood and let her smile fade when he didn't. 'My dear Win, we came here to represent the will of the council of High Lords. It is our duty to return to them with news of House Sapphire's recent changes. What your lord desires or does not desire is irrelevant here. Now you have a simple choice to make. Either you order the gates open for us, or we will open them ourselves. Rest assured, whatever position you take will be noted and reported to the council when we see them.'

Win nodded rapidly. 'Ah, yes. Well in that case,' he turned and raised his voice to a hoarse shout. 'Open the gates!'

She patted him on the shoulder. 'Much better.'

With a lot on his mind and nothing immediate to do Sa-at had returned to the courtyard, keen to make new friends, but he found himself dawdling on the edge of the crowd. Now that they couldn't see him, they didn't seem as happy as before. He saw they had broken up into lots of smaller clumps. Many of the groups had their heads close together so they could talk without being overheard.

As Sa-at worried about what that meant he saw the gates swing open and Win hurrying inside. Following behind him were two more Deathless. Their armour was reminiscent of the Sapphire suits he'd seen recently but the shapes of the plates were curved, more rounded, though just as elaborate.

These glowed with a soft blue-violet light of their own and were, to Sa-at's mind, equally beautiful. One of them cast an imperfect aura, the light dimmer on his chest and right wing, which was broken.

The Sky-legs they walked on seemed to have a life of their own, like beasts straining at the leash, and the Deathless almost tottered in their efforts not to run Win down.

He didn't recognize the man, but the woman he knew instantly.

The one with golden lips is here! He mouthed her name: Lady Pari Tanzanite. This was both exciting and worrying. She was yet another of Rochant's enemies. But she had saved his life from the Red Brothers, and he had taken her safely out of the Wild. That made them nearly friends.

Why is it always so messy? Why can't my friends be friends with each other too?

The two Deathless were met by a group of people in similar colours and he could see orders were being given.

Sa-at stepped out of his hiding place and was about to wander over when Win caught sight of him and hurried to intercept. 'What are you doing here?'

'I was going to ask the people some questions but they didn't look very happy and—'

'Not now,' Win hissed. 'Just stay out of sight.'

'What are you going to do?'

He staggered slightly as if struck by a strong breeze and stopped to lean against the wall. 'I don't know. This is too much for me. I never knew being a seneschal would be so difficult!'

Sa-at nodded. *It's hard for everyone here,* he thought.

Because of all the people. People make things hard. Lots of people make things really hard.

Win started to mutter under his breath. Sa-at found it hard to hear but he wasn't sure Win was actually directing the words at him. 'If I interfere with them, I'll be drawn up before the High Lords, but if I don't Lord Rochant will have me cast out! He says they aren't to be trusted but how can that be? And how can I obey him when he has ordered he is not to be disturbed? It's impossible! My task is impossible!'

Sa-at wondered if he were about to cry again. 'Would you like a hug?'

'A what? No! Just leave me alone. I need to think.'

Win pushed off from the wall and rushed, unsteady, into the castle. Sa-at wondered what to do. Win had told him to stay out of sight, but he hadn't told him not to go near the lady with the golden lips.

So long as she doesn't see me, I can go and see her.

He crept forward, using the crowd as cover, stalking them as he might a potential meal in the Wild. The Tanzanite staff were hurriedly preparing a carriage while the two Deathless spoke easily with one another. He couldn't hear what they were saying but he caught the sound of their laughter.

There wasn't much cover between him and them, but if he stayed where he was, he'd never know what they were laughing about or what their plans were. In that moment, Sa-at wanted to know very much. Moving around so he could approach from behind them, he edged forward.

As long as they don't turn round, they won't know I'm there.

'You're right,' said the Deathless man. 'It is like that time with the Hedgekin. Except that, as I recall, you got impatient and scared it away.'

'That's an interesting piece of fiction, my dear. If I remember rightly, what happened was . . .' she leaned forward and lowered her voice.

The man chuckled. 'Oh yes, I'd forgotten about that.'

Forgotten about what? Sa-at kept low and crept closer, using the two armoured figures to shield him from the view of their staff.

'Yes,' continued the lady with the golden lips. 'I thought the Hedgekin was cute but I had no interest in hunting it. I was after something else entirely.'

'What was it again?'

'Oh Arkav, you really don't remember? It was a crafty little thing but not especially bright. It actually thought it was hunting us that day.'

'I remember now. It was quite small, wasn't it?'

'Yes. Small and rather out of its depth.'

'What did we do with it in the end? Did we eat it?'

'As I recall, we toyed with it a little first and then we caught it.' They both turned and loomed over Sa-at. 'Rather like this.'

There was a pause.

'Hello,' he said.

She frowned. 'You seem familiar. Have we met before?'

'Yes, you helped me once and I helped you. That makes us nearly friends.'

The two Deathless exchanged a look. 'Does it now?' asked the woman.

'I hope so.'

She gave him a half smile. 'What's your name?'

'Sa-at.'

'Well, Sa-at. I am Lady Pari Tanzanite and this is my brother, Lord Arkav. We'd very much like to know why you were spying on us.'

'I wanted to know why you were here.'

'That's public knowledge.'

'Not to me.'

Pari looked at him more closely. 'Yes, we have met before. But not here.' Her eyes widened. 'It was in the Wild.'

He nodded. 'You fought the Red Brothers and saved me.'

'And it was you that took me back to the Godroad afterwards.'

'Yes!' He grinned. 'That was me.'

Arkav studied him for a long moment. There was an openness in his gaze coupled with an intensity that Sa-at found unnerving. It was like being stared at by Crowflies or Murderkind. 'You're a long way from the Wild, Sa-at.'

'Brother dear, don't you think he's the exact replica of the body Lord Rochant has just been reborn into? They could be twins.'

'No,' replied Arkav. This close, Sa-at could see a dark line that marred the light of his chest plate. 'They're nothing alike.'

Sa-at wasn't sure what to do. He was talking to Rochant's enemies. That would make Rochant angry. Should he call Win? Or call the guards? It was so hard to know how best to help his friends. Was Pari really his friend or was she his enemy too?

'Oh, come now,' continued Pari, 'don't be stubborn. Cut his hair and dress him appropriately and they'd be identical. I feel like we're missing something here and I know just who will have the answers.' She cast her eyes over the tents and traders lining the courtyard. 'Typical. He's never around when you need him.' She looked back to Sa-at. 'I don't suppose you've seen any large white five-legged Dogkin recently?'

He shook his head.

'Arkav, you really don't see the resemblance?'

'No.'

Sa-at found himself agreeing, the image of the imposter, his body all strange and twisted, alive in his mind.

'Well I do. It's almost as if Chandni and Mohit had two children. Is Honoured Mother Chandni your mother?'

'They say she is.'

'Then you must be an Honoured Vessel.'

'Yes! That's what Lord Rochant called me.'

'The man that looks like you called you that?'

'No, not the demon, the real Lord Rochant.'

The two Deathless exchanged another look. Sa-at felt a strange sinking sensation in his stomach. Had he said something wrong?

'We need to go,' said Arkav.

'I couldn't agree more.'

They signalled to their servants and the carriage was suddenly moving. Arkav bounded past it towards the gates and demanded they be opened while Pari kept her attention on him.

'It's a shame that our conversation is being drawn to a close. I'd very much like to speak to you further.'

'I'd like that too,' he said, and then wondered if he was letting Rochant down.

'Why don't you come with us?'

'Now?'

'Why not? There's space in our carriage. We could show you the lands of House Tanzanite.'

He saw Arkav forcing the gates open with superhuman strength. The guards were protesting but none dared stop him. As soon as the gap was wide enough, the carriage began to trundle through.

'I can't,' he replied. 'This is my home.'

'I understand.' She gave him the kind of smile that made his toes tingle and so it was something of a shock when she scooped him up in one arm.

The next thing Sa-at knew, he was sailing through the air with Pari in great, gliding bounds. He was so surprised and so torn between the awe of travelling in this fashion and the anger at having been taken against his will, that he simply stared.

There were shouts and movement. People were protesting but they all flashed by in a blur. Three more bounds and he was by the gates. Another two and he was through them.

Arkav held up his hands when he saw them. 'Suns, Pari! What are you thinking?'

'I wasn't really,' she replied. 'It was more of an impulse.'

'We're here to stop a war, not start one!'

'Yes, but I have to see him with my own eyes and this will bring him out.'

'Pari!'

Guards were tentatively pouring from the gate behind them. Sa-at wondered what was going to happen. Win came bustling out shortly afterward his eyes nearly popping from his skull as he saw them. 'In Lord Rochant's name, I demand to know what is happening!'

'Please don't fight,' begged Sa-at.

'Oh, there's no need for all this fuss,' Pari replied. 'I'm just showing the Honoured Vessel how much fun Sky-legs can be.'

'You're not . . .' Win paused and smoothed down his tunic self-consciously. 'Taking him away?'

'Of course not. What a foolish thing to say.'

Sa-at noticed the carriage was on the bridge now. Arkav still stood by their side. *She's just like Rochant. Saying one thing and meaning another. She's tricked me and she's tricked Win. But why?*

'My lord's order was very clear. The gates were to stay closed. Why have you forced them open? Why have you taken the Honoured Vessel outside the castle?' His voice cracked a little. 'What is all this?'

Rochant appeared at the battlements. He no longer wore his armour but was wearing a long wrap of blue and gold spirals. 'It's all right, Win. I'll take it from here.'

'Lord Rochant,' Pari smiled 'I must say I did not expect to see you again so soon.'

'Nor I you. It seems you can't keep away.'

'You know me,' she replied, and Sa-at saw her glance down at him. 'I can't resist a good mystery.'

'Then perhaps I should appeal to Lord Arkav instead. You have business with the High Lords. I will not interfere in that, so long as you return to me what is mine.'

The two Tanzanite Deathless exchanged a look.

'Remember your place, Rochant,' said Arkav. 'You cannot interfere with the will of the High Lords. Our duty is to report to them what we have found.' He gestured to Sa-at. 'We believe the council will be most interested in what he has to say.'

'Well,' added Pari, 'that was put a little more directly than

I would have done, but yes, my brother has the right of it. We will take our leave now, and we will take Sa-at with us. When the High Lords are finished talking to him, he'll be set free.' She put a hand flat across her chest. 'Believe me when I say that Sa-at has absolutely nothing to fear. Sa-at will be quite safe. Only those that have betrayed the sacred duties of our kind need worry.'

They're talking about me. They're going to take me away. But I don't want to go away! I want to stay with my new friends.

'Are you sure you want to pursue this approach?' asked Rochant. His tone and manner were still calm but Sa-at saw there were many spears outside now, all poised and ready to throw on his command.

'Come on, my dear,' said Pari, holding out her hand to Sa-at. 'It's time for us to go.'

Sa-at took a step back. 'But Rochant is my friend.'

Her voice became gentler. 'Believe me when I tell you, he is not what he appears to be. You said we were nearly friends. Why don't you give us the chance to become true friends?'

This made him falter. A part of him dearly wished to be Pari's friend. Even when she was in her armour she didn't seem scary like the other Deathless he'd seen.

'I don't think I can be your friend and Rochant's friend at the same time.'

'No, my dear, you have to choose.'

He looked back towards the battlements. Rochant still stood there, calm as ever, but Sa-at knew better. *He won't show his feelings while his enemies are here. I know he wants me to come home.*

Pari was still holding out her hand as Arkav leaned in and said quietly. 'The carriage is across.'

'Last chance, Sa-at,' said Pari.

'I can't!' he blurted, and ran for the gates. Win stepped aside, the guards parted, and he dashed between them, not stopping until he was within the walls of the main keep.

Behind him, the gates shut with a resounding *thud*.

Safe, he thought. *I am safe again.*

CHAPTER EIGHT

They had walked for the rest of the day, following the pack as they padded through the trees. Chandni would have enjoyed the experience more if she wasn't still feeling light-headed from blood loss. Still, Varg and Glider were with her, and Crowflies came and went, bringing her little gifts; a variety of nuts and berries.

The way seemed easy. No branches scratched at her; no roots snatched at her feet. She wouldn't describe the forest as friendly but she wouldn't say it was hostile either. It tolerated their presence.

A chill took the air as the suns began to set. Something told Chandni that they would not want to be wandering the Wild for much longer. 'Excuse me,' she said to the lead Dogkin. 'How far is it?'

The old white muzzle swung back in her direction for a moment. She met the creature's eyes but could read nothing of value in them. Then it turned away and carried on walking.

'I don't like this,' said Varg.

'Nor do I,' she agreed. 'We don't know where we're going. We don't even know where we are.'

'And it's getting dark. Do you think we can trust it?'

'I think they are bound by our agreement to serve me, but I'm worried they could twist it somehow.'

'What do you mean?'

'I'm not sure.' She tried to recall the exact words she'd used, but fatigue was making her mind foggy. They had agreed to serve her but her experience with staff was extensive, and she knew that a bad servant was worse than none at all. 'What if they are obeying my order but in the worst possible way?'

'Nah, I don't get it. You saying they don't have to obey you?'

'No. I'm saying that while they *are* helping me find Prince Kennelgrove, they might be taking the longest route they can. Or they might be leading us through a dangerous part of the Wild so that something else can get us.' She threw up her hands. 'Or I could be completely wrong. I don't really know what I'm doing, Varg. And I'm tired.'

He stopped and drew her close. She rested her head against his chest and closed her eyes. *Just for a moment,* she promised herself. When he spoke, she could feel the rumble of his speech against her ear.

'Well, you could ask.'

'Ask who? Crowflies isn't here.'

'That's a good thing if you ask me. But I ain't talking about Crowflies. I'm talking about the old Dogkin. It's gotta do what you say, so ask it what it's doing. I don't think it can talk but it understands you well enough.'

'Yes, but she could lie to me and not break our agreement.'

Varg frowned as he thought that over. 'Shit.'

'Quite.'

Glider barked and the other Dogkin stopped and waited for them, their eyes making pale glimmers in the fading light.

Just a moment more, she thought. Varg's chest seemed to generate an impressive amount of heat. His arms were snug across her back. *Just another . . . moment . . .*

A wet nose on her cheek snapped her awake.

It was Glider.

'Was that really necessary?'

Glider gave an earnest bark.

'All right,' she said, pushing Glider's head out of the way.

They walked on still surrounded by trees. The colour had leeched from them now, telling her that the suns must have recently set.

She caught glimpses of a black shape flying from tree to tree. *Crowflies.* There was a conspiratorial nature to its movements. Each time it landed, it paused to whisper something that set the leaves quivering, like someone trying to suppress a chuckle. But as soon as she got closer to any given tree, it silenced the motion, like an actor snapping back into role. *What is it up to?*

They hadn't gone far when the gaps between the trees narrowed, and the trees themselves started leaning towards one another, their branches intertwining like lover's hands. Beneath the arch they made was a natural tunnel of wood and mud, sloping down. The Dogkin pack sat in a half circle around it.

Their leader looked at Chandni for a long moment, then padded inside.

Glider whined and sat down. When Varg took a step towards the tunnel, all the Dogkin growled at him.

'I think I have to go in alone,' said Chandni.

'Well I fucking don't!'

'That's sweet, Varg, and I truly would rather you be with me. But this is the Wild. There's a way to do things and I feel that this is right.'

'How long?'

Chandni frowned. She couldn't make out his face any more and wasn't quite sure what he meant. 'How long until what?'

'Until me and Glider come in there to get you.'

'Oh. If things go badly you should probably leave, but—' she added quickly '—as I know you won't do that, take your lead from Glider. If she wants to go in, you come as fast as you can. You'll be able to find me in there, won't you?'

Glider barked affirmatively, though this was undermined by the whine that accompanied every glance towards the tunnel.

She gave Glider a hug and Varg a kiss. It was hard to pull away but she made herself do it.

I have never backed down simply because something is difficult. If the creature I seek is down there, then that is where I will go.

Chandni stood as tall as she could and walked towards the tree-tunnel entrance. The old Dogkin went in ahead of her and was swallowed almost instantly by the darkness.

A second later, it swallowed her just as swiftly.

Satyendra woke up slowly. It occurred to him that he wasn't dead, which was a surprise, but one that was hard to take much pleasure in. Apart from the place where Rochant's gauntlet had gripped him, most of the pain had gone. Five finger-sized sores still burned whenever he moved. His body felt wrung out and stiff. Exhaustion clung heavy to his bones.

And he was cold. Most of his clothes had been stripped from him and the stone floor was sucking the heat from his skin.

More than anything else though, he was hungry. And he was alone. The room he was in was small. There was little in the way of furniture or decoration. Just rough-hewn rock and a bit of light from outside that managed to illuminate the gaps where the door had warped in its frame.

I am in a cell. Wait. I know this place.

He gave a grim laugh as he realized this was the same cell he'd been keeping Pik in. *An unhappy accident or a deliberate bit of spite on Rochant's part?* He decided it was probably the latter. If the Story-singers were to be believed, Rochant never did anything by accident.

A voice came from nearby. A woman's voice, laced with age and bitterness. 'Care to share the joke?'

'No.'

'Fine. I doubt I would have laughed.'

He tried sitting up and failed, only getting halfway before collapsing again. As he lay on his back, panting and feeling sorry for himself, it occurred to him that the woman didn't sound like a guard or a servant. 'Who are you?'

'A prisoner of Lord Rochant, same as you. What did you do to gain his ire?'

He considered lying but what was the point? They'd got him now. And besides he was too tired to lie. He was almost too tired to think. 'I pretended to be him.'

That made her laugh for quite a while. 'You pretended to be a Deathless?'

'Yes,' he smiled at the incredulity in her voice. 'It was easy. At least, it was until the real Rochant showed up. How did you become Lord Rochant's enemy?'

'I rejected him in a previous lifecycle.'

'You're a Deathless?'

'I was, once.'

'Which one?'

'Nidra Un-Sapphire.'

'But you're dead! They sent you into the Wild before I was born.'

'My brother, Yadavendra, sent me but I didn't oblige him by dying.'

Suddenly it made sense. 'Now your son is High Lord you've come back. But Rochant doesn't want you to come back.'

'It's complicated. He doesn't want me to come back on my own terms.'

'Well, he doesn't want me to come back at all.'

'Then you should ask yourself why you're still alive. There will be a reason.'

He frowned. Nidra was making sense. His frown deepened as he considered all the reasons why Rochant might have kept him around. None of them were good. 'I'm more interested in why he put us together. Seems sloppy.'

'Oh, that's easy,' Nidra replied. 'It's to allow us to talk under an illusion of privacy and give away our secrets.'

'In that case we should talk about how annoying he is.'

Nidra laughed again. It wasn't a nice laugh but he liked it. He'd made his mother laugh once but that seemed like a long time ago. 'Actually, he'd enjoy that. He enjoys the challenge. It's better not to talk about him at all.'

Satyendra nodded. 'How did you survive in the Wild?'

'That's a pertinent question. If he doesn't kill you, exile is your most likely fate. I survived by skill, luck and sheer bloodymindedness. It's hard to find food and it's hard to avoid the predators, but that isn't the greatest threat. The Wild has a presence of its own. It's like someone is pressing down on your chest making it hard to breathe. They don't push hard but they never let up. If you relax or drop your guard, they squeeze a little more and they never give back what you've lost. Just being there is a slow death. If you ask me, you'd be better off with execution.'

'Easy for you to say.'

She didn't reply to him immediately, then asked: 'What's your name? Your real name?'

'Satyendra.'

'Hmph. I remember now. Always said it was too long. Satyendra sounds like a high lord's name.'

'It's supposed to. I was born on the same day as Yadavendra. Apparently, he was so pleased he gave me a name as long as his.'

'With a start like that, it's no wonder you've ended up here.'

Satyendra's temper began to flare. 'What, the same place as you?'

'Don't confuse us, boy. We are not in the same place. I've managed to fight my way back from the dead. I will rejoin the ranks of the Deathless soon, one way or the other. I have options. You are dead. The only questions for you to consider are what does Rochant want to squeeze out of you before he kills you. And how long and painful does he intend your death to be.'

He had nothing to say to that, so he went back to lying there, cold and tender and hungry. He clenched his jaw, squeezed his fists, and wrapped himself in a cloak of self-pity.

But Nidra was not done.

'What I don't understand is why you're just waiting for it to happen.'

He didn't answer her.

'If I was in your position,' she continued, 'I would be thinking of ways to escape . . . or to make him suffer.'

He licked his dry, cracked lips, answering despite himself. 'Why are you saying this if you know he can hear us?'

'Oh, he *was* listening. He's not now. An urgent matter drew him away not long before you woke up. The guards went with him in a fluster. All of them,' she added with a note of delight, 'so it must be very taxing indeed. I'd love to know what it is, but you can't have everything.'

'Why are you doing this?'

'Simple. I want revenge. On Rochant. I imagine you want the same. Find a way to make him suffer and if I can, I'll find a way to spare your life.'

'How can I trust you? And don't give me anything about Sapphire honour. I know how much that's really worth.'

'If you won't trust my word, trust my hate. I would give anything to see it satisfied.'

He could feel her hate as sure as the stone beneath him, and recognized something of himself in it. Whatever else she was lying about, her enmity with Rochant was undeniable.

Why not? he thought to himself. *I have nothing to lose.*

'Very well. I'll take you up on that offer, though I hardly see how it's relevant here. I'm beaten. Powerless.'

'He needs you for something, and in the right hands, that need can be twisted. Stay alert and a chance will come.'

She's right. I have faced death every day and won. I tricked all the Sapphire Deathless for years by cunning alone. I can beat Rochant as well, but only if I stop whining and start thinking.

But as he tried to take comfort from that thought, another came: This idea of self-reliance, of him tricking everyone with his brilliance, was merely a comforting lie.

All these years, Mother protected me. Perhaps only so that I could be sacrificed for Rochant's benefit but, without her, I never would have got this far. I wasn't alone until I sent her away. And how long did I last after she left? One day. One miserable day. Perhaps this is justice.

His features twisted into a mask of hate and he forced himself to sit up, wincing as the burned skin pulled tight on his back.

I spit in the face of justice.

I spit on the Deathless.

I spit on them all.

For a moment he managed to convince himself, and then he sagged down again. Even in his own mind the words had a hollow ring.

I am doomed and alone. Is hurting Rochant really all I have to live for now?

It was easy for Nidra to talk of hate and battle. That was her world. She had survived terrible things but always with the promise of a return to glory. She was Deathless, destined for greatness. He, on the other hand, was something else, something outside the natural order. Perhaps he'd find a way to make Rochant pay. Perhaps he wouldn't. Either way, Satyendra held no illusions about his own fate.

Vasinidra flew through the night. The only light was the Godroad, cutting an arrow-straight path ahead of him. Either side of it was the Wild, a vast sea of darknesses, all twisting together.

For him, flying was the purest of actions. It focused his mind and body totally, devoting both to the moment. He had worries about what he would find in the Ruby Lands. He had worries about his mother, about his ability to lead the house, about a hundred things. But in these moments, all he thought about was the dip and rise of his wings, of essence currents playing over his armour, and of moving onward.

The vagueness of the dark below and the unchanging road contributed to an odd sense of going nowhere. As if he were hovering in the sky, not diving through it.

Time passed.

Vasinidra flew.

When at last, the sky began to lighten in anticipation of the sunsrise, he saw the lands of House Ruby laid out before him. Forest had given way to a rising swamp that threatened to submerge the Godroad in places. It seemed the denizens of the Wild had not been idle in his absence. For each settlement that he passed intact, there was another abandoned or in the midst of being repaired. Most of Raften had been ripped from its stilts and dragged down into the muddy waters, leaving only jagged stumps and a single house behind. Fourboards remained, but it looked more like a battleground now than a home, its people grim faced as they sifted through the rubble. None of them looked up as he passed. None saluted. It seemed they lacked the energy for hope.

House Ruby had been teetering on the edge when he left. Now it seemed to have fallen.

I've been gone a matter of days. If I'd stayed, could I have prevented this?

Soon, the floating castle of the Ruby High Lord came into view. In the twilight it was a heavy blot against the clouds, like a rough-edged smudge on a painting. The High Lord herself was between lives but her daughter, Lady Anuja Ruby, had taken the role temporarily. During his last visit, she was the only active member of the house remaining. He recalled her desperation, and her plan to bring her mother back early.

He dearly hoped she hadn't followed that plan.

It wasn't until he was close that he saw the guest flags flying, four colours, four of the seven houses present to aid their wounded ally – Tanzanite; Peridot; Opal; and, at last, Sapphire.

He came down to land where the Godroad ended. The guards didn't challenge him as they had before, but they didn't welcome him either. Their expressions were tired, old before their time.

Vasinidra stopped nonetheless and gave the proper greetings as the cage was winched down. He climbed in and ascended alone, the cage swinging in the wind. There was plenty of time for him to examine the old pulleys and chains.

The metal is as worn as its people. When was the last time these were changed?

It felt as if House Ruby had been under too much pressure for too long, and the cracks were starting to show.

In previous lifecycles, the castle had been a proud and happy place.

I will make it so again, he promised himself.

At the top, servants in ruby livery tried to direct him to the Gardener-smiths, but he waved them away. 'There's no time for that. Is Lady Anuja here?'

'Yes, High Lord Vasinidra. She is meeting with your family as we speak.'

'Good. Take me to her.'

He marched down narrow corridors, having to twist awkwardly at times to accommodate his wings, as the servants struggled to keep pace. It pained him to be breaking with protocol and not remove his armour. It pained him further to feel like he was repeating Yadavendra's behaviour. He knew he'd been exalted for too long, and that such a state could become addictive. But he also knew that time was of the essence. The Corpseman was on the move, and they had to act before it did. He was sure that the demon had a plan, and that it centred around House Ruby.

As he drew closer to the room, he could hear the sounds of argument. There were lots of voices, but two rang out more clearly than the others: Lady Anuja Ruby and his uncle, Lord Umed Sapphire.

His heart sank.

Given his attire, he did not dare break tradition further by entering without permission. But waiting as the servants announced him with song, and waiting still longer for an invitation was painful.

When it came, he strode in. There were many Deathless present: Umed, Yadva, and Gada from his own house, a single noble from house Tanzanite, and then one from each of the minor houses, Opal, Peridot, and Ruby.

Though both the Opal and Peridot were dressed in their finest and painted for the occasion, no amount of artistry could hide their injuries fully. Lord Lakshin Opal's long face was swollen on one side, the glittering lines around his eyes sagging with exhaustion. Lord Quasim Peridot remained upbeat, despite the fact that one of his arms was bound to his side.

Lady Anuja was on her mother's throne. The gold star around her right eye flashed angrily with each flick of her hand. However, the aggressive movements were testing her injuries, the pain plain on her face. 'Talk of the future all you want, Lord Umed. My people's end is coming now. Tonight. And I will not be sitting in this chair when it happens. I will be out there. With them.'

Quasim and Yadva nodded approvingly, but Umed raised his hands. 'If my understanding is correct, the demons are looking for your people, for you above all. If you go out there and die, all this fighting will have been for nothing.'

'If I don't go, I am nothing.'

Any surprise Umed showed at Vasinidra still being armoured was matched by relief. 'Ah,' he said. 'If you won't listen to me, then please, listen to my High Lord.'

Vasinidra bowed to her, though technically he no longer had to.

Anuja appraised him coolly. 'I see you have come back as disrespectfully as you left. Two days you have been gone, and two nights. They came for us that first night, so on the second day we hunted them. But on the second night they came back even stronger. Demons have entered my settlements, walked into houses as if they owned them. Demons!' she exclaimed. 'In my streets! So many that we have had to go down and fight them in the dark or else risk losing everything. So many, that the road-born fear to sleep in their own beds. They watch from the Godroad as their livelihoods are destroyed . . . As my hunters are destroyed. Now my forces are too broken and tired to hunt any more. The demons know it.' She slumped back in her chair. 'They know it.'

It took him a while to find the right words to respond. 'Please forgive my absence and my entrance. All I can say in my defence is that both were to serve you.'

'And how does this insult serve me? You refuse to do battle by my side, yet come to my home, to my hall, dressed as a conqueror!'

'I left alone so I might come back with the combined might of House Sapphire. And I came back in this manner for two reasons. The first is time. Your people have run out of time and, as soon as we conclude this talk, I will ask your permission to take wing once more, to fight for your noble house. The second is to make a point.'

Her eyes narrowed but she said nothing.

'You and I have talked about the Wild changing. The demons are no longer simply dangerous entities. They are organized and they have adapted to take advantage of our traditions. Don't you see? We have become predictable to them. Quiverhive has been wearing you down with its forces, but that was only the beginning. It has been in communication with the Scuttling Corpseman, who is active once more. The Corpseman is the true threat. My hunters and I went to its lair but by the time we arrived it had already fled. It is coming here, to join its strength with Quiverhive's.'

He pointed a finger at her. 'When the Corpseman arrives, it and the demons will destroy your settlements. They will drive your people onto the Godroad, and then they will slaughter them.'

The other Deathless looked puzzled aside from Anuja, who looked like she might be sick. 'That is why Quiverhive was sacrificing demons on the Godroad. It was experimenting, testing the limits of our defences. Yes, you understand. They mean to use the Godroad against us.'

'Impossible!' said Quasim. 'The Godroad is poison to them.'

'It is,' agreed Vasinidra, 'but Quiverhive can pile enough bodies onto the Godroad to make a carpet. I saw him use Murkers for that purpose. The Godroad turned the Murkers to ash in seconds, but for those seconds, Quiverhive could travel. Imagine if it used human bodies instead. A whole settlement's worth of bodies that won't burn.'

There was consternation in the room.

Vasinidra held up his hands and they fell silent. 'The Wild has changed, it has become intelligent. Not like you and I, but it thinks now. It plans. It has watched us, learned our ways, and adapted, and we have suffered for it. If we are to survive, we need to change too.' He gestured to his uncle. 'Lord Umed was right when he said that they are targeting the Rubies over all others. I don't think they're attacking randomly any more. I think the Corpseman is trying to break House Ruby entirely. No, not break it, remove it from existence. They are hunting your people to extinction.

'I believe all this is to draw you out of the castle, Lady Anuja. The Corpseman knows how you think. It will be expecting you to die alongside your people. And that is why you must go out there again, tonight. You, and Lords Quasim and Lakshin. They will see how tired you are, how vulnerable, and they will attack.'

Anuja nodded. 'That they will. How will we turn it to our advantage?'

'We will choose where the fight will be. They will think they are hunting you but in truth, we will be hunting them. When you have drawn them out, House Sapphire and House Tanzanite will come from the sky and crush them. Above all else, the Scuttling Corpseman and Quiverhive must be destroyed.'

He turned to the Tanzanite Deathless. She was a tall, solid woman, with twists of gold threaded through her thick, curly hair. He knew her by the stud-like tattoos on her knuckles and the aloof expression that followed her from one lifecycle to another. 'Lady Farida, I understand your High Lord sent three of you to aid the Rubies, are the other two still with us?'

'Still in their bodies, yes, but I came alone to relieve the hunters here. They continue to patrol the border.'

'With Lady Anuja's permission, I would ask you to fetch them. We need everyone we can get.'

'You have it,' Anuja said. 'Lady Farida, go now and swiftly. The rest of you, prepare yourselves for one last hunt.'

CHAPTER NINE

Vasinidra stood on the edge of the battlements, waiting for the signal. The Wild had attacked again. Once more, Fourboards was the target, a beleaguered settlement that had been battered more times in the last few weeks than it had in its whole history. Lady Anuja had led a group down to face them. A joint force of Ruby, Peridot, and Opal, the minor houses standing together as they had always done. But all three Deathless were injured and in no fit state for a prolonged fight. They were bait, nothing more.

Lord Gada came and stood next to Vasinidra, close enough that his right wing ran parallel to Gada's left, the thin slice of air between them humming with energy. 'Any word, High Lord?'

'No, brother,' replied Vasinidra. 'When there is word, I will tell you.'

'I'm sorry.' Gada paused, but there was no doubt he was going to continue. 'Don't you think it's been too long? What if something's happened? What if they weren't able to give the signal?'

'If Lady Anuja has been overrun, we've already lost.'

'Yes, you're right.'

He was worried though. So much of his plan relied on timing and half-baked theories about the Wild's new tactics. *Would Anuja even give the signal? What if she has just gone out there to die?* He shook his head to try to dispel the fear but it had little effect. Waiting had never been his strength.

Gada pointed down towards the swamps below. 'Was that the signal?'

'What?'

'There. I thought I saw something.'

Vasinidra leaned out, feeling the strong currents tug at his wings. He saw endless swamp dotted with islands and ragged patches of trees. There was the Godroad, shining brightly as ever, and distantly, gathered along its edge, the nearest of the Ruby settlements. All as it should be. 'I see nothing, brother.'

'Oh.'

He was just trying to think of the best way to send Gada somewhere else when Lady Yadva came and joined them. 'I never liked this plan,' she said, settling her huge frame on the other side of Vasinidra. 'It seems wrong to be up here while the minor houses take all the risk. I should be fighting alongside them. The only robust thing about Lord Quasim is his smile, and Lord Lakshin doesn't even have that. Lady Anuja would last a lot longer with me and my hunters at her side.'

'We have to give the Wild what they expect,' replied Vasinidra. 'There will be plenty of work for you to do soon, believe me.'

She only grunted in reply, unconvinced.

'Was that it?' asked Gada, pointing at the land below.

'No,' snapped Vasinidra.

'You're sure?'

Yadva shook her head. 'I didn't see anything.'

'Oh,' said Gada.

But it won't be long now, thought Vasinidra. Somewhere out there, much further along the Godroad would be Lady Farida and her fellow Tanzanites. They too would be waiting for the signal. When it was given, they would join his Sapphires in flight, becoming the other half of a pincer that would trap Quiverhive and the Scuttling Corpseman between them. Or so he hoped.

Lord Umed arrived and joined them in a line. 'Enjoying the view?'

'No,' replied Yadva.

'Receiving last instructions from your High Lord, then?'

'No,' she repeated, a little more testily than the first time.

'Then why are you standing here? Should you not be with your hunters? And you, Lord Gada?' They did not immediately reply. 'I see. Do you believe that by standing here and bothering your High Lord, the signal will be given faster?'

'Fine,' muttered Yadva, and bounded back towards her people.

Gada inclined his head. 'Wise words, Uncle.' As he allowed himself to be led away by Umed, Vasinidra saw it: A distant shaft of red light flickering into the sky, like a sunbeam cast in reverse. 'There!' he yelled, pointing.

'What?' said Gada, but by the time he'd turned to follow Vasinidra's instruction, the shaft had vanished. 'I don't see anything.'

Vasinidra raised his spear. 'Deathless Lords, hunters of the Sapphire, with me!' And he leapt from the wall.

After only a few steps Chandni had lost all certainty in her surroundings. She assumed there were trees on either side of her and mud beneath her feet. But was that true any more? She felt her way forward, forced to inch along. More than once she was stabbed by a branch, or tripped by crumbling earth or treacherous roots.

Don't fall, Chandni, she urged herself. A fall could scrape knees or hands and the slightest hint of blood would bring all manner of creatures down on her. The Dogkin was panting ahead of her but the sound was picked up by the trees and passed by on her left and right.

I wish Varg were here. Or Glider. Or even Crowflies.

It was strange. They hadn't known each other long but she felt an affection towards the Birdkin. She suspected it liked her too, and that it was helping more than Murderkind had ordered it to.

Why do I think that? And why with such surety? Is the Wild playing tricks on me or am I starting to learn its ways?

Whenever she strayed from the path that she couldn't see, the trees prodded at her. When she tried to get her bearings, the trees tricked her. And when she stumbled and tripped, which was often, they laughed at her. At least, the branches shook and the leaves rustled in a manner that brought the blood to her cheeks.

After what seemed like an interminably long time, the slope levelled off. There was a pressure on her sleeve and the old Dogkin led her several paces forward before letting go. No sunslight penetrated this far down, and the air was bitingly cold. The trees whispered amongst themselves. It reminded her of the times she'd been scrutinized by her mother and various family friends. All talking about her but not to her.

Chandni lifted her chin and waited.

She was sure that there was something more than trees out there. The chill air stroked her skin, making the fine hairs rise and the breath catch in her throat. Her hands began to shake. *Something is here with me. It's close!*

Still she waited.

Let it watch if it wishes. I will not flee.

The voice that spoke came from in front of her. It sounded like a young man but she was sure that it was neither of those things. 'To flee, to free. Ah, to be free! I will tell you one thing for free and one thing only: Your black feathered friends have no power in this place. They cannot protect you.'

'I understand.'

'That, I doubt. You stink of neediness. You stink of Birdkin. Of needy Birdkin, you stink. It is not a pleasing scent.'

She knew she had to forge an alliance with Kennelgrove but she instinctively felt it would not be as simple as laying out terms. There were some old grievances between it and Murderkind that would need careful handling. She needed to impress it but she didn't know how. She didn't even know if the thing in front of her was Kennelgrove, though she suspected it was. 'May I ask you a question?'

'A question? Just one? No, don't answer. I will not take your charity. I too have questions and you too have answers. Let us trade. A question for a question, until I grow bored or one of us loses.'

'How do we lose?'

'A good first question. You agree to my terms then?'

Chandni did her best to stop her teeth from chattering. 'When you have given me your answer, I'll give you mine.'

It laughed. 'I see why Murderkind likes you. Very well. The first to ask a question the other dares not answer, wins. If I grow bored, then neither of us lose.' It murmured something so quietly she didn't hear it the first time, but one of the trees slipped the information to her. *'Unless I grow bored too quickly . . .'*

'What is your answer?'

'I accept,' she replied, 'as soon as we have had a proper introduction.'

This was met by another laugh. 'So be it. I am Kennelgrove, I am The Curious, I am prince and changer.'

I have found it! Now I need to find a way to win it over. And, after the style of its introduction, it seemed that simply giving her name would not be enough. 'I am Chandni. I am the Iron Purebird. I am an Honoured Mother.'

She had the sense it was waiting for something more but she had no idea what it was.

'You may ask the first question, Iron Purebird.' Kennelgrove's footfalls were soft and all around her, making it sound as if it were many creatures rather than one. And all the sounds were moving closer. 'If you wish, you could ask me what your other names are.'

I have other names? She wondered if this were a trick on its part but now that it had put the idea in her head, she found she had to know the answer. 'Yes. I want to know my other names.'

'You are also Soultorn, the beloved of Prince Murderkind, and Packstealer.'

There were too many reasons why she could have the first of those names, but the other two were obvious. 'Thank you.'

'How did you bind this white-furred creature to your will?'

'I tricked her into biting what wasn't hers.'

'A clever trick. Will you tell me the how of it?'

'Yes . . . if you want that to be your next question.' She held up a hand even though it was dark. 'And now it is my turn to ask.'

'So it is.'

'Are you willing to consider an alliance against the Scuttling Corpseman?'

'I might be.'

'That isn't much of an answer.'

'It is the best I can give to such a poorly worded question. You have said nothing of terms nor participants, nor even what gifts might be given to sweeten your words.'

'What kind of gifts would please you?'

'Now that is a question I would enjoy very much,' came the sly-voiced reply. It moved closer again, close enough now that she could smell damp wood and fur and something reminiscent of spiced wine. 'But you have jumped ahead. Our agreement was a question for a question. You would do well to stick to the rules, Packstealer, they are all that protect you here.'

'My apologies.' The pressure and the cold were starting to get to her. She wondered if its plan was to keep her here until she passed out.

'Rather than ask you two questions with my words, I would ask you one with my hands. A generous offer, I'm sure you'd agree.'

It was getting harder to talk. The tip of her nose and her lips had gone numb. 'Y-yes.'

She'd been expecting to be groped or squeezed but she barely felt anything, Kennelgrove's fingers ghosting over like Mothkin wings, tickling, tingling and gone. 'Such pain! Such a heart! You grip yourself so tightly it has barely room to beat.' He fell silent. 'Well? What else would you ask of me?'

'You may have another q-question. I too am feeling g-generous and want to ask a question with my hands. It is only fair.'

It hesitated. Only briefly but it was there. 'Of course,' replied Kennelgrove, though it sounded less sure of itself than before. 'Whose suffering is more painful to your ears than your own?'

'A few days ago I would have g-given you a long answer. Now it is brief. My son, my lover, my friends, the people in the sky that I w-watched over, and Lord Rochant Sapphire. My turn.'

Again, there was hesitation. 'Mmmn.'

Her right hand was always numb and she was losing sensation in her left but she allowed both to roam over Kennelgrove. To her surprise she discovered something very much like a man. Two arms, two legs, slender like a youths. There was a coating of mud on its body and leaves worn almost like clothes but beneath them she felt human skin, alive and warm. It radiated heat in fact, enough to take the sting from her fingers and thaw out her lips. She felt a rent in the leaves and skin, and Kennelgrove stiffened as her fingers drew close. There was a hot damp under her fingers, like blood but thicker. *It's hurt. It didn't want me to know.*

'It is your turn,' she said.

'Tell me why I do not go above and feast upon your lover?'

It's angry with me and Varg will be the one to pay for it. She refused to be afraid. Those times were behind her. The Wild might be terrifying but she was Sapphire, born and bred. 'Because he is mine, and if you hurt him, Murderkind will come for you, and you are in no condition for such a fight. I think I know who you are, Kennelgrove. I've heard of you before, a man dressed in mud and leaves who helped a group of exiles long ago. Because he was curious. Because of a woman named Rayen.'

Chandni had forgotten about the old Dogkin but at the mention of that name, it howled, long and loud and sorrowful. This time it was not the cold that made Chandni shiver. 'You took that woman as the price for your knowledge. And you took away the group that tried to attack you.' She was onto something; she knew it from the way Kennelgrove's demeanour had changed. 'When Rayen came back for the last time her hair was white . . .' She thought back to when Fiya had told the story. *White as the fur on your Dogkin.* 'You changed her hair . . . you changed her.'

The old Dogkin howled again and Chandni thought her heart would break at the sound.

'By the suns, you changed them all. They are the Dogkin. Their souls are in the Dogkin!'

Kennelgrove suddenly sounded tired. 'That isn't a question.'

'No. My question is . . . what hurt you?'

The warmth that had been so close to her receded. 'I have grown bored. This game is over.' Kennelgrove spoke over her shoulder. 'Take her from here, Rayen. Do not bring her back.'

The Dogkin padded over, but when Chandni felt the tug on her sleeve, she planted her feet firmly. 'No.'

'No?' asked Kennelgrove.

'We agreed to the rules in front of witnesses.' The trees rustled agreement as she pointed a finger to where she thought it was. 'You are not bored. You are afraid. So either answer my question or declare me the winner.'

There was a long pause. Everything fell silent. She could hear nothing save for the beating of her heart and the grinding of Kennelgrove's teeth.

'Damn you, damn you, damn you!' It came close again, and whispered: 'The Scuttling Corpseman did this to me. Many of mine were slaughtered, but I got away.'

The trees began to whisper. '*Corpseman, Corpseman, Corpseman.*'

'Wait!' hissed Kennelgrove. 'Do not summon that abomination here. Hush your leaves! Stop! Why are you betraying me?' Its voice softened as he addressed the forest. 'Whatever price it has offered, I will match. You know this. We have entwined together for so long and I have always been kind, have I not?' A cold wind blew through the trees. 'Mostly kind, then. Sometimes kind. I could be so kind if you gave me a chance.'

'*Damn you, damn you, damn you,*' came the echo of Kennelgrove's own words, repeated over and over.

'I have to run!' exclaimed Kennelgrove. 'To flee far and wide and hide and wait.' It gave a cry of self-pity. 'But it hurts to run.' And then it was in front of her again. 'You, Beloved of the Prince. Take me to Murderkind. It will listen to you. Yes. Tell it to shelter me. Together we might stand against the Corpseman. But we must go. Fast! Now. Now, I say!'

This is my chance, she thought.

'If I do this for you, in return, you will treat fairly with Prince Murderkind, and you will restore the Dogkin to their original shapes.'

'You ask too much.'

Chandni could hear a faint sound beneath the continuous whisper of the trees. It was a buzzing sound, the kind made by hundreds and hundreds of wings, all humming together. 'You're right,' she said. 'Goodbye, Kennelgrove.'

She began to feel her way towards the exit but she'd barely gone three steps before it replied.

'All right! Thrice curse your hair and feet, all right!'

'I have your word?'

The buzzing was getting steadily louder. 'Yes, may a thousand Wormkin lay eggs in your ears, you have my oath. I swear it on my blood and bones.'

As he said those words, the buzzing stopped, as if all those Flykin had been murdered in the same instant. Though the resulting quiet was a welcome respite for her ears, it was not a true silence. She could make out a rustling of leaves, a nasty chuckling coming from the trees themselves, accompanied by a single Birdkin. She couldn't see it in the light, but the voice was familiar.

'Crowflies? Is that you?'

'Cha-aan,' replied Crowflies.

It seemed as if they were sharing a joke, and she had a

suspicion it was at Kennelgrove's expense. She waited and listened again. Where moments ago there had been a swarm, now there was nothing, not even a single Flykin. 'The Corpseman isn't really here,' she said. 'You've been tricked.'

'You dare to trick the trickster!' Kennelgrove exclaimed, which only set them to all to laughing louder. In response, the demon spat on the floor. 'May your seeds find only hard earth and the bellies of hungry creatures. May your roots wither and your boughs sag. May—'

'Crowflies!' snapped Chandni. The cold was getting to her again, sapping both strength and patience. 'Stop laughing and take us to Prince Murderkind.' The Birdkin gave a chastened squawk and leapt from its perch. 'Kennelgrove, please stop cursing and come with me.'

'For now, I will stem the flow of my hatred, though this will not be forgotten, nor forgiven.'

Chandni ignored the comment, and was relieved to find that when she left the circle of snickering trees, Kennelgrove came creeping after her.

Vasinidra heard their roar of assent as they followed, and behind it, a more ragged cheer from the people of House Ruby. There was no time for drums or speeches or song, as there would have been with a normal hunt. This meant they had to rely on the power of their Sky-legs alone to launch them, and skilled use of their wings to make the best of the essence currents.

The floating castle was quickly left behind, replaced with sky and screaming winds, and the blurred rush of the swamp beneath. There were two things that would make Lady Anuja give the signal. The first and most preferable was that

Quiverhive or the Scuttling Corpseman had been seen. The second was if her forces were being overwhelmed.

Like a hail of glittering arrows, they shot across the land, riding the energies of the Godroad. It did not take them long to reach Fourboards. The swamp bubbled with activity, and he could plainly see the three Deathless and their people, all fighting for their lives. As they suspected, Lady Anuja had the worst of it, and he directed his Deathless to go to her, signalling with his spear. Umed, Yadva, and Gada each saluted him and then began to dive, their hunters following, one rank after another.

He was not surprised to see so many demons here, but there was no sign of either Quiverhive or the Corpseman.

They are here, somewhere. They must be!

Only one lifecycle ago he would have plunged into the fight without a second thought. After all, the situation was dire and he would not want to bring dishonour upon himself. Now though, he saw things differently. *Before, Quiverhive hung back, watching. It's here, somewhere. I know it is.*

He continued to follow the Godroad, flying over the heads of the people of Fourboards. They had all retreated from their homes and gathered in several messy clumps along the road's surface. Even from above, he could see how drawn and thin they looked. *If the demons don't kill them soon, the stress will. I have to end this.*

He was only a little further along when he saw something strange ahead, a break in the light of the Godroad. At first it looked as if a hill had sprung up overnight, swallowing a section of the glowing crystal. But as he drew closer, he saw that it was a pile of bodies, not stacked like a carpet as he'd feared, but as a barricade. There was no sign of flame nor flash of power. These were ordinary human beings, not demons, and the Godroad's power could not touch them.

Half a settlement's worth were there. Good people reduced to macabre bricks. He felt sick at the sight of it. It was a monument of sorts. A vile proof of the failure of the Deathless.

But what is it for? To stop people getting here or to stop them getting out?

Tell-tale ripples in the surface of the swamp told him there were demons below. He stared down hard, straining his eyes to see if one of them was long enough to be Quiverhive, but all he could see were Murkers, their bloated bodies paddling lazily around the spot where the sides of the 'hill' joined the swamp.

He banked round in a wide arc, signalling his hunters to follow. They hadn't anticipated this but his instincts were telling him to go the other way. As he returned to Fourboards he saw three more Deathless in the sky opposite, each backed by a full flight of hunters, and the familiar violet glow of House Tanzanite. He waved his spear, hoping to catch Lady Farida's attention, but it was too late. As per the plan, she was diving to attack the demons in the swamp. Whatever was happening here on the Godroad was up to him to deal with.

And then he heard the screams. There was a distinctive quality to them: Terror and shock rolled into one. A horrible mismatched chorus of misery heading his way; made by the people of Fourboards as they ran towards him. Small children were being carried. Others were being dragged. The thick groups he'd seen before had strung out into lines, those at the back pushing those in front, desperate to get away from . . .

Vasinidra's eyes widened. *By the Thrice Blessed Suns!*

He had to look a second time to make sense of it. A thick bloated wormlike thing was snaking its way after the mob. A demon without doubt, but one that traversed the Godroad without injury. Something in its movement reminded him of Quiverhive but it looked so odd, so changed, that he wasn't sure at first.

The outer layer of the beast seemed to be made of corpses, their arms and legs threaded together, linking them in bands that ran from the demon's tip to its tail. A row of bodies flopped over the front of the demon's mouth like a fringe, bobbing obscenely with each forward movement. The bodies were as pale-skinned as those on the barricade, road-born that had been killed and left too long under water.

With horror, Vasinidra realized what he was seeing.

It is Quiverhive! It's using them as armour! Quiverhive is wearing our people as armour.

Smaller demons swam nearby, braving the edge of the Godroad's energies for the chance at scavenging whatever Quiverhive discarded.

Vasinidra had seen enough. He ordered half of his hunters to form a wedge between the demon and the people of Fourboards. The other half he called to follow him and attack.

They swooped down together, stabbing at the demon as they flew by. Vasinidra's own spear caught at one of the bodies but failed to penetrate deep enough to do any real damage to the creature beneath.

For its part, Quiverhive ignored them and barrelled into the hunters on the road. The first was scooped up and bitten in half; the legs and lower body swallowed, the upper body, with wings still attached, was spat away into the swamp.

As Vasinidra turned for another pass, he tried to think of a way to counter the new threat. It was all happening too fast! *I have to do something about that armour* – he felt another urge to vomit at the thought of the armour's nature – *but what?*

Four of the hunters on the Godroad set their spears, trying to stab at Quiverhive's mouth. It didn't try to bite them this time but just set its head forward, and charged, butting into them. Spears stabbed into dead flesh and stuck fast, their owners swung on the end of them like Purefish in a Birdkin's beak. In seconds, spears ripped from hands, and all four were flung into the swamp.

The second rank of hunters stepped in and quickly suffered the same fate.

The third rank leapt back on their Sky-legs in a succession of little hops, stabbing futilely to try to slow Quiverhive down.

The barricade was in sight now, and the people of Fourboards had seen it. They were running ahead of the hunters and had been putting space between them and the demon but now they slowed, a great moan going up among them.

'Follow my lead!' shouted Vasinidra, using the currents of the Godroad to climb as high as he could before diving down, spear first. He used every bit of momentum, every bit of strength, and plunged his spear as deep as it would go. The point pierced one of the corpse's bellies, going through with barely any resistance, then further, into hard scale. Not enough to break Quiverhive's hide, but enough to get the demon's attention.

Vasinidra didn't wait to see what it would do. Standing on its back now, he used his exalted strength to tear the skewered body free, exposing a row of scales. Several of them flipped over to reveal eyes that glared upwards, hateful.

He was aware of his hunters also trying to attack the armour and that they were struggling. Even as he was worrying about this, he raised his spear a second time and drove it into Quiverhive's back.

The eyes flipped back to scales again, but it didn't matter. The glowing sapphire tip was anathema to all things of the Wild and it sunk deep, burning as it went.

Quiverhive twisted angrily, trying to shake him off, but he simply hopped upwards, hovering there until it had stopped. The moment it did, he attacked again. While the other hunters were not as effective as him, they continued to bother the demon, distracting it, slowing it down.

He put his weight behind the spear, driving it slowly deeper as Quiverhive bucked in agony. Then, when he had gone as far as he could, he pressed the trigger on the shaft, firing the point still further. Around the edge of his spear, the scales flipped, revealing eyes fixed on him, thoughtful, despite the pain. Then they flipped back.

Before he had time to wonder what that meant, the demon was moving, rolling its great bulk sideways. Vasinidra went with it, gripping his spear tight as the world lurched. Quiverhive kept rolling, not in an attempt to shake him off, but to leave the Godroad entirely.

One moment Vasinidra was the right way up, the next, he was upside down, one wing sparking off the corner of the Godroad as they fell off the side of the road. The moment after that was marked with a splash as his back broke the surface of the swamp. Everything went black, save from the glow of his armour. Even if the sunslight had been strong enough to penetrate the murky water, the sky was blocked by Quiverhive's vast bulk.

They sank together, towards the bottom.

Vasinidra kept one hand on the spear, and gouged at the wound with the fingers of the other, his sapphire gauntlet burning the demon just as easily as his spear did.

Quiverhive began to curl, wrapping itself around him. Normally such an action would be suicide, but with its corpse armour protecting it, the demon had nothing to fear. It was so huge, it covered him in a single loop of its body, pinning his arms and legs. He felt the spear handle slip from his grasp, he felt the horrific pressure begin to build on all sides, and he fought back.

And so it went until, with an almost gentle bump, they reached the bottom, Deathless and demon, superhuman strength pitted against inhuman power. Vasinidra struggled with everything he had, but he knew he was outmatched. As the seconds ticked by it got harder for him to breathe, and he could feel the strain on his armour. Any moment now, the crystal would crack and snap, and he would be killed.

While he did not fear death, he feared delay. To be between lives for any length of time could spell disaster. And so he fought and strained, trying to find his spear again. It had moved in their struggle, still buried deep in Quiverhive's flank, the glow only just visible through the layers of demonic flesh. It would be killing the demon slowly from the inside. Perhaps, if he could hold out long enough, the wound would finish it off completely. It was too far to grab now. Even if he had full movement of his arm, it was beyond his reach. So instead he worked to free his legs.

Meanwhile, Quiverhive continued to crush and squeeze. A gap appeared in the glow cast by Vasinidra's armour, mirroring the first crack in his breast plate. First one, then two, then more, tiny little breaks all reaching out to one another.

And yet he felt Quiverhive weaken, just for a moment, and in that moment he swung out and kicked the spear, ramming it so far inside the demon that only a short stub of silver remained visible.

The next thing he knew, everything was in motion as the demon went rigid, flinging him aside. He struggled away, fearing that he would be trapped under its body, then tucked his Sky-legs beneath him and leaped – only to find the swamp bed sucking at his legs, stealing his momentum.

He kicked and swam, doing all he could to go up, aware that his strength was giving out.

Just as his fingers were about to break the surface, he felt something snag on his ankle, trapping him. It wasn't Quiverhive – the demon was surely dead – but a simple tangle of weeds.

So close! he thought, but it gave him no comfort to be nearly free, to be almost alive. He gave a weak kick but the thing would not budge. He gave another, his last he suspected, and still it would not budge.

In desperation he reached for the surface again, trying to find purchase on the high sides of the Godroad. But it was smooth and straight, perfectly so, and his fingers slid down the sides, frictionless.

Then, a blue glow tinged the murk above, and a gauntleted

hand closed around his. He felt his arm jolt in its socket and his hip complain at the pressure, and then the weeds tore free and he was moving upwards.

'Got you!' shouted Yadva.

He dangled from her arm, blinking in surprise. 'You . . . saved me?' Barely a day had gone by since she'd tried to destroy him and take House Sapphire for herself. He still had the bruises to prove it.

She laughed. 'I've decided that I don't want to be High Lord any more. You're welcome to it.' She set him down on the Godroad next to her, though she didn't let him go. 'Besides,' she added, 'now I get to be part of the legend of Quiverhive's defeat.'

'How—' he began, then stopped as something came rushing up his throat. After hauling off his helmet, he coughed up filthy water and a few nameless globs that he couldn't bear to examine. 'How are the others.'

'Your plan worked perfectly. We slaughtered them. Took some losses though.'

'Lady Anuja?'

'She was alive when I left her, but I don't think she'll last much longer.'

'Take me to her.'

Yadva nodded and helped him to walk along the Godroad. The swamp was quiet once more. Hunters waded on their Sky-legs through droves of Murker corpses, prodding them with their spears. The people of Fourboards were safe, huddling together in relief. And yet he could not relax. 'Did you engage the Scuttling Corpseman?'

'There's been no sign of it. Maybe it's scared of losing another arm to you.'

He failed to muster a smile in response, not least because his mother had taken the Corpseman's arm and given him the credit. 'I was sure it would be here!'

Yadva shrugged.

'It was supposed to be here.'

She shrugged again.

'Where is it?' he asked, as much to the air as to her. 'Where is the Scuttling Corpseman?'

CHAPTER TEN

They made an uneasy fellowship: two humans, a pack of Dogkin, a Birdkin, and a demon prince. Chandni knew she wasn't the only one who felt it, the tension hung between them thick as Spiderkin silk. She'd hoped to ride back to Murderkind on the Dogkin, but while Glider was happy for this to happen, the rest of the pack had bristled at the idea of carrying Kennelgrove anywhere. Though the demon had grumbled at having to walk, she suspected it was relieved to be able to keep its distance from the victims of its curse. Their slow pace obviously irritated Crowflies, who was getting further and further ahead.

All I have to do is get to Murderkind. Then Kennelgrove will transform the Dogkin back to their original form, and I will be free to enjoy my time with Varg.

As if sensing her joy, Kennelgrove drew closer. Weak sunslight filtered through the canopy to pick out the shape of a man much like Chandni had imagined. However, there was something odd about it. The joints seemed to be backwards at the elbows and knees, and the cant of its head was more animal than it was human. Moreover, it carried itself awkwardly. Mud and leaves were packed around a belly wound, and fresh scars adorned its arms and shoulders.

'To be taken to Murderkind in this way is painful, shameful, woeful! I have changed my mind. I will not go another step.'

'You swore an oath.'

'Surely an oath sworn under false circumstances, brought about by false friends, is no oath at all.'

Chandni shook her head. 'The oath is as good as you are, Prince Kennelgrove.'

'I do not feel good at this moment, and neither should you.'

'What is that supposed to mean?'

For the first time since they'd left its domain, she saw some of the old cunning return. 'It was but half a trick they played on us when they pretended the Corpseman was coming. These trees can steal sounds but they cannot conjure their own. It may not have been hunting us, but it is hunting.'

'Hunting who?'

It looked away, almost coy. 'I do not know, but you could find out. That buzzing was fresh. Not here, but near, and close enough to feel.'

She took a step towards it. 'Me?'

Kennelgrove looked her in the eye and smiled. In that instant, her thoughts became ghostlike, pale and half-remembered, all her attention snared by the creature in front of her. It had rich walnut eyes that she'd never really appreciated before this moment. She found herself smiling back, which felt wrong though she couldn't in that moment think why.

'Yes,' it continued, 'you want to please your Prince, don't you?'

'Yes.'

'And surely you want to stop the Corpseman destroying all those you care about?'

'Yes.'

Its eyes seemed to sparkle with approval. 'Of course you do. When you learn what our enemy is up to it will be easy to upset its plots.' Kennelgrove smiled again. 'We will wait here for you.'

Again, something didn't feel right, but she found herself nodding in time with Kennelgrove's words. 'Yes. I'll go and see.'

'Yes, you go and see and I'll see you go. What a wonderful idea. Be sure to take a good close look, but do be careful. It would be a terrible shame if something awful and visceral and painful and permanent were to befall you.'

'Yes,' agreed Chandni, still nodding.

'And perhaps you should take your lover with you.' Its smile widened. 'For protection.'

'Yes,' she murmured. 'For protection.'

'I think the buzzing is coming from over there.'

Kennelgrove gestured towards a slender path, the kind worn down by irregular travellers that is easily swallowed by the Wild. Chandni nodded and called Varg to her. After a quick discussion, the two of them leaped onto Glider and set off.

It was not long before they could hear the buzzing for themselves.

'You know,' said Varg, 'this part of the woods is familiar. I ain't travelled here from this direction but I'd swear I've been round here before.'

Glider barked affirmation.

'Shit.'

'What's wrong?' asked Chandni. It seemed a pertinent question because she had the feeling that something was terribly wrong, but she couldn't think what it was.

'Well, I don't travel the deep Wild, so that means we're probably not far from the Godroad and people. And if you think the Corpseman is around, that's gotta be real bad for someone and I'd rather that weren't us. You sure you want to keep going?'

'If my people are in trouble, we can't just abandon them.'

'I'm sorry, Chand, but they ain't your people any more. You don't owe them anything.'

She sighed. 'It doesn't feel that way. If I don't even go and see . . . what kind of person does that make me?'

He kissed her cheek. 'I won't stop you looking so long as you come back with me if I reckon things are getting too dangerous.'

It was an effort to turn round on Glider's back and kiss his cheek in return, but she managed it. 'Agreed.'

The path joined another wider one and Glider raced along it until a settlement could be seen up ahead. Varg was the first to recognize it as Sagan, one of Lord Rochant's. To protect it from meeting a similar fate as Sorn, the elders had erected a gated wall around the outer perimeter, so that the only way to approach was from the Godroad. A no man's land of scorched earth created an open space between the wall and the edge of the trees.

Glider came to a skidding stop and began to whine. The buzzing was louder now, much louder. Chandni frowned. Despite the noise she couldn't see the Corpseman nor any of the many creatures she could hear. *It sounds like they should be all around us but there's nothing here. Is this another trick of the trees?* She considered turning back but Kennelgrove's words were loud in her mind. Murderkind would want to know what the Corpseman was up to.

She dismounted Glider and was about to go further when she felt Varg's hand on her shoulder. 'You sure about this?'

'I need to have a good long look.'

'What?'

'I need—'

Before she could speak again the trees around her shook, their interwoven branches tugging and creaking.

Glider whined again.

With a great groan, the trees all disentangled and leaned back, opening their canopy to the sky. But Chandni made out no sky, just a mass of hard-edged clouds, buzzing, glistening, too close.

Her first thought was Flykin, but they were too big, even the smallest were as big as her. Human legs and arms hung loose from their carapace, and a human head sat atop each one, though the eye sockets were empty and the jaws slack. Semi-transparent wings blurred at their backs, flickering softly, swiftly, holding them there. Then something else, something much bigger, began to descend. She recognized it instantly from the Story-singer's tales: the Scuttling Corpseman. Its body was covered in living armour, black, save for patches of bone dotted across back and chest. She saw five plated limbs, multi-jointed, long, and a stump at the right shoulder where the sixth had once been. A human skull sat atop its shoulders, too small, almost comical against the bulk. Antennae extended out from the eye sockets. All of this, she had heard before. But none of the stories described the vast wings, nor the swirling patterns that drew the eye to them, demanding to be examined, curve after curve of organic spirals, where the end of one took the observer to the beginning of another.

Down they came. Down like a great cloud of menace, turning the protective wall of Sagan into a kind of pen, the gates into prison doors.

She tried to go closer for a good long look but Varg's hand clamped down on her shoulder, hard enough to bruise. She barely noticed.

'Chand!'

She wasn't sure how long she watched the Corpseman float down upon Sagan or how long she struggled against Varg's grip, but at some point Crowflies flew down in front of them. It looked from her to Varg and back to her in three quick twitches, and then pecked at the meat of her leg.

There was a flash of pain, of shock, and then sudden awareness.

What in the name of Blessed Suns have I been doing? Focus Chandni! she told herself, tearing her gaze away.

The two guards on the wall could have used the same advice. Their heads were still tilted upwards, with expressions both awestruck and despairing. They had lit a sapphire beacon to summon aid, and it was well known that in Lord Rochant's absence, the other Deathless kept a close watch on Sagan. But as she looked about, she saw no Deathless of House Sapphire in either the sky or on the Godroad and not even a single hunter. The people of Sagan were alone.

Chandni cupped her hands to her mouth. 'Run!' she shouted. 'Run!'

But the guards did not run. They did not even register her warning. Perhaps it could not be heard over the din. Perhaps they were too entranced by the hypnotic patterns on the Corpseman's wings.

A moment later both were plucked from their posts by giant Flykin and taken behind the wall, out of sight.

'Oh fuck,' said Varg. 'We gotta go!'

And they did, back into the cover of the trees. Noises followed them, of humming and buzzing, and breaking and movement. But of the human residents of Sagan, she heard no sound.

The bed Sa-at was on was big and squishy. At first he liked it. There was lots of space to move his arms and legs, and it reminded him of the many times he'd lain in the soft earth, only this was better as his clothes stayed dry and he didn't have to worry about getting eaten.

When he actually tried to sleep, though, it wasn't as good. The bed didn't hold him in the way the friendly tree used to. It would have been better if Tal had been here to share it but despite there being plenty of room for the two of them, Win had refused, mumbling something about it being improper given his station.

Sa-at had no idea what the old seneschal was going on about but he hadn't argued. Instead, he'd tossed and turned and waited for his eyes to get heavy. But they didn't. Though the day had been long and eventful, sleep would not come. To make matters worse, his mind was very active.

He knew there was more going on than he understood. Win seemed to know some of it but Lady Pari and Lord Rochant knew more. He wondered where Lady Pari was now. *Should I have gone with her?* He was fairly sure that staying had been the right thing to do, and so couldn't understand why he felt so glum about it.

Gradually, the castle settled. Outside in the courtyard, he could hear the chatter of small groups. Their words wafted towards the window, not quite audible but of a furtive nature. He recalled the crowds when he'd first arrived and they'd sounded different. They'd been louder, more raucous. The noise had scared him at the time, but now he missed it.

Have I only been here for one day?

So much had changed his head span with it.

Eventually, the number of voices thinned out and the castle fell silent. To compensate, Sa-at's thoughts got louder.

Why did Lady Pari say that Lord Rochant isn't my friend? Was she playing a trick?

Why was Win so upset when we handed Nidra over?

Why can't Tal be here?

Why did that demon look like me?

Without really thinking about it, he slid out of bed and crept out. Unlike in the Wild, the castle never got truly dark, instead it became more twinkly and soft, which he liked a lot. He ran his hands over the gemslights as he passed, making the glow dance and flicker.

One of the guards came marching over. He looked both tired and grumpy. 'What are you doing?'

Sa-at shrugged.

'Oh, pardon me,' said the guard as he got closer. 'You're Honoured Vessel Satyendra.'

'No, I'm not.'

The guard frowned. 'Yes, you are.'

'No, I'm a different Honoured Vessel. I'm Sa-at.'

'Sa . . . what?'

'Sa-at. Can I ask you a question?' The guard looked slightly confused, but nodded. 'What's a cell?'

'It's a room for prisoners in the deepest part of the castle. We're keeping that thing down there now.'

'Why don't you call it a room?'

'Because it's different.'

'How?'

He watched the guard's face squish with thought. 'Well, a cell is made to keep people who are too dangerous to be free.'

'What do you mean?'

'I mean the person inside the room doesn't get to choose when to go in or out. The door only opens from the outside and there are no windows.'

'But how does the sunslight get in?'

'It doesn't.'

Sa-at thought about this. He'd first found Rochant when he'd been trapped in Nidra's house. He'd been a prisoner and Sa-at had hated it. Not to be able to look where you wanted or walk where you wanted was just . . . wrong.

'Thank you,' he said.

As much as the imposter bothered him, it also fascinated him. He wanted to understand it and he wanted to understand what was happening here in the castle. At first it had overwhelmed him, but now the initial awe had passed, he felt frustrated. It wasn't in his nature to sit around. It was in his nature to explore and question. After all, Rochant had told him it was important to think about things.

Of their own accord, his feet retraced the route that Roh had taken them earlier, down into the depths of the castle.

Though the corridors were empty, the castle seemed to hum to itself, which made Sa-at feel like he was in the company of a giant friendly demon.

The evenly set gemslights came to a stop, but he found a crystal lantern hanging on the wall next to the entrance to where the cells were. He glanced about but saw nobody. After a little indecision, he took the lantern, assuring the castle that he would replace it as soon as he returned.

It didn't take long to reach the cells. He moved up to the first one and listened. It was very quiet but he thought he heard the soft sounds of someone asleep inside. Very carefully, he tried the door. It didn't budge. Locked doors were new to him and the novelty was already wearing thin.

He tried the second cell but it too was locked. Then, when the door rattled, he heard someone stir inside.

Sa-at decided there was only one way to find out who. 'Hello,' he said.

'It's you, isn't it?' replied a young man's voice.

'Yes.' The voice sounded familiar to him because it sounded like his own voice! 'You're the imposter, the one who looks like me. Who are you really?'

'I have been thinking a lot about that myself but I don't see why I should tell you anything. Why did you bother coming here? Did Rochant send you?'

'But,' said Sa-at, 'you haven't answered *my* question.'

He heard a frustrated sigh from the other side of the door. 'My name is Satyendra.'

'I like that name.'

'You would,' came the sarcastic reply. 'It's yours.'

'No, it isn't, my name is Sa-at.' But he didn't feel as confident of that fact as normal. *The guard called me Satyendra as well. Have they stolen my name and replaced it with another?*

'Your name,' said Satyendra, 'is whatever they say it is. You'll be Satyendra from now on, at least until . . .' he trailed off.

'Until what?'

'It doesn't matter.'

'Tell me.'

'First, you tell me, are you proud to serve Lord Rochant?'

'He's my friend.'

'And you like being his Honoured Vessel.'

'It's nice. Everyone smiles at me and makes me feel like when the sunslight is on my skin, but it's in my heart.' Satyendra muttered something under his breath. 'What was that?'

'I said, how lovely for you.'

Whatever Satyendra said the first time had sounded very different. Sa-at scowled. He didn't like being lied to.

'Except,' Satyendra continued, 'it's not lovely. It's not lovely at all. Oh, they're all smiles now. They'll all want to be your friend and then one day . . .' he brought his hands together in a loud clap. 'Gone.'

'Gone?'

'Yes. Gone. You really don't know, do you?'

'I've only been here a day.'

'Come closer to the door and I'll tell you the truth.'

Sa-at frowned. This felt like a trap but he couldn't see one anywhere. Cautiously, he approached the door, and placed his ear against it. 'I'm here,' he said softly.

'That's better. Do you know what a vessel is?'

'No.'

'It's a jug for storing liquid in. And that's what you are. A very rare jug, except instead of liquid, you will store a soul. Rochant's soul.'

'I don't understand. He already has a soul.'

'Yes, a very old one in a very young body. When his current body gets old, he'll need a replacement. A new vessel to house his soul.'

Sa-at's heart sank. *He means me.*

He heard Satyendra draw in a long, deep breath. 'Mmmmmn.'

'But if Rochant's soul goes in my body, what happens to my soul? Do we squish up together?'

Satyendra laughed and then laughed some more. 'That's adorable. But no. Rochant is too greedy to share. He'll push your soul out to make room for his.'

'But what about my soul?'

'Truly, I don't know, but I'd wager nothing good. Crushed or shredded I imagine.'

Sa-at stepped back from the door. *Crushed? Shredded?* 'But . . . Rochant is my friend.'

'Let me tell you a secret. There are no real friends in this world. Just people who want what you have. The only difference between a friend and an enemy is that a friend will rob you with a smile on their face and you'll thank them for it afterwards.'

'No, that can't be true. He's my friend.'

'If you don't believe me, ask anyone, they'll tell you what an Honoured Vessel is for.'

'But I don't want my soul to be crushed!'

'I completely understand. I once stood where you're standing now.'

'What did you do?'

'I tried to run away, but I was caught. Escape is your only chance to live. Come closer again and I'll tell you all the tricks. You'll be able to slip away and Rochant will be none the wiser.'

It won't hurt to listen, he told himself as he stepped up to the door. *Listening isn't the same as doing anything.*

'That's it,' said Satyendra. 'We don't want anyone else to hear what we're up to. Now, this is what you need to do . . .'

'. . . And after that, you're on your own,' Satyendra concluded.

'Thank you.'

'You can thank me by not getting caught. Go now, while your body is still your own.'

He fell back from the door and sat heavily. Nidra had been right. An opportunity had presented itself and he hadn't even had to leave his cell to find it. It had come right to him. He could still taste that delightfully bitter moment when Sa-at had realized he'd been used. He almost felt sorry for the other boy. They shared the same fate after all. True vessel or not, both were destined for destruction.

If only I could be there to see Rochant's face when he learns his precious vessel has escaped.

The victorious thought was soured somewhat by the pain in his side. Though he'd taken a small amount of sustenance from Sa-at's shock and misery, the wounds made by Rochant's gauntlet seemed resistant to his supernatural ability to heal.

Not long after, he heard more footsteps, soft and sure,

and then the sound of a key in the lock of the adjacent cell. Satyendra pressed his ear to the door and listened as hard as he could.

'My lady,' whispered a voice, female, that he did not know. 'Are you fit to move?'

'Yes. Though I thought the days of crawling through those damned tunnels were long behind me.'

The other woman said nothing as Nidra got to her feet.

Satyendra knocked on the door. 'Lady Nidra, wait. Take me with you.'

'No,' Nidra replied in a dry whisper.

'You're just going to leave me here? At least open the door. Give me a chance to escape.'

'Help you? Tell me, did you impersonate Rochant for the good of House Sapphire or for yourself?'

'For the house,' he lied.

Nidra gave a cynical bark. 'I liked you more when you were honest and defiant. The difference between us is that I was branded a traitor and you, actually, are one. We may both have been thrown in a cell but my path and yours go in different directions now. May they both bring Rochant pain.'

'At least tell me how. We still have that desire in common.'

She paused. 'You have the trust of Rochant's Honoured Vessel. His last and only chance at rebirth. Kill him, and you kill Rochant.'

'Why don't you kill him?'

'He already knows not to trust me. But you? You could get in close and do it easily.'

'It doesn't matter. Sa-at is helping me escape tonight.'

He heard her joyless laugh. 'You think Rochant won't just

find him and bring him back? All you've done is waste a bit of his time, and he has plenty to spare. If you get the chance, kill the boy, and make sure to check you've done the job properly.'

And with that they were gone and Satyendra was alone.

For a while he was furious with Nidra. How could she abandon him like that, knowing what Rochant would do to him? But in the end, he couldn't blame her. After all, what she said was true. He was a traitor and he didn't care about House Sapphire or its people. He cared about himself. He'd only ever cared about himself and nobody had ever cared about him.

Apart from Mother, he thought miserably. *And I destroyed her for it.*

He sat down, his mind desperately turning over different ways to survive what was coming, but his options were so few, so pathetic.

For a while, he lost himself to despair, until a faint nervousness in the air got his attention. Yes, he could sense . . . not fear, but . . . an anxiousness. Moreover, he recognized it. Sa-at was outside the door.

'I've got the key. We can escape now.'

Satyendra found his usual eloquence had deserted him. 'You're really going to help me?'

'Yes.'

His lip curled in a sneer. 'Why?'

'Because you're like me.'

'Oh, but I'm not. You've seen what I am.'

'Yes. You're a thing of the Wild. So am I. I thought I had family here but my father is dead and my mother has been sent away. I'm going to find her.'

Mother! He felt a keen stab of loss. It had been a mistake to send her away. Perhaps they could find her again. *But if she meets her real son, she'll have no time for me. But then, if I found her, alone, I could tell her that my body rejected Rochant's soul. I could tell her anything I wanted.*

'Do you still want to come?' asked Sa-at.

'Of course I do! Hurry up and let me out.'

Sa-at laughed. 'No. If you want me to let you out, you'll have to make a deal.'

Perhaps we are more alike than I thought. 'What do you want? I don't own much at the moment.'

There was a pause on the other side of the door. 'I don't want your things. I want your oath.'

Words! He'll give me what I want for words? This is too good. 'Well, that depends. What do you want me to swear?'

'To help me escape. To never hurt me, and to answer my questions truthfully.'

'Of course. I agree to your terms.'

There was a pause, then: 'You have to swear it.'

'Yes, yes. I swear it.'

He heard a snort on the other side of the door. 'That's not how it's done. You have to say the words aloud and you have to swear it on your blood and bones. We don't have any trees to witness it, but we're from the Wild so we don't need them.' There was some scuffling and then the sound of something being pushed under the door. 'Prick your finger on this first.'

Satyendra felt around at his feet until he found the tip of something sharp protruding under the door. He did as he was told, feeling the tiny prick of pain as he did so. 'I, Satyendra, agree to help Sa-at escape the castle. I swear to never harm him and to answer his questions with truth.'

'On your blood and bones,' whispered Sa-at.

'I swear it on my blood and bones,' added Satyendra.

As he finished a shiver ran down his spine. *It's nothing. A coincidence. Words are just words after all.* But deep down he wasn't so sure. He began to worry if perhaps Sa-at wasn't as naive as he'd first thought.

He heard scuffling and movement back and forth, and the sound of the key in the lock. The door opened and a shaft of sapphire light shone through, stabbing at his eyes. *The sooner I am gone from this place, the better.*

Sa-at was standing on the other side. Again, he felt a stab of profound hatred. A part of him wanted to tear at the other's face and rip it off. To pound on the body until it was pulp. Satyendra often disliked people, but this was something else. As if the need to hurt was too big to be his alone. And yet alongside it was an annoying sense of kinship. Sa-at had seen him, really seen him. *And he accepts me, like Mother did but without the guilt or the shame.*

He played up the pain of his injury to disguise his reaction.

'You're hurt,' said Sa-at.

'Obviously. But don't worry, I'm more than capable of keeping up.'

'That's good. Before we go, I want to see Tal.'

'Who?'

'He's my friend. I think he'll want to stay but I'm going to ask him to come too.'

'Don't. If he betrays you, we'll both be stuck here.'

'But he's my friend!'

Satyendra grit his teeth. 'Then we'd best be quick about it. We have to be gone before the guards get back.'

Sa-at nodded and they began to head out.

If our escape fails, thought Satyendra, *I'll have to kill them. Oath or no oath, Rochant must be made to pay.*

But, as he watched Sa-at move away, he found the thought of killing them, of hurting them at all, left him profoundly conflicted.

CHAPTER ELEVEN

Pari and Arkav put a good amount of distance between themselves and Lord Rochant's floating castle before stopping to rest. Normally, they would stay at one of the settlements, but Pari opted to wait on the Godroad instead. She didn't anticipate the road-born giving her trouble, but she wanted to be able to move quickly, should Rochant change his mind and come after them.

Both she and Arkav had decided to remain in their armour, and the Dogkin were still partially harnessed to the carriage, just in case.

She didn't like waiting, especially when it felt like other people's plans were in full motion, but it wouldn't do to over-extend themselves this far from home.

'Well,' she said, looking back down the empty Godroad. 'That was interesting.'

Arkav came over and put a hand on her arm. 'Are you all right?'

'Me?' she asked with mock lightness, a hand across her chest. 'I'm fine.'

He didn't say anything, just gave her a sad smile.

The emotions she'd thought had been buried for good threatened to emerge. Rochant had been her lover once. They had flouted the laws of their people to be together in secret. And the risk had been worth it! Such excitement she had not known before or since. But then she had learned that Rochant had taken a similar approach to other sacred laws. He'd betrayed his own people to the Wild and the reasons he'd given were damning at best.

After that, she'd cut her ties with Rochant, and helped Nidra Un-Sapphire get her revenge. She thought this was all behind her. The worst of it was that when she'd seen Rochant on the battlements, a part of her was relieved. A part of her still cared for him.

Sometimes, she thought, *I'm my own worst enemy.*

She gave Arkav the brightest smile she could muster. 'There are bigger things than me to worry about, and you know I don't say that lightly.'

'Our duty is clear. We must report to the council of High Lords.'

'But report what? I'd thought House Sapphire had got through the worst of its madness but now I'm not so sure. Rochant is back. That means Nidra has either taken the last breath of her last life, or she's in terrible danger. High Lord Vasinidra is also in danger, and without him House Sapphire will fall apart.'

'You're suggesting we save House Sapphire?'

'Well, my dear, they're not exactly capable of saving themselves, are they?'

He suppressed a chuckle. 'I suppose not. That boy is another puzzle. I didn't agree with your kidnapping him, but it's a shame he got away. I would have liked the chance to talk to him further.'

She nodded. 'Indeed. We have too many puzzles and not enough time.' An image of High Lord Priyamvada Tanzanite came into her mind, stern as ever. 'But you're right, we go to the High Lords first.'

They decided to enjoy a light meal before travelling on. Throughout it, Pari kept watch on the road behind them and the castle above it. Just as the servants were preparing the carriage for travel, Arkav came and stood next to her. 'See anything?'

'No. Should we be insulted that he hasn't come after us?'

'Do you want him to come after us?'

'It just bothers me that I don't know what he's up to.'

With a shrug, Pari ordered them to keep going, hoping to leave Rochant and his plans behind. They got back into the carriage and set off.

A little time passed.

Arkav held up a hand. 'Do you feel that?'

She immediately looked back the way they'd came. Again, the Godroad was empty. If anyone was following them, they were risking the edges of the Wild to do so. 'Feel what?'

'I don't know . . . It's . . .'

'Come on, Arkav. The suspense is killing me.'

He lapsed into silence and she went back to looking out of the window. The forest running parallel to the Godroad looked quiet. They didn't meet any other travellers, and while this meant they made good time, it gave her a desolate feeling inside.

Up ahead, she could make out a beacon of blue piercing

the sky. Despite its distance, she could see it clearly, where the settlement it was coming from was only a grey silhouette. Normally, a village in need would make an offering to their Deathless Lord and request a hunt. However, in the worst of circumstances, they could use the beacon for a more direct summons. The light was visible for miles around, a call to any Deathless in the area.

'Have you seen the trees?' asked Arkav.

She cast her eye over the dense expanse of forest. 'You're going to need to be more specific.'

'Just watch.'

She did so and her eyes widened. 'It looks like they're trembling.'

'Yes. The forest is afraid.'

A growing sense of horror rose in her stomach. *The settlement ahead, the one calling for aid, is Sagan. It's one of Rochant's.*

She leaned out of the window and shouted to her driver to go faster whilst knowing, in her heart, that she would be too late.

Sa-at hurried to keep up with Satyendra. They darted through the castle like thieves, swift and silent. Satyendra seemed to possess a sixth sense, knowing when to wait and when to move. Avoiding guards and the few people still walking the corridors with ease.

It's like me, he thought. When I'm in the Wild.

It occurred to him that he didn't know where he was, that he was completely reliant on his new ally. Satyendra may have sworn an oath, but oaths could be twisted in the right hands. It would not protect him forever.

Satyendra stopped at the doorway to a small room. There were no guards in sight and nothing to stop them going inside. 'Wait here,' he said to Sa-at. 'Keep an eye out, I won't be long.'

'What are you doing?'

Satyendra paused, a brief flash of uncertainty on his face that went as quickly as it came. 'Gathering my strength.' And with that, he slipped inside.

Sa-at watched him from the doorway, though he often paused to glance up and down the corridor. Inside the room slept a sad little ball of skin and misery in the shape of a boy. He was tossing and turning, clearly in the grip of a bad dream. Satyendra was standing over him, his hands hovering over the boy's head.

A few seconds passed. Sa-at wasn't sure what was about to happen but he didn't like it.

Satyendra took a breath, and then put his hands firmly upon the boy's throat and squeezed, leaning down to whisper in his ear: 'Weep for me, Pik, you traitorous little shit!'

Immediately, Pik's eyes sprang open, and he began to struggle. He clawed at Satyendra's hands, but to no avail.

Satyendra held Pik's gaze, an unpleasant sneer on his face and an unnatural light in his eyes. With each second he seemed taller somehow, stronger.

The urge to enter the room and confront Satyendra vanished. It was not that he was surprised by the display of power. After all, there were many things in the Wild that were far stronger than they appeared. It was that he was surprised by it here in the castle, which had seemed so solid and free of peril. A part of him had started to let his guard down, to believe that he had found a sanctuary. Those illusions scattered like dust on the wind.

He's going to die. The boy is going to die!

Sa-at cried out, and stepped forward, uncertain of what to do.

At the sound of his voice, Satyendra jolted, and looked shocked, snatching back his hands as if he'd only just become aware of what they were doing.

Sa-at went to the limp body. 'Did you?'

'No. He's alive.'

'But you were going to kill him.'

'I . . .' Satyendra looked away then added in a smaller voice. 'Yes I was. He sold me out and I hate him. The funny thing is, it isn't really his fault. He was just following orders and, to be honest, I was never a particularly good friend.'

'You took something from him, didn't you?'

'Rochant had weakened me. I needed to be strong again for our escape.'

'And are you? Strong again?'

Satyendra gave him a nasty smile, the glimpse of vulnerability gone. 'Oh yes. It's time to get your friend and get out of here. Where is his room?'

Sa-at shrugged. 'I wanted him to share mine but they wouldn't let us.'

'Perhaps he has been assigned his own one now. How does he serve Lord Rochant?'

'He's a Gatherer.'

'A castle has no need for Gatherers.'

Sa-at thought hard. Rochant normally got Tal to carry things but that didn't seem like a job on its own. Then he remembered. 'Oh! What's an apprentice ship?'

'It's when you learn a trade. Why?'

'When we were putting on Rochant's armour, Tal said we needed a Gardensmith and Rochant said this was his apprentice ship.'

'It's Gardener-smith!' tutted Satyendra. 'I know where he might be. Follow me.'

He followed Satyendra through the castle. The corridors were empty, and felt very different to how it they had in the day. *Like the Wild!* he thought, convinced now.

'That's odd,' murmured Satyendra. 'There should be guards here.'

Sa-at shrugged.

'It serves us for now but I have a feeling it won't later.'

The main gates of the keep were shut, but they were able to go out through the kitchen entrance. It was still warm inside, the great slabs of crystal radiating heat long after sunsset. Satyendra pulled a cloak from a hook on the wall, putting it on as he walked to the door. But it was locked and bolted.

'Do you have the key?' Sa-at asked. It occurred to him that Roh probably had it. Then he remembered her staring eyes and felt sad.

'I don't need one,' replied Satyendra. He grinned, then flexed his arms. The door groaned, then tore free, hinges and lock still attached.

They rushed out into the night, crossing the courtyard towards another building with doors of glass. Satyendra pointed towards it. 'See? There are still lights on inside.'

Sa-at nodded.

'There shouldn't be. Something strange is going on.'

Wagons and tents were packed along the walls, the traders

still trapped here by Rochant's edict. A few of their tethered Dogkin perked up as they went past, but soon decided the two small figures were of no interest and settled again.

They pushed open the doors and were blasted by a wave of heat. Sa-at saw Satyendra flinch away as if stung, then brace himself and go inside. It was even warmer than the kitchen in here. There were two large pools of glimmering sapphire water, one on each side of the room. Huge plant-like structures grew from them. He could see crystal leaves that were teased into different shapes. Some were being curved into tubes, while others were being stretched flat.

Tal was also there. He'd been dusting an empty armour stand but turned as they entered. His brief joy at seeing Sa-at was swiftly eclipsed by shock when he saw Satyendra was with him.

'What are you doing here?'

'I—' Sa-at began, but his old nervousness overcame him again. How could he explain things to his friend when it was all so tangled in his mind?

'We're leaving,' said Satyendra. 'Sa-at wants you to come with us.'

Tal took a step backwards, starting to circle behind one of the pools. 'I'm not looking in your eyes, I'm not listening to what you're saying. Let my friend go, demon, and I won't sound the alarm.'

'No,' said Sa-at. 'It's not like that. He told me what Rochant is going to do, Tal. He's going to kill my soul!'

Tal continued to back away, glancing towards Sa-at but steadfastly not looking at Satyendra. 'What?'

'When Rochant dies, he's going to put his soul in my body and my soul is going to be all shredded and crushed!'

'Yes,' said Tal, 'I know.'

'But I'll die!'

'That's what being an Honoured Vessel is. You give your life so our Lord Rochant can come back. It's a sacrifice for your people.'

Sa-at gasped, unable to understand how his friend looked so calm. 'But . . .'

'They're all in on it,' said Satyendra softly. 'All your so-called friends will give you up the moment Rochant asks them.'

'You won't come with me?' asked Sa-at.

'No.' Tal smiled proudly. 'I'm going to live with the Sky-born now. I'm going to be a Gardener-smith. We'll get to see lots of each other because . . . Actually, let me show you something. You'll like this. But tell that demon to stay back.'

Satyendra leaned in so close that his breath tickled Sa-at's ear. 'We're going to have to kill him to get out of here.'

Sa-at shook his head. 'Promise me you won't kill Tal.'

'That's a stupid promise.'

'Promise or . . . or I won't help you any more.'

'Don't be a fool. I'm trying to protect us.'

'Promise!'

Satyendra shook his head in disgust. 'I promise I won't kill him.'

'Good. Wait here. I want to see the thing.'

With a hiss of frustration, Satyendra nodded.

Sa-at followed Tal over to the far side of the chamber. The ex-Gatherer went to a veiled object that was at least six foot tall and nearly as wide. 'Ready?'

'Yes,' said Sa-at, unable to stifle his curiosity.

Tal pulled away the veil to reveal a suit of sapphire armour. It looked exactly like the armour Rochant wore except it was smaller, and some of the plates weren't fully formed, leaving gaps on the chest and one of the shoulders. 'This is your set.'

It was beautiful. Sa-at momentarily forgot himself; all his attention had been stolen by the armour.

'You'll have to come down for fittings. It's not finished yet and it needs lots of work to fit properly.' He smiled. 'Which means we'll be spending lots of time together.'

'But . . . I have to go.'

Tal's smile vanished. 'You can't go. We all have our duties. Mine is to learn this trade and help the other Gardener-smiths make weapons and armour to fight the Wild. Yours is to learn all about Rochant and be there if he needs you.' He put a hand on Sa-at's arm. 'Don't look sad! This is what you wanted. You're going to have lots of friends now and a really good life. You'll never have to worry about food or being safe or having—'

Tal's eyes rolled up in his head and he collapsed. Satyendra was standing behind him. Sweat glistened on his face and his breathing was heavy. 'Before you say anything. I haven't killed him.'

Sa-at checked to see if that was true. As he did so there was a flash of anger towards Satyendra, followed by a flash of anger at himself.

I should have made better rules when I bound him. I should have told him not to hurt Tal too.

When he found his friend still breathing, he let out a sigh of relief. Then, the sadness came back. 'He knew what was going to happen and he didn't care.'

'Nobody will. You're the first person I've met that understands. That's why we need to stay together. No more distractions. No more so-called friends. It's just you and me.'

Unable to find the words, Sa-at just nodded.

'The tricky part will be escaping the main wall. I used to have rope prepared for this purpose, but it was taken from me by a traitor.'

'We could use the hole.'

'What hole?'

'The one Rochant showed me. It's how we got in.'

'That might get us outside but,' Satyendra paused to wipe the sweat from his brow, 'we still have to get down the mountain. With the castle locked tight, the roads will be empty. When the suns come up, we'll be seen by anyone who cares to look.'

'And you can't use the Godroad,' said Sa-at. 'It will kill you.'

Satyendra nodded, fear in his eyes. 'You're probably right. I wouldn't know . . . I've never left the castle. Not since I was a baby anyway.' He slumped and looked away, all the vigour he'd shown earlier gone. 'I hate this room.'

Sa-at shook his arm. 'We have to go before the guards find out.'

'It's not the guards that worry me,' Satyendra replied. He glanced at the larger, empty armour stand and his hand went to the small of his back. 'Rochant is out there somewhere. Oh, this is hopeless. We'll never get clear in time . . . There's nothing else to do but . . .'

Sa-at didn't like the way Satyendra was looking at him. 'I know how we can get down the mountain really fast.' He went and put his hand on the smaller set of armour.

'No, that won't work.'

Sa-at grinned at him. 'I'm good at falling.'

'No.'

'I'll carry you.'

'No!'

Sa-at lifted the wings from the stand. 'Yes.'

Pari had the carriage stop a safe distance away from Sagan. Though her brother followed – the two of them advancing in bounding, gliding strides – his damaged wing meant that she soon left him behind. The light of the beacon was beginning to fade. Were it not so quiet, the outside of the settlement would appear almost normal.

Like most settlements, Sagan was built alongside either side of the Godroad for protection. The houses were closest, then the working buildings, then the thin stretch of farmland. After its closest neighbour, Sorn, had fallen prey to the Wild, Sagan had taken on the refugees, growing in size. It had also erected wooden walls for extra protection. They still looked to be in good repair, though it bothered her to find nobody manning them. She'd got used to being challenged by House Sapphire's overzealous guards and their sudden absence was startling.

Up ahead she could see bodies on the Godroad. These were people who had followed the normal protocols, fleeing the settlement for the safety of the crystal road.

She landed alongside them in a crouch. The nearest body belonged to a middle-aged man. He had the pale skin of the road-born, and the hands of a Cutter-crafter. He also had a spear sticking out of his chest. It was embedded deep, so deep that if she didn't know he was still in his castle, she'd have wondered if Rochant had thrown it. There was debris around the bodies. Stones and tools. Small but weighty objects.

The people fled here and were attacked with projectiles.

She could see the scrabble marks in the earth to either side. Clearly those who had not been dropped in the initial volley had tried to jump to safety.

But there was no safety. Those poor souls must have been plucked from the ground the moment they left the Godroad. Who did this? What did this?

She got up, unfurled her whip, and continued into Sagan.

The gates had been opened to allow people to escape and she entered without challenge.

Inside was a scene of carnage. She and Arkav had stopped here on their way in. It had been an overcrowded place of problems, but also of industry and people fighting adversity together.

Now it was a place of the dead.

It looked as if a storm had swept through, tearing chunks from the mud roofs and pulling several of the houses over entirely. Carts were overturned, personal possessions strewn randomly, abandoned.

A few of the bodies had been stripped of clothes and skin, their scattered skeletons clean. She couldn't be sure but it seemed to her as if each one was missing a bone or two. Other bodies were virtually untouched. These were being gathered together by a group of six demons, who fluttered over a growing pile. She recognized the flying mishmash of human and Flykin. They had once been the people of Sorn. She'd seen them cocooned in slabs of amber, buried in the hillside. They hadn't been fully transformed then. Now they were. *The children of the Scuttling Corpseman.* She did not like to think about what they were up to, and she most certainly did not like the idea of letting them continue.

Six seems a bit much though, even for me. Come on, Arkav!

As she waited, she saw four of them scoop up bodies and take to the air, while the remaining two went back to building the pile. She only had to take one glance at the fliers to guess where they were going.

Sorn. Or more likely the hill outside Sorn. It seems the Corpseman wants to grow its family further.

There was still no sign of Arkav or the carriage and she decided that these were probably the best odds she was going to get. Her opponents were partially armoured, but their arms and legs were still recognizably human, with patches of pale skin exposed beneath holes in the chitin.

She leapt forward, her whip flashing out ahead of her. The Tanzanite barb sunk into the back of one of the demon's knees and nestled in. Flames immediately flickered around the wound. Before it could react, she pulled hard on the whip, taking its legs from under it and bringing it out backwards to the floor.

Pari leapt forward again, driving her knee into the prone demon's back, cracking carapace and wing case as she did so. It made a distressed buzzing noise which she had no desire ever to hear again.

As the second demon turned towards her, she grabbed the face of the first one with her crystal gauntlet and squeezed, breaking and burning until the noise stopped.

It bothered her deeply that once, this had been a loyal servant of House Sapphire, betrayed by Rochant and corrupted by the Corpseman. She hoped that the man the demon was made from had died long ago, but she couldn't be sure.

May you have some measure of peace now.

She looked for weak points as the second demon approached, its wings flickering angrily at its back. This too was not completely covered by natural armour, but instead of skin she saw flecks of white where pieces of whittled bone had been used to plug the gaps.

There was no expression on the demon's face and the jaw hung loose. There were no eyes either, but the eye sockets weren't entirely empty, something rounded sat deep within the recesses of the skull.

She jumped back as it approached and lashed out with her whip. The demon seemed to anticipate the attack, twisting clear without losing momentum.

She jumped back again, whipping for its legs this time. It leapt high and kept coming.

It was nearly on her.

When she'd fought the Corpseman before, it had sensed her with its antennae, and she suspected that it detected thought as much as movement. She wondered if this demon worked the same way, and noticed how it held its hands forward, as if the fingers themselves were tasting the air.

Her third jump put her back to the wall. It was time to test her theory.

She whipped the fingers of its right hand, and was pleased to see it overreact to avoid the blow, jerking backwards in alarm.

Before it could recover, she pressed it, switching from whip to boot, to fist, as she spun and attacked again and again. At last, she made contact, slicing into its hand with her blade-sharp wings. For a moment it was stunned, and in that moment, Pari spun again, snipping its head cleanly from its body and setting both aflame.

A noise from behind soon got her attention. She turned just in time to see Arkav charge into Sagan. 'Pari! Are you all right?'

'I'd have been much better if you'd arrived five minutes ago.'

He stopped and snorted. 'Yes, you seem fine.'

'I wish I could say the same for everyone else. Come over here and look at this. I want to know what you think.'

She waved him over to where the bodies were. Where the swarm had picked the others clean, these were all intact. 'I'm not even sure what killed them.'

Arkav squatted down on his Sky-legs. 'That's because they're not dead.'

'What?'

He held his bracer over the mouth of the nearest victim. 'It's barely discernible, but do you see?'

She had to crouch down and crane her neck, but she saw; a weak puff of mist. 'But they seem more than asleep. They seem . . . gone.'

'Perhaps they are,' he mused.

'I want you to examine them further. If they are still alive, see if you can save them from whatever this is.'

'It's making servants. Breeding them from these bodies.'

'You're saying that these people are being turned into parts?'

Arkav nodded grimly. 'Yes. Like eggs that have yet to be

fertilised. The Scuttling Corpseman is trying to recreate itself. And the people of Sagan are paying the price.'

'No,' replied Pari. 'Sagan is just the latest part of the price. It's happened before, in Sorn, and it will happen again.' She clenched her fists and looked him in the eye. 'Unless we can stop it.'

CHAPTER TWELVE

The suns had set some time ago but the Wild remained quiet. Nobody was taking any chances however. Hunters from five of the Crystal Dynasties patrolled Fourboards' perimeter. The road-born that lived there, no longer sure of the Godroad's protection, huddled in their homes, waiting for the Deathless to make things right again.

In his exalted state Vasinidra did not feel tired, but he was starting to feel stretched, a sure sign that when he did take off the armour, the exertions of the past few days would hit hard. But he did not dare take it off, not yet, not with things still so tense.

One of the biggest buildings had been cleared for their use and the Deathless filled it easily. Yadva nearly filled it on her own! Of the ten immortals that had joined the battle, only eight remained in their bodies, and only six of them looked to for much longer.

The minor houses had taken the worst of it. Lords Quasim

Peridot and Lakshin Opal were now between lives, all but a few of their hunters dead. Lady Anuja Ruby was still breathing but her condition was uncertain. She was too weak to move, and had slept for most of the day. Nobody had dared try to wake her.

Vasinidra looked at the faces of his peers. *None are behaving as if we had a victory. They know that things are different now. We are like children who have just lost our parents. Nothing makes sense any more and we don't know what to do.*

'We should be having a feast now,' grumbled Yadva. 'Not squatting in this hovel.'

'Ssh,' said Gada, his long face creased with disapproval. 'You disrespect House Ruby.'

'House Ruby is comatose,' Yadva retorted. 'I don't see the point of staying here. We need warm beds and good food and a break from this swamp. How anyone lives with this smell is beyond me.'

As Gada shook his head, Umed lifted a hand. His uncle's body was nearing the end of its natural life, and it had cost him to put it into battle. Though his armour sustained him, Vasinidra suspected this would be Umed's last venture until his next rebirth.

'Yes, Lord Umed?' he asked.

'While I may not agree with Lady Yadva's use of words, High Lord. She is right to point out the need for a plan.'

'We are in Ruby lands, Uncle. It is for Lady Anuja to make a plan, not me.'

'Time is against us. The people of Fourboards will struggle to sustain themselves given their losses and there is no way they can host a force of this size for long. Moreover, the longer we remain here, the longer we leave our own lands undefended. You said yourself that the traditions no longer serve our needs, so I urge you to take action now.'

The other Sapphire murmured assent. Having seen how dangerous the Wild had become, they were all keen to return and check their homes were safe.

He looked over to Lady Farida Tanzanite. 'What do you think?'

She tilted her head. 'I think House Ruby would rather a little disrespect than lose any more of its people. My High Lord told us to help Lady Anuja. So long as I believe you are working to the same goal, we will do as you suggest, High Lord Vasinidra.'

'Thank you. We know that the Wild has been behaving oddly here for some time. We know that Quiverhive has been directing the attacks on House Ruby. We also know that they have been targeting the Rubies above all else. I think Quiverhive's goal was to wipe them out entirely.'

'I think,' said Yadva, gesturing towards Anuja's prone form, 'that it succeeded.'

'The question is, why? Why go to all this trouble? What was the point?'

Umed closed his eyes. 'Many have gone mad trying to fathom the Wild.'

'But that was when the Wild was unfathomable. It is behaving differently now. It's thinking, reacting, it's becoming more like us. They've adapted to the Godroad, and to our hunting tactics.'

'They had, you mean,' said Yadva. 'Quiverhive is slain.'

'Yes. I'm hoping that means that the relentless attacks on Ruby settlements will end. It still doesn't answer the question of why. And it doesn't explain where the Corpseman is or what it's doing.'

Gada sighed. 'I wish we could give you insight, High Lord, but you know more about what's going on than we do.'

He's right. I won't get answers from them. I'm going to have to find them myself, and until then, guess. How has it come to this? Gambling our futures on shreds of evidence and half-formed ideas.

'Lady Farida, I'd ask that you and the rest of the Tanzanite force remain in Ruby lands and patrol the Godroad. It might be that the Wild will go for easier targets. Keep on the move. There's no telling where the enemy might strike next.'

'As you wish, High Lord Sapphire.'

She rose and the other two Deathless rose with her, leaving the Sapphire alone with Lady Anuja.

'Lord Umed, it is time for you to return home. You've done enough here.'

'Yes, High Lord.'

He was about to say more when he saw Lady Anuja begin to cough violently. They all waited respectfully until the fit had passed. Though she didn't open her eyes, her lips parted and she began to speak. 'Has there been another attack?'

A couple of strides and he was by her side. 'No. Your people are safe.'

'Vasinidra?'

'Yes.'

'My house . . . has fallen?'

'No, my lady. It stands, held up by its allies until its suns rise again. We will watch over your lands while your High Lord returns to the lands of the living. Rest now. You've earned it.'

She shook her head. 'The Bringers do not answer my call. I sent for them urgently and there has been no sign of them. Not even a message.'

'Rest,' he said again. 'I will deal with this.'

'Swear it.'

'I swear it on my house and my honour and our friendship.'

'I will hold you to it,' she replied, closing her eyes and drifting away while his thoughts whirled.

If something has happened to the Bringers then none of us will return. Have they abandoned us? Are they victims of the Corpseman? What about Mother? If they haven't answered Lady Anuja's summons, perhaps they haven't responded to mine either. I'll find them and drag them to her rebirth ceremony myself if I have to.

He was halfway to the door before he remembered himself. 'I have to investigate this further. Lady Yadva, Lord Umed, you will remain here and represent House Sapphire. Lord Gada, gather your hunters. We're going home.'

Varg and Chandni rode on Glider's back, following Crowflies back to the others. They had gone until the buzzing of the swarm could no longer be heard behind them. Then they had rode on some more.

At last, she ordered Glider to stop and catch her breath. The Dogkin obeyed immediately, falling onto her belly to pant, while Crowflies perched on a nearby branch to glare at them, impatient.

'I don't think those things are following us,' said Varg.

She just nodded, her jaw clenched.

'What's up, Chand?'

'Kennelgrove. It tried to kill us!'

'How?'

'It spoke to me, bewitched me somehow so that all I could think of was the Corpseman. I thought we had won Kennelgrove over and I let my guard down. Even our youngest children know the rules for demons: Don't listen, don't make eye contact, don't let them touch you. How could I have been so stupid?'

'I reckon it's hard not to look a demon in the eye or listen to its voice when you're living with them. We either gotta get away from all of this or find some new rules.'

'There's no getting away, Varg. It's too late for that. And I need Kennelgrove to undo its curse.'

Varg looked worried. 'What curse?'

She lowered her voice. 'Kennelgrove cursed Rayen and her people, and Glider, turning them into Dogkin. The deal I've made with Kennelgrove is to change them back. I'm not sure if the others even remember what they were, but Rayen does.'

'Which one is Rayen?'

'Their leader. I'm worried about her.'

'Yeah?' He sounded disbelieving. 'She was trying to kill you yesterday.'

'She had good reason. Fiya was one of her descendants and I murdered her.'

Varg held up his hands. 'All I'm saying is that it's fucking weird. I don't get why you're trying to help them. They're not your responsibility.'

'They're mine for a year, Varg. And when that year ends, I intend to leave friends behind me, not enemies.' She shook her head. 'None of this was Rayen's fault. It's hard to put into words but . . . I want to change things. I don't know how yet or even what I'm aiming for. I just know I want to make things better.'

'I thought you wanted a life with me, and to have a family.'

She found his hand with her good one and their fingers laced together. 'I still do. More than anything.'

'I don't see how you do both. If you go about trying to change things, you'll get changed too. That's how the Wild is.' His voice cracked. 'I'll lose you again.'

'Before I came here, I was an Honoured Mother. At the same time, I was the seneschal for Lord Rochant Sapphire. Parent and leader. I did both. I will do both here. You have to understand, we are part of the Wild now. We're living inside it. I already have relationships with demons and Dogkin.' She bit her lip. 'This may sound arrogant, but the more I see of the Wild, the more I think that we could do things better.'

'Fuck me, you want to organize the Wild! Pari was right. You Sapphire are insane.'

'I bargained for this time, Varg. I don't intend to squander it hiding in a little hole with you. I'm going to make a life for us. A good one.'

He sighed. 'I must be insane too because I'm not running away. I'm never leaving you again.'

She decided it was time to kiss him.

And so she did.

'You know, I used to hate the way Mohit smelled when he was sweaty, but I don't mind it with you.'

He kissed her forehead. 'I like the way you smell.'

'Even now?'

'Yeah. Wish I could say the same about Glider.'

They both laughed and Glider gave a little whine. 'Sorry,' she said, giving the Dogkin's head a gentle stroke. 'We love you too.'

'Yep, we love everything about you except your farts.'

'Oh, Varg!'

'Come on though, those things can fell a fucking tree!'

Glider gave a snort and tucked her nose under her tail. Her eyes were drooping with fatigue, but just before they could close, Crowflies screeched indignantly and took wing again.

'Sorry, Glider,' said Chandni, 'we have to keep moving.'

When they got back to the rest of the Dogkin pack, Chandni went straight to Kennelgrove, though she was careful not to look it in the eye.

It spread its hands in a gesture of mock surprise. 'How unexpected to see you back unharmed, unharried, and still in the same number of pieces. I am *beyond* happiness.'

'You betrayed me!' Crowflies cawed agreement but Kennelgrove simply laughed.

'I gave a trick for a trick, all within the rules, all for the good. Like the one your feathered imp played on me.'

'That was different. How would my death have helped this alliance?'

It made a show of looking her up and down. 'You do not seem dead to me. Did your lover not protect you as I suggested?'

She fought to keep her expression calm. Obviously it was twisting things. It had probably hoped for Varg's death too, but what Kennelgrove said was undeniably true. The demon took her pause for agreement.

'And did you not learn something to please your prince?'

This question also led to a frustrating answer. 'Yes.'

'What did you learn?'

'That House Sapphire have lost Sagan, another of Lord Rochant's settlements. The attack occurred in daylight. That's never happened before, and in such numbers! It will make a tale the Story-singers will dread to voice. I don't understand why the Deathless didn't come to protect their people.'

'Another trick, I'd wager. The blue-winged ones have flown away, lured by other bait. But there's more, isn't there? I see it by the wrinkling of your forehead.'

'The Corpseman has changed from the stories into something new. It can fly now, and its wings have these patterns that . . .'

'Do not speak of them. The memories are painful for poor Kennelgrove.'

'Very well. I saw its army too.'

'It sounds like a most useful excursion.'

'I'm still angry about what you did.'

'Good.'

It took all her self control not to meet its eye with a wrathful stare. Instead, she maintained an appearance of calm and asked, 'When are you going to restore the Dogkin to their true forms?'

'It was the second thing I promised and the second thing I'll do. First, I will treat with your prince.'

'Then we should go immediately.'

'We are of one mind.'

I sincerely hope not, thought Chandni.

Satyendra watched as Sa-at struggled to get into the armour. A day ago, he had been lord of this castle and now he was having to flee in the most ridiculous and dangerous manner. Any second, he expected someone to burst into the Chrysalis Chamber and throw them back in a cell.

'I can't reach the strap,' said Sa-at. He'd managed to get the back plate and chest plate into the right place, but he couldn't hold them and secure them at the same time. 'Can you help me?'

'No.'

'What?'

Satyendra looked away. 'I can't. I don't get along with that armour.'

'This won't work if you don't help.'

'I told you it was a stupid idea.'

He heard Sa-at sigh. 'What idea do you have?'

The question made him furious because he had no ideas. The majority of the castle's guard had been posted on the outer wall, making any escape attempts impossible.

Sa-at was still looking at him, the wings hanging lopsided on his back. He wanted an answer Satyendra didn't have. 'You swore to help me escape. If you don't have an idea, you have to do mine.'

'Fine,' he shot back. 'I'll help you but it's going to cost me. You remember that.'

Sa-at frowned. 'You swore. That's not my fault.'

I hate him so much, thought Satyendra as he moved over to fix the wings back into place. They weren't active yet. No blood had been daubed on them, but there was a dormant energy in the crystal that set his teeth on edge.

'Ow!' cried Sa-at. 'That's too tight.'

'We don't want those wings falling off when we're in the sky, do we?'

'No.'

'Then they stay tight.'

Between them, they got him into the rest of the suit. Sa-at offered his hand without hesitation for Satyendra to take some blood, and between them, they applied some to each piece. Perhaps it was because they weren't Gardener-smiths and they didn't know the proper way. Perhaps it was because Sa-at was not a Deathless and it needed Rochant's blood. Perhaps it was because the armour was not fully grown. But when they were done, the armour did not glow in the way Satyendra expected.

'That will have to do,' he muttered. 'If this ends with us leaping to our death, I'll . . .' He was going to issue some kind of threat to Sa-at, but anything he could add would be irrelevant at that point so instead he said, 'It doesn't matter. Wait here.'

There were two ways out of the Chrysalis Chamber. The main door that led out into the courtyard, and a set of steps that led out onto a balcony. On hunting days, Lord Rochant would leap from there. Satyendra ran up the stairs. The doors to the balcony were made of coloured glass. They weren't locked and he was able to slide them open with ease. The wind blew cold and bitter on his face, a welcome change from the cloying air of the chamber. He stepped out and looked down. The drop was significant. Story-singer Ban told him that when Rochant leapt, the songs of his people carried him out and over the main wall.

I doubt the snores of a bunch of trapped merchants is going to suffice.

He ran back down the stairs. 'That way isn't going to

work. We need to get you onto the battlements and jump from there.' He felt a wave of irritation. 'This is impossible!'

'I don't care,' said Sa-at. 'You swore to try.'

There was an unpleasant tingling in his stomach. Not enough to convince him that his oath was binding, but enough to make him think twice about ignoring it.

'Stay here,' he replied. 'I'll clear a way to the battlements. When you hear a commotion, I want you to come as fast as you can, go up the stairs to the top of the wall. I'll be waiting for you there.'

Satyendra checked Tal was still unconscious and then left the Chamber using the same doors they'd come in. He took in a deep breath of clean air to clear his head. There were no guards immediately between him and the stairs. But he could see a hunter at the top, several others posted at nearby intervals, and a pair of guards making a circuit on this quarter of the wall.

His mind worked quickly as he began to ascend.

Nothing I say will persuade them to leave their posts. I have no authority any more and if they realize who I am, they'll attack. But I refuse to die here. I refuse!

As he got closer, he recognized the hunter. A plan formed in his mind but his feet hesitated on the steps. He didn't know the hunter well, didn't particularly care for him either way, but what he was about to do was horrible. *Is this really who I am? A monster. Why do I have to be like this?* But even as a part of him reconsidered, wanting to flee back down the steps, the other part of him began to stir.

Satyendra lowered his head as he reached the top to keep his tattoos hidden in the shadow of his hood. 'Excuse me, it's Jir, isn't it?'

The hunter turned in surprise. He had long hair as was the fashion and it shone beautifully black in the gemslight. 'That's me. Do I know you?'

'I'm just one of Roh's boys,' he replied, dipping his head even lower. 'But I saw your partner just now. She was in the kitchens with another hunter. They were . . .'

He had Jir's attention now. 'They were what?'

'They were . . .' he dragged out the moment, savouring the rising anxiety in the other man, 'touching each other.'

Jir ran a hand through his hair. 'You're sure it was her?'

'Yes, sir.'

'No, it can't be true.' He looked around as if seeking confirmation from the air, then smiled. 'That can't be. All the hunters were posted on watch by Lord Rochant himself. You're mistaken, boy. And if you make up lies about my partner again, I'll give you the sharp end of my spear.'

Satyendra risked making eye contact. 'Begging your pardon, sir, but it wasn't one of Lord Rochant's, it was Zax, that big one that used to serve High Lord Yadavendra.'

Jir's smile vanished. None of Rochant's hunters liked Zax. The man had kept a low profile since Yadavendra had died but he hadn't been forgotten. The hunter snatched up his spear. 'I'll kill him.'

The sense of betrayal, the hurt, it all pulsed through Satyendra's body. But he needed more. 'Wait, you can't. They haven't done anything wrong. She was willing.' He paused again. 'Very willing.'

Jir no longer saw Satyendra, his eyes were staring, unfocused, imagining the worst. 'No . . . No, no, no . . .'

Satyendra drank in the man's mounting despair, feeling his muscles swell and his senses sharpen. The Sapphire placed their lights so meticulously that there was nowhere on the wall where his actions would not be observed, but now the rush was setting in, he didn't care. They wouldn't be able to stop him now. No one could.

He grabbed Jir by the leather straps that crossed his chest. Hunters trained hard and considered themselves strong and capable. Satyendra was several inches shorter than Jir and of a slender build, so the older man was taken completely by surprise when he was picked up as easily as a babe and slammed against the wall.

Pain. Fear. Shock.

The spear fell from Jir's fingers.

More fuel for Satyendra's growing power.

He slammed Jir against the wall again, and this time, there was a crack as his delicate wings broke apart. As soon as he heard that, Satyendra hurled him over the wall.

Jir plunged, screaming, into the darkness and was gone.

It occurred to Satyendra that he had killed another person, but it was a thought rather than a feeling – *shouldn't I feel bad about this?* – but it barely registered as he absorbed Jir's last moments of shock and terror, the ecstasy eclipsing any guilt.

The two guards were now charging towards him and a cry of alarm had gone up. To Satyendra it looked as if they were moving in slow motion. He had plenty of time to look for Sa-at as they approached.

There he is, he thought with disgust, *wobbling on those Sky-legs like a newly born Cattlekin. He needs to be faster!*

Satyendra picked up Jir's spear and hurled it at the first of the two guards. They barely registered the motion before the shaft was protruding from the woman's chest. The second guard looked over his shoulder, trying to understand why she had fallen. When he looked up again, Satyendra was in front of him.

'Wha—'

His hands closed on the guard's throat and squeezed. The man's eyes rolled up into his skull, but not before he'd given up a delicious fizz of panic. Satyendra felt stronger still.

His body hummed with energy.

His bones twitched.

His face began to open.

No! No, I don't want this!

But his body was shifting of its own accord now, gathering a momentum he neither understood nor could control. Meanwhile, more hunters were approaching him at speed, spears ready. They were coming from both sides, moving in together to flank him.

He shook his head, the guard still dangling from his grasp, and his cheeks swung oddly, sending a chill down his spine.

What's happening to me! I want it to stop.

Out of the corner of his eye he saw a spear coming towards him. It sailed slowly, leisurely, almost as if it had been tossed for him to catch, but there was no doubt that its intent was to kill.

He plucked it from the air with his free hand and sent it on its way twice as fast, causing those behind him to fall back with a cry. Then, he launched the guard he held at those in front of him, turning the approaching hunters into a heap of struggling limbs.

Moments had been bought. He used the reprieve to probe at his face and found his cheekbones too far apart. Horrified he tried to squeeze them back together, his stomach lurching as they moved on some new hinge within his skull.

Sa-at was on the stairs now, moving with a lot of energy but little skill, jumping three at a time, then slipping, then jumping again.

Satyendra wanted to shout at him, but he dared not speak. Instead he held down a hand. Sa-at saw it and nodded, scrambling to close the gap between them.

The hunters were regrouping. Satyendra noted the slow looks between them as they took positions and advanced. They were more cautious this time, and he could see they were using forms usually practised against demons of the Wild. None met his gaze now, their attention was on his arms and legs. The next attack would come from both sides simultaneously.

Come on! he thought, though even he didn't know if he was urging the hunters to commence the fight, or Sa-at to enable their escape. His mind was working so fast, the feelings so powerful, that things felt like a blur, like he could be anything he wanted. And he wanted many conflicting things all at once:

He wanted to get away and hide and be alone.

He wanted to make people suffer.

He wanted it to stop!

It was all getting too much. His vision began to flicker, the gemslights becoming burning points of blue, the people distorted shapes. He swayed for a moment.

And that was when the hunters attacked.

And that was when Sa-at's hand found his.

Satyendra grabbed hold and stepped up onto the battlements, raising Sa-at above his head. To an observer they would look like partners performing a difficult lift in a dance. He didn't like the feel of the armour being so close but it did not radiate malice, at least, not yet.

The hunters were gathering at their heels, thrusting for him with their spears. As he jumped, he felt a point of pain in the back of his thigh, sharp and bright.

Then they were in the air, him dangling from Sa-at's arms much like prey would hang from a Birdkin's talons.

Sa-at said something that he couldn't make out but it sounded nervous. He looked around for trouble but there were no immediate threats. Sa-at spoke again, clearly worried, and this time Satyendra didn't need to hear him to understand.

They were not flying. They were falling.

CHAPTER THIRTEEN

When Sa-at had watched Rochant fly, it looked easy. Of course, he'd never seen Rochant try to carry someone else. And Rochant's armour shone bright like a star up close, whereas the armour he was wearing glowed like the last embers of a fire.

He was falling fast. Satyendra was gripping his wrists so tight it hurt, and with his arms locked straight down, there was little he could do to alter their trajectory.

They fell past the outer wall. Luckily, Satyendra had pushed them far enough away that they cleared the rocky skirt that flashed out at the base. As they passed that, they fell into a current of essence that wrenched at his wings. For a moment they slowed, even started to rise a little, and then they slipped sideways out of it and fell again, spinning crazily.

Satyendra was shouting at him but he couldn't hear a word of it over the roaring wind. In the dark, he was just a shape. But there was something about the shape that he found unsettling.

If I was alone, I could do this, he thought.

He considered letting Satyendra go. After all, *he* hadn't sworn any oaths, and he hadn't made up his mind about Satyendra yet. Surely it was better that one of them survived?

'I'm sorry!' he shouted.

It was hard to tell if Satyendra understood, but the grip on his wrists tightened still further, threatening to crush the bones. *Even if I let go, he won't.*

He tried kicking his legs and tilting his body, doing all he could to re-enter the currents, but it was an impossible task. Between the extra weight, the unfamiliar armour, and the constant spinning, he could barely see, let alone fly.

But, by chance, they fell back into the currents beneath the castle naturally. He felt the armour press painfully into his chest as their momentum was forcefully checked. Before he could process this, he was tossed about like a leaf in a storm, and it was all he could do not to throw up in his helmet.

All around him was dark, save for the castle's lights that he glimpsed occasionally as he was flipped over and over.

Are they above me?

Below me?

Up and down ceased to have meaning. Time ceased to have meaning. His panic became a single moment in time, as constant as the pain in his arms and the tight clenching of his stomach.

And then, there was a more defined movement, as if the essence currents were some great beast that spat them out.

He felt a great jolt run through his body and then he was lying on his back. It took him a while to realize that his mind was spinning rather than the world. And it took a while longer than that for it to stop.

When he sat up, his shoulders, elbows, and wrists all protested. He didn't care about them though, being too busy pulling off the helmet so that he could vomit without obstruction.

After having emptied his stomach, he felt much better, though the pain in his arms was suddenly much more pressing. He lifted his head and looked around.

The castle was far, far above. From this angle, the man-made structure was completely obscured. All he could see was the rocky base lit by soft veins of sapphire.

To his right, directly beneath it, was a large rent in the earth. A chasm with perfectly smooth sides that led down into the darkness. Just looking at it made him shiver.

The ground around him was mostly dry earth, odd tufts of grass, and a few plants that were too stubborn to die. Satyendra was standing a few feet away, facing away. He was barely visible under the starlight.

'What happened?' asked Sa-at.

'I saved you.' There was a tightness to his voice that spoke of pain.

'How?'

'By taking the fall for both of us. I caught you, I stopped you smashing into pieces on the rocks. I kept my promise.'

'Sort of.'

Satyendra's silhouette half turned towards him. 'What?'

'Well, you did help me escape the castle, like you promised.' He held up his hands. 'But you hurt me.'

'That wasn't my fault!'

Sa-at frowned. 'An oath is an oath.' Before Satyendra could

answer, he became distracted by something. The glow from his bracers was irregular, smudged in places. He peered at them and realized that there were burn marks on the crystal. Black hand-prints left by a layer of seared skin.

Maybe he was squeezing so tight because it hurt.

'Are your hands okay?'

'Why would you care?'

'Are they?'

He heard a bitter sigh. 'No.'

'Can I see?'

'No.' Satyendra tucked them into his armpits.

'If we can get into the Wild, I know things that will help.'

'Why do you assume I'm going to come with you? I've helped you escape. You don't have any hold on me now.'

'What's "assume"?'

'You think you know what I'm going to do when you don't know me at all.'

Sa-at thought about this. 'What are you going to do?'

'Whatever I want.'

'Oh . . . What do you want?'

Satyendra turned his back again. 'I don't know. But you should take off that armour.'

'Why?'

'Because it can be seen from miles away, especially at night.'

Sa-at took off the Sky-legs. He liked their bounciness but didn't like the way it made his legs feel out of control. He took off the greaves and the wings and the chest plate. He took off the vambraces and the gauntlets. It would be wrong to return to the Wild in Deathless armour, he knew this. Better to go back as a friend than as a wound.

He stood up and took off the cloak he'd been given. Beneath it he still wore his coat of feathers. He hadn't realized it until now but none of the things he'd been offered had felt right. They had been exciting for their newness, but they had not been his.

'Do you want my cloak?' he asked.

Satyendra took it without a word, knelt down, and began tearing it into strips. He fastened one around his head like a scarf and pulled up his hood. The others, he started to wrap around his right hand. Then he stopped and muttered something under his breath.

'You shouldn't cover them up,' said Sa-at. 'Not until we've found the right juices.'

'I need to use my hands.'

'But—'

'Don't interfere!'

Satyendra struggled for a while. It was painful to watch.

'I can help, if you want,' said Sa-at.

Satyendra nodded, but didn't look in his direction.

It was difficult tying the bandage in the dark, but Sa-at had a lot of experience of doing things by touch, and so he managed. When that was done, he bandaged Satyendra's left hand as well. 'When we get into the Wild we can do better.'

'Yes,' agreed Satyendra.

He isn't my friend. I don't think he'll ever be my friend. But I feel sorry for him. He's like me. Even though he grew up in Rochant's castle and I grew up in the Wild, we're both lonely.

They began walking away from the chasm towards the dark of the forest. Sa-at's sadness was mitigated by the thought of seeing Crowflies again. *I've missed it. It will be pleased to see me, and it will help me find my mother.* He wondered if Satyendra and Crowflies would get along. He imagined them meeting and a smile broke out on his face. *Probably not,* he thought.

They were only just on the border of Sapphire lands when Vasinidra brought his flight down to land. He told himself it was because it wasn't fair to push his hunters all the way through the night, but deep down, he was feeling his exertions keenly.

Given the late hour, they landed on the Godroad. Nobody commented about the fact that it no longer guaranteed their safety, but it weighed heavy on them all.

While his people enjoyed a respite from the weight of their wings, their chatter a balm of comfort in the night air, he saw Gada coming in to land. His brother's flight was close behind, and soon the two groups of hunters were mingling freely.

Vasinidra moved away down the Godroad so that he might speak with Gada in private. The two clasped arms. Though the light from the Godroad was comforting, the darkness on either side of it was not. *I try to avoid the Wild at night. It's bad enough in the day, but after the suns set it becomes something else entirely.*

'Please don't take this as a complaint, High Lord, but why have we stopped? I thought you were keen to reach Lord Rochant's castle.'

'It's just us here, brother. You may speak freely and without fear.'

Gada nodded, but his expression remained guarded. 'I thought I was, High Lord.'

We were never close but there is a distance between us now. How can there not be? It struck him then that he had authority over Gada. He decided which Sapphire Deathless got to return, when they got to return, and in which body. As High Lord, he chose what was added to their legend for good or for ill. He held his brother's future lives in his hands. How then, could he expect his brother or any of the other Deathless to be without fear in his presence?

'Of course you were, Lord Gada. To answer your question, I am playing the long game, tempering my desire for speed with the need to keep our hunters from exhaustion. The fight with Quiverhive may be over but the Corpseman remains at large. And in truth, I am tired too.'

Gada removed his helmet, there was concern in his eyes. He pulled nervously at his beard. 'Forgive the bluntness of my question but how long have you been exalted?'

'Since we began the hunt for the Corpseman.'

'That's what I feared.'

'Believe me when I say that I want nothing more than to take off my armour and sleep. But there's no time. I can't doff it here, so the best thing to do is to push on to Lord Rochant's castle.'

'I thought you said we were going home.'

'I meant back to our lands.' He pulled off his own helmet and shook out his long hair. It was good to feel the air on his face. 'There are some things I need to tell you. The others don't know and I would prefer it to stay that way.'

Gada nodded. 'You can trust me, High Lord.'

I hope so, thought Vasinidra. He could tell his brother was pleased to be taken into his confidence. There was a little puffing of his slender chest, and a crease of the mouth, mostly hidden by his beard.

'While you went directly to the Rubies, I took Mother from her exile in the Wild and returned her to Lord Rochant's castle. With luck the Bringers will be seeing to her rebirth as we speak.'

'I wondered if she was the cause of your absence.' He leaned closer. 'When you announce her return to the others, I will stand with you.'

'It warms my heart to hear that. I'm hoping that the reason the Bringers haven't responded to Lady Anuja yet is they're busy serving me, but I'm worried, Gada. With everything we've seen lately . . .'

'What do you fear, High Lord?'

Vasinidra shook his head. 'The Corpseman and Quiverhive haven't just been attacking settlements, that would be bad enough. They're attacking our way of life. I think they meant to wipe out the Rubies entirely. I'm hoping that they don't understand how we return, that they were just obsessed with destroying every Ruby they could find. But what if the Corpseman does know? If it can get onto the Godroad, where else can it get to? What other refuges of ours are no longer safe?'

Gada's long face looked drawn. 'You think it could attack one of our castles?'

'Perhaps. Or the Bringers themselves. I'm saying that we need to be prepared for anything.'

'But Vasinidra—' Gada caught himself, 'High Lord. How does the Corpseman know these things? Is this all from when Samarku Un-Sapphire betrayed us? Or did Mother . . .' He couldn't bring himself to say it out loud.

'Not Mother. Perhaps this came from Samarku, but I believe the true traitor is Rochant.'

'Lord Rochant!'

Gada took breath to start talking. Knowing his brother's penchant for being long-winded, Vasinidra held up a hand to silence him.

'Listen. There are things you need to know. Honoured Vessel Satyendra's rebirth was a failure. Rochant's soul never entered his body. I don't know why the Bringers didn't spot it, but they didn't. Satyendra pretended to be Rochant but that was a lie. The real Rochant is still alive and in league with the Scuttling Corpseman. He betrayed our mother and the house in order to gain power. He betrayed Samarku as well.'

'What?' blurted Gada. 'He . . . Surely not?'

'Yes. I think it is Rochant's aim to destroy us all. We need to remove Satyendra from his post and reassign Rochant's Godpiece to Mother. And we need to do it quickly.'

'Yes. Yes, of course, but why are you telling me this, High Lord? All this is within your power.'

'Because if something happens to me, I need you to be ready.'

Gada just nodded, dumbstruck.

'Things have not always been good between us, brother. That is my fault as much as yours. Now we must be our best selves. The house and its people must come first.'

After a moment, Gada approached and tentatively put a hand on Vasinidra's shoulder. 'I agree with everything you say, High Lord. But please, I beg you, take off the armour. Rest. Allow us to escort you back to the castle. You've been wearing it for too long and it is taking a toll on you.'

'A little rest and something to drink is all I need. The suns will be rising soon. We'll continue onto the castle and then, I promise, I'll do what you ask.'

Gada patted his shoulder. 'Very well. I will leave you to your thoughts.'

Vasinidra watched him go. *He's worried about me going the same way as Yadavendra. Is this how it started for my uncle, I wonder? Did he think that he'd just wear the armour until the threat had passed? And the right time never came.* He stared out at the impenetrable border of trees, unsure if he would ever feel at peace again.

Varg and Chandni rode on Glider's back alongside the pack. This pleased Crowflies, who could make greater haste, and irritated Kennelgrove, who struggled to match their pace. Chandni found she was content with both those outcomes. Despite Kennelgrove's constant muttering about his injuries they made good time and nothing opposed them, and yet there was something in the Dogkin's tense manner that made her feel uneasy. 'Does anything seem wrong to you?'

'Yeah,' replied Varg. 'It's quiet. Too bloody quiet if you ask me.'

'What do you think it means?'

'I think it means the rest of the Wild knows something we don't. I ain't seeing any bodies, so I reckon whatever normally lives round here is either hiding, or gone.'

She looked round, half expecting to see some horrific demon bearing down on them, but there was nothing save for a sense of emptiness. Even the trees seemed further apart from each other in this part of the forest, each one standing alone, their branches not touching their neighbours, not even reaching out to them.

It feels so . . . sad.

'This is awful!' announced Kennelgrove. 'Such loss, such emptiness. And I fear it is only the beginning of the long and final end.'

'No,' said Chandni. 'We'll find a way to make this better.'

'We will?'

She was careful not to meet its gaze, though it made her feel as if she were being disingenuous. 'Yes.'

'Such hope! Oh, how poor Kennelgrove could use some of that. Perhaps we might barter again when I'm done with your prince . . .'

'Perhaps,' she replied with a shudder, and urged Glider to put some more distance between them.

'I don't like the way this is going,' said Varg, keeping his voice low and to her ear. 'These demons are trying to snare you up in their schemes.'

'I promise you, we'll make something good out of this.' Privately, she had started to plan. To think about ways to live within the Wild, to change it even. She suspected Varg just wanted them to have a quiet life in the woods somewhere. *Is that what I want though? Is that enough?* Certainly, the futures she envisioned were all broader in scope.

Sometimes, the pack diverted off to hunt. Pickings were slim, a few Ratkin, and some nuts scavenged from a dying bush, just enough to remind them of their bellies but not enough to satisfy them.

By late afternoon, they arrived at the edge of the forest to find a field of tall grass. Each stalk was pale yellow, with ear-shaped buds at its tip. An old dirt road ran along by the far side of the field.

Chandni gasped. 'I know this place!' She looked up and was rewarded with the distant sight of Lord Rochant's castle hanging in the sky, black against the pale red of Wrath's Tear.

'Yeah. This is where I took you after we first met.' Varg pulled at his beard. 'Funny to think how much has happened since then.'

They moved back between the trees but didn't go deep, following the lines of fields until they came upon a strange sight. In the middle of the last field was a circle where no grass grew. The circle was fifty feet across and so perfectly round, it could have been created by a Sapphire artisan. The soil was thick and moist and black, with a rich, fertile smell. She saw shapes sliding through it, hundreds of them, the smallest Wormkin she'd ever seen. Each was no longer than her little finger, and they lacked eyes and claws. She didn't for an instant consider them harmless, but she wondered if they had stumbled across a group of newborns, and if the mother was nearby.

A flock of young Birdkin came swooping down, just old enough to fly but not yet full grown. They swept some unlucky Wormkin from the soil and banked away towards the forest. Crowflies gave an approving chirp and gave chase.

These Birdkin won't be far from a nest. We're close to Murderkind's domain. 'Follow them,' said Chandni, and the Dogkin broke into a loping run, plunging into the welcoming trees.

CHAPTER FOURTEEN

Satyendra squinted up through the canopy. The suns had risen, but down here their light did not jab at him the way it did in the castle's courtyard. He still didn't like them, but they were much easier to ignore. The trees helped too, shielding him from the worst of the heat.

There are no walls here.

He turned on the spot, appreciating for the first time the sheer amount of space there was. He could walk through the forest in any direction, and not reach the end of it. Only the mountain at his back formed a true barrier, and he had no intention of returning there.

Breathing was easier too. Perhaps it came with the sense of freedom, but he suspected it had as much to do with being out of the castle. It had always constrained him somehow, the sapphires in the walls and floor were like little needles, stabbing at his mind.

The high from the previous night had worn off, leaving him with a clear head. The burns inflicted by Rochant's gauntlet still plagued him whenever he bent forward or twisted his body, and his hands stung terribly from where he'd had to grip Sa-at's bracers. It was hard to be grateful for the fact that his other injuries – the ones sustained when they had landed – had all miraculously healed.

Since their landing he'd said little. To speak meant working his jaw, and that felt dangerous. He was worried that his face might move in other ways. He was worried he might not be able to move it back. That wasn't the only way he'd changed. The knobby bone on the end of his wrist poked out from the end of his sleeve and his trousers kept untucking themselves from the top of his boots.

My limbs are longer. I am longer.

When he clenched his fists – which made his palms burn – the skin stretched painfully tight over his knuckles. It was as if his bones were growing too fast for the rest of him to keep up. Using the last of the strips from the cloak Sa-at had given him, he bound his wrists and the space where the cuffs of his trousers met his boots. There was nothing to do about the physical changes, but he could at least stop the cold from getting in through the gaps in his clothes.

At least, that was his intention. Tying his legs was possible, if painful, but tying his wrists one-handed with bound palms was beyond him. Out of the corner of his eye, he could see Sa-at watching him, an expression of pity on his face.

'Do you want me to help?'

'No, but . . .' Satyendra forced the words out. 'It would be quicker, and we need to get moving before Rochant comes for us.'

He watched as Sa-at set to work. Side by side, their hands were quite different. His skin was no longer as dark as

Sa-at's, and it wasn't as rough. He had all his fingers too. Sa-at was missing the little finger on his right hand, and there was a pale circle of smooth burnt flesh in the middle of his palm.

'How did you lose that?' he asked. He wasn't sure if it was curiosity that drove the question or an unconscious desire to stir up some long-buried pain.

'The Red Brothers took it from me when I was very small.' He looked up, his eyes unusually hard. 'They're all dead now.'

'And that burn?'

'A bad bargain.' He was still staring. 'Why are you hiding your face?'

Satyendra turned his head away. 'None of your business.'

'If it's to protect you from cuts, you need to cover your ears more, and your fingers. The Gatherers wear thicker boots than yours and they have big gloves. It makes them clumsy though.'

'I know,' he snapped. 'I've been planning to come here for years. You think I didn't try and learn about it first?'

'You've never been here before!'

His incredulity annoyed Satyendra for reasons he couldn't articulate. It was as if he was at fault somehow. 'I was Lord Rochant's last remaining Honoured Vessel. They kept me in the castle for safety.'

'So . . . you don't know anything.'

'I do!' he protested. 'I told you, I learned all I could.'

'People told you things?'

'Yes. Story-singers, hunters, travelling merchants. I spoke to everyone I could.'

Sa-at frowned. 'You heard things?'

'Yes.'

'But you don't know anything.'

A flash of anger went through him. *How dare he speak to me like that!* There was an impulse to rip his hands free of Sa-at and storm off. Another one to give him a good kick as he did so, but it soon faded.

I hate him for it, but he's right. This is all new to me. I need him. At least until my injuries have healed. Yes, I must keep him close until I can survive on my own.

He let his head hang down in an act of contrition. 'It's true. I don't know the Wild. Will you help me understand?'

Sa-at didn't immediately reply. He continued binding Satyendra's wrists. When he was finished, he sat back and frowned. 'I can help you.'

He sensed there was a catch. 'But?'

'I want to ask you something.'

Satyendra hid his irritation. 'Of course. Whatever you want.'

'You swore on your blood and bones that you would answer my questions truthfully.'

'Yes, yes, I know.'

Sa-at nodded very seriously. 'And now the trees do too.'

There was no change in the trees, nothing to indicate they'd heard or even cared what was being said. Still, Satyendra couldn't help but feel uneasy. *Whatever this is, he believes it's true.*

He gestured for Sa-at to continue.

'Do you know what you are?'

A number of responses came to mind, few of them pleasant. 'No.'

'You're a demon.'

'. . . What kind of demon am I?'

Sa-at shrugged. 'I don't know but I have friends who will. I can ask them for you but it will cost.'

'Cost what?'

'That's up to them.'

'And what will your help cost me?'

'That depends. Are you my friend?'

Just saying no seemed too blunt but he could at least soften the truth. 'I don't know you.'

'Do you want to be my friend?'

'It's too early to say.'

'Then, I want you to save my life.'

He made an exaggerated show of looking around. 'You're not in any danger.'

'Not now. But the Wild is full of dangers.' He looked directly at Satyendra again. 'I know you're strong. For saving your life now, you owe me until you've saved mine. That's my offer.'

'I already saved your life when we landed.'

Sa-at replied immediately. 'That was part of the old deal.'

'Fine. I swear that if you save my life now and help me survive in the Wild, I will save yours.' He saw Sa-at's expectant look and added, 'I swear it on my blood and bones.'

Perhaps it was coincidence, but as he finished a breeze stirred the leaves at his feet, and it seemed to him that his words were carried with them, passed from tree to tree.

'Good,' said Sa-at. They gathered their things and set off into the woods trying to put the castle as far away as possible. 'As part of our deal I'm going to find us something to eat.'

It was only when Sa-at mentioned food that Satyendra

realized he wasn't hungry. Not even a little bit. He tried to think of the last time he'd eaten a meal. It was at least a complete rotation of the suns ago.

He took another deep breath. The air tasted different down here. It had a taste of its own. A musky, nuanced quality. Much more interesting than what he was used to. *The air above was just cold and sharp. Empty. There is life down here, and I am part of that life.*

Despite the strangeness and the fear, a part of him had relaxed. It had already realized what was only just dawning in his conscious mind: He had come home.

The Godroad stretched ahead, its soft light comforting. If Pari stayed on course for long enough, it would take her all the way back into her own domain. Already, the trees had begun to change, spreading out a little, becoming less oppressive. It was still the Wild of course, but it was the Wild of House Tanzanite. An altogether more palatable thing in her opinion.

On her left she could see a stone road that joined the Godroad. It was marked out by crystal beacons. Though these lacked the power to destroy, their glow was enough to dissuade any minor demon from venturing along it. There were six other stone roads like this one, one for each of the Crystal Dynasties, and they all led to the same place: The House of Seven Doors.

Pari ordered the carriage to turn, and she felt the clunk as the crystal-tipped wheels left the buoying energies of the Godroad behind. She also heard the grunts of the Dogkin, who would now have to work much harder to move them.

Arkav looked out of the window and sighed.

'Something wrong?' she asked.

'I was just trying to remember the last time I was here. I'm struggling.'

'I'm not surprised, my dear. Why don't we agree that it's been too long and leave it at that.'

'All right.'

'No need to be gloomy about it. You'll be a novelty. Just remember to say lovely things about me in your report.'

That got her a reluctant chuckle. 'Same goes for you.'

Since Arkav was still looking out of the window, Pari decided to do the same. The view she got was reassuringly familiar. Barely touched by the years or the elements, the House of Seven Doors was a large heptagonal building constructed of black and white marble. It had a pointed roof, and though it was impressive on the outside, the inside was even more so: Whoever constructed it had excavated as deep into the earth as they had built upwards. As a result, only half of its grandeur could be appreciated on the approach.

Very little grew in the few miles around the building, mysterious forces holding back the Wild to create a sanctuary of sorts. Much of the time, the House of Seven Doors was unoccupied, save by the Bringers themselves, and they had little appeal to the outside world.

The second and fourth roads came in gently on her left and right, their beacons a gentle flicker in her peripheral vision. At the end of the road was a marble door, at least a foot thick, that only moved by some secret artifice of the Bringers. There was talk among the Deathless that if the door did not open, it meant you would not live to see another lifecycle. There was also talk that if you took the wrong road, something dire would happen. And, while Pari was often tempted to try the Sapphire road to see for herself, even she had never quite found the courage to experiment.

As ever, the heavy marble slid soundlessly aside to admit them, and, as ever, Arkav and Pari breathed a quiet sigh of relief. The carriage passed through and came to a halt. Being careful not to catch her wings, she stepped out of the carriage and into the greeting chamber, which was a large triangular space. There was a door at the narrow end of the wedge for the Deathless and a few chosen attendants to proceed. The fat end of the wedge was for carriages, Dogkin, and the majority of the entourage.

Theirs was not the only carriage here. She recognized High Lord Priyamvada Tanzanite's banner alongside an impressive number of staff. She quickly identified the Gardener-smiths and was about to approach them when Arkav set off at a brisk pace towards the heart of the building.

'Brother dear, what are you doing?'

'Reporting in,' he called over his shoulder.

'Aren't you forgetting something?' She tapped at her chest plate for emphasis, making the crystal sing. Tradition dictated that they should doff their armour and cleanse themselves before proceeding, to be in the right mindset for harmonious discussion. Being clean and fragrant in social situations was one tradition that Pari fully supported.

'We don't have time for that. Sagan has fallen and the Corpseman is on the move, we have to . . .'

She lost the last part of his sentence as he stepped out of sight. With a shrug, she bounded after him, leaving both her staff and Priyamvada's to gawp in their wake.

As she moved into the next chamber the floor sloped gently down below the level of the earth. This was where visiting Deathless would prepare themselves. A luxurious basin had been carved out of the marble, allowing one to bathe. Alcoves lined with shelves flanked it, containing perfumes and ointments. One had been disturbed by the speed of Arkav's passing. She arrived too late to catch it, and winced as it shattered on the floor, scattering shards of coloured glass, and the scent of yellow berries.

A bad omen if ever I saw one.

They came to the corridor that led to the main chamber. It seemed longer to her than usual, and Arkav had extended his lead. As she hurried to keep up, she worried for her impetuous brother, and, belatedly, for herself.

Another step and she was through. The path continued to slope down, leading to a platform where one could address the assembled. Next to it was a curved table and long bench. She had spent many hours sitting at this bench, and had seen to it that the Tanzanite one had more cushions.

The acoustics of the chamber were excellent, so she heard the gasps of indignation with terrifying clarity. Putting on her best smile, she joined her brother and bowed, prompting him to do the same.

Behind each of the seated figures, great banners were hung to denote the presence of Houses Tanzanite, Spinel, Jet, Peridot, and Opal. Five of the seven High Lords coming together to deal with the rising threats to their world.

Unfortunately, in this moment, they were coming together to deal with her and Arkav. There was a flurry of words and outrage at the sudden intrusion, the presence of two armoured Deathless, and the lack of cleanliness. And then

High Lord Priyamvada stood up. She was amongst the oldest of all the Deathless, and favoured large vessels. Her current body was broad, the gown she wore hanging down like the front of a fortress. Even out of armour, she made Pari feel smaller somehow. 'I will deal with this,' she stated before pointing an unfriendly finger in Pari's direction. 'Explain.'

'We come from the Sapphire lands. As you requested, we went there to escort their High Lord, Yadavendra, to the House of Seven Doors for judgement. However, he refused the summons and became rather violent, breaking tradition and trying to send us both onto our next lifecycle.

'With help from loyal members of House Sapphire, we were able to overcome Yadavendra, and, when he saw that his cause was lost, he took his own life.' She paused to let them take that in. 'The Sapphire then chose Lord Vasin as his succesor, who has taken on the name High Lord Vasinidra.'

'The significance of that name is not lost on me,' Priyamvada replied. It was clear this was not a good thing.

'Well, you see, Nidra Un-Sapphire was falsely accused of treachery by Yadavendra. The new Sapphire High Lord is honouring his mother and clearing her name by taking it as his own.'

'Be that as it may, it does not explain the manner of your arrival, nor the absence of the Sapphire High Lord. He should be explaining this to us in person.' She looked about the chamber. 'Your mission was to bring him here and yet I see only you and Lord Arkav.'

At this, her brother bristled. 'There's no time for this! The Sapphire High Lord isn't here because he's hunting the Scuttling Corpseman. We're here because the threat did not die with Yadavendra. There is another traitor: Lord Rochant Sapphire. He has betrayed us all to the Wild.'

Hearing the words out loud, in this place, made them all the more real to Pari. It still hurt that Rochant had fallen so far and she hadn't realized. Still hurt that someone she loved could be so corrupt.

In as level a voice as she could muster, Pari explained. 'I believe that Lord Rochant traded with the Scuttling Corpseman to trick his way into joining our ranks. In return, he gave it Sorn. That's why no Deathless responded when they made tribute. The Corpseman came and took the people away. But it didn't kill them. It . . . changed them, somehow. Twisted their bodies more into line with its own. It has an army now, made of Sapphire road-born. And while the Sapphire have been fighting elsewhere, that army has fallen on Sagan. We've just come from there. Like Sorn, it was defenceless. Like Sorn, Sagan's people have been stolen away, no doubt to allow the Corpseman to enlarge its army further.'

'To what end?' asked Priyamvada.

To that, Pari had no answer.

Arkav spoke into the silence. 'House Ruby teeters on the edge of extinction and the Corpseman grows ever stronger. As we speak, people are dying and new enemies are born from their suffering. The Godroad failed to protect Sagan. We—' he hammered his gauntlet into his chest, making a resounding clang '—have failed Sagan. The Wild is spreading, from Sapphire and Ruby settlements to the rest of our lands, and we come to you for guidance. There is no more time. We have squandered too many years. This is the time to act and so I ask you: What should we do?'

There was a pause and then, to Pari's great surprise,

Priyamvada smiled. 'It brings me great pleasure to hear you so restored, Lord Arkav. Consider me satisfied.' She gave Pari a meaningful look.

Thank the suns! She sees Arkav is himself again so she will sanction Arkav's rebirth. And that means she will sanction mine as well.

'Now,' Priyamvada continued, turning to her peers, 'let us discuss a stratagem. Lord Arkav, Lady Pari, stay with us. We would have your counsel.'

They both bowed, and as the High Lords began to deliberate, she glanced at Arkav, and the two of them shared a brief smile. Now there would be concerted action across the houses. Together, they would find a way to stop the Corpseman and undo the whole horrible mess that Rochant had created. She was just starting to wonder how best to bring up the issue of the Bringers of Endless Order, when the room shook to the sound of thunder above, of thick marble groaning, cracking, and shattering like glass.

Vasinidra did not sleep, nor did he dream, but his eyes were closed, and his mind wandered. Memories of past lifecycles came and went, disjointed ghosts and poignant moments were all jumbled together: Yadavendra, Umed, and Nidra all laughing at some shared joke, and laughing even harder when he asked them to share it . . . Gada teaching him the rules of the hunt . . . Fumbling the steps of his first dance . . . Singing old songs and hearing his castle sing back . . . The thrill of catching a demon . . .

Always before, he had played the role of the youngest Sapphire Deathless, even when Rochant had joined them. In the end, age didn't really matter, it was all about perception.

People liked to put you in a box and keep you there. But gradually, that box had got too small for him, had stifled him. He'd become more reckless in response but that too had been in keeping with an immature soul.

Another memory surfaced, this time of his mother's voice during her exile in the Wild, dissatisfied, critical. *She wants to keep me in my old role. She wants to keep me down.*

'High Lord,' said a voice. It sounded far away.

I cannot allow that. I must make her see that I have changed.

'High Lord.'

The others have accepted it. Even Gada.

'High Lord!'

A hand gently shook his shoulder. He opened his eyes to find Gada staring back at him. Gradually, he took in their surroundings. They were standing on the Godroad. All three suns had made their way into the sky. It was morning.

How long have I been standing here?

He blinked. His body did not feel tired but neither did it feel refreshed, and his mind still felt fuzzy, and mired in the past. 'Lord Gada? Is something wrong?'

His brother took a little too long to reply. 'I am sorry to disturb you, but this is no place to linger. Our hunters need to eat and rest properly.' He didn't add that Vasinidra needed this even more but it was in his eyes.

Vasinidra nodded. 'Yes, of course.'

They set off, bounding along the Godroad at a good but measured pace. If he were alone, he could take to the air and arrive in half the time, but he didn't. For one thing, it would embarrass Gada, and for another, he was High Lord now. Young, impetuous Deathless might have the liberty of zooming off on their own but not him. Not any more.

Up ahead they could see Lord Rochant's castle, glinting in the sky. Gada was on one side of him, Mia on the other. His brother kept giving concerned glances, which was both touching and irritating at the same time.

Mia however, was looking up and pointing. 'Hunters!'

She was right. He could just make out a stream of winged shapes, blue wings stark against grey stone. At their head was a Deathless. He frowned. 'It can't be.'

'We've enjoyed a long peace at home, High Lord,' replied Mia, 'but the Wild always comes back. Did you suspect?' she asked. 'Is that why you kept Lord Rochant behind to lead a hunt?'

He didn't answer. As far as he knew, the armour being grown for Satyendra wasn't finished yet. *The rest of the house is elsewhere. Mother can't be reborn, and even if she was, she has no Gardener-smiths of her own. It will be years before she has wings again.*

A horrible certainty formed in his mind.

'That's Rochant.'

Mia nodded. She had no reason to think this was a bad thing.

Gada continued to look worried. 'Does this change our plans, High Lord.'

'Yes. Mia, keep your eyes on them. We will follow on the ground. Lord Gada, tell your hunters to stay close. Tell them to trust in my orders, no matter how strange they might sound.'

He and his brother nodded slowly to each other.

'Is there something I should know?' asked Mia.

'Yes. Listen closely, but keep your eyes on the sky.'

And he began to tell her. As he did so, their quarry started to dive. He wasn't sure what they were after, but it was clear they'd seen something and it wasn't far from the castle.

But if Rochant has returned, Mother is in terrible danger. Perhaps she is the thing being hunted.

He began to accelerate forward, taking them all by surprise.

'High Lord?' asked Mia.

'High Lord!' called Gada.

'Come as fast as you can,' he called back, making one bound, two, his wings finding the currents of the Godroad and lifting. 'I'll need you!'

And then he was in the sky.

Hold on, Mother. I'm coming.

CHAPTER FIFTEEN

Sa-at rejoined Satyendra and the two hurried on. He'd managed to scrounge a few things to eat as they travelled but the forest had been unusually quiet. There were no animals around, which was always a bad sign, and the trees were refusing to talk to him. He wondered if his time in the sky had changed him somehow. Perhaps they sensed the not-Wild on him. Perhaps they just weren't feeling talkative. The only way to be sure was to get back to a part of the forest he knew, preferably to his friendly tree.

The thing that really bothered him was that Crowflies hadn't shown up. He was worried about the Birdkin. It had been so distressed when he'd taken the Godroad that Sa-at worried something had happened to it. He wasn't sure what, but the more time passed, the more he began to feel a horrible twisting in his belly.

What if I never see Crowflies again?

His worries weren't eased by Satyendra, who had gone ominously quiet.

'Do you want some nuts?' he asked, holding out an open hand. 'We can share.'

'You keep them.'

Sa-at didn't need to be told twice and began stuffing his face. It didn't do much to fill his belly but he relished every chew and crunch. 'Oh,' he added, swallowing the last bits down, 'I found these.' He pulled out three thick leaves. 'For your hands. Come and sit with me.'

It was hard to read the expression behind the scarf but Satyendra came. Sa-at unwrapped the bandages and examined the damage. The burns stood red and white on the insides of his hands but the skin around them was odd too. It had paled significantly. He fancied that in the right light he'd be able to see the outlines of the bones beneath. Working swiftly, Sa-at tore the three leaves in half, pressed them against the worst injuries, and rewrapped the bandages around his hands. Throughout the process Satyendra sat very still, his jaw set, his gaze averted. When Sa-at was finished Satyendra reached out to him as if to rest a hand on his shoulder but he paused halfway through the gesture before lowering his hand. Eventually he said in a quiet voice. 'Aren't you scared of me?'

'No.'

'I could kill you. You know that. You've seen what I'm capable of.'

'That's why I made you swear.' He smiled and though he couldn't see much of Satyendra's face he knew it wasn't reciprocated. 'I've seen what happens when a demon tries to get out of an oath.' He let his smile drop. 'You wouldn't like it.'

Having made his point Sa-at set off in the direction of

the friendly tree. He'd only got a few steps when he realized that Satyendra hadn't followed. He turned back to see him looking up through the trees in the direction of Lord Rochant's floating castle. Despite their long walk, it remained visible, a solid slab of blue and grey against the sky.

'Do you miss being up there?' asked Sa-at.

'No. Do you?'

'No . . . Yes.'

'Which is it?'

Sa-at shrugged. 'Both. I liked the people.' Satyendra made a dismissive noise. 'I liked when they smiled at me. I liked how safe it felt. But it wasn't real. It was just a big clever trap, wasn't it?'

'Yes. They didn't care about you. The moment Lord Rochant needed a new body, your life would be over. I say life, but that's a stretch. You wouldn't even be yourself.'

'Why?'

'Because—' Satyendra broke off and pressed the sides of his hands against his cheeks. 'Because,' he repeated slowly, as if feeling each sound and syllable, 'they would make you be like him. Talk like him. Move like him. Even think the same way.'

'But . . . Rochant made me feel nice and he said I was clever. He said I just had to be myself.'

'Of course he did. He wouldn't just tell you the truth. When did he call you clever? I'll bet it's when you did something the way he liked it.'

Sa-at sank to the ground. *It's true. He taught me to think one thing and say another. And he got me to keep secrets from Tal. And . . .*

All his conversations with Rochant came back to him, this

time in a new light. He felt sick and stupid and angry. Tears pricked at the corners of his eyes, and his throat burned with words unsaid.

Satyendra took in a deep breath. 'Mmmn. You understand now. He was never your friend. Neither was Roh. None of the Sky-born were or the road-born for that matter. Not even Tal. You're not a person to them.'

The tears were blinked away. 'It hurts.'

'Yes. Do you want to hurt them back? I know a way but I'll need you to agree to it.'

Sa-at shrugged. He was confused. Mostly he wanted to find Crowflies and curl up in the branches of his friendly tree. 'Do you?'

'Of course I do. The good news is, we are hurting them right now. Until he manages to father another child, you are his only hope for coming back. Do you understand? Simply by being out here, you are killing him. That's why I . . .' Satyendra paused and his hands bunched into shaking fists. 'That's why *we* have to keep moving.'

Sa-at stood up and had one last look at the castle. It had seemed so incredible when he first saw it. How he had longed to explore it! Now, it loomed there, like an unspoken threat. A distant play of sunslight on the castle made him squint. *Something's fallen off.* It was too small and too far away to make out clearly, but as he watched he saw another movement, and another.

And another.

'What is it?' asked Satyendra, but he was already looking for himself. 'We have to go. Now!'

They turned and moved deeper into the forest. Thoughts of Rochant in his armour flew through Sa-at's mind. Of his impossible strength and speed. He thought of all the hunters – the spears – at Rochant's command.

We will need help.

As they ran, he took breath and called, 'Crowflies! Please! I need you. I'm sorry. Murderkind! Murderkind! Murderkind!'

The trees rustled at the name, like drunken men trying to stir. They took his words awkwardly, turning them into an uncertain whisper.

'Crowflies needs you.'

'Murderkind? Murderkind? Murderkind?'

Sa-at didn't understand why the trees had taken his words in this way. But he realized that while he was away something fundamental had changed, and no help was coming. They were on their own.

Satyendra had been forced to exercise a lot in his life as an Honoured Vessel. Injuries aside, he was in good physical health, and no stranger to running. However, try as he might, he could not keep up with Sa-at.

He watched, awed, as the black feathered coat snapped and rippled in front of him, it too, struggling to match the twists and turns of its owner. While Satyendra barrelled through, his arms high to protect his face from the spiteful branches, Sa-at flowed around the obstacles like a river around rocks.

'Murderkind?' whispered the trees, each repetition of the word a little quieter.

There was a soulful note in their voices that spoke to his heart.

Then, from above, an explosion of leaf and bark rained down as the first hunter broke through on their left.

Sa-at pivoted right and kept going without losing momentum while Satyendra nearly crashed into a tree, pushing off from it to change direction.

He risked a look back over his shoulder and saw that the hunter had landed in a heavy crouch and was already rising, long spear in hand.

Satyendra didn't look back a second time.

More noises came from behind them: The screech of trees, the thump of Sky-legs connecting with the ground and absorbing the impact. *More hunters!*

And yet more, from the right this time, closing them off.

Much as he hated himself for it, Satyendra's thoughts had been trained to move like Rochant's. He imagined things from the point of view of the Deathless. The hunters would form a perimeter, a walking net that would close around the quarry. Rochant himself would be able to fly the furthest, so he and his best hunters would have flown ahead to close the trap.

We're probably being guided towards him right now. If we face Rochant, we're dead.

'This way!' he shouted.

Sa-at slowed but did not stop. 'What?'

'We go our way not theirs. Which way are your allies?'

'Through them,' replied Sa-at, pointing at a pair of hunters bounding towards them from the left.

Satyendra nodded. 'Follow me.'

As soon as the hunters realized what was happening, they took defensive positions and raised their spears. *They don't need to kill us, just hold us here long enough for their master to arrive.* He knew the first bit would be the hardest. If he could get past their guard and hurt one of them, that pain would fuel him, make him stronger. Then he would be better able to escape. But that was easier said than done.

The only thing in his favour was that he knew Rochant's hunters, much better in fact than Rochant did. So when he rushed towards them, he made eye contact with Ila, the woman on the left, whilst actually planning to attack Fom, the man on the right. Fom was a good hunter, the kind that would instinctively move to protect his partner even if it meant putting himself at risk.

Satyendra knew that he only had one chance. He sprinted as fast as he could, locking eyes with Ila, giving every impression that he was about to jump at her.

As he coiled his body to leap, the sunslight flickered above him. He saw a winged shadow cast three times, blocking out his own. For a split second he felt a familiar choking aura descending, then a tremendous force crashed into him, slamming his face into the dirt.

Sa-at skidded to a stop. Rochant had dropped through the canopy in front of him, feet first, onto Satyendra. Branches had cracked, leaving a ragged hole above. Bones had cracked below, then creaked as Rochant stood and stepped off the body.

Sa-at had to take a hurried step backwards as Rochant turned to avoid being swatted by the long sapphire wings. Sa-at could see hunters all around him now. While their spears did not point at him directly, they were ready.

There were so many thoughts and feelings leaping round Sa-at's mind that he had no idea what to say or do, so he just stood there.

Rochant regarded him, his expression cool. 'When I heard

that you'd gone, I assumed that this one,' he pointed his own spear at Satyendra, 'had taken you against your will. Then my people reported that you had stolen my sacred armour and helped him to escape. They told me that you had worked together. Tal says that you attacked him. Several of my loyal hunters cannot speak, their voices silenced by your actions.' He paused, continuing to study Sa-at in a detached manner. 'What do you have to tell me?'

'I . . .' Sa-at tried to find the words. In its own way Rochant's calmness was brutal. He looked around, confirming that there really was nowhere to run. 'You lied to me!'

'That is a grave accusation, and one that you could have made in the castle. If you had concerns, you should have come to me.'

He sounded so reasonable that Sa-at felt doubt flicker in his heart. 'I know what an Honoured Vessel is for.'

'Tell me.'

'It's for killing.'

Rochant nodded. 'Ah, I understand.' His spear moved to Satyendra again. 'He told you that, I presume?'

'Yes.'

'And you believed the imposter, a demon of the Wild, a known enemy, over me? You took his word without even thinking of talking to me about it?'

Sa-at looked down.

'People have been injured and killed. Good people. Their blood is on your hands. Do you understand?' A single step brought him close. 'When a Deathless is sent between lives, they need a new body to return. We call that person an Honoured Vessel. They have to be related by blood. If, when this body dies, you were needed, you would be expected to sacrifice the remainder of your life. That is true.

'Did he tell you that there can be more than one Honoured Vessel?'

Sa-at shook his head.

'Did he tell you that my current body still has fifty, sixty, perhaps more years left in it?'

Sa-at shook his head.

'And did he tell you that if I have other children, or if you have children, or if they have children, any of them could become an Honoured Vessel?' Rochant leaned down and pitched his voice low. 'It is just like any deal. It has a benefit and a cost. With me you will enjoy a long and fruitful life. Everyone will love you. You will have incredible opportunities to learn and train. I have so much to show you, Sa-at. So many wonderful things. Do you really think you'd have a better life down here?' He tilted his head the tiniest fraction. 'Or a longer one?'

It had all made sense before but now nothing felt certain. *Have I got it all wrong? Did Satyendra trick me or is Rochant tricking me again? I don't know!*

'I'll take your silence for agreement,' continued Rochant. 'I know this has been a hard time for you and I'm sorry I've had other matters that have taken me away. You've been misled by a demon and I have to accept some responsibility for that. If I'd destroyed it immediately, none of this would have happened.' He held up a finger. 'Pay attention, Sa-at. Everyone makes mistakes. That is part of life. But one must always learn from them. Let me show you what I have learned.'

He turned back towards Satyendra and shifted the grip

on his spear, spinning it in his hand so that the sapphire tip was facing down. 'I realize now that nothing this creature can teach me is worth what it has already taken and I vow that it will take nothing from me again.'

'Wait!' said Sa-at, finding his voice at last. 'Don't kill him, please.'

Rochant glanced back at him. 'There is still a great deal you don't comprehend. You have no authority here. Your job is to watch and learn so that you never allow yourself to be used in this way again. Do you understand?'

'No! I don't. Don't kill him, he's just like me.'

'Observe, Sa-at, and you will see just how wrong you are.'

He raised his spear high. If Satyendra had any awareness of his impending doom, the only evidence he gave was an incoherent groan.

Sa-at didn't know what to do. It seemed like there was nothing he could do. As Rochant turned his attention back to Satyendra a small object flew through the air towards him. It was a sapphire spear head, similar in design to the one Rochant carried, but this one trailed a slender silver chain that ran into the trees above.

The spear head punched through Rochant's right wing and lodged there. Dark circles appeared in the crystal, radiating from the impact with thinner, crazier lines around them.

Another Deathless followed the spear head, also decked in glowing blue armour. *Vasinidra!* He was in a sharp dive, skimming over the heads of the hunters to land nearby.

Rochant paused, his helmet moving to track the newcomer.

The silver chain went tight.

And then Rochant was ripped off his feet.

Vasinidra swung his spear overhead, like a fisherman casting a line, adding power to his momentum. Rochant flew through the air on the end of the chain and was slammed into the nearby trees with a thunderous crash.

The hunters cried out in surprise and horror.

Sa-at looked from them, to Vasinidra, and back again.

He doesn't have any other spears with him. Rochant has lots. It that good? Is it bad?

Sa-at looked to where Satyendra lay, the crumpled figure making a pitiful attempt to rise. One of the hunters had noticed too and was moving to intercept.

Should I help him or stop him?

There was a break in the circle of hunters now.

Should I run? Should I stay?

But he did none of these things. Indecision had gripped his heart. The only thing that he knew with any certainty was that there were no right answers, just a series of miserable choices that he didn't want to make.

Vasinidra released the trigger on his spear and the chain vanished into the shaft once more, the sapphire head snapping back into place with a neat click. He moved forward, intending to make good on his surprise. Rochant would not be down for long and he had no desire to face the other man in an even fight.

But before he could close, hunters beset him on all sides. None actually went as far as to attack him, but they interposed themselves between him and their lord nonetheless.

'Listen to me, faithful servants of House Sapphire. Lord Rochant has betrayed us all to the Wild. I do not expect you to understand but I do expect you to stand aside. I am stripping Lord Rochant of his status, here and now, as is my right as High Lord.'

To his surprise, they didn't move.

He could see their hands trembling and the stress of the situation plain on their faces, but he saw Sapphire resolve there too, stubborn and unshakable.

'I say again, stand aside. Everything I do is to restore us, I have no wish to hurt loyal members of the house.'

For a second time they did not move.

Behind them, he saw Rochant sit up. 'It's too late, Vasinidra. They know the truth.'

'That you're a traitor?'

'That you were raised to your new position with the support of an imposter.' He pointed towards the spot where Satyendra lay. 'A demon of the Wild. The very same demon I was about to slay and that you have rushed to save.'

He's not speaking for my benefit, Vasinidra realized. Each of the hunters in front of him stood a little straighter, their doubts banished by Rochant's words.

How does he always manage to twist things?

'That's a lie and you know it!'

'What I know,' Rochant replied, stooping to collect his spear, 'is that you don't talk to demons or their allies. You destroy them.'

On his order, the hunters closed in, their spears like teeth in a giant's mouth. But they were only there as a distraction. The real threat, Rochant, was watching, waiting for an opportunity to do more serious damage.

Vasinidra was trapped. He used his own spear to make some space, thrusting randomly to keep the hunters at bay. As they'd been trained, each pair fell back as he attacked, while two other pairs would come forward and harry him. Their weapons scratched at his armour, marring the polished surface as they searched for a weak point.

Out of the corner of his eye, he saw one of the hunters had been separated. The hunter was moving strangely, struggling to remove some feathered creature from its back.

Then his attention was back to his own survival as a fresh attack came from the hunters. He ducked, pressing down on his Sky-legs to store energy, and jumped.

For a blissful moment he was free of them. A few spears followed him into the air but they simply glanced off his armour. There were essence currents in the Wild, strong enough to allow flight, but they were treacherous. No wind swept through to lift him to safety and he soon found himself gliding back to earth.

Rochant's spear shot like a thunderbolt over the heads of the hunters. He saw it coming but there was nothing he could do. There was the clash of sapphire on sapphire, the ringing crack of armour breaking, and then the flash of pain as it buried itself in his side. In his exalted state the pain did not overwhelm him, but he knew he was in trouble.

The impact twisted his body, turning his landing into a sliding shuffle. He kept his feet, just, but by the time he'd righted himself, the hunters were on him again, Rochant at their heels. One of them passed Rochant a new spear.

They didn't attack immediately. As always, their first priority was to reform a perimeter to ensure he couldn't escape.

Vasinidra held up a hand. 'I give you . . . one more chance. Lay down your weapons and I will spare your lives.'

They didn't even dignify him with an answer.

The wound in his side was nagging at him but he didn't dare look at it. One lapse and he was finished. They'd got him now. All they had to do was take their time and he'd go down.

So this is what it feels like to be prey.

He shifted his thinking. Perhaps he could not hope to win this fight, but he could afford to die. Rochant couldn't. If he could make an opening, he could sell his own life to end the madness. Though everything seemed to revolve around the Scuttling Corpseman, he was convinced that all House Sapphire's problems stemmed from Rochant.

All he needed was one chance.

No doubt they are thinking the same.

As he studied them and they studied him, so absorbed in each other they were almost like one creature, there was a scream.

It was a human scream, just. It rose and fell unnaturally, as if it were being controlled, dragged out. And it was close.

At first they all ignored it, training and respect for their enemy demanding no less. But as the scream continued, eyes reluctantly began to flicker in that direction.

It was coming from where the lone hunter had gone down. From the spot where Rochant had landed on Satyendra. A hunter lay in the spot where Satyendra had been. Mounted on his Sky-legs, Vasinidra could see him, his eyes staring straight up, his mouth stretched wide. There was blood spreading across the hunter's chest.

And we are in the Wild!

Two figures stood next to the hunter. One, smaller, was dressed in black feathers. The eyes of the other figure, the taller, burned bright with hatred, its face obscured. They both seemed familiar. The taller one's right hand was soaked in fresh blood, and its fingers were wrapped around the shaft of the hunter's spear. *That's Satyendra.*

The shorter of the two was trying to leave but Satyendra would have none of it.

'Hey, Rochant!' he called, and threw his spear.

Vasinidra didn't wait to see what would happen next. He jumped. Straight up this time, high enough to have a clear shot at his enemy.

Rochant was already twisting to avoid Satyendra's spear, but it flew as fast as anything a Deathless could throw, faster even than Rochant could handle, and found a place just under his ribcage.

Lifecycles of training took over for Vasinidra. He saw how the blow had struck Rochant, saw the forced step, knew where he would be standing in two seconds time and threw his own spear with everything he had, aiming for the space between helmet and chest plate.

Even so, Rochant saw it coming.

He couldn't move aside, but he lifted a hand. Vasinidra's spear punched straight through the gauntlet and plunged into Rochant's neck. Not as deep as he would have liked. But deep enough. Their eyes met, Rochant's widening with shock, and in that moment they both knew they had killed the other. It was just a matter of how long it would take for their bodies to realize and stop working.

Rochant took a few drunken steps.

Vasinidra landed, his own wound roaring at the impact.

Then, all became chaos.

Hunters threw themselves at him.

Hunters broke off to attack Satyendra.

Hunters rushed to Rochant's side.

Vasinidra fended off their blows, trapping spears, hurling back his aggressors. Others found him. One struck his helmet, making it ring like a bell. He stopped thinking. At least, he stopped thinking about the present.

His body fought on, detached, while his mind drifted. *I'm going to die again.* He worried about what would happen in his absence. He worried about his mother. Had Rochant managed to destroy her, or would he return to find her waiting, smiling and strong?

Something sharp stung his right wrist. Something heavy struck the back of his leg, bringing him to his knees. Blows struck his back and wings. *Not my wings!* he thought stupidly.

And then the blows stopped.

He blinked. He was on all fours. Sweat and blood was running off his face and collecting on his visor.

There was fighting all around him, and shouts.

'Protect the High Lord!'

His brother's voice. Gada.

A strong hand took his arm, half lifting him. 'I'm here, Vasin. I'm here.'

Mother?

He smiled and told her that Rochant was dead. Except when he tried to speak, something was in the way.

Nidra's face filled his vision. She looked worried.

Don't worry about me. I'll come back. I'll be sad to miss the years with you, but I'll come back.

'Don't worry,' she said. 'We've got you,' and again, 'we've got you.'

CHAPTER SIXTEEN

They all flinched at the sound of the outer door being breached, as if the blow to the marble was a personal one. And in a way, it was. The House of Seven Doors was a sacred place to all the Deathless, and the idea that a demon of the Wild was here, that it had forced its way into a place of peace, shook Pari to the core.

Though there were many Deathless present, between them representing countless lifecycles of wisdom, none responded immediately. This experience was shocking in its newness, and they had no reference for response. Instead, the five High Lords present, and Pari and Arkav all turned, stupefied, towards the sound. It did not surprise her that the noise came from the Sapphire passage and she gave a small thanks for the fact that no delegates from House Sapphire were present, and therefore none of their entourage would be facing whatever had just broken through.

And something had come through. They could hear them now. A great cacophony of wings, angrily buzzing, growing louder, closer. Pari recognized the sound from her visit to Sagan. 'It is the Corpseman!' she cried. 'It's here.'

High Lord Spinel was the first to recover his wits. 'Quickly, my friends, we must prepare for battle.'

The others nodded and began rushing to their respective exits. Pari had never seen High Lord Priyamvada move so quickly. 'Lord Arkav. Lady Pari. Hold them off until we are ready to join you.'

'Yes, High Lord,' they replied. Pari began unfurling her whip as she moved across the walkway to stand before the entrance to the Sapphire corridor. Arkav came and stood next to her. There was no time for discussion, not even a quick quip. For the swarm was already upon them.

Like a river of wings and clawing hands, they came, heedless of their own safety. There were too many to hold back. Too many to fight. She could barely distinguish one from another, let alone pick out a target as they slammed into her. Body upon body. A senseless, angry mass. She reeled back, teetering, almost falling, before she managed to kick backwards, gliding back to the central stage. Arkav was not so lucky. She could see him on one knee, the Flykin crashing around him like a wave on a rock. And they kept coming, some splitting off to attack the fleeing High Lords, others vanishing up different corridors, still more racing in circles around the perimeter, ripping at the banners as they passed, shredding reds, greens, purples, and whites with careless ease.

The High Lords needed her. They all needed her, but in the end she went to her brother. How could she not after all they had been through? With exalted strength, she grabbed the Flykin that crawled over him and hurled them away until he was able to regain his footing. They didn't fight her.

They didn't fight him either. It was more like they were obstacles to be got past than enemies to be defeated. As soon as she threw one of the demons clear, it flew off, as if she wasn't even there.

'Are you all right?' she asked.

He blinked a few times, then looked past her, his eyes widening in horror. A new presence had entered the chamber.

The Scuttling Corpseman.

She knew the demon was here even before she saw it, some sixth sense bringing her head round. It snatched the fleeing High Lord Spinel off the ground and raised him so that his eyes were lined up with the holes in the Corpseman's skull, its antennae only inches away. Two black-armoured hands gripped the High Lord's shoulders, while a third held him by the chin. His purple robes were long, obscuring his feet, making him look curiously doll-like. His hair was tied in a series of tight spirals, each laced with fine silver jewellery that trailed ribbons.

The force of the swarm circling them made those ribbons flicker violently, in contrast to the absolute stillness of the two figures. High Lord Spinel was not dead however, his eyes twitched as they matched the tiny movements of the Corpseman's antennae.

She had been in a similar position in her previous lifecycle when the Corpseman had touched her mind. Whatever it had found there had persuaded it to spare her. It had even been gentle in its own way. The feelings in her gut suggested High Lord Spinel wouldn't be so lucky.

Was it fear of the Corpseman or loyalty to her house that made Pari turn from the sight and look for her High Lord? Pari wasn't sure. Using her Sky-legs, she leapt from the platform at House Sapphire's end, sailing over the central well to land on the matching platform for House Tanzanite.

As she waited for Arkav to catch up, the swarm continued to buzz and circle and bustle in and out of the chamber. They all ignored her. So much so, that she had to duck to avoid several of them as they flitted past. If it had just been her, she'd have assumed that she was benefitting from Rochant's misplaced love, but Arkav was also being ignored. *Could it be our armour?* she wondered. *No, that didn't stop the Flykin in Sagan attacking me. We're not being attacked because we're not the targets.*

High Lord Priyamvada hadn't got far. They found her body behind the bench for Tanzanite delegates. The Flykin had caught her trying to flee and dragged her back to the main chamber. Her tall hat had fallen off, and the great tent-like robe had been torn from her and dumped nearby. There were no obvious wounds on her body, but the woman was frighteningly still, her eyes closed.

Pari knelt down beside her and noticed an odd glistening on Priyamvada's skin. As Arkav joined her, he held a bracer over the High Lord's mouth to see if there was still breath to steam it.

Nothing.

Leaning in closer, however, she saw a slight pulsing at the vein on Priyamvada's neck, but that wasn't the thing that drew Pari's attention. *There's something wrong with her eyelids.*

She reached out and tried to open them. There was resistance, some kind of film that covered her from head to toe. It was tacky to the touch, a near translucent yellow that put Pari in mind of the amber set into the Corpseman's hill. Gradually she eased the sticky lids apart.

In her many lives, Pari had seen a lot of things, a lot of grim and disturbing things. It was inevitable when dealing with the Wild. But nothing had unsettled her stomach more than what lay before her.

There was no eye in the socket. Something had removed it. In its place, deep inside Priyamvada's skull was a plug of amber. The amber had not fully set and she could see little grubs about the size of her eyelash wriggling around inside it.

No.

She jumped up, needing to put some space between her and the body. Her High Lord wasn't dead but given what she could see that seemed like a bad thing. As she stood there, stunned, the nightmare continued to unfold around her. Some of the swarm flitted in and out of doors carrying bodies, hunters and servants, and the other High Lords, their proud house colours reduced to rags.

Very slowly, as if by its own accord, her head turned to look back at the Corpseman. It had pulled High Lord Spinel close. From the right angle it would look as if they were kissing. From Pari's angle she could see the antennae buried deep in the man's skull.

Once again, bile stirred in her stomach.

The Corpseman let go of his head with its third arm and began running it over the High Lord's face. She could see some kind of secretion passing from the feelers on its knuckles onto his forehead.

Think, Pari. Think!

No plans came, but her final conversation with Samarku Un-Sapphire came back to her. The ex-High Lord had been a prisoner of the Corpseman until Nidra had set him free. His words rang fresh in her ears.

'It wants to know how I think, Lady Pari . . . It is learning from me, learning our ways, but for what purpose, I do not know.'

She looked across to the other High Lords who had been present: Jet, Opal, and Peridot. Each of them had met the same fate. Not quite dead but certainly not alive either.

It's stopping them from coming back. How long would it take before we'd have realized? How many years? How many failed rebirths? More than enough for whatever the Corpseman is planning.

It had hit them in a place they felt safe, used their own ways against them. Pari spun back towards Priyamvada and lifted one of her Sky-legs. She'd often imagined doing something like this to her High Lord, but in the fantasy it had been pleasurable. Now, in reality, she felt only sickness and grief. *At least this way Priyamvada will return one day.* She brought the Sky-leg down on her High Lord's neck.

The crack of bone rang out, cutting through the other noises with remarkable clarity. As one, the swarm stopped, some landing on the floor, others attaching themselves to the nearest wall. All of them were looking at her. Meanwhile, the Corpseman continued to coat High Lord Spinel in a layer of yellow discharge. Out of the corner of her eye she could see that he too had lost his robe and undersilks at some point in the proceedings.

'Your turn,' she murmured to Arkav.

He leapt across to where High Lord Opal had been left, and she was painfully aware of all the heads following the movement. As he closed the last few steps to the body, several of the swarm dropped from the ceiling to create a living, and to Pari's mind, hostile, barrier.

It's one thing to laugh at death when you know you're coming back. It's quite another when you're facing being entombed in your own body for an undisclosed and possibly endless amount of time. Pari felt a sudden reluctance to fight the demons. All her instincts were telling her that if she sent another High Lord to their next lifecycle, the swarm would make her pay for it. And, at some point the Corpseman would finish its business with High Lord Spinel, and then she'd be in real trouble.

Still, the thought of leaving anyone trapped between lives was too much to bear. While Arkav held the swarm's attention, she hopped forward, landing in a low crouch alongside High Lord Jet to build the energy in her Sky-legs while bringing her right hand down sharply on his windpipe. 'Forgive me,' she murmured, then kicked off again, towards House Jet's door.

Her plan was to keep moving, keep the swarm confused, and then send as many High Lords as she could between lives. But as she glided forward, a larger, darker shape landed in her path: the Corpseman. It still carried High Lord Spinel from two of its arms. His skin now glistened in that odd way and the man's eyes were closed now, halfway between sleep and death.

She had too much momentum to stop, so instead she pivoted in the air, drawing her knees to her chest, and used the Corpseman as a springboard from which to kick off. It made no move to stop her so she was able to sail backwards to the central platform, returning to her brother's side.

'Now what?' he asked.

'I don't know.'

All seven of the exits were blocked. They were hideously outnumbered. In the absence of a strategy, Pari did what she always had when things were bleak: she bluffed.

'Good afternoon,' she said to the Corpseman. 'I suspect you remember me. I certainly remember you.'

It held out its three arms to her, making High Lord Spinel sway like a ragged doll. Even the stump of the fourth shifted in her general direction. The smaller antennae on its knuckles drifted for a moment, then flicked towards her. The larger antennae that protruded from its eye holes also strained in her direction, as if reaching out.

She realized it had changed in other ways since their last meeting. It was bigger for one thing, and its lower legs were distinctly different from its other limbs. Longer, thicker. It had always been able to jump but now it looked . . . *By the Thrice Blessed Suns, it's become more like us. The curve of its feet matches those of my Sky-legs. The carapace is like a mirror to my own armour.*

'It seems time has been kind to both of us. I do like your wings by the way. What do you think of my new body? I'm rather fond of it myself.'

It was hard to tell if the Corpseman understood her or if it had ears to hear the sound of her voice. But so long as it was attending to her, she and Arkav were safe. Very slowly, the Corpseman moved one of its arms, the gesture so languid it looked like it was being made underwater. It was beckoning her.

'No, thank you. We're very happy over here. Actually, I was wondering if it might be possible for us to go?'

The Corpseman didn't respond. In fact, it was ignoring her altogether. Its antennae moved in the direction of a new buzzing coming from the direction of the House Sapphire doorway.

Instantly, all around her was in motion, the chamber full

of leaping bodies and wings snapping out with furious energy. The Corpseman spread its wings and left, taking High Lord Spinel with it. The others followed, pouring down the corridor like water through a crack. A few seconds later they were gone.

The Corpseman and the swarm had abandoned them. While relieved, she was somewhat insulted to be so easily discarded in the middle of a conversation.

Arkav went to High Lords Opal and Peridot and put them out of their misery. It obviously pained him, just as it had pained her to send her own High Lord and High Lord Jet to their next lifecycle. But it had to be done.

She gestured in the direction the swarm had gone. 'Shall we?'

'What are you hoping to find?'

'I'm hoping the Corpseman will discard High Lord Spinel so we can help him without a fight.'

Three bounds took them straight through the preparation chamber. The air was cloudy with perfume and the floor covered in a carpet of broken glass that crunched beneath their Sky-legs. It looked as if a storm had passed through House Sapphire's entrance chamber. Hangings were shredded beyond recognition, and the soft crystals that provided illumination had been smashed from their housings, plunging the space into a gloomy half-light.

What was left of the great door was closed, but sunslight peeked through the many holes. Chunks of marble lay scattered; the smallest was as big as her head and many were bigger. She stepped through the remains and Arkav joined her outside. The swarm were still visible, a dark cloud flying too low in the sky, skimming over the treetops. They gave chase, though it was clear that they would never be able to keep pace with the demons. When they reached the edge of the forest, the trees still trembled to an echo of that awful buzz and, on the edge of her perceptions she could hear their faint whisper: *'Rochant . . . here . . . here . . . here . . .'*

She gave Arkav a sad smile. 'It seems that, for once, Rochant's arrival has been to our advantage. The Corpseman dropped us like a pair of hot stones as soon as it heard his name. A shame it didn't drop High Lord Spinel.'

Arkav was still looking in the direction the swarm had gone. 'You want to follow it.'

'Naturally.'

'And then?'

'I don't know if we can stop the Corpseman or its army, but we can beat Rochant. Perhaps that will be enough.'

Vasinidra threw up for the third time. Blood and bile soaked into the ground between his hands. Mia stood behind him, holding back his hair, while another hunter stood nearby, carrying his helmet.

They'd pulled out Rochant's spear. The layers of silk worn beneath his armour had stopped the tip penetrating his flesh, but the whole area around the impact was swollen and unhappy. Deep inside, something was not right. It hurt to bend forward, it hurt to turn his torso, and even if he didn't move, his stomach throbbed in an alarming manner.

He'd lived and died enough times to know that this injury would be the one to send him on. Gradually though, the convulsions in his stomach settled, and he felt the pressure on his throat ease. His throat felt burned and raw, but the air passed through it again. He had a little time at least.

Around him were a ring of hunters, and around them he could see more pairs patrolling the area. Bodies wearing Sapphire livery could be seen lying next to each other, united again in death. His heart sank. *Our best people killing each other. How has it come to this?*

But he did not have the luxury of mourning. Too much time had already been lost.

'Where is Lord Gada?' he asked, wiping his bloody lips.

Immediately, his brother landed in front of him. 'Here, High Lord.' Nidra came and stood at his side. Seeing her there, alive and standing among Sapphire without shame made his heart swell. She looked tired but alert. He gave her a bloody smile. 'I thought I'd imagined you.'

'No, my son.' She gave him a strange look. 'My High Lord. I was there when you fought Rochant, and I saw the defeat in his eyes. What a gift you delivered me! I will treasure it for all my lifecycles.'

The praise warmed him despite the pain.

She knelt down beside him, pulled off his helmet, and put something into his mouth. He recognized the taste. It was a form of Tack. Usually he smoked it, but he'd heard there was a much more potent form that could be chewed. He shook his head and went to spit it out. Tack brought oblivion, a sweet escape that had nearly destroyed him in the past. He'd vowed never to take it again.

Nidra clamped his jaws shut. 'Eat. It will help you through the pain. I've seen enough suffering for a thousand lifecycles.'

Slowly, he chewed. Between the last energies of his armour and the potency of the drug, the agonies of his wounds receded enough for him to think again.

'Tell me our situation, brother.'

Gada's hesitation meant things had not gone well. He gritted his teeth and prepared for the worst.

'Lord Rochant's hunters refused to stand down.'

'You gave them a chance to surrender?'

There was a pause. 'We did what we had to do to save you, High Lord.'

'And they fought you? Even though we had two flights to their one?'

'To the last. They gave their lives to cover their master's escape.'

An image of Rochant returned to him, one spear through hand and neck, the other through his side. The man had been barely able to stand straight. 'He . . . escaped . . . and you didn't pursue?'

Gada gave a nervous swallow. 'Our priority was your safety.'

A flash of anger came and went. *There is no point in yelling at Gada, he acted to protect me and minimize further risk to our hunters.* He forced his hands to relax and his breathing to steady. 'Of course. Thank you, Lord Gada.' He reached out for Mia and she took his hand, helping him to his feet.

Fatigue seeped into his body. The aura of his armour was damaged, how badly he wasn't yet sure, but his exalted state was diminished. Pain was that little bit sharper, more distracting. His thoughts mired in a thickening fog. 'Do we have a trail?'

'Yes, High Lord,' said Gada.

'Good,' added Nidra. 'We'll all sleep easier once we've found the body.'

He took a spear from the ground and snapped off the

head in a single motion, turning the shaft into a makeshift walking stick. *There was something else . . . what was it?*

'What about the others?'

'Others?'

'Yes. Two young men. One wearing house colours, the other dressed in black feathers.'

Gada shook his head. 'I've seen no sign of them, but there are many in house colours here.'

'Not hunters. He was wearing a servant's cloak, the kind favoured in the castle.'

'Then no, High Lord. There is no one of that description here.'

'No matter.' He tested his weight and tried taking a step. The injury in his side complained, but with the right posture he could mitigate it. 'Lord Gada, you will take your flight and follow the trail. We will do our best to keep up with you.'

'And if I should catch Lord Rochant before you arrive?'

Vasinidra raised his voice so that the others would hear. 'Rochant Un-Sapphire is to be taken down any way you can. Catch him or kill him, whatever you like, but we give no more of our house's blood to that traitor. Do you understand?'

Gada nodded and sprang forward, spear held high. His hunters immediately formed up behind him. He watched their bouncing forms flit between the trees and vanish.

In a much more stately fashion, Vasinidra followed, his own flight forming protectively around him. Mia marched proudly at his side. The hunter carrying his helmet offered it to him. Chunks of crystal were missing from the back, and it looked like a light touch would be enough to shatter the visor. The inside was still smeared with his blood. He was almost better off without it. Nevertheless, he put it back on, squinting through the cracks.

With a flick of his head, he gestured for Mia to come close. 'How bad is the rest of the damage?'

'The wings are not safe to fly on, High Lord, and most of your armour is dark from the back.'

Soon, he thought, *it will fail entirely, and when it does my body will follow.*

The sensible thing to do would be to retreat. It was unlikely but just possible that his body would survive with the proper care. Nevertheless, he wanted to see Rochant's end with his own eyes. The man might be even closer to death than Vasinidra was, but they'd underestimated him before at great cost.

And while it seemed quiet for the moment, they were in the Wild now. They were the enemy. Trails could be lost or hidden. Other traps could be waiting. He'd told Gada to make sure there were no more deaths, but the longer they kept going the more impossible his order would become.

Fortune's Eye shone bright and gold above them, the two red suns already starting their descent towards the horizon. *We have an hour to find Rochant, perhaps two and then we'll have to return to safety.*

Mia remained at his side, as did Nidra. For this he was glad, as he had more questions for her. 'What happened after I left you at the castle?'

'Rochant happened. He was already there, waiting for me. It was unpleasant but what's one more bit of suffering, eh? In a few years' time I will be reborn and he will be nothing more than a story.' She made a cutting gesture.

'Forget Rochant, there is another problem. A smaller group of his hunters found me before I found you. Yi led them away but she hasn't returned. I need her.'

Vasinidra frowned. 'It will be hard to find her, and even if we do it might be too late.'

'It can't be!' Nidra reached up to grab at his arm. 'She's all I have. Do you understand? We need her.'

It took a few moments for the import of her words to sink in. 'Yi is your descendant?'

'My last. Without her, I am lost. Do this one last thing for me, my son, and our fortunes will truly be restored.'

'I could find her. Yes. I can do it. We still have a little light. She would be visible from the sky.'

'But Vasinidra,' Mia protested, 'my High Lord. Your wings . . .'

'Are you worried that I cannot fly?'

'No. I am worried you will fly to places we cannot follow. You have already fought so hard and for so long. What if you fall somewhere in the Wild? What if I cannot find your body?'

'Then I will return to a new one, to a house kept strong by you, Nidra, and my brother.'

'Do not worry for him,' Nidra replied. 'His future is secure. Mine is not.'

'But it will be, I swear it.'

Mia saw the determination in his face and stepped aside with tears in her eyes. 'We will watch for your signal.'

It was a strange mix of sensations. Satyendra's burns still nagged at him. The imprint of Rochant's gauntlet stubbornly refused to heal. His palms remained tender where he'd gripped the sapphire bracers and the bones on his ribcage grated as they tried to slot themselves back together.

And yet, the deeper they went, the easier it got to breathe. When he'd fed on the downed hunter, the flow of strength had been faster, the effects more immediate, more potent. He was both high and in pain, suffering and transcendent all at once.

Out of the corner of his eye, he could see his hands swinging back and forth. The fingers seemed too long for his palms, as if they had been stretched, and his wrists protruded from the bandages once more. A look down confirmed his legs and body were also longer than before. Where his cloak had hung to his ankles, it now came only to the back of his knees.

Sa-at was much shorter now. A child next to an adult. But Satyendra didn't have the width to go with his new height. He felt stretched out, elongated, but strangely hollow. Mostly though, he felt vengeful.

They had stolen away from the fighting and into the quiet of the Wild. He had grown up on tales of the place. Storysinger Ban was forever banging on about the dangers. Why were there not stories about the beauty of the Wild? The freedom to walk and walk without coming to a wall or a drop was wonderful.

When he adjusted his hood, cheekbones jutted out at odd angles beneath his fingers. He sucked in a panicked breath and pulled his scarf up further. 'Well? Do you know which way Rochant went?'

'Yes,' replied Sa-at. He gestured with a mud-stained hand. 'But we shouldn't go that way.'

'Why?'

'Because the suns are setting and Rochant's bleeding.'

Satyendra paused to consider this. Deep down, he knew that Sa-at was right, the sensible thing to do was to find shelter. Let other creatures finish Rochant off. But the hunters' cries still echoed in his skull, making his fingertips tingle and his bones sing. He did not need to fear the dark.

'I want to kill him.'

'But—'

'He wants to kill both of us, remember that.'

Sa-at looked down, his lips twisting unhappily. Then he nodded. Out here in the Wild, emotions were easier to identify. Or perhaps Satyendra's senses were no longer muffled by the non-stop dirge of the castle.

He agrees with me but is reluctant. A strange mix of bitterness and sadness . . . and guilt. One breath in and Sa-at's emotion was his to consume. There was a loud click as a rib popped back into place.

'Take us after Rochant.'

'But the trees were calling his name. We shouldn't interfere.'

'I'm not letting him get away!'

Sa-at shook his head. 'He's done now.'

'Oh yes, because your trees did such a good job last time he was here.' He leaned down so that his eyes were on Sa-at's level. 'If we kill him, we're free. There are two of us. He's weak and alone.' He tapped his head. 'And we know how he thinks.' *And he will be thinking. Even if that evil shit is dying, he'll be hatching a plan of some sort.*

'He's going away from his castle,' said Sa-at.

'That's what I'd do in his position. Go deep and try to outlast Vasinidra and his hunters out here. Most things of the Wild won't touch him in that armour.'

'Most things,' echoed Sa-at.

'My point is, he has a chance against demons. He has none against two flights of hunters and two Deathless.'

Sa-at nodded but he'd already started to look about nervously, as if expecting trouble.

'What is it?'

'The forest goes quiet when trouble is coming.'

'It's been quiet since we first came here.'

Sa-at gave a solemn nod and drew his coat tighter about his body. 'I know.'

CHAPTER SEVENTEEN

Night was coming on fast. Vexation and Wrath's Tear had dipped below the tree-line, and Fortune's Eye seemed in a hurry to join them. Despite having survived several nights out here, Chandni still found herself instinctively fearing the dark.

Crowflies had raced ahead, and she hoped they were still going the right way. Murderkind's domain had to be close but such things mattered little in the Wild. Around her, the trees stirred. Borne on the wind came the sounds of violence and pain. The *thwack* of person striking person. A scream, too long to ignore. Other shouts, their echoes all blended together.

Varg gripped her arm. 'What the fuck is that?'

She looked around. *Is this a trick?*

'Rochant . . .' said the trees. *'Here . . . here . . . here . . .'*

In seconds the wave of sound had washed over them and continued its swift journey.

'Where is that coming from?' asked Chandni.

'I dunno. Knowing this place, probably anywhere but where we think it is.'

'Can you tell, Glider?'

Glider barked affirmatively, her nose pointing confidently into the distance. Rayen and the rest of the pack barked agreement.

'They seem keen,' said Varg. 'But I reckon that if we go chasing whatever this is, we're going to be heading away from Murderkind.'

'I know, but I heard it say Rochant. I have to know what that means.'

'Sounds like a trick to me.'

'I agree with your hair-bound lover,' said Kennelgrove.

'But what if it's not?'

Varg just looked at her. 'What if it is?'

She patted Glider's flank. 'Then whatever is waiting will get a nasty shock. I have to see.'

Wind rushed through her hair as Glider charged onwards, she and the pack seeming to know instinctively where they were going. Varg sat behind Chandni, his arms tight around her body.

As the golden light faded from the canopy roof, she began to make out a glowing shape ahead. It reminded her of the time Lord Vasin had come to her aid. The pack had been against them then. Perhaps they were reminded of that time too, as their pace slowed dramatically and more than one of the Dogkin whined.

But where Lord Vasin had been a blur of motion, like a shooting star, this was static, and the light uneven. It was blue though, an unmistakable sapphire glow. She bid Glider stop, and dismounted. 'Wait here.'

'Even me?' asked Varg.

'No. I want you with me.'

'Good.'

'I do not take orders from you, Packstealer,' retorted Kennelgrove. 'Yet your fortune is blessed, for I have decided to rest my aches and pains here. Let Murderkind come the rest of the way, for I have travelled far more than my share already.'

Chandni decided that argument could wait.

The other Dogkin were sitting back on their haunches. 'Do not approach unless I order it,' she said. Rayen and the others may have agreed to serve her, but she knew the stories. If she wasn't clear, they would do as they pleased.

'You sure about this, Chand?' whispered Varg.

She knew what he meant. If this was a Sapphire Deathless, they would see her as the enemy. To approach was a risk. To not approach was cowardly. Besides, she had information that House Sapphire needed. Though she no longer served, she would not turn her back on her former people.

With Varg alongside her, she weaved her way through the last of the trees. The ground was bumpy beneath her feet, treacherous roots and malevolent divots in the earth were doing their best to ensnare the unwary. The figure ahead seemed to have run afoul of the Wild's tricks. As she drew closer, she could see that one of their Sky-legs had sunk too deep and become trapped.

What drew her attention however, was the design of the armour they wore. The simple lines, less elaborate than other Sapphire Deathless, identified them immediately.

Lord Rochant!

But this was not the body of her son that stood before

her. This was an adult, tall and broad. This was Honoured Vessel Kareem's body, the one that had vanished from the castle immediately after rebirth sixteen years ago.

As her mind tried to manage the ramifications of that, she also saw that Lord Rochant was not in a good way. One of his wings was almost black, and looked ready to shatter at any moment. A spear shaft protruded from one side, and it shocked her how much of it she couldn't see for that meant it had gone deep. His right hand was raised in a frozen wave, held there by a second silver-shafted spear that had gone through the palm and into his neck.

She recognized it instantly. *That spear belongs to Lord Vasin. Why would he be trying to kill Lord Rochant? What is going on?*

If the pack had not been so afraid, she might have assumed this was a trick of the Wild, but no, the armour was real. This man before her was her Lord Rochant.

She stepped into his line of sight and bowed. 'Your seneschal is here, my lord. How can I serve you?'

Eyes that had been half closed against the pain sprung open. '. . . Chandni?'

'Yes. Yes! I am here. Let us tend to your injuries.'

Unable to nod, he gave one slow blink.

She turned to Varg. 'I need your help.'

'Yeah.' He looked Rochant up and down. 'Fuck me, what a mess.' Chandni gave him a hard look and he mumbled an apology.

Together, they freed Rochant's Sky-leg from the earth and helped him to sit. Varg cut a length from the wooden spear so that only a foot's worth still protruded. The silver spear could not be cut, but it had not gone deep. Chandni pulled the spear from his neck while Varg staunched the flow of blood. Then, they threaded it through his hand and again bandaged the wound.

Rochant made very little noise throughout, though his eyes often closed tightly and his head lolled with fatigue. Every so often though, he would snap awake, his gaze intent on the darkness around them.

She wondered if he was aware of the pack nearby and felt a wash of shame at all the deals she had made, followed by anger. *I don't know if I could stand to be judged again. The first time nearly destroyed me. But I do not regret my actions.* She squared her shoulders. 'Do not worry about the Dogkin, my lord. They pose no threat.'

'I fear no Dogkin,' he replied.

'Who attacked you, my lord?'

His attention flicked back to her. 'Our enemies, traitors to House Sapphire.'

For a moment she thought he was accusing her, but then it passed. *He has been away. He does not know what I have done.* She made a guess based on the spear. 'You mean Lord Vasin?'

'Yes. He betrayed High Lord Yadavendra and took his place. He is known as Vasinidra now. He intends to reinstate Nidra Un-Sapphire and destroy me.' Rochant paused. 'Your son, your real son, is in grave danger.'

'You've seen him?'

'Yes. Like you, he is a good person. Without him, I would still be rotting away in the ruins of Sorn, but he is being misled by the thing you raised.'

Her hand went to her chest as it clenched. 'Tell me what to do.'

'Like my enemies, they are here in the forest too. We must find your son whilst avoiding capture. Then we need to free him from the demon's clutches. As you can see, I am in no position to fight. Our first task is to move away from here while obscuring any tracks we've made.'

'I have an idea of how to do that, my lord.'

She thought she detected the hint of a smile behind the visor. 'I have come to be unsurprised by your excellence, Honoured Mother. Do as you see fit. I will trust in your wisdom.'

Chandni moved back to where the pack was waiting. Varg was right behind her, bending down to hiss in her ear. 'He ain't going to like it when he finds out about all of them.'

'I'm not worried about myself, Varg. I'm worried about Lord Rochant. The pack can obscure our passage with their own. I'll handle that. I want you to stay close to Lord Rochant and support him as best you can.'

'So, are you back to being a Sapphire now?'

'In my heart, I never stopped being one. Please, I know you're worried, but I have to do this. We can discuss the future if and when we get there.'

'I thought we were done with serving them. I thought . . . I dunno. This makes things different.'

She tried not to feel annoyed. In her mind there was a clear way forward, but she realized that Varg was not part of the house. He had no reason to do any of this except for her. 'Nothing's different between us, I promise.'

'Because I didn't walk away from Pari just to help some Sapphire Lord.'

'I know you didn't. I couldn't go back to the Sapphire now, even if I wanted to. This is just the right thing to do. Helping Lord Rochant will also help find my son.'

His expression became marginally less grumpy. 'All right then, let's get to it.'

Having brought Varg into line, she turned her attention to the pack. And they ignored her completely. Where Glider and Rayen had been on their bellies, they were now standing, their ears pricked up and their teeth bared.

Something was wrong.

Chandni looked around for the source of the danger, making sure to scrutinize the canopy above for any sign of enemy Deathless and their hunters. But the only thing she saw was a single Birdkin sitting on a nearby branch. It was reminiscent of Crowflies, but she knew immediately that it was a different creature. There was something unpleasant about it, a malevolence that made her shiver. Like the Dogkin, it was ignoring her and its attention was fixed on Lord Rochant as Varg helped him to stand.

'Come on,' she said. 'We need to go.' She looked towards Rayen and said, 'Lead us to a place of safety.'

The old Dogkin made a grumbling noise in her throat and turned first left, then right, then whined.

Another Birdkin arrived, black winged, with compound eyes. It perched next to the first, and quickly assumed the same position.

Then another came, and another.

She picked a direction at random and set off on Glider's back. Rayen went ahead while the majority of the pack brought up the rear, allowing Rochant and Varg to stay in the middle. If her lord thought the pack's presence odd, he gave no sign. She hoped – knowing it was futile – that he was too concerned with his injuries to notice them.

The four Birdkin gave chase, moving in lazy flights to catch up every so often. Up ahead, more Birdkin were waiting, as if they'd known she'd choose this route. Crowflies was among them. She saw its pale beak in the light of Rochant's armour. Like the others, it had eyes only for Rochant.

Increasingly, they looked less like a collection of distinct creatures and more like one. Their postures were identical, their demeanour the same. A tension was building in the air. She could feel it, and in her heart, she knew what it was.

Murderkind is coming.

Slipping off Glider's back, she looked from the fractured light of Rochant's armour to the growing shadow ahead, and moved into the space between the two.

Vasinidra flew. Just. It was hard to maintain height, let alone gain more, and he battled to get his head above the tree line. Mia was right about his wings. They were in pitiful condition, almost as bad as he was.

Even in his exalted state, he was aware of the pain. His body was trying to tell him that it needed rest. That he needed to stop. And while the Deathless could push their bodies beyond their limits, there was always a cost. He didn't like to think of what it would be like to take off the armour, nor, if he survived somehow, what tomorrow's price would be.

The suns were getting lower, but he caught their red-gold rays illuminating a set of wings down on the ground, then a second, then a third, like the gleeful fingers of a child playing hide and seek.

Got you.

He didn't have the height or the speed to dive effectively, so he turned his body in their direction and fell towards them as gracefully as he could muster. The three hunters were advancing on a figure who had to be Yi, his mother's protector and last descendant. She was hiding in a cluster of dense trees. They could not move into them easily because of their wings nor could she leave without being run down.

As he got closer, he saw a fourth hunter crouched over the body of a fifth, a knife handle protruding from an eye socket. They were trying to stem the blood before the Wild came, not knowing that there was an abundance of blood nearby. But not a single demon had come to claim it.

Why was that?

He'd planned to land between them and Yi but the currents were too weak and he came down behind the three instead. 'Stand down,' he said. 'Or be forever known as traitors.'

They did not pause. Whatever Rochant had told them left no room for doubt in their minds. When they looked at Vasinidra, they did not see their High Lord. They saw the child of Nidra Un-Sapphire, an enemy.

Even as his feet touched the ground, they were going for him.

He did not have his own spear, but he had the shaft of one that he'd been using as a walking stick. He swung it at the head of the first hunter whilst stepping forward to grab the second. There was a satisfying thump as wood met forehead but the second hunter seemed to move too quickly or his hand moved too slowly. In either case he grasped empty air.

The two remaining hunters hopped back and forth, dancing away from his swings while stabbing at him with quick, stinging attacks. He was aware that the fourth hunter had stopped tending their dead companion and was standing up, ready to join the fray.

I am in worse shape than I realized, and getting worse by the moment. I have to end this quickly if I am to have a chance.

He forgot about the new hunter coming behind him and blocked out the one on his right. The next time the one on his left began to jump forward, he moved to meet him. He knocked the hunter's spear aside with his stick and put his other fist into his chest, using their momentum to add weight to the blow. Bones cracked beneath his gauntlet, organs ruptured, and the man, who had been loyal and good, an asset in any other time, was reduced to a lifeless bundle.

It occurred to him that the hunter on his right had not attacked. This was odd as he'd expected him to take advantage of his open flank. However, that hunter seemed to have his own problems. He caught a glimpse of Yi on his back – her fingers sliding into his eye sockets – as the two went down in a heap.

Before he could go to help, he felt a sharp pain in his back. Nothing had distracted the last hunter who'd taken the opportunity to plunge her spear through the cracks in Vasinidra's armour and into the the flesh beneath. He now turned with such force that he tore the weapon from her grasp, coming face to face with a young hunter. She was determined, focused, reaching for a weapon even as she sought to leap away. It reminded him of Mia when they'd first met.

He grabbed the end of one of her Sky-legs as she leapt and swung her into the nearest tree, killing her instantly.

When it was clear that Yi was not in danger he sank to his knees, wondering if he had it in him to rise again.

More good people gone by my hand. Rochant has set House Sapphire upon itself. Truly, the man is poison.

He stayed on the ground for a while. At some point he closed his eyes.

Time passed, thoughts drifted, and then he heard leaves crunching nearby, the sound of many hunters, and then his mother's voice by his ear. 'You did it, Vasin, you can rest.'

'It's . . . Vasinidra now.'

'Yes. High Lord Vasinidra.'

'Can you do something for me, Mother?'

Her voice was rough with emotion as she replied. 'Name it.'

'Gather the others. I have some things I'd like to say before I go.'

CHAPTER EIGHTEEN

While the forest itself was quiet, the night was alive with sounds. It made Sa-at nervous. He knew the animal kin and the demons and the blends of the two, and he knew that what he could hear was none of those things. The whisper of wings cutting the air, of feet kicking off from the ground with such long gaps in between that they were leaping rather than running. Hunters.

And so many of them!

Perhaps the Wild was playing its usual tricks to confound the senses, but Sa-at suspected it didn't need to. He'd seen how many of those blue-winged men and women there were.

He looked at Satyendra. It was difficult to make him out in the dark, and it was getting harder for Sa-at to match his own image to the shape in front of him. 'I want to stop.'

'Not until we find Rochant.'

'I can't see and the trees aren't talking. I want to stop.'

Satyendra moved past him. 'Let me lead then, there's still a little bit of light.'

No there isn't! Thought Sa-at. The three suns had gone down some time ago. Even if they weren't beneath the canopy, any residual light had faded from the sky. Only his familiarity with the Wild allowed him to navigate at all, and that was offset by the strange atmosphere.

The trees are scared. That makes me scared.

All his instincts were telling him to find a hiding place and stay there until morning. But as he squinted into the night, he couldn't be sure exactly where they were or how to get to any of the havens he knew.

What was clear, though, was that they were moving deeper into the Wild, into the places he would normally avoid regardless of the hour. Increasingly, he felt a resistance to their progress. The signs were subtle, but the usually supportive environment began to tug at the two of them, slowing them down. Maybe this was because the trees were trying to protect him, maybe it was because they wanted to get between them and Rochant. Either way, any sensible person would take the hint and turn back.

Satyendra did not even seem to notice.

A couple of times, they caught glimpses of distant lights through the trees. Some of the hunters had caught up and were moving parallel to them. Sa-at didn't think they'd been seen, not yet, but it was only a matter of time.

After all, they were both tracking the same person. Except that as far as he could see, the trail they'd been following had vanished, replaced by multiple Dogkin tracks all moving in different directions.

The hunters also seemed to be confounded. They had

spread out like a long string of pearls, and were calling to each other, staying in contact and checking in. None seemed happy. One of the hunters was awfully close too.

He crouched down behind the nearest tree with Satyendra and whispered, 'What are we going to do?'

For the first time since they'd fled the fight, Satyendra hesitated. 'I thought Vasinidra would have retreated by now.'

Sa-at waited for a better answer. He decided that if he didn't like it, he was going to follow his own path.

But before Satyendra could say anything further, Sa-at heard a faint sound, almost hidden by the hunter's movement. It was a soft, sliding noise, of fabric brushing the ground, and something else reminiscent of a long, endless sigh.

And it was coming from behind them.

Sa-at spun round and was rewarded with the sight of a creature. Tall, ghostlike, more a suggestion of a presence than an actual thing. Before he could reconcile the shape, it had vanished again, but only from view. It was still there. The raised hairs on the back of his neck told him that much.

He reached out and tugged on Satyendra's sleeve. 'We're being followed.'

'Yes . . .' all the usual confidence had gone from his tone. 'What is it?'

Sa-at shrugged. 'I don't know. It looks big. We should keep away.'

'No.' Satyendra's confidence had returned as fast as it had broken, icy and brittle. 'Maybe this is a good thing. That demon might distract the hunters. Come on, we keep after Rochant.'

The demon might distract the hunters, he thought sullenly as they continued. *But what if it wants us as much as Satyendra wants to kill Rochant?*

Do I want to kill Rochant?

He tried to think about what he wanted but the only thing that came to mind was something nice to eat, and the sense of safety that came from being curled in his friendly tree with Crowflies nearby.

And then, amid the sounds of hunters prowling, and the demon's hushed pursuit, he heard a more familiar flap of wings.

Crowflies?

A Birdkin flew over their heads, fast and intent. Sa-at turned to go after it. 'It's this way.'

'You have Rochant's trail?'

Sa-at decided that he wouldn't lie. He just wouldn't answer the question. That much at least, Rochant had taught him. 'It's this way,' he repeated, and set off at speed.

Satyendra followed him without another word.

Lord Rochant's return had thrown Chandni's plans into disarray. Whatever may have happened, she still loved her former lord and felt loyalty towards him. Nevertheless she had made a pact with Murderkind, one that bound her body and soul. To navigate a path that met her duty to both of them seemed impossible. But that was what she must do. Anything less was unthinkable.

There were so many Birdkin now they were beyond counting. They lined branches, filling the gaps left between the trees until it felt more like they were inside a large feathered dome than out in the forest.

The only light came from Rochant's fractured armour and its reach seemed to diminish with each new arrival, as if the combined mass of Birdkin were pushing back the aura with their very presence.

Varg stood next to Rochant, and Glider stood next to her. Neither seemed to be very happy about it, and she was terrified that her friends would be caught up in whatever was about to happen. Of Rayen and the rest of the pack, there was no sign. She suspected they were nearby, doing their best to obscure their tracks through the forest and confound their pursuers. Whatever her hold over them, there was no way they'd interfere in Murderkind's business.

From the deepest shadows came a change, as if something were pushing through a curtain, its shape gradually becoming recognizable. Humanoid, with a long beaked head, multifaceted eyes that ate the light, wrapped in feathers that sprouted high on its shoulders and pooled heavily at its feet.

Chandni bowed low. 'Prince Murderkind.'

'Iron Purebird,' chorused the Birdkin, all speaking with one voice, 'you smell of Kennelgrove and death.'

'Yes, I met with both yesterday.'

'Tell me of them.'

'The Scuttling Corpseman came on strange wings with a great host to attack Sagan. There was nothing I could do.'

The Birdkin gave a single, incredulous squawk, 'You desired to help the ones who abandoned you?'

'Nobody deserves the Corpseman's justice.'

'Truly said and truly felt. Where is the Kennelgrove? I smell but do not see it.'

'Close by. Kennelgrove is willing to make an alliance.'

'Then your desire to help me against the Corpseman has been doubly met.' It gestured towards Rochant with a feathery arm. 'For you have brought the Bane-friend to me, broken in all the right places. I would have his tongue and mind for my collection. Give him to me.'

She tried to think of how to turn the situation to her advantage. She had dealt with many powerful and dangerous individuals before and found ways to persuade them to her point of view. However, unlike Kennelgrove, there was no game to play here. And with the other Deathless, even the mad ones like Yadavendra, she knew them and their foibles.

'What if I asked you to release him?'

'What would you offer? I have all of you already.'

As she tried to think of something, anything, Murderkind spoke again, 'This is not a matter for dealing and twisting and thinking and speaking. This is war and he is my way to win. Strip away his poison shell, and I will taste his bitter tears.'

'My Prince, I . . .'

How can I convince Murderkind to spare Rochant?

'You cannot,' replied the chorus of Birdkin. 'Bane-friend is our enemy twice-fold. Once, for hunting us from the sky. Twice for bringing back that which should have stayed dead. Calm your heart, Iron Purebird, for it is misled once more. Bane-friend is your enemy too.'

'Because my body and soul are yours?' She hated asking the question in front of Rochant, but a man of his brilliance must already know she had sold out to the Wild. She would bear his judgement if she could spare his life.

The Birdkin all laughed. 'Your heart, always true, cannot see what lies and lies and lies before you. Without Bane-friend, the Corpseman would not be. Without Bane-friend, the peoples of Sorn and Sagan would live uncursed and free of mind. Your lost child would still be yours and you would not be mine.'

'I don't understand.'

Murderkind moved closer until it could wrap her within its winged darkness. 'A man of the road helps a corpse to live and a man becomes a hunter. A hunter helps a corpse to scuttle and a hunter dies but comes back, endless, Deathless. A Deathless helps a corpse to fly, to breed, to destroy those of wood and sky, and even I know not what that man will gain from it.'

The idea that Lord Rochant, wisest of all the Sapphire, would be a traitor was ridiculous, and yet she turned away from Murderkind's embrace to look into his eyes, hoping to find denial there, or even outrage.

But, despite the situation, Lord Rochant's eyes were as calm as ever. 'Honoured Mother, you are far from home, but don't forget what I taught you. The Wild weaves many tricks that do not bear scrutiny. Hold the demon's words in your hand and see if they outweigh the years we have served together. You were the best of all my students and even the worst knows better than to trust the tale of a demon.'

It was true. The stories were clear with their warnings: Do not look into the eyes of a demon. Do not speak or listen to them. Do not let them touch you.

And yet, the Birdkin laughed, and Chandni laughed with them.

Rochant's brow creased with a frown. 'You find me amusing?'

She remembered what Murderkind had told them on their last meeting. 'My heart and Prince Murderkind's are too close together for lies to fit between them. You are lying, my lord, no more. Not the demon. I'm laughing because for years I have been afraid of your judgement and all the while, you have been hiding far worse crimes. I'm laughing at the absurdity of it all, because what else is there to do?'

'My bidding,' answered the Birdkin.

'Yes,' she agreed and walked over to Rochant, reaching out towards his helmet.

'You forget yourself,' said Rochant. He stood faster than she thought possible, his hands moving for her throat and she suddenly regretted her close proximity. 'For I am Deathless, and beyond your—'

Rochant screamed and doubled over.

As the great wings dipped, she saw that Varg was standing behind him, both hands on the shortened spear handle protruding from his side. There was a murderous look on his face that Chandni had not seen before.

Glider leapt forward, landing on Rochant's back, and pinning him to the floor. The force shattered his already damaged wing, and the rest of the armour began to disintegrate into fragments.

Chandni took advantage of the moment to complete her action, pulling the helmet from his head. The glow, already diminished, faded still further, as Glider stamped and butted and Varg tore off chunks of armour with his bare hands.

'Enough,' she said at last. She was burning with rage at Rochant's hypocrisy but she knew better than to cut off a source of information.

What was revealed of Rochant's body spoke of deprivation. There seemed to be little meat on his bones. But somehow, even stamped down, in broken armour, defeated, there remained some last dignity in the man. As a Sapphire, she could not help but admire that. She was not sure if she would be the same with Murderkind looming over her.

At the Demon Prince's gesture, Crowflies flew down and landed next to Rochant. It marched up and down the length of his body, inspecting it on both sides, and came to a stop next to the wound with the spear jutting from it. Varg's recent treatment had widened it considerably and caused a wash of fresh blood to flow. The Birdkin opened its beak and its proboscis levered free, drinking deep of the easily available blood.

As it gulped, Murderkind spoke through the other Birdkin. 'Bane-friend, you are. Traitor, you are. Now tell us, what do you dream to be?'

Rochant said nothing, but Crowflies lifted its head and croaked: 'The lord of all the sky. The lord of life and death, highest of the high.'

'The thing that should not walk, is the Corpseman. What does it dream to be?'

Crowflies drank a second time, then said, 'The mother of mothers who makes a dead race fly, the killer of killers, the ruler of all the Wild.'

While the shock of what she was hearing and seeing rolled over her, Chandni could not help but feel something was wrong. Even for a Sapphire, Rochant seemed to be facing his end with incredible calm. She knew how tired and beaten he was, and now he was about to meet some terrible fate at the hands of Murderkind. She didn't know what the demon would do exactly, and for that she was glad.

'Why do this?' she asked.

Rochant simply looked at her and something in his expression suggested that she could not understand. This made Chandni even more angry.

'You have nothing to say for yourself at all?'

With what seemed like a great deal of effort, Rochant moved his right hand in a half circle across the dirt until it came to his face. Still looking at her, he raised his index finger and put it to his lips.

For a moment she thought he was telling her to shut up. Varg had obviously come to the same conclusion because he took an angry step forward.

'Wait,' she said.

'What?' replied Varg.

Murderkind turned its attention to her, and so did the rest of the assembled Birdkin.

She held up a hand, held her breath, and listened.

On the very edge of her hearing, far away but gaining steadily in volume, was a low-pitched buzzing. The kind made by hundreds of flickering, transparent wings.

Now she understood. Rochant hadn't given up, he'd been biding his time, waiting for the Scuttling Corpseman to come back for him.

Satyendra was scared. The bloodlust he'd felt combined with the need for revenge had taken him a long way, but now it was fading. He realized his eyes were handling the dark surprisingly well. Though he couldn't make out colours or specifics, he could make out Sa-at's shape with ease, and those of the trees and the undulations of the earth.

He caught only glimpses of the thing that followed them. It wasn't a hunter, wasn't even human, but it wasn't an animal either. Its presence was like a person sighing on the back of his neck. Except that when he turned, there was nothing there except an echo. No, it was more than that. It was communication. He was sure the demon was talking to them, but whatever it was saying was beyond his ability to decipher. In his guts though, he had the feeling it was calling out, asking them to stop and approach it. It seemed almost friendly, and that scared him far more than any screech or war cry.

Up ahead, the darkness was changing. He no longer saw trees and the void between them; now it was taking on a solidity, like a flexing, fluttering skin. He had the sense that he was looking at one massive creature, some fusion of bark and blood and . . . feathers? The sight of it mustered a very different kind of fear. The deep primal kind that told him to run as far away and as fast as he could.

Satyendra grabbed Sa-at by the arm. 'We need to go around.'

'No, we don't,' he replied, 'that's my friend. We're safe now.' Sa-at's tone, annoyingly cheery and utterly at odds with everything else, seemed so out of place.

'It doesn't feel safe.'

'It's safer in there than it is out here. Come on!'

And with that Sa-at sprinted forward, and into the dark, which fluttered like a curtain to admit him.

When Satyendra went to follow, his foot sank between tangled roots that immediately tightened around his ankle. He tried lifting his leg but had no luck. He crouched down and tried to prise open the roots with his fingers only for the earth to slump beneath him with a sudden burp. Now, his leg was buried up to the shin, and his hands were between the roots, which curled like manacles about his wrists.

There was nothing to draw from here. No fear save his own, no pain. Without a way to make himself stronger, he was trapped.

'Help!' he called into the dark. 'Sa-at! Help!'

No answer came.

While he tried to think of a plan, he became aware that something was watching him. It approached from behind, and he was unable to twist far enough round to see it. Whatever it was moved as quietly as the sigh of a sleeping child. He felt the chill of its proximity, and struggled in vain to free himself.

Its shadow loomed over him. He couldn't see it of course, it was too dark, but he felt it all the same.

He heard a sound, like air rattling in a dead throat, a threat, but it wasn't directed at him. The tree shivered, and the roots released him, retreating still deeper into the moist earth.

His immediate thought was to run but his body had other ideas. Slowly, achingly slowly, he turned around until he came face to face with the thing that had been following him.

It was right there. No longer a ghost or a hazy image. It was nearly three times his height and twice as wide, and it exhaled at him in a soft, almost tender manner. It seemed to be made of bones, stretched long and thin and draped in rags. Up close, he was no longer sure the rags were actually fabric. Some bile stirred in his stomach as the creature's name came to him from the Story-singers' tales: A Whispercage.

I should run.

But his legs refused to obey. In fact it was all he could do to stop himself making eye contact. The old lessons were loud in his head now. *Do not face a demon alone. Do not look it in the eyes. Do not let it touch you.*

It reached out towards him with one pole-thin limb. There

was no violence in the gesture, but he shrank back regardless.

'What do you want from me?'

Air hissed from whatever served as its mouth and he had the sense it wanted him to look up and meet its gaze.

He did not want to look up.

He did not want to know what it looked like.

But it was as if invisible fingers had slipped under his chin and were slowly lifting it up.

There were holes in the rags that allowed him glimpses of ribs within. Slender, knifelike bones wrapped around a hollow core. The face was not the skull he had been expecting. It was buried deep within a hood, but he saw four petals made of pale flesh pressed together like hands in prayer. And he saw eyes like smoke trapped in glass, and he saw enough to know that he was looking at a mirror of his future.

He screamed then, but it was no ordinary scream. When he opened his mouth without care, it swung wide in four places, not one. Such was his horror and revulsion that he lost himself. He screamed and screamed while the Whispercage waited, patient as stone.

Soon, the volume diminished, became muted, as if his throat were collapsing, his voice dying.

When he finally stopped, the two stood together, not quite in silence. Not quite. Something unnatural was coming.

A question managed to form itself in the remains of his consciousness. *What is that?*

The Whispercage had noticed too, its head canting slightly.

Satyendra could hear buzzing. The sound of a great host. Immediately, he knew two things. It was close, too close. And it was wrong.

CHAPTER NINETEEN

Sa-at stumbled into a strange gathering. Rochant was on the floor, and in bad shape. Only a few bits of his armour remained intact, and in what was left of its light, he could see Rochant's thin and battered body. Crowflies stood next to him, blood glistening darkly along its beak.

Murderkind loomed nearby, its host of Birdkin packed in around them all, and there were others too. A bearded man and a giant, five-legged Dogkin. But his attention was drawn elsewhere.

A woman stood barely twenty feet away with her back to him. She had long dark hair that swept all the way down to her ankles. He knew it instantly.

It is like my hair!

A memory flashed into his mind of the same woman on a wagon, of the way his heart had leapt and he had yearned to reach out to her.

He reached out to her now.

Though his voice failed him, as it often did at times like

this, his feet were already moving towards her, his hands raising of their own accord.

This is her. This is my mother. My mother!

He knew it with unshakable certainty.

As if sensing his approach, she turned, displaying strong, proud features. Emotions crossed them. First surprise, then confusion, and then the beginnings of realization. Sa-at was nodding, excitement growing inside.

She knows me!

Everyone else was still, tense, even Murderkind. As he pondered this, he drew closer to his mother, a few more steps and he would be at her side.

Her eyes were wide now, the beginnings of a question on her lips.

There came a buzzing, muted at first, then shockingly loud, as if someone had suddenly opened a box full of Flykin.

And then, everything exploded.

Birdkin filled the air, some flying, some falling, screeching chunks of shrapnel blown inwards as some alien force pressed in from all sides. He felt several of them bounce off his back and shoulders, felt the prick of talons and the accidental slash of a beak against his thigh.

Without thinking, Sa-at dropped to the floor, making himself as small as he could. Through squinted eyes and splayed fingers he could see chaos playing out above. Things with human shapes and Flykin bodies crisscrossed overhead. Some had nets, others had spears, the kind carried by Sky-born hunters. Amid the madness, patterns formed, the swarm moving in units that seemed to blend and shift in the blink of an eye.

Directly overhead the Birdkin circled in formation, like a

gathering storm. Three lights appeared in their centre. Three glowing points of blue. For a moment he thought they were eyes, but no, they were spear heads of purest sapphire, each one mounted on a long shaft. Each carried in the arms of the Scuttling Corpseman.

The great host of Birdkin swirled round it lazily, lulled by the pulsating spirals on the Corpseman's wings. A natural space appeared around it, allowing the demon to descend uncontested.

Sa-at found his gaze was also taken by the spirals, his eyes rolling in their sockets as they followed the strange curves, tracing them, over and over.

Shrieks and clicks and violence faded away.

Time faded away, taking conscious thought with it.

It was peaceful. His eyes were moving with the patterns. The Birdkin were moving the same way, all together, in one big mindless harmony.

Chandni had thought there was someone behind her. A figure she'd seen before, that she knew. They had appeared from nowhere and had then vanished just as quickly, leaving demons with human shapes and insect wings in their place. This new enemy was everywhere. In front, behind, to the left and right, on her level, above; too many for her brain to manage.

For every demon there were a dozen Birdkin, pecking and slashing, but in a frenzied way. The buzzing of the swarm was painful to her ears and it seemed to drive everything else mad.

She caught a glimpse of Varg running towards her, then he was obscured by angry flying bodies, then another glimpse, closer now but with blood on his face. Something flashed by, too fast to see, and Varg stumbled, then vanished from view again, what little light there was flickering madly, weakly, between the struggling figures.

'Varg!' she shouted, though even she didn't hear it over the other noises. 'Varg!'

Then, miraculously, he was back, still running towards her, running so fast, she realized he wouldn't be able to stop.

'Varg?'

He ducked down, putting his shoulder into her stomach, and took her with him. Abruptly, her view changed from the fighting to Varg's back as the breath whooshed from her body.

Something made Varg lurch to the side but he kept going, on and on, until all of a sudden, she was aware they were moving clear of the fighting. The buzzing, though still horrible, was less invasive. Free of the sound, her mind started working once more and she tried to lift her head to see what was happening.

But it was no use, the trees and dark conspired to hide everything. All she knew for sure was that the fighting continued, fast and fierce, and that she was powerless to do anything about it.

Something had interposed itself between Sa-at and the Corpseman's wings. A big, scary, familiar, friendly shape, but flowing faster than he'd ever seen it move. *It is Murderkind,* he thought sluggishly. *Murderkind is fighting.*

His eyes still slavishly tried to trace the patterns he'd been looking at, but he couldn't recall the lines properly. As their image faded from his mind he blinked, then blinked again, his thoughts slowly becoming his own once more.

Gradually, he became aware of the terrible noise all around.

He lay on his side, curled up into a ball. He hurt in several places. He was bleeding! Sa-at knew that he had to do something about this but everything still felt strange and surreal like a dream.

'Crowflies?' he murmured. Always in the past, his friend had been there when he'd got hurt, ready to tut and shake its head and pinch shut the wounds.

He blinked again.

Three angry blue eyes were staring back at him. They were in a triangular formation and had opened in Murderkind's back.

Like his own, these blinked too, vanishing one by one to reappear with breathtaking speed, but in different places.

The eyes are moving?

With horror, he realized they weren't eyes at all. They were spear tips of sapphire, their touch anathema to the things of the Wild.

Murderkind began to change. A lump twisted free of its shoulder and fell to the floor next to him. It was a Birdkin, dead, the compound eyes smoking and sightless. A second followed the first, then a third, and more, as the great demon prince collapsed in pieces.

Murderkind? No!

The three spears remained lodged in what was left of Murderkind, leaving the Corpseman's hands free to scoop Rochant from the floor. When it leapt into the air, the swarm flew to join it, and they ascended together.

Sa-at could not help but watch, mesmerized by the sight.

So absorbed was he in the beating of the Corpseman's wings, that he barely noticed that Rochant was looking down at him; nor did he register that Rochant was speaking and urgently pointing his way.

When the swarm flew off to be swallowed by the night, he did not realize that one had stayed behind, and was coming back.

Only when it landed in front of him did he snap back to consciousness. But his legs refused to obey his commands and he lay there, helpless as the demon reached down for him. In places, its skin was soft like his own, in others it had been replaced with a hard, black shell. It lifted Sa-at as easily as if he were a feather, and with a single leap, sailed above the level of the canopy.

His first instinct was to struggle and fight, but as they rose higher, it was matched by a fear of falling. The wind blew his hair behind him in a horizontal line, chilling his skin and making his eyes water. Then, something violet flashed up to meet them.

Another Deathless, armoured as Rochant had been, but in different colours and softer edges. A Deathless that he had met before. *Pari, the lady with the golden lips!* She kicked off from a tall oak to fly straight for them. She was calling to him, but he couldn't make out the words.

He stretched out a hand towards her.

She echoed the gesture, the gap between them closing rapidly.

The demon immediately swerved away, so that her gauntleted fingers closed inches away from his.

He stretched and reached again, but it was too late, her upward momentum had already run out, leaving her to glide in their wake, not falling, but not climbing either.

Suddenly, there was a whip in her hand, flicking out

towards the demon. The barb stung its foot, causing a hum of alarm, but it did not find purchase, slipping out of the wound as easily as it had slipped in.

And then they were too high and too fast for her.

Sa-at watched with a sinking heart as the glowing figure got smaller and smaller, lower and lower, until she was swallowed up by the darkness of the Wild.

Branches snapped and trees groaned as Pari broke through the canopy to land heavily on the forest floor.

Despite pushing herself for hours, she'd arrived too late. The Scuttling Corpseman had come and gone, taking Rochant with it. She hadn't even managed to save Sa-at.

For a few minutes she did nothing but catch her breath.

Even exalted in her armour, there were limits. She did not have it in her to chase the swarm, and alone there was no point in pursuing. So she waited, panting and muttering to herself.

She was still doubled over, her hands on her thighs, when Arkav came bounding through the trees. He skidded to a stop next to her and put a hand on her shoulder.

'You know, my dear,' she said. 'This habit of arriving after the event is most unbecoming.'

'I'm sorry, but someone had to tend to our people when you rushed off. I've sent them home. They'll be safer there.' He frowned up at the night sky. 'For now, at least.'

She shook her head. 'I wasn't fast enough, Arkav.'

'I know.'

'Other people might be expected to mess up on occasion, but I really can't abide doing it myself.'

'Yes.'

She looked up at him. 'I am impressed you found me though.'

'It wasn't down to my skill. It's the Wild. Don't you feel it?'

To her annoyance, she didn't. 'Feel what?'

'When I was coming after you, it didn't intervene. Usually, I'd expect to be misled, or meet obstacles. But the Wild is quiet. It's like it's . . . in shock.' He let go of her shoulder to make a slow circle. 'Grief stricken. I don't think we are the only ones being shaken to our very hearts.'

'Interesting, but I don't see how that helps us.'

'Nor do I. I saw Sapphire hunters on my way to you, a whole flight's worth. They're not far from us.'

She straightened. 'Perhaps you could have led with that, my dear.'

It didn't take long to find them. The hunters were arrayed in two loose circles, one inside the other. Each stood wingtip to wingtip, their spears pointing outwards, ready to impale anything that got close.

Crouched down in the middle of the circle was a Sapphire Deathless. He appeared to be examining something but the many bodies obscured whatever it was.

'That's Lord Gada,' said Arkav. 'Do you want to handle him or shall I?'

She gave him a smile as she took the lead. 'I'm surprised you need to ask,' then lifted her voice and made it more resonant. 'Greetings to you, Lord Gada, child of the Sapphire Everlasting. Greetings to you, Lord Gada, welcome light in this dark place, and thrice greetings.'

Gada stood abruptly at the first mention of his name, bouncing gracelessly on his Sky-legs a few times before regaining his dignity and drawing it around himself like a second layer of armour. 'Greetings to you, Lady Pari and Lord Arkav, children of the Tanzanite Everlasting. What sanctuary I and mine can give, is yours. May our spears find your enemies and our songs find your hearts.'

The three Deathless all bowed to each other, Pari and Arkav going a fraction lower than Gada. Their exact status was a little grey. Technically, this was his domain. Pari could argue that being this deep in the Wild meant that they hardly qualified as being on Sapphire land and she could also point out that this section of Sapphire land didn't even belong to Lord Gada, so their standing was equal. She decided it more prudent to appeal to his ego for now.

Gada made a gesture and his hunters parted for them. He then looked down. 'What do you make of this?'

At his feet were several bodies, humanoid in shape but twisted and covered in a black carapace. In places it had been cracked open and she could see wasted flesh beneath. Torn wings sprouted from their backs, semi-transparent, slim, almost delicate.

'We encountered a host of them just now,' Gada continued. 'They flew through us without a care in the world. Luckily, we were not their target.'

Pari glanced at the hunters. 'Are you sure you want my answer? It is not an easy one to hear.'

His tone was typically Sapphire. 'We will not be broken by words.'

'Very well. You are looking at your own people. These were once the residents of Sorn and Sagan, given to the Scuttling Corpseman by Lord Rochant Sapphire, and turned into . . . this.'

'We are aware of Rochant Un-Sapphire's treachery. My High Lord sent me ahead to capture him.'

'I'm afraid you're too late.'

'He's dead?'

'No. The Corpseman stole him away. If High Lord Vasinidra is here, I would speak with him.'

Gada's long face stiffened but he kept his composure. 'Of course. Allow me to escort you.'

'He's awake!' said Gada.

Faces peered down at him. His brother. His mother. Mia. Both had removed their helmets and wore expressions of grave concern.

'Come closer,' he said, and they hunkered down low. This was not easy on Sky-legs and impossible to do without looking comical. Despite himself, he chuckled.

They smiled back at him, though he caught the worried look that passed between them.

'Don't worry. I haven't gone quite yet. Listen to what I am about to say. You won't like all of it but I haven't time for argument.'

'Yes, High Lord,' they said together.

I wish I had more time to get used to that.

'You were right to advise me to be more cautious. Yes, yes, I should have followed your advice. But I didn't. In my folly I ignored your counsel. I've pushed myself too hard for too long and now I have to pay the price. My armour is crumbling and my body is dying. There's nothing we can do about that but I promise I will be more open to you when I return.'

Gada looked stricken. 'But we need you, High Lord.'

Vasinidra silenced him with a look, then moved his gaze onto Mia. 'I've had many consorts over many lives, but none who brought me joy on earth and in the sky. I hope to see you again, but if I don't, know that you will never be forgotten. In what is to come, you will command my flight. And afterwards, I leave the care of my hunters to you.'

'Yes, High Lord. It will be as you say.'

He saw tears in her eyes but she let none slip her guard. Pride for her welled up inside. *What a Deathless she would have made!* For the briefest moment he thought of ways to keep her longer, perhaps elevating her with Rochant's Godpiece, but then thought against it. What if the artefact had been corrupted through his treachery? What if the others disputed the ruling? No, new Deathless were delicate things that required a High Lord to be present to oversee their ascension. And in any case, such an act would condemn them to be forever close and forever apart, for relationships between Deathless were forbidden.

No. It is better this way. For both of us.

'There are things I must say to my family, alone.'

She lifted his hand and kissed it, then laid it across his chest.

The exertions of travel had faded the paint on his brother's face. As a result, his fear was all too easy to see.

'How long do you have?' Gada asked.

'Long enough. Heed well my orders. Rochant Un-Sapphire must die.'

Nidra's face twisted at the mention of his name. 'We must allow no chance for Rochant to return. You, Gada, must ensure that his line is cut. I wouldn't put it past him to have a vessel tucked away somewhere.'

'It will be done, I swear it.'

'Good,' replied Vasinidra. 'Both of you, raise my children well. Of course I wish them to fly, but they must have a head for ruling too, and for listening.' They both nodded as he spoke. 'Make sure they have room for me to grow when I come back. There is so much we could do better . . . that I could do better. Can you do this for me, brother?'

'Yes, yes of course.'

'There is more. Mother must be reborn soon. Do what you can to speed the Bringers of Endless Order to this task. I wanted to tell the other Deathless the news myself but that will be your job now. Assist her restoration.'

Some of Gada's consternation eased at the mention of Nidra's return. He turned to their mother and smiled, the two clasping hands. It was a beautiful moment. It made what Vasinidra had to say all the harder.

'Gada. I am leaving stewardship of the house to you.'

Nidra's brief moment of joy faded and she let go of Gada to turn a hard stare in his direction.

Gada meanwhile flapped his mouth like a breathless fish. 'I . . . you . . . honour me, High Lord. But I don't understand. Why not Lord Umed? Or Mother? Both are more experienced than I.'

'Umed is a good advisor but he's no leader. He proved that when Yadavendra took us on this path. He could have taken the position of High Lord many times but he has always let it go. His nerve is broken.'

Nidra grunted agreement at that.

'And Mother?' asked Gada. 'Her nerves are nothing but steel.'

Again, Nidra grunted agreement.

Vasinidra was suddenly so tired that he felt all he had to do was let go and sleep would rush to greet him. 'That's true. But I fear that is not what we need right now. Her name is controversial and that will not serve my vision for the house.'

Nidra folded her arms. 'Which is?'

'To restore our relationship with the other Crystal Dynasties. House Sapphire is the cause of all of this. We can blame Rochant all we like, but he is our fault. We must put things right as best we can.'

'Surely Mother is better placed to—'

'I can speak for myself,' interrupted Nidra. 'Our High Lord is right. I am not yet restored. My wisdom alone will serve the house for now, but you must lead it.'

Vasinidra felt relief flood through him. He lacked the strength for an argument. 'Yes. This is how it must be. I want to restore balance and trust. We are forever diminished from seven to six, Yadavendra saw to that. He has made us a house that is neither greater nor lesser. A misfit house. But perhaps, in time, we can reclaim our honour, and do right by those that have suffered for our folly.' He wanted to take his brother's hand but the effort of lifting an arm seemed like far too much, so he tried to make contact with words instead.

'You asked why I have chosen you for this task. Your legend is based around loyalty. I believe you will serve us best and for the future. If all of this seems impossible, take comfort in the fact that it is a temporary burden. And Gada, one more thing.'

'Yes, High Lord?'

'Listen to Lady Pari Tanzanite.' He saw the question

coming and intercepted it. 'On all matters. Trust me, she knows better than us what she's doing, and you will need advice from outside the house if we are to move forward. Am I clear on this?'

'As crystal, High Lord.'

'Good. Now, bring me something to drink, the best of whatever we have with us, and send Lady Pari over. I fear I don't have long and I need to consult with her before the end.'

Gada sprung up and leapt away. *Was that a bit of hurt in his eyes that I dismissed him for a Tanzanite?* He found himself smiling again. *What fools we are. Gada and I have clung to our identities for too long. He as the older responsible brother and I as the carefree and troublesome one. But we are not children, not even young men. We are ancient. Stuck in our ways. Strange how I only realize that now. But if I can change, so can he. And if we can change, perhaps there is hope for the Sapphire after all.*

Seeing Lady Pari approach him through the trees with his brother, Gada, he was reminded of a similar meeting sixteen years previously. Then, it was her body that moved slowly and relied on a stick for support. Now she seemed sprightly and it was he who stood at the gates that led from one life to the next.

'Are you sure she is on our side?' asked Nidra. 'She still has feelings for Rochant. I think she was behind his escape.'

'You're wrong.'

'Ha! How can you be so sure?'

He sighed. Death would take this body soon, and he needed his last breaths to talk to Pari. 'If you cannot trust her, Mother, trust in my judgement.'

'And if I'd rather trust my own?'

'Then consider this an order from your High Lord.'

There was a pause and he found his eyes closing, but very faintly he heard her bitter reply.

'Very well, High Lord.'

When Lord Gada came to speak to Pari, she'd already guessed what was going on.

The knowledge of Vasinidra's imminent death was passing between the hunters too. A muttered gloom flitting from mouth to ear. It was a strange time. The Sapphire High Lord had not died yet, but they were all waiting for it to happen.

'He wants to speak to you,' said Gada.

'Vasinidra honours me.'

Gada's mouth formed a thin line. 'He does.'

She went over to where Vasinidra had been positioned. The worst of the damage on his back and side was hidden by dirt and tufts of wild grass. His armour was giving off very little light, and the fracture lines in the crystal looked ready to give up completely at any moment.

Nidra stood over him like a protective Birdkin. She gave Pari a cool look.

Vasinidra's eyes were closed, but his lips curled in a drowsy smile as she approached. 'Pari.'

She ignored Nidra and crouched down next to him, wobbling a little as she settled her Sky-legs. 'Vasinidra. I do hope I'm not disturbing your sleep.'

'In your case I'm happy to be disturbed.'

'Then, can I disturb you back onto your feet and into battle?'

He smirked at that, then sighed. 'It wasn't supposed to be this way.'

'I know. How can I help?'

'You've already helped me a great deal.'

'But? You didn't call me here for a last cuddle to warm you between lives. Better ask while you can, my dear.'

His eyelids flickered, then opened. She felt a pang of sadness at the effort it cost him to focus on her. 'I've warned the others that our enemy is different, but you're the only one that really understands. I've told Gada he will speak for House Sapphire in my name, but I want you and Mother to guide him. Do what's right.'

She glanced at Nidra. 'What's right for who?'

He managed a smile. 'For all of us.'

'I'll do what I can.'

'Be gentle with Gada. He's not ready for this.'

'I'm always gentle,' she winked. 'Except when I'm not.'

'And please, help Mother. She's been through so much.'

Nidra tutted. '*She* is standing right here.'

'I have no doubt that Nidra will be fine as soon as she's returned to her proper station.'

'Yes.' His eyes closed and for a moment she thought he had slipped away. 'Pari?'

'I'm still here.'

'I'm sorry. For leaving this all to you. It's too much for anyone to manage alone but you're the only one left that can.'

She put a hand over his. 'I'm not alone and neither are you, my friend. Remember that when you come back.'

He tried to nod but though she saw the muscles flex in his neck, nothing happened. 'Looks like I still have a lot to learn . . . Funny how that never changes . . . So many lifecycles and we still . . . act . . . like . . .'

The end of the sentence vanished in a sigh.

Vasinidra had gone.

'I'll see you on the other side,' she whispered.

CHAPTER TWENTY

It was only when all traces of the swarm had gone that Satyendra dared to move. Fear had gripped him so tight that he'd thrown himself into some bushes and stayed there, as unmoving as death.

Now, at last, it felt like he could breathe again, could think again. Though in truth, he did not want to think about what had just happened.

The Whispercage was nowhere to be seen, reclaimed once more by the shadows. He had a feeling he would see it again soon enough.

I have seen my future and it is worse than I could have imagined.

He picked his way closer to where the fighting had been. Mostly, he saw dead Birdkin, but here and there he also saw the strange corpses of the humanoid Flykin. And in one place, faintly, was an intermittent buzz, a spasm of broken wings.

Life.

He went over to find a Flykin on its knees, its body bent over backwards and its head thrown up towards the sky. A Birdkin's body and talons protruded from one eye socket.

Even alone, harmless, the sound of its buzzing made him wince. It was painful somehow, and he had a powerful urge to leave. This was countered by an equally powerful urge to investigate further. To act in spite of fear. For fear and Satyendra were intimate friends, and there was much give and take between the two of them.

The demon was so far gone that it did not register his approach. He lifted one if its hands, marvelling at how human the fingers were. He bent one back to see how far it would go. The thin plating had grown hard over the joints, restricting the movement. Satyendra continued to bend and was rewarded with a sense of its pain. Not quite as pure as that of a person, but something he could feed from nonetheless.

The shell cracked around the knuckle. Only the stutter of the Flykin's wings gave any outward indication that it suffered. Next, the finger popped from its joint and he felt the familiar rush as the demon's pain was absorbed by his body.

The fear he had felt drained swiftly away and was replaced with the need to take more. To fill himself up again. With increasing vigour, he set to work finishing off the creature as painfully as he could. By the time he was done, his wounds were gone, save for some scarring, and his bones tingled beneath the skin.

What do I do now?

Though he was no longer afraid, he was alone in the Wild. Aimless. Friendless. There was no sign of Rochant nor Sa-at, and he had no idea how to find his mother.

But he was different now. A predator. He instinctively tasted the air. It was full of blood and suffering. Moreover, he could see it like strands of smoke in the air, could tell one from the other.

Sa-at's blood was shed here.

Rochant's too.

He studied the strands, realized that he could follow them. Realized that they were travelling in the same direction.

The grin that crossed his face felt wrong and too much air came into his mouth. At some point his scarf had slipped down, and he self-consciously pulled it up over his face whilst tugging his hood forward.

Then he set off.

Satyendra told himself that he was going for vengeance on Rochant, and perhaps, to pay off his debt to Sa-at. After all, he had sworn to save his life, and the oath bound him, he knew that now. Beneath it all, however, he felt something else. Loneliness and the need for a friendly face. A human face that would not turn from his in revulsion.

And he ran faster.

Chandni clung to Varg in the dark almost as tightly as he clung to her. Neither spoke. They stayed as small and quiet as they could, cheeks touching, eyes closed, barely daring to breathe.

The notion of the Wild being a home seemed foolish now. It was incomprehensible and dangerous and terrifying. What arrogance she had displayed to think that she, a mere mortal, could tame it when the Deathless themselves did little more than hold the borders.

Time passed.

She knew that Varg was cut and that his blood would make them a target, but nothing came. The forest was silent. She realized that the last time she'd come here it had been full of noise: The scampering of tiny feet, the flutter of wings, the call of one animal to another. All of it had gone.

It reminded her of the time she'd first struck a deal with Murderkind, how the whole Wild had seemed to hold its breath in anticipation of her sacrifice.

Once or twice, she dozed, or at least her tired mind stopped thinking, giving her some measure of peace. Then, at last, the stars faded to be replaced with a brighter grey. With the light came a little of her usual resolve.

We are going to live.

The thought made her grip Varg with renewed vigour. 'Thank you,' she whispered.

'Yeah.' He planted a soft kiss on her cheek.

'Let go, I need to see you.'

He released his grip and sat back. She got him to shuffle into what little light there was and started examining him for injuries. He was covered in scratches and cuts and bruises. The cuts were scabbing over. Not ideal, but much less alluring to the demons than flowing blood. Then she turned her attention to herself. Mercifully, her numb arm had not been badly damaged during their flight. She found a number of superficial injuries dotted about her person but could not remember getting any of them.

'We need new clothes,' said Varg. He raised one arm and the sleeve that hung from it was more holes than fabric.

She nodded, her practical mind reeling with lists of all the things they'd need to find if they were to survive. 'Did you see what happened to Glider?'

Varg shook his head. 'Nah, was all I could do to keep an eye on you.'

'We need to go back for her.'

Getting up was harder than expected. The cold of the night had stiffened their limbs, forcing them to stamp and stretch and flex their bodies. They moved slowly, like people decades older than they were. For Chandni, every movement took effort. How was she going to build something from this? How would they even survive?

'Varg, there's something I need to say.'

An expression of worry immediately settled on his face. 'All right.'

'Whatever happens, I won't serve under Rochant again.'

'I, uh, kinda figured that out on my own.'

'If the Corpseman takes over the Wild, I won't bow to it either. I just want to be free to live my life with you.'

He took her hand and brushed it with his thumb. 'You know, the Wild is fucking huge. We could find some place where no demons go and make a home. If Glider and the others survived, they could come too. All this,' he spread his hands, 'is bigger than us. Like, this is between giant demons and Deathless. We should stay out of it.'

She didn't reply for a moment. Varg was right. It would be wiser for them to do nothing, but doing nothing felt wrong. It wasn't who she was. Neither of them were in a position to stand against the Corpseman, so she just said, 'Let's find Glider and go from there.'

It didn't take them long to make their way back, the distance seemed much shorter now they could see. As they began to make out the edges of the carnage, Chandni's eyes were drawn to one of the nearby trees. It stood alone, as if the rest of the forest had pulled back in disgust. Every leaf had been torn away, and every branch snapped so that they dangled from threads of bark like arms on impossibly thin elbows. The breaks glistened with daubs of a dark resin. The same resin could be seen leaking from a number of holes bored deep into the main trunk. Powerful hands had dug down to the roots, cutting and coating them too.

Immediately, she knew that the tree was dead.

On the other side of the clearing, she saw a second tree that had suffered the same fate. It too, stood alone, a wide circle left around it.

This is more than just an attack. These trees have been made into warnings to the others. The Corpseman isn't just going to war with us, it's going to war with the Wild as well.

The air smelled of blood and death, and yet no scavengers had dared to appear. The Birdkin and Flykin bodies had been left unmolested in their death poses. There were feathers everywhere and small forms, twisted, crushed, broken. In the middle of them all was a great mound of the dead, pierced by three spears. As Chandni moved over to it she saw Glider, half-buried, lying on her side.

Varg instinctively moved over to the Dogkin while Chandni continued towards the mound. A long dark beak jutted from it, too big to belong to anything other than Murderkind itself.

She gave a bow of respect, manners coming to the fore even here, then crouched alongside it. 'Can you hear me?'

The great beak did not move, but she heard a smaller voice reply, 'Cha-aan . . .'

'Crowflies? Is that you?'

She dropped onto her knees and began to search for signs of a white beak and talons among the black. Gore seeped through the fabric of her clothes as she worked.

'Cha-aan!'

She could hear it more clearly now and pushed aside mud and other matter to reveal the Birdkin. It had been pinned down, but as soon as she lifted the dead weight from its body, Crowflies sprang up and shook out its wings, examining them with a compound eye.

'Is Murderkind dead?'

Crowflies looked up at her sharply but said nothing.

She turned back towards the demon prince. 'Murderkind! Murderkind! Murderkind! Murderkind!'

All around her, there was clacking as a hundred dead beaks opened and closed. Together, they let out a pained wheeze. 'Iron . . . Purebird.'

'Yes. I'm here.'

Crowflies cawed as if to say that it was there too.

'We are broken and beaten . . . We are . . . done. Be gone, Iron Purebird. Be free if that is your wish. We . . . release you from your obligations.'

'You can't die,' said Chandni. 'Not now.'

'Open your eyes to the truth. We are dead and we will not rise again.'

Chandni curled her hands into fists. 'You don't understand. I do not release *you* from *your* obligations. We had an accord, sworn under the eyes of the Wild itself. Until it is fulfilled, your blood,' she picked up some mud and feathers from the ground, 'your body, all of you, belongs to me.'

The Birdkin all wheezed together, a failed attempt at a laugh.

But Chandni was not laughing. 'You promised me vengeance and a life of my choosing, a good and long life. If you cannot deliver that, then you must give me what I need to take it for myself. There are far worse things than death, even for you, Murderkind.'

There was a long pause.

Crowflies' beak hung open in astonishment.

When she had spoken the words, she'd realized that this was how she truly felt. Living in fear in some corner of the Wild was no life at all. She wanted more than that. She'd rather risk it all than settle for scraps.

Slower now, the dead Birdkin spoke as one. 'Take my mantle if you will. But . . . beware . . . You will be pure . . . no longer . . . Only iron and murder and—'

'How? Just tell me how.'

'Reach inside . . . take my heart . . . taste its last beat . . . take it down . . . take it . . . all . . . take it . . . take . . . it . . .'

This was it, she realized. The point of no return. She'd crossed lines before, made pacts, done things that most honest folk would never dream of doing, but always before it had been to save lives in the moment. This was different.

This is for me. It is not necessary. There are other ways, but all of them involve running and hiding, or giving up my dreams. I have had my fill of waiting and serving the unworthy. Of others not delivering on their promises. Of lords and princes failing their people. I paid for Murderkind's support, and if it no longer has the power to help me, then I will claim that power and make it my own. I will make a better world from the ashes of their failure. I will make this better. Otherwise, what was the point of it all?

She reached between the spear shafts, into the feathered darkness below the beak. There was resistance but not as much as she expected. It was more like putting a hand into a wet lump of mud than a person. Gradually, it gave way to pressure and she felt around. It was hard work.

Once or twice, she thought Murderkind had died, but then she'd hear breath rattling in the corpses around her, and redoubled her efforts. Finally, her cold fingers closed around an object that flexed in her grasp.

Pulling it free was much harder.

She considered asking for help but this felt like something that had to be done alone. Inch by inch, she pulled her arm free until she could hold her prize up to the light. The organ was bigger than her fist and half of it hung down past her wrist, to brush at her elbow.

A fresh flutter of wings caught her ear. When she looked up, she saw a new Birdkin had arrived, much like those that served Murderkind but very much alive. A few more soon joined it. She noted some were injured and that most were young. They weren't the only ones watching her. It seemed that the trees leaned in in a way they hadn't been when she arrived. Glider sat up, her mismatched eyes fearful, and Varg . . .

Oh, Varg.

There was such sadness in his face that he seemed to have aged ten years. His head shook naturally, almost of its own accord.

The heart beat against her palm. A single, feeble kick.

It has to be now. There is no other choice.

Chandni raised it to her mouth. She had endured so many things before and come through to the other side. She would endure this. Whatever she was now, whatever she would become, she had been born and raised a Sapphire.

I will not bend nor break. I will do what must be done.

The flesh of the heart was thick and rubbery. It resisted her teeth. When she clamped down on it and pulled, it stretched, resisting her efforts to tear it.

I will do what must be done.

More Birdkin came to watch. Not the great host that had come before, but a number. Their compound eyes glittered as the first rays of Vexation shone red through the trees.

At last, she tore a chunk free. It sat bitter on her tongue. With deliberation, she chewed and chewed.

And chewed.

Perhaps her efforts made it smaller but it did not feel that way to Chandni. Gathering her courage, she took a deep breath, and swallowed. It slipped down slowly until it reached her chest, where it sat, resolute.

There was a lot of heart left in her hand.

The watchers continued their vigil, intent. Whatever they were waiting for had not happened yet.

She brought the heart to her mouth once more.

CHAPTER TWENTY-ONE

Chandni's heart beat. Beat.

Beat-beat-

-beat-beat.

Beat-beat-

-beat-beat.

Twice as many beats as there should be, a second set answering the first.

She was on her knees still and the numbing cold was creeping up to her waist. For once her legs were as senseless as her right arm. Mindlessly, her jaw worked, chewing and chewing.

As she came back to herself, she realized there was nothing in her mouth any more. It was both a surprise and a relief. Some part of her had been convinced that her teeth would be worn down to stumps long before that elastic flesh yielded.

It is done. It is finally done.

She stopped chewing.

The pressure she had felt, the intense scrutiny of both

Birdkin and the trees, had also eased. They still watched her but in a different way. It took her a while to understand what exactly they were after, but though they were demons rather than humans she knew what their manner was communicating.

They are waiting for my word.

Determined to show strength, she drew herself to her feet.

The many sets of compound eyes tracked the movement. A breeze like a breath taken in, stirred her hair. Varg too, watched her, as did Glider, but she wasn't worried about them.

Beat-beat-

-beat-beat, went her hearts.

She pointed to Murderkind's remains and the many, many dead around it. 'This cannot stand.' She pointed to the stripped, destroyed tree. 'This cannot stand. I will not allow it.' Her finger moved to a group of Birdkin to her left. 'Find the Scuttling Corpseman, find Rochant, then return to me with their locations.'

They watched her as her words sunk into their bones, then scattered in a flurry of wingbeats.

She pointed to another group on her right. 'There is a Deathless in this forest, Lady Pari Tanzanite. Find her, and lead her to me.'

'And give her this,' added Varg, holding out a golden earring.

These Birdkin went off swiftly too, plucking the jewellery from Varg's outstretched hand.

'Glider,' instructed Chandni, 'stand up.'

The Dogkin did so.

'Summon the pack. I wish to see what I have left.'

Glider threw back her head and howled. After a few moments, other voices joined in, scattered in a loose circle around her.

Good.

She returned her attention to the remaining Birdkin. 'Varg and I need food and clothing.' More of them left, leaving only a handful behind. 'There is something I wish to know.' The remaining heads all canted to one side. 'Rochant said my son was here in the Wild. Is that true?'

Crowflies hopped forward. 'Sa-aat.'

'Are you talking about my son?'

Crowflies gave a sharp nod.

'You know him?'

It gave a second, more emphatic one.

She crouched down to be close to Crowflies' level. 'I need to find him and I need to know everything you can tell me about him.'

Crowflies tapped her right hand with its beak. She held it out and it gently nudged under her thumb until she turned it over. Then, with a quick motion, it stabbed her palm, dipping the tip of its beak inside the wound.

With it being her right hand, she didn't feel any pain. But a moment later she felt many things, as moments and memories flowed through her, of a baby growing in the Wild, becoming a boy, and then a young man that she recognized.

It is him! He was right here. But where is he now? Where is my son?

The vision came instantly – it was another of Crowflies' memories and a very recent one – of her son being swept away by one of the swarm.

She opened her eyes again as Crowflies pinched the wound

shut. 'Do the same for Varg's wounds. And I want him armed.'

'Why?' Varg saw the expression on Chandni's face and his eyes widened. 'Oh, shit.'

'Because we're going to war and we're not going to stop until it's won.'

To her surprise he folded his arms. 'I didn't come with you to fight and die. I came with you to have a life. With you. Not a servant's life neither. A life of equals.'

'I'm sorry, Varg, but my son's in danger. This is not the time.'

'Yeah, it is. It's time to make a deal.'

She looked at him in shock. 'You wish to make a deal? With me?'

He nodded, his expression set. 'You've made deals with everyone else so why not me? I've given you everything without asking for anything back, but that was before. You're as much Wild now as you are Sapphire. So, if you want me to fight for you and risk our future, if you're gonna start being some kind of . . .' he shrugged, exasperated, '. . . whatever it is you are now, I want a deal.'

All of a sudden, she saw herself through Varg's eyes. A strange and terrible thing, and the sadness hit her like a punch in the gut. She sighed. 'What do you propose?'

'I want a life with a family, and I want you in it. And I want you to talk to me about what we're doing, not just make decisions as if I don't matter. You're not running a castle any more and I'm not a servant any more.'

'Yes. What else?'

He frowned. 'Uh . . . and I don't want to live in some fucking tree. I want us to live in a house.'

'A life. A family. A house. You wish to be involved in discussions concerning our future. Is there anything else?'

He shook his head.

'If I agree to your terms, what are you offering me?'

'What I always offered. Me. I'll fight with you. I'll make a life with you.' He nodded to himself, then added: 'It'll be good.'

She gestured for the Birdkin to begin tending to Varg's wounds as she accepted the offer. 'Yes. Yes, it will.'

A slim, leaf-dressed figure slipped from between two nearby trees: Kennelgrove. She scowled. 'Where have you been? Murderkind might have survived if you had come.'

'But that is why I have come. For Murderkind's power still lives, beating madly in your strange heart.' To her surprise the demon knelt before her, the knees flexing backwards, folding underneath it. 'As promised, I have come to seek your protection, and to make fair terms for an alliance against the Corpseman. Though poor Kennelgrove is too weak to fight, there are still some who answer my call, and they are yours to use if you would have them and me.'

'Very well,' she said, and this time she looked it in the eye without fear. 'Let us talk.'

Sa-at woke slowly, the nightmares unwilling to let him go without a fight. But, as consciousness returned, he began to wonder if he'd rather have stayed asleep. The first thing he became aware of was discomfort. His legs were at a strange angle and one was crossed under the other, putting a strain on his hip. There was pain in his shoulders and chest where he'd been gripped too tight and a number of minor cuts and bruises that also made themselves known.

The second thing was hunger. His lips were dry and his belly was empty. It gurgled and groaned at him like a disgruntled old man. The last thing he'd eaten was a handful of nuts and that had been nearly a day ago.

The third thing was that he had no idea where he was. A soft glow outlined the space he was in. It was some kind of intersection between a series of low-roofed tunnels. They were circular and relatively smooth, and coated with a substance that seemed to provide stability to the loose earth.

Larvae were making the light. Their semi-transparent bodies glowed with a soft energy. Each one was about the size of his fist and they slept together in clumps that were packed into the tunnel walls. They gave off heat too. The one thing Sa-at couldn't complain about was being cold. If anything, the opposite was true; the heat was stifling and turning the air stale.

Sa-at had the feeling that it would be bad if the larvae woke up.

Moving slowly and quietly, he uncrossed his legs and flexed his toes. It felt horrible but the feeling soon came back to them and he was relieved to find he still had full use of his limbs. To leave, he was forced to move on his hands and knees. The floor was tacky and pulled at his fingers, but not enough to stop him. Four tunnels met in the space where he was, but only one of them had any light at the end of it. He took that one.

To his dismay he found that it led downwards.

As he crawled, his hands came into contact with something smooth buried in the rough earth. By pressing himself against the wall, he was able to let a little of the light from the larvae behind him shine on it. He could see a thick amber block with an almost skeletal human silhouette inside. It was hard to make out details but Sa-at thought there was something familiar about them. He brought his face nearer to the floor to try to get a better look. The hands were clasped together in an odd way.

Like someone who had caught a baby Flykin and was about to shake it to death.

He remembered the time he'd first met Tal and the other Gatherers from Sagan.

Oh no. This is Rin.

Rin, who had looked after the group. Who Sa-at had dearly wanted to befriend. Rin, who had thrown stones at him but only to protect Tal, who he had always treated with kindness.

Tal would be devastated to learn about this. Then it struck him that he would probably never see Tal again, and that Tal would hate him after what he and Satyendra had done.

Sa-at suspected that Rin was preserved inside the amber. Not dead but not alive. Perhaps the Corpseman intended to feed upon him later, but Sa-at doubted it. He had the feeling that whatever remained of Rin would rise again to join the strange Flykin like the one that had brought him here.

Rin had once called the names of his Gatherers to be sure they had returned safely. Would anyone be calling his name now?

'Goodbye,' Sa-at whispered, touching the amber above Rin's arm before crawling on.

He was led to a chamber with a slightly higher roof. There was another tunnel on the opposite wall that led sharply up. It was significantly wider than the one he was in. The chamber itself was empty save for Rochant, who had been partially packed into the left wall. Parts of his body were covered in a thick amber resin that seemed both to glue him in place and form a kind of cocoon. One arm dangled free of the wall, and his head was only partially covered, allowing him to breathe and move his eyes freely.

The light Sa-at had seen before was coming from the resin itself. Whereas the amber that encased Rin had been dull and quiet, this seemed vibrant and very much alive.

Of course, Rochant had already seen him. Sa-at stopped and settled his back against the opposite wall. He felt he should say something, though he had no idea what. Despite everything, he still didn't really know what he felt about Rochant. Or rather, he didn't know which of the many things he felt was dominant.

'I'm reminded of the time we first met,' said Rochant. 'I was a prisoner then, if you recall, and you were as skittish as a Ratkin caught sniffing through the pantry.'

He didn't know what a pantry was, but he checked his normal desire to ask. It felt dangerous, like he was skirting around the edge of a Spiderkin's web.

'You were reluctant to speak then, too,' added Rochant, 'though I see the curiosity burning inside you now, bright as ever.'

'Why has the Corpseman trapped you? I thought you were friends.'

For the barest second, Rochant's expression shifted, but Sa-at could not tell what it was trying to change to, only that it was nothing like the calm face being presented. 'We are. It is . . . complicated between us.'

'Tell me.'

'There are other things I'd rather discuss.'

'I don't care. You swore to tell me about the Corpseman.'

'So I did.' He favoured Sa-at with a smile. 'We are more alike than you know. Your mind is quick and you stay focused on your goal.'

Sa-at simply folded his arms behind his back and waited.

'Very well. The Corpseman brought us both here to keep us safe. It is trying to do for me what I did for it all those years ago.'

'Healing you?'

'In its own way, yes.'

Sa-at knew there was a lot more to the words being said, but rather than ask he decided to have another look at Rochant's body. Through the amber he could only see an outline, but it was wrong; too thick across the chest and too thin at the waist. The arm that was in the wall also seemed odd, the elbow joint much thinner than the upper and lower arm.

'It's fixed the broken bits of you with bits of itself.'

'Yes.'

'And you're not happy.'

There was a pause as Rochant watched him intently. 'No.'

'Why?'

'That's a question about me and not the Corpseman. If you want the answer, you'll have to offer me something in return.'

'No, I don't. This is like . . . this is like that time with the oak, when we had to bargain to get Tal's boots back. You taught me that I don't need to give things up. I need to think about what you want and I need to think about what I know.'

He stopped talking and did just that. *Rochant wants to be alive but not like this. And he wants me to be like him so that he can have my body when he dies. But if the Corpseman changes him too much, he won't be like me any more.*

'The Corpseman is saving your life but if it hurts your soul you won't be able to come back into my body.'

'That is my fear.'

A very worrying thought occurred to him. 'Is the Corpseman going to make my body like yours?'

'No. I've only asked it to keep you safe. It knows how important you are to me.'

'What if it doesn't listen?'

A hint of concern appeared in Rochant's frown. 'It must listen, you're our last hope.'

'I thought you could have other children?'

'You think Nidra left me fertile? That was one of the first indignities she put me through when I was under her care.'

'But you said I wouldn't have to be the Honoured Vessel. You said that maybe you would have other children and they could be your vessel instead. That was a lie.'

Rochant started to reply, then caught himself, cutting off whatever he was going to say in exchange for a simple nod.

'You said that if I had children or grandchildren, they could be the Honoured Vessel. Was that a lie too?'

'No. That is true.'

Sa-at thought about this. *Do I believe him? Do I want my children to die for him? I thought he was my friend but now I don't know. I'm not sure he's anyone's friend.*

'Sa-at, I want us to make a new deal.'

'How can I trust you?'

'I delivered on the last one, didn't I? I answered your questions and I took you to my castle.'

This was true, though Sa-at suspected that there were lots of things he hadn't been told. Rochant was clever with words, too clever to be trusted. 'What deal?'

'I want you to help me get free and talk to the Corpseman. I need it to undo what it's done before these changes become permanent.'

Sa-at peered into the amber again. 'I think it's too late.'

'No, the physical changes can be removed, even if there isn't much of me left. But it has to be done quickly, before they become part of my self-image.'

'I still think it's too late.'

'That's my burden to bear, not yours.'

'And if I did free you, what would you give me?'

'What do you want? Soon, I'll be in a position to give you so many things. We could return to the castle. I could teach you about the world. I could teach you to fly.'

The idea of learning new things and flying appealed to Sa-at a great deal, but in the same way as a nice piece of fruit did. He enjoyed the idea of it, but he did not need it. Moreover, he didn't need Rochant to give it to him. He could feel words bubbling up inside, far more than he'd usually say. 'I don't want to die now and I won't ever want to die. And I don't understand why I should have to die just for you to live.

'What I've always wanted are friends. I thought you were my friend but you're not. You were never my friend. You've already changed the way I think but I don't want to change any more. I don't want to be like you.'

'But you already are,' replied Rochant.

Sa-at shrugged. 'I'm not making a deal. I'll find my own

way out. If the Corpseman is really your friend, you don't need me anyway.'

'Please, Sa-at, there's so much you don't understand. Take me with you, I could give you so much.'

'Goodbye, Rochant.'

'Listen to me!' cried Rochant, his voice lacking its usual calm. 'I just need you to help me get free and I'll give you all the friends you want, and I'll find a way to . . .'

Sa-at ignored him and started crawling over to the other tunnel, the one that went sharply upwards, and examined it. There were no handholds for climbing, and the sides were rough and coated with the same tacky slime as the rest of the area. But it wasn't sheer and, if he leaned forward, he could brace his feet against one side of the tunnel and his hands on the other.

Still, before he could start the climb, he became aware of something coming at speed down the tunnel towards him. He threw himself away from the entrance and against the nearest wall, hard enough to bruise his back.

A moment later, the Scuttling Corpseman landed exactly where he'd just been standing, its wings folded around its body like a cloak of office. It immediately dropped onto six legs and skittered towards Rochant.

Sa-at saw that its missing arm had been replaced with a human one and, while parts of the skin were covered by grafts of bony shell, he still recognized the thin appendage immediately. *It's Rochant's arm!*

The demon paid no attention to Sa-at at all, its attention was very much focused on Rochant, who was also ignoring Sa-at now. 'Wait, wait!' Rochant squealed. 'This isn't what we agreed.'

Its antennae curled down to gently brush Rochant's eyes while Sa-at crept over to the tunnel and began to climb.

'No, you can't have any more! You can't have my . . . have my . . . have . . .'

And then Rochant fell silent.

Sa-at tried to be silent too as he climbed. He tried very hard indeed.

It was a strange situation. High Lord Vasinidra had gone between lives, leaving his brother, Lord Gada Sapphire, in charge of two flights of hunters and the future of the house. But his last orders had been for Pari to lead the attack on the Corpseman, for him to defer to her.

Nidra was also there to advise, but also to defer to Pari. *At least that's how I interpreted the High Lord's words. I'm not so sure Nidra has come to the same conclusion.*

She suspected that as long as she could keep up the appearance that Gada was in charge, he'd do what she wanted. He might be a proud Sapphire, but he was also terrified of his new responsibility. She could use that. Nidra was harder to predict and would be impossible to control. Luckily for her, Nidra's body was old and exhausted, and was currently dozing on Gada's back.

They'd sent a pair of hunters home with Vasinidra's remains and strict instructions to return his shattered wings to the Gardener-smiths, while the rest of them continued to hunt the Scuttling Corpseman and Rochant. The Wild remained strangely quiet, almost dead, and they were making good time towards Sorn. She was aware that this was not their first trip and all of them were tired. In her case dangerously so.

If I'm not careful I'll end up going the same way as Vasinidra.

A Birdkin flew overhead and dropped something small and golden that landed at Pari's feet before landing on a branch just ahead of the lead hunters. She realized it was the first creature they'd seen in hours of travel. Its eyes were strange, multifaceted things that glittered as it shifted its gaze rapidly from one to the other.

The nearest hunters readied their spears but Pari's attention was on the object dropped by the Birdkin. She scooped it up and recognized it instantly. *This looks like my earring. One that I gave to Varg to use as a signal. I do hope he hasn't got himself into trouble.*

'We have a demon,' said one of the hunters, 'should we dispatch it?'

'Of course,' said Gada.

The Birdkin looked at Pari and made a flicking gesture with its beak, as if to say 'Follow me'.

How odd, she thought.

The hunter threw her spear and the Birdkin hurled itself into the air to avoid being skewered. It cawed angrily, then nodded at Pari and made another flicking gesture before flying away.

Pari turned to Arkav. 'If I didn't know better, I'd think it was trying to lure me away with the most childish of tricks.'

'Lucky for us you know better.'

She gave him a mock scowl.

They hadn't gone very far when the Birdkin returned, though not as close as before. It had brought others with it, a black feathered host. They all had the same type of eyes. As one, they flicked their beaks.

'Oh, now this is getting ridiculous,' said Pari.

'I don't like it,' agreed Gada. 'They could be spies for the Corpseman.'

'Unlikely,' she replied. 'The Corpseman's followers don't look like this, at least not the ones I've seen.'

'High Lord Vasinidra believes it has been working with other demons. He told me that Quiverhive's attacks on House Ruby were part of a larger plan. Either way, they're demons. We'll see if we can scare them off.'

Before he could give the order, however, the Birdkin scattered.

Arkav watched them go with a thoughtful expression on his face.

Pari gave him a gentle prod. 'If you don't tell me, I won't be able to appreciate how clever you are.'

'I don't know. It may be nothing.'

'But?'

'I think I've seen feathers like that before.'

Her eyes widened. 'Come to think of it, so have I! Sa-at. His coat was made of them.'

'You should follow the Birdkin.'

'I think I'm a little busy right now.'

He smiled at her. 'You're right. I suppose we'll just have to accept that we'll never know what it was all about.'

'That's low, dear brother, even for you.'

He started to move off in the direction of Sorn. 'Perhaps it's for the best. I know how much you love an unsolved mystery.'

'Stop that!'

'It will give you something to ponder when you get bored.'

'If you don't stop right now, I'll—'

'Go after the Birdkin?'

She scowled. 'I hate you sometimes.'

'Hurry. I'll make sure we don't start our attack on the Corpseman until you catch up.'

'Lord Gada will be livid.'

'I'll handle him. You handle this.'

She trusted her brother's instincts as she did her own. Perhaps more so. On impulse, she took his hand and kissed it. 'I really am glad you came back.'

His eyes misted, and the skin at their edges crinkled around his smile. 'Thank you for having the strength to bring me back.' He gently turned her towards the trees. 'But your new friends are getting away.'

'True. What are you going to tell Lord Gada?'

Arkav laughed. 'Something brilliant.'

She laughed too and gave him a final wave as she sprang forward on her Sky-legs.

It didn't take long to catch up. The Birdkin were waiting for her. As soon as she got close, they took wing, leading her towards a clearing. There were two larger things waiting for her there, a man in black and a white-furred Dogkin. Though she recognized them immediately, a part of her refused to believe what she was seeing.

'Varg?'

'Yeah.'

She looked at him a second time as the Birdkin took up posts in the trees around him. *Almost protectively.* He was dressed in armour that seemed to be woven from roots and vines. Feathers sprouted from the shoulder plates and made a long skirt around his legs. There were fresh scars on his face and he looked taller somehow. In his hand was a sapphire-tipped spear. Two more spears were crossed on his back.

Glider sat next to him, looking more wild than ever.

'On a normal day, I would positively enjoy picking apart what all this means,' Pari began, 'but time is rather short, so I'd appreciate it if you'd just tell me what in the name of the Thrice Blessed Suns is going on. Oh, and if there are any good reasons why you are dressed like that and obviously collaborating with demons, and why I shouldn't execute you . . .' She gave him her sweetest smile. 'I'd start with those.'

Varg scratched at his beard. 'Well, me and Glider don't work for you any more.'

'Not the best start, Varg.'

'Look, you ain't like the other Deathless. I've done a lot of things for you that don't exactly follow the rules, so I reckon you understand that sometimes the rules don't work.'

'Keep talking.'

'Things are fucked. Like, really fucked. An' it seems to us that Rochant and the Corpseman are gonna destroy everything unless we work together.'

'Who is this "we" exactly?'

'I'll show you, but you gotta promise not to attack.'

'Do I receive the same promise in return?'

'Yeah. We just wanna talk.'

'Very well, lead on. Just be quick about it.'

Varg didn't turn to leave, he stood aside. More Birdkin had gathered behind him, and with them was a woman wrapped in a dark robe. Feathers formed a high crest behind her head. Her slender arms seemed almost like wing bones from which long sleeves hung. A white-beaked Birdkin perched on her shoulder, its head tilted to one side. Again, Pari recognized her. Again, it was hard to believe.

'Honoured Mother Chandni? I suppose with Varg here, I shouldn't be surprised.'

She didn't bow in Pari's presence but for some reason that didn't feel as odd as it should have. Chandni had always been poised, but there was something different about her now, something regal. 'I am Honoured Mother no more. I am Chandni of iron and darkness, I am a two-hearted queen, a packstealer, and this is my flock. I know that I have crossed a line and I know that we will never again be friends, but hear me: Our enemy today is the same, and I believe that alone we will die fighting it.'

'What are you offering?'

'I can tell you where the Corpseman is.'

Pari laughed. 'You'll have to do better than that.'

The Birdkin scowled down at her, shrieking, and Glider growled low, as if daring Pari to try being disrespectful again. Chandni simply raised a hand and they all stopped. 'I can tell you exactly where it is and the positions of its children. I will show you where best to attack from, and send my followers to aid your flights of hunters in battle. We can mask your approach until you are in a position to strike.'

'And what do you want in return for all of this?'

'Only a Deathless can face the Corpseman directly. We can open a door for you, but we cannot go through it.'

Pari nodded. She knew how overpowering the Corpseman was, even for those protected by tanzanite armour. 'I take it this is your first hunt, my dear?'

Chandni stiffened. 'What of it?'

'I've fought the Corpseman before but I've never come

close to defeating it. And now it has wings and an army. We need a strategy.'

'What do you suggest?'

'We keep the Corpseman busy. It won't kill me or Nidra. At least, not unless we really annoy it. If we can engage its forces and keep them distracted, you can strike at its weak spot.'

'I wasn't aware the Corpseman had one.'

Pari grinned. 'Of course it does. Rochant. Get your hands on him and the Corpseman will back down. At least that is what my instincts tell me.'

'What if you're wrong?'

'Then we try to win the traditional way. Why do I feel there is more you're not saying?'

'The Corpseman has taken my son, his safety is a condition of my support.'

'You mean Sa-at?'

Some of Chandni's steel wilted as she took a step closer. 'You know him?'

'A little. I like what I've seen so far. Given that we have some history and I have nothing against him personally, I will agree to your terms.'

'Swear it before the Wild.'

'Oh, I think not. You may have sold your soul to this place, but that is a path I will not be following.' *If Rochant had been as discerning,* she thought bitterly, *none of us would be in this mess in the first place.* 'If you wish me to trust you, you must take me at my word.'

Chandni inclined her head, and the Birdkin did the same. 'I haven't forgotten how you saved my son and I all those years ago. We will trust you, Lady Pari.'

'While I am incredibly open-minded about things, I doubt my companions will be able to manage it, so please keep your communications subtle, and when the fighting starts, keep your . . .' she gestured to the Birdkin '. . . companions out of our way.'

'I understand.'

'Please also understand that I am not condoning your life choices.' She raised an eyebrow in Varg's direction. 'Nor yours. When this is all over, you will be treated just the same as any other traitor.'

Varg seemed saddened but there was resolve in his eyes as he moved to Chandni's side. *He knows too much about me, but there is nothing I can do here and now.*

'This is the last time you'll see me, Lady Pari,' said Chandni, 'I promise you.'

Pari had the sudden and unwelcome sense of being dismissed. She quickly quashed the urge to get the last word. *Just focus on the world-shaking problems for now, Pari,* she counselled herself. And with a bow grand enough to be mocking, she left to catch up with her brother and the Sapphire.

CHAPTER TWENTY-TWO

Satyendra was close, he could feel it.

Ahead of him was a steep hill. From a distance it looked like some gnarled and knobbly piece of fruit. As he got closer, he could see mud-smeared bumps of amber all over it. The humanoid Flykin were crawling from one to the other, fussing over them. Though he couldn't make out any entrances from where he was, it was clear that the Flykin were moving in and out of the hill from several different places.

The constant buzz, though unsettling, did not distress him as it had before. It was softer, more peaceful, and didn't cut into his thoughts. And yet, his instincts still told him to keep away.

He came to a stop at the edge of the trees and scowled up at the sky. The three suns shone down angrily. Intellectually, he knew that their rays were not as strong here as they were in the courtyard of Rochant's castle, but it didn't feel that way. To him, their light seemed sharper than ever, stabbing at his eyes until he looked away.

Why am I here? he wondered. The idea of getting revenge on Rochant remained but he struggled to recall why it was so important. *What does it even matter now?*

Rochant had hurt and humiliated him. In return he had drawn the man's blood, but that wasn't enough. He had to do more.

But why? he asked himself. There was no articulate answer, just the overwhelming need to make Rochant suffer, the kind that didn't need a reason. It simply was. And while a very small part of him recoiled from it in horror, he already knew that he was going to see his desires through.

Vengeance was not all that drove him though. He was also here for Sa-at. A part of him still wanted to hurt Sa-at, like a reflex, but another part of him wanted to talk to Sa-at and be reassured. It had been a while since he'd last seen himself and he knew his body had undergone significant changes since then. The idea of his reflection scared him now. *Would he find a taller version of Sa-at staring back at him or a smaller one of the Whispercage?*

Turning away from such thoughts, he continued to study the hill. Standing there in the shadows of the tree he was all but invisible, his body slipping into an unearthly stillness.

There were bonds between the Flykin demons and the mounds in the hill, and bonds between each member of the swarm to each other. He saw as much as felt them, new senses picking out the ghosts of essence that ran from one to another. *That is what allows them to coordinate so effectively. Perhaps it could also be exploited.*

The swarm remained unaware of his presence, busying themselves with the movement of bodies and the reengineering of the hill. Gradually, their patterns started to make sense to him, and he was drawn to the strange, almost maternal way they treated their charges. There was tenderness to match their efficiency.

Interesting.

Safe from the glare of the suns he continued to observe. There were far too many for him to face alone but Satyendra felt no concern. From here, he could watch and wait, unnoticed. Sooner or later an opportunity would come.

'You okay?' asked Varg.

They were both sitting on Glider's back, Chandni in front and him behind. The pack, swelled with Kennelgrove's own Dogkin, padded alongside and her Birdkin glided above, a great host that moved at her command. 'We're together, aren't we?'

The compliment earned her a gentle squeeze. 'Yeah, it's just . . .'

'You can speak freely to me.'

'When you were talking to Pari you didn't sound like you. You sounded like one of them.'

'I am one of them. Murderkind's power is mine now, Varg.'

'Yeah.' He sounded crestfallen.

'But I'm still me.'

She only caught the end of his answer as the first part was muttered into his beard. 'Don't see how you can't be changed by . . . what you did.'

Chandni could understand Varg's point of view, but he was wrong. Strictly speaking she had changed. Her heart beat differently, and she was connected to the Wild in a way she'd never been before. She could feel how the trees had fallen silent, driven into hibernation by fear. The pain of her flock, bloodied and diminished, was written in every flap of their wings. Rochant and the Corpseman had destroyed the old order and everything had withdrawn to see what the dawn would bring.

But she felt no different in herself. She had taken Murderkind's authority, not the other way around. Her wants and needs remained the same. In an odd way, she felt more like her old self than ever, for now she had a domain to protect and a score of individuals all dependent on her guidance. The only real difference was that she used to serve the lords of House Sapphire, and now she served no one.

'Varg, if you aren't happy, I won't force you to stay.'

'I'm with you to the end, Chand. You know that. I just worry. You keep getting closer and closer to the Wild and I'm scared you've gone too far, like too far to come back. There's always a price, you know?'

Chandni wasn't so sure. She suspected the Wild was more complicated than a simple trap that consumed everything it came into contact with. And anyway, she was tired of living in fear. Varg may not understand now, but he would in time.

She drew the pack to a halt when the trees began to thin out. Ahead of her was the hill that held Sa-at. On the other side of it one of her Birdkin was leading Lady Pari and House Sapphire into a position to strike.

A single gesture brought the flock down. They clustered close together, forming a big plump rug of feathers. She slipped from Glider's back and walked among them, letting her hands brush the backs of their heads.

Beat-beat-

-beat-beat.

Beat-beat-

-beat-beat- went her twin hearts, whispering to each other, sharing secrets. Like any power of the Wild, she could give and take as she pleased from those beholden to her. With each touch, she took a Birdkin's hearing, and the flock's world grew quieter.

Don't worry my, children, she soothed, *this will not be forever.*

When she was done, she helped Varg put hoods on the Dogkin, then they helped each other fasten their own headdresses. She doubted it would be enough to cut out the sound of the swarm entirely, but it would help them to resist.

When she was done, Chandni climbed onto Glider's back and raised her arms.

As one, the flock took wing.

Chandni watched them go with pride. *Has any flight of hunters ever flown with such unity of purpose, such perfect formation? I think not.*

What was coming scared her, but she had a plan, and she had her people, and she was ready.

Be patient, my son, I am coming.

Pari walked through the Wild with Gada and Nidra, the hunters strung out behind them in two formations. It was hard talking to them whilst keeping a subtle eye on the Birdkin leading her through the trees. Or at least it was hard doing both things at once without getting irritated.

'No,' she said 'that's not what I mean. High Lord Spinel is not actually dead, though he may well wish he was. The Corpseman has trapped him in his body. If it wasn't for our intervention it would have done the same to High Lords Jet, Opal, Tanzanite, and Peridot. Ultimately it means to end the cycle of rebirth for all the Deathless save for,' she paused, 'myself and Rochant and Nidra.'

'Forgive me,' said Gada, 'but why you three? And how do you know this?'

She looked at Nidra who nodded permission for her to answer. 'Through bitter experience. As to why, I believe love is to blame. At the time Rochant made his pact, he loved your mother and me,' she gave another glance towards Nidra, 'despite our rejections. He probably still does. Because of this, the Corpseman will not hurt us, though I'm less sure about its . . . I want to say children, but I'm not sure that's the right word.'

'We can use that to our advantage,' said Nidra.

'Perhaps. Have you heard about Sagan yet?'

Both Gada and Nidra shook their heads.

'Sagan has been destroyed. Those who weren't killed have been harvested, I suspect to make more children for the Corpseman. I think that is what the Corpseman wants: To breed.'

Gada cleared his throat. 'This is all very useful information, Lady Pari, but how do we destroy it?'

'My dear Lord Gada, I'm not sure we can. The Scuttling Corpseman has been stealing memories from Samarku Un-Sapphire for years about our ways, and it has been making plans with Rochant Un-Sapphire for at least as long. It knows how we think and it knows how our society works. I wonder if the question is not so much how we beat the Corpseman but whether it is possible to stop it beating us.'

'No,' said Nidra. 'The Corpseman can be beaten. It allowed me to hack off its arm.' Gada's eyebrows shot up, but a quick gesture from his mother was enough to ward off any interruption. 'That means you can attack it, Lady Pari, maybe even kill it. You must try, for all our sakes. We have four Deathless and two flights of hunters, enough to give you a chance. If the Corpseman means to make its forces larger, then we have every reason to strike now before it becomes overwhelming. House Sapphire will hold off the enemy's troops while you cut out its heart.'

I agree with you, she thought. *So long as we're talking about Rochant. He's the Corpseman's weak spot.*

'Are you sure about this?' asked Lord Gada.

'I am,' replied Pari, doing her best to give him due attention and keep an eye on the small, feathered guide flitting just above the canopy. 'Give me the chance and I'll bring down the Corpseman.'

'Actually, I was referring to this route. As you know, I have been to the Corpseman's lair before, and I'm not sure this is the most direct way.'

'Fear not, Lord Gada, for I too have been here before in my previous lifecycle. I know where I'm going.'

His long face was perfectly shaped to display polite disapproval. 'Forgive me, Lady Pari, but that was some time ago, and the Wild is fond of changing its pathways. My hunters and I came here mere days ago, which is why I believe . . .'

He was still talking but Pari did her best to tune him out. In situations like this she found it easiest to make pleasant noises that suggested agreement while getting on with the work herself. Besides, she could hardly explain to Gada that she knew better thanks to a demon of the Wild.

As the trees gave way to thick tufts of grass and the ground began to slope upwards, Pari gave Gada a satisfied smile. 'Here we are, just as I promised. Are your people ready?'

'Yes. Suns shine on you, Lady Pari. I hope we all see each other in the same bodies when this is over.' He raised one hand to his head, which was the signal to make preparations. Mia, who was leading the other flight, made the same gesture, and all the hunters put in their ear-plugs.

Another gesture, and the hunters spread out, each flight forming a semi-circle of spears. Pari took a moment to appreciate the pretty formations while she could.

Arkav came to join her, clearly intending to have a last word before the battle. She stepped away from Gada to join him.

'I know,' she said. 'I'll be careful.'

He raised an eyebrow at that. 'Whatever happens out there, we stay together.'

'Agreed.'

He nodded, then asked, 'Are you sure this is the best way to take on the Corpseman?'

'I hope so, dear brother, given that you thought it was a good idea!'

'Yes. Yes, I think it probably is. Although I'd rather it were us going after Rochant. It seems very risky to leave our fates in the hands of our very dubious allies. What if they fail? What if they betray us? If we die here, there won't be anyone to deal with the Bringers.'

'Maybe you should stay back? I can handle the Corpseman, you can handle the Bringers.'

'No. It beat you the last time you were alone, remember?'

'I rather wish I couldn't.'

'Perhaps together, we'll be able to take it down whether they find Rochant or not.'

She peered through a gap in the trees in time to see the Birdkin begin its dive. 'I believe it's time to go.' She signalled

Gada to begin the attack. 'No dying,' she said to Arkav, 'Okay?'

'I won't if you won't.'

'Deal,' she replied, and the two of them broke cover and started to race for the hill.

Sa-at was out of breath by the time he reached the top of the tunnel. His arms and legs were tired too. Though the tacky substance that coated everything gave him some purchase, the sides were smooth, and the earth beneath his fingers soft. A trail of feathers stolen from his coat now lined the tunnel walls, marking his route.

He emerged at a point on the top of the hill but not, as he expected, into open air. Around him was a dome of hard amber that turned the sunslight a strange orangey yellow. It was warm, soporific, and after all his excitements, sleep was very tempting. The Scuttling Corpseman was still lurking below though, and he knew that it would make short work of the climb if it had a mind to do so.

He reached up and pushed. Immediately, cracks appeared above him. The dome was already broken, and each of the pieces had been rearranged together like a jigsaw. He pushed harder, standing on tiptoes to send several of the chunks toppling over, then hauled himself out of the hole in the dome and dropped down onto soft wet grass.

The fresh air was cool on his face and he took in a long deep breath, immediately feeling more awake. Silver birch trees dotted the top of the hill, and beyond them he had a view over the Wild in all directions. In places he could see gaps where lone leafless trees stood and a sad feeling settled in his gut.

Some of the trees have been killed.

But why have the others left them there?

Usually a dead tree would fall but these remained upright. And usually, the Wild reclaimed its own with great speed unless there was some other power involved.

As he tried to work out what this meant he became aware of a low humming all around him. Though it did not sound aggressive, it put him on edge. The demons that served the Corpseman were here, weaving in and out of the hillside. He only caught glimpses, most were hidden from his view, but he could tell they were very close and that, as yet, they were unaware of him.

Sa-at considered his options. Below him was the Scuttling Corpseman. At some point it would conclude its business with Rochant and come back up the tunnel. He did not want to be anywhere near the hill when that happened, but to leave the hill he would have to go through an army of demons.

Neither choice seemed very appealing.

While he stood there, a great black cloud rose from the trees to his left. It was made of Birdkin, and it was coming at great speed. *Crowflies? Is that you? Have you come for me?*

He wasn't sure how this could be so. With Murderkind dead, the flock had no leader, but he couldn't deny the evidence before him.

And then, to his right, he saw two glowing violet figures emerge from the trees, and hunters were following, blue wings flashing on a hundred backs.

The lady with the golden lips!

He knew that the Birdkin were enemies of the hunters. But he also knew that both were enemies of the Corpseman.

And the Corpseman is in the middle!

Though his friends might end up fighting each other, they would attack the hill first. As he frantically tried to think about what to do, he heard the tone of the swarm change. Soft, rhythmic humming cut off, to be replaced with a moment of blessed silence, and then an angry, alien roar.

Sa-at crouched low and moved to the edge of the hilltop. Below him, the swarm was in motion. Some were throwing themselves into the air, their transparent wings a blur at their backs, while others were diving into holes on the hillside, to emerge a moment later with weapons in their hands. Sa-at recognized some as the kind carried by road-born – simple sticks, slings, and spears – as well as a smattering of crystal-tipped weapons that must have been scavenged from dead hunters.

In seconds the sky was filled with humanoid bodies, so thick that they became like a living wall. So thick, that Sa-at could no longer see or hear any of his friends. Their buzzing filled his senses, overwhelming – wrong! – rooting him to the spot. He stopped worrying about his friends or the Corpseman or how to escape, and began to scream.

Rayen led the pack, a white arrowhead of Dogkin, speeding under the black cloud above. Chandni sat in the middle of them on Glider's back, Varg behind her. She leaned forward, keeping as low as she could. The swarm of demons didn't notice her at first, distracted by her army of brave Birdkin.

Everything around her was muted, giving it a sense of unreality. She looked up once, and saw the initial contact between her forces and the Corpseman's. The last time the flock had faced the swarm, it had been maddened by the noise, but this time, the Birdkin were able to fight with precision, each one a tiny dagger thrown at the heart of the enemy.

The swarm adapted swiftly. She saw them splitting into smaller formations, throwing knives and spears, raising nets between them . . .

Fighting like we do. Like our hunters.

She didn't look up again. Whatever was going to happen would happen, regardless of her worrying. For better or worse they were all committed to the plan now.

As they passed underneath the swarm, a unit of demons detached and dived down towards them. Varg's hand was firm on her back, keeping her down, and Chandni clung tighter to Glider's neck. She was aware of Varg moving behind her, his body twisting as he stabbed at something that had got too close. Chitin-coated hands grasped for her, then there was a flash of white, as a Dogkin leapt next to them, and the hands were gone.

All around her, teeth flashed and bodies crashed together, soft white and shiny black. Some went down, some kept going. She saw weapons flash in the sunslight and red streaks bloom on fur. She saw a Dogkin pounce on a demon, ripping it from the sky, only to be surrounded by more of them that danced above it, each dip accompanied by a spear thrust.

And then they were through, and running towards the base of the hill.

Varg tapped her on the shoulder and pointed towards a hole directly ahead. She nodded and they went for it, leaping from Glider's back as the Dogkin skidded to a halt, and diving inside.

* * *

One of the swarm came towards Pari at blistering speed. To her horror, she realized that the spear in its hand was tipped with a ruby head and was glad Vasinidra wasn't there to see it. *All our worst fears are confirmed.*

Her whip flicked out and the barb tore one of its wings off like paper. The demon spun wildly, crashing into the floor at her feet but before it could recover, she stamped down on its neck.

Another two were already on her, trying to flank her position. Pari allowed herself a slight smile. She recognized the manoeuvre. *How interesting.* This time her whip snared one by the ankle, allowing her to swing it into the second. As the two demons crashed to the ground, Arkav came leaping down onto them, fists first. His gauntlets flashed as they made contact. There was a distressed buzzing, a sharp cracking sound, and then a wet squelch. The buzzing cut off abruptly.

'I wondered where you'd got to,' she said.

Arkav tapped the side of his helmet and shouted something. She couldn't hear him over the sound of the swarm, which was, she thought, rather the point of his communication.

She nodded to show she'd understood, and gestured for them to continue. Arkav held up a finger and then pointed back to where the bulk of the Sapphire hunters were. They'd been arranged into two flights and, spread wide, were forcing the swarm to thin out in order to block their approach. She didn't like the restraint the swarm seemed to be showing, nor did she like the odd formations they were taking up.

'I have a terrible feeling that the Corpseman has been teaching its children how to fight us.'

Arkav glanced at her and tapped his helmet again.

'Sorry, it's hard to break the habit of sharing my wisdom.'

Arkav raised an eyebrow and she mouthed 'sorry' at him.

Lord Gada and Mia were using traditional tactics. However, these normally assumed that the hunters would outnumber the prey, and that the prey would not be using the same weapons. It was also uncommon to find so many demons that could fly.

If we don't do something, they'll be overwhelmed.

She could already see that fighting had started in places, that demons were flying overhead and hunters were leaping into the air to stab at them. Neat lines were disintegrating into clumps, as the swarm's units dropped down among the hunters.

Though her helmet muted the sound of the swarm it was still distracting. Neither she nor Arkav realized that more demons were approaching from behind until their shadows fell across them.

Pari didn't have time to use her whip, doing her best to twist as a thrown spear glanced from her side. Luckily it only had a wooden head, and did little more than scratch the tanzanite plates. She grabbed at the demon's face as it flew over her, gathering antennae in her fist and allowing its momentum to rip them free. It crashed nearby, and lashed out wildly at the air.

Arkav had managed to dispatch two more, but at a cost. His other wing had gone dark and the armour's aura had started to flicker.

Chandni needs to find Rochant and end this sooner rather than later, and I need to draw the Corpseman away. Come on, Pari. Think!

But it was hard to think. For one thing, there was a lot going on, and for another, she was beyond tired. The only thing she was sure about was that they had to finish the Corpseman here and now, before it had a chance to strengthen its position. In the years it would take the other High Lords to return from their enforced trip between lives, the balance of power would swing still further against them.

So, she carried on towards the hill. Arkav stooped to collect the ruby-tipped spear and came with her. She suspected she could reach the top with a good run up and a single jump but she leapt onto the side of the hill instead, landing next to one of the person-sized bumps of amber. Putting away her whip, she grabbed it with both hands and pulled, exposing about a third of it to the air. Inside was the silhouette of a body, slowly changing from corpse to demon.

Arkav landed next to her and plunged the spear into the thing with all his Deathless strength.

Some of the swarm nearest to them paused in the air, as if someone had just slapped them across the back of their heads. She moved to the next block of amber and did the same. Arkav destroyed it just as fast.

By the fourth, large chunks of the swarm were breaking off and heading towards them.

'Well,' she shouted amiably. 'That got their attention.'

'Agreed,' Arkav shouted back. 'Now what do we do?'

She shrugged. 'Keep going, sooner or later we'll annoy the Corpseman into appearing.'

CHAPTER TWENTY-THREE

Satyendra slipped from his hiding place. Nearby, hunters and demons fought each other in clusters, formations breaking and re-forging, the piles of the dead slowly growing, their patterns showing the ebb and flow of battle.

Amid the buzzing and shouting and thud of weapons he was a quiet shadow moving within the greater shadows of the hill. Nobody was looking for him. Nobody was expecting him. As he moved further from the fighting, the oppressive noises eased and it became easier for him to think.

Somewhere inside he would find Sa-at.

Somewhere inside he would find Rochant.

None of the swarm had stayed behind and he was aware of another battle happening on the far side of the hill. There was nothing to stop him going inside. But as he studied the different tunnels and tried to decide which one to take, he felt a twinge of fear. A primal instinct was telling him to run, to put as much distance as he could between himself and this place.

Satyendra ignored it and held fast to the twin desires of

hope and revenge. They were the stars he navigated by now. It was easy to insert his long, slender frame into the tunnel, though he had to crawl to make progress. The darkness did not trouble him as much as it used to, and he found he could still make out shapes quite clearly, the colour leeched from them. He caught a glimpse of his hands as they moved in front of him and felt his heart clench. The fingers protruded from the bandages, impossibly long, nearly twice the size they had been before, and the skin was stretched so thin over them that it had paled, becoming almost as white as the bones beneath.

But they felt neither frail nor brittle. If anything, they felt stronger. Before, his body had only changed when he had fed upon the emotions of others, but now the transformation seemed to have acquired its own momentum, twisting him even as he stood and waited.

And I didn't even notice.

There was a haze in the air in front of him, vibrant against the greys of the tunnel. He realized it was not a physical thing, but the faint edges of a collection of emotions. Ones he knew, and from a person he knew.

Fear. Frustration. Despair. Anger. And the source is Rochant!

The instinct to run remained, but now he could feel that special hunger, and it soon eclipsed his fear. *Oh, to feed on Rochant, that would be the sweetest meal of all.*

He was aware of other things close by. A multitude of beings living within the hill, some large, some small, their individual scents too small to identify, that formed a backdrop to Rochant's. By contrast, these were docile; quiet dreamers with unformed thoughts.

And laced on top of them was the hint of something more predatory, the Corpseman itself. It was hard for him to detect. Not so much a set of emotions as a presence. He had no idea how it felt nor where it was, only that it was *here*.

For a moment, the fear overtook the hunger once more. He stopped.

The hunger urged him on.

The fear urged him to flee.

And for a while, in the dark, he waited.

Sa-at could not say how long he'd been lying on top of the hill. He watched as the clouds twirled above him in a slow, unconcerned manner. After a while, the sound of the swarm had become too much and he'd simply stopped thinking.

In its own way, it was strangely peaceful.

He knew that his ears hurt, and that in various places his body did as well, but these things were far away. He also knew that there was fighting going on all around him, and yet that felt far away too.

A thought gradually came to him, though it was sluggish and took him a while to understand.

Those aren't clouds.

He looked again and realized he was right. The grey shapes above were not clouds, they were wings. And the shapes they were making were not in his imagination, they were spiralling lines that seemed to twist and ripple, trapping his thoughts within.

The clouds – *the wings* – moved together and the Scuttling Corpseman rose higher into the air. He remembered now that he'd been screaming when it emerged from the wrecked dome, and that it had opened its wings and the screaming had stopped. It wasn't that he'd stopped suffering, more that it had ceased to be relevant.

The antennae that sprouted from the eye sockets of the Corpseman's skull tested the air for a moment, then it began to dive. Closer and closer it came, until it was all Sa-at could see. Until it was his world.

Wind buffeted his face and made his eyes water.

And then it was gone, diving past him down the side of the hill.

He blinked, enjoying a moment of peace, before the sounds of the swarm and the fighting and the pain returned in full force.

Here it comes, thought Pari.

In destroying a few of the Corpseman's unborn brood, they'd succeeded in drawing it out. Now came the hard part. She was fairly sure that it wouldn't kill her but Arkav would enjoy no such protection. She hoped that Chandni would be quick, for all their sakes.

She reached for her brother's hand and then raised it with her own until it was at eye level. By glancing at the bracers she could see the reflection of the Corpseman's shape growing larger. Muted by the tanzanite plates, the image lacked the power to mesmerize.

She crouched, pressing down on her Sky-legs so that their blades curved and began to store energy. All the while, the Corpseman's image grew on their bracers, becoming more distinct.

The two of them waited, lifecycles of shared experience putting them in tune.

A little closer.

When its reflection covered the surface of the bracer completely, Pari sprung to the left, while Arkav leapt to the right. She felt hard-tipped fingers glance her shoulder, and just had time to feel relieved that it had gone for her and not her brother before she was sent corkscrewing through the air and into the hill. Sacrificing dignity for survival, Pari scrabbled against the earth, trying to right herself and avoid a tumble. On her second attempt she managed to get her legs under her and kick off from the hill, gliding in a tight circle back towards the Corpseman.

She got a brief view of the other fight taking place beyond the hill. It was a crazy mess of dark spots fighting smaller dark spots, and impossible to tell who was winning. As she wheeled round she saw the Sapphire hunters engaged with the other half of the Corpseman's spawn. The fighting was fierce, brutal, less a case of winners and losers, and more one of who survived and who did not.

Then she came back to the hill and realized she'd been wrong. The Corpseman had not been going for her after all. It was flying upward, its thick wings moving in slow, powerful beats. Higher than her, higher than the hilltop and still climbing. Two of its hands gripped the stub of Arkav's remaining wing. She could see the strain forming, the cracks rushing out across the surface of the dimmed crystal. Any second now, it would break, and her brother would fall.

'No!' shouted Pari.

The Corpseman continued to ascend.

There was a palpable shift when the Corpseman left. Satyendra felt it go, and with it, a lessening of pressure. He knew it was still close by but it was no longer in the hill and that was enough.

Even better, Rochant is still here.

He began to make his way through the tunnels. Though he didn't know the layout, he could tell when he was getting closer to his prey, and it didn't take long before he emerged into the chamber he sought. To his delight he found his enemy in a profound state of unhappiness and it only took a glance to understand why.

Rochant was struggling to pull himself free from one of the walls but the amber that coated him stretched with his efforts, sticking to him like glue. One of his arms did not match the other, and what was visible of his body was the wrong shape: The flesh was drawn too tight around the spine and the shoulders had bulked out. A black exoskeleton covered his torso and one arm but it had not yet hardened, reminding Satyendra of the top of a newborn baby's skull.

There was a delicious moment when Rochant became aware he was being watched and froze in place.

'Would you like me to help?' asked Satyendra, but his voice came out as barely more that a whisper.

Rochant simply stared at him and continued to work himself free.

'Yes. You keep going,' he murmured. 'I'll wait.'

Though Rochant's face gave nothing away, the pain and the rising fear rolled off him in waves. Satyendra let the emotions seep into him. Each one gave him a rush of strength and awareness. Despite this, he couldn't help but give Rochant his grudging respect. The man was still going despite the lack of hope and the terrible odds.

The membrane finally tore, spilling a thick amber liquid

and Rochant onto the floor. He lay there, apparently too weak to move, and turned his head to look up. 'Perhaps we could discuss a deal?'

Satyendra laughed. 'What could you possibly offer me that I couldn't take for myself?'

'Survival. If you do anything to me, the Corpseman will destroy you.'

'Look at me.' Satyendra crawled closer. 'Do you think I fear death?'

'Look at me,' replied Rochant. 'Death is the least of your worries.'

'I can see why the Corpseman would have to restore your body, but why take your arm?'

Rochant said nothing.

It doesn't matter, thought Satyendra. *I know how best to hurt him now.*

'The Bringers of Endless Order might be stupid, but even they will know you for an abomination. You're not coming back from this life.'

'We'll see.'

'Yes. We will. Don't worry, I'm not going to kill you.'

Satyendra reached out with such speed that Rochant did not even register what was happening until he heard the sound of his own arm being broken. The scream was perfect, just the right mix of surprise and horror, that he was overcome by ecstatic bliss, his eyes rolling back into his head.

Rochant's other arm twitched at his side, but the new connections had not yet formed, leaving him powerless before Satyendra.

'I imagine that when the Corpseman finds you, it will want to replace your other arm now, yes?'

Rochant didn't answer.

This time, he grabbed Rochant's leg, placing both hands either side of his knee, but he didn't break anything, not yet. 'Legs next, and then your jaw. Unless you have something better to offer me?' He had no intention of making a deal, but the chance of it would allow him to milk an even sweeter bounty from Rochant's misery.

'Wait. Wait! There is much I can offer you. Tell me what you desire and it's yours.'

Satyendra smiled and nodded, for this was what he'd been waiting to hear. He made a show of considering what he might say, then twisted his hands in opposite directions, grinding the leg bones in his grip as he did so. While Rochant writhed in agony, he very slowly, very deliberately reached for his other leg.

'Uhhnhn . . . wuuhn . . . wait!'

'What I want,' said Satyendra, 'is to make you suffer for what you did to me.' His eyes narrowed. 'You are just as bad as I am. Worse! I never had a choice, but you did.'

'Tell yourself that if you want,' gasped Rochant. 'But there are always choices to be made. I don't regret mine but it's clear yours haunt you.' He carried on quickly as Satyendra's hands began to tighten. 'You do have a choice. You don't want to be a monster of the Wild any more than I do. What if I told you there was a way to change back?'

Satyendra stared at him.

'That's right,' continued Rochant. 'You don't have to be like this. You could have your normal body again and a happy life.'

'How?'

'Ah well, that's the real trick. I alone can make it happen, but only if you help me.'

With effort he checked the urge to twist and break. Was this all he was now? A thing that caused pain? *And if I do take revenge on Rochant, what then? What kind of life is waiting for me out there?* Somewhere beneath all the surging power came a note of despair. As much as he'd hated being an Honoured Vessel in the castle, it was what he knew.

Rochant was watching him. There was pain in his eyes, but no fear. Satyendra took the thoughts to their conclusion. *If I agree to his terms, I will be beholden to him. If I give up on the hunger, I will also lose my strength, my speed, my new senses. But if I ignore his offer they will be all I have. I . . . am tempted by this offer.*

A voice spoke from the tunnel at his back, and the blood froze in his veins. It was both familiar and not familiar, and its authority spoke to both his heart and his hunger.

'The Wild always demands a price for its power and there is no going back for any of us.'

He turned to see his mother at the tunnel's entrance. Often he'd found her frustrating, but on her good days, she was fierce. This was her at her best. The steel in her gaze shook him, and her presence filled the chamber almost as much as the Corpseman's had. He could see it now, a swirling pattern of essence spilling in front of her, edged with feathers.

She pointed a finger towards Rochant. 'He lies to you, as he has lied to all of us.'

He turned back to Rochant who remained unfazed.

'Chandni was always a great follower because she lacked imagination. Just because she cannot conceive of a solution does not mean that there isn't one. Destroy her, help me, and I will grant what you truly desire. I'm the only one who can.'

Again, he was tempted.

Had he not hated his mother as much as he'd hated Rochant? Wasn't this what he'd have done anyway, regardless of Rochant's offer? And yet . . . if he was going to kill Chandni, he felt it should be on his terms. And when he thought of her voice, of the aura around her, he wasn't sure that killing her was even an option.

'He's using you,' said Chandni.

He didn't look at her when he answered. 'You'd know all about that, wouldn't you, Mother?'

'Judge me as you wish, but I did what I did to serve House Sapphire and our people. He serves only himself.'

Rochant's reply was swift. 'She doesn't understand us. Like you, I was born into a position where the only option was to fight or be discarded. Like you, I had to be clever against overwhelming odds. Like y—'

With a quick twist, Satyendra broke his other leg.

Why did he do it? He wasn't sure. An impulse had moved to his fingers before he'd had a chance to consider further, and after that, nothing mattered but the sudden rush as the swell of Rochant's pain made his smile spread wide, then wider, then wider still, opening in four directions. Horror and exultation gripped him in equal measure. He felt his strength growing, his bones growing, his senses changing again. But something was slipping from his face and a panicked voice told him he was losing a vital part of himself.

It was hard to appreciate that, increasingly hard to think about anything other than the rush.

Only one thing remained clear. The man before him needed to suffer. But as he reached for Rochant's jaw he heard Chandni's voice again, saying his name.

'Satyendra.'

Not now, Mother, he went to say, but only a hiss emerged from his throat; his mouth was no longer able to form the shape required for speech.

'Satyendra, look at me.'

Her words were like a hand gripping his skull, twisting him round with force. He tried to resist, but it was no use. She was still crouched down in the entrance, a small woman at her smallest. And yet she was not small. She was vast. A giant before a speck.

He saw her in all her dark glory, and he knew that she saw him.

And the feelings that bubbled up inside were too much to bear.

With an inhuman screech of shame, of self-loathing, Satyendra spun away and fled for the other tunnel, the one that led upwards and away from his past.

Pari watched as the Corpseman flew higher and higher, taking Arkav with it. Experience had taught her that the demon was hard to read but she had a nasty feeling she knew what it was planning.

There were no such doubts with her brother. Though Arkav was caught, he was still conscious, and as he shifted his grip on his spear, she knew all too well what he was about to do.

'Don't be an idiot!' she shouted helplessly.

Arkav stabbed upwards, aiming for a spot where the Corpseman's leg met its hips.

Two of its four arms snapped down, catching the shaft and wrenching it from Arkav's hands.

It seems it can read my brother as easily as it does me.

Then, without ceremony, it dropped Arkav, tilting in the air so that it could dive towards the Sapphire hunters.

The essence currents above the Wild were weak and unpredictable. Even a Deathless would struggle to manage them for long. With only one damaged wing left, Arkav was doomed. He tumbled slowly as he fell but he did not fall slowly.

Pari backed up across the top of the hill. Out of the corner of her eye, she glimpsed a small figure writhing amid the grass – *Sa-at!* – but she paid him no mind. All her attention was on the sky, the distances between her and her brother, the best angles to try for . . .

She knew she only had one chance and she knew that was all she needed.

Come on, Pari. She told herself. *It's time to be brilliant.*

A short run, three bounding strides and she was in the air, arcing up as her brother arced down. There was a chime of crystal as she tackled him midair – that rang out – giving a brief respite to the background buzzing of the swarm.

Their arms automatically laced around each other, Arkav doing his best to make the movements of his body complement hers as she tried to bring them down safely.

She'd been confident that she'd catch him, but was less confident about the landing. The base of the hill was coming at them too fast. Still holding each other tightly, they bent their knees, preparing to come down heavily on their Sky-legs. Ideally, they'd make several bounces, each one stealing a little more of their momentum until they came to a stop.

The first bounce did little to slow them, sending them off

at a wild angle. Arkav's one wing was unbalancing them and neither of them had compensated enough for it.

Oh, no.

The second bounce was little better and the trees were suddenly close. Awfully close. One in particular seemed to have placed itself directly in their flightpath.

Oh, dear.

She let go of Arkav on the third bounce, so that they could glide parallel on either side of the tree, missing it by inches. A second later, with barely enough time to think about how close that was, something snagged her wing and the world became a blurring spin of greens and browns.

The next thing Pari knew she was on her back. It was suspiciously comfortable. *I really have been pushing myself too hard lately. It would be so easy just to lie here, to let go.*

But she thought of Arkav and all those brave people fighting and dying nearby. She thought of the Corpseman and how she was the only one that could stop it, and she got up.

By some miracle, her armour appeared mostly intact. The crystal had been chipped in places, and she was far from her best, but there were no major fractures or breaks.

'Arkav?' she called.

'Here,' replied her brother as he limped over.

His fall had been worse than hers. The armour on his right leg barely glowed, and the blade of his Sky-leg wasn't fully extending. 'Honestly,' she said, 'this really won't do.'

'It's just a scratch,' he replied, holding out a hand, 'shall we?'

'Yes.'

Together they leapt from the trees. Arkav had to favour one leg, and Pari lost some momentum in order to keep him with her, but they managed. As they returned to the battle, her thoughts raced.

The Corpseman knows it can't hurt me but it also knows how to manipulate me. I've shared its thoughts before, and while I've learned something of its nature it must have been learning about me at the same time. It's already used Arkav against me once. I have to make sure it doesn't again.

While she had been rescuing Arkav, the Corpseman had not been idle. The battle of the hunters and the swarm looked very different to Pari as they emerged from the trees.

The Corpseman hovered directly above a central block of hunters, its great wings spread wide. All the nearby hunters had stopped fighting; their collective gaze was being drawn upwards, unwilling, by the strange swirling designs, allowing the swarm to smash through their defensive line.

Lord Gada Sapphire had become aware of this, and was bounding to that position to give support. Unlike the hunters, he would not be swayed immediately, but he would be facing the demon alone.

'Gada! Stop!' she shouted. 'That's just what the Corpseman wants!'

But it was no use. She was too far away and the swarm's drone drowned out her words.

Long before Gada got within range, and just after he had committed to a leap, the Corpseman threw the ruby-tipped spear it had stolen from Arkav. It flew so fast Pari could barely track it in the air. Gada didn't even see it until after it had hit.

One moment, Gada was mid-bound, readying his own

spear. The next, he was on his back, nailed to the earth by one wing. *The Corpseman doesn't care about hunters, it wants to destroy us! Not just kill us. Remove us entirely.* She remembered the other High Lords, trapped in their bodies between life and death and knew it planned the same for Lord Gada.

As if to agree with her, the Corpseman dived down towards the prone Deathless.

'Catch up,' said Pari, letting go of Arkav. 'I'll need you.'

Freed of the encumbrance of her brother, Pari shot forward, doing everything she could to reach Gada before the Corpseman did. However, several of the swarm saw her coming and moved to intercept. Despite their alien appearance, she noticed that they flew together in the manner of trained hunters, only these ones could fly as well as glide.

Interesting. The Corpseman has imparted some of its knowledge to these . . . children, but they remain predictable.

She couldn't read much in their faces nor their posture, but the pattern of flight, the way one demon mirrored the movements of the other, told her that they were using a modified version of a classic Sapphire attack pattern. Pari was careful not to let anything show on her face as she approached, lest they be as good at reading opponents as the Corpseman itself.

They came in fast, one slightly to her left, one to the right, accelerating rapidly in the moments before impact.

Keeping her eyes ahead, she flicked out her whip to the right, lodging the barb into an old knotted stump in the ground. The whip went tight and wrenched her round, out of their path. The two flew past with a frustrated buzz and she made a fast turn, releasing the whip as she came full circle to continue towards Gada unimpeded.

Still, she had been too slow.

The Corpseman landed in front of her, completely obscuring Gada's body. It raised its four arms in what Pari considered to be a most ominous manner. Mercifully, the back of its wings were less hypnotic than the insides were and she could still focus.

Before she had time to react, and before the Corpseman had time to strike, another figure took action. Nidra had been close by, and when her son had fallen, she'd moved from her hiding place to get to his side. Now she stood before the Corpseman, a living barrier. Her eyes were squeezed shut and one hand was held up beseechingly.

Very gently, the Corpseman reached out and began to slide her out of its path. Nidra touched its arm, the human one that looked fresh, unarmoured, and then pulled her sapphire-bladed knife from behind her back and lodged it deep in the meat of the shoulder.

The Corpseman reared away, twisting its body to protect itself from further assault, and Pari took advantage, flicking out her whip at the back of its head.

The two thick antennae flicked vertical in alarm and the Corpseman whirled round to face her, forcing her to turn her head away to avoid being mesmerized.

'Hello again,' she said, doing her best to sound like she had happened across an old friend on the road. 'So sorry to interrupt but I really can't let you do that. Lord Gada isn't my favourite Sapphire, not even my second favourite, but we must maintain some standards.'

She was babbling, saying anything to stall it. As she talked the Corpseman's antennae drifted down until they were at a slight downward angle. Pointing at her.

'You know, on reflection, I think you could do with a new name, don't you? Scuttling isn't exactly your preferred method of transport any more and I—'

Perhaps a heartbeat before it moved, Pari's instincts told her to jump back.

She did, using her wings to glide away, but the Corpseman had also leapt, further and faster, closing the gap.

She spun in the air so that she could flee more effectively, aware that she would buy herself seconds at the most.

One jump, and its shadows were at her back. Two and its hands reached out for her.

But now Arkav was in sight, leaping for her as she leapt for him.

'Close your eyes!' she shouted, and whether he heard her or not, he complied, extending both fists. She watched her own fractured reflection in his chest plate grow, and the Corpseman's, larger, behind it, and gave her brother a nudge in the right direction as they crossed paths.

There was the beginning of a screech as sharp fingers ran down the plates on the back of her shoulder, then a thud as Arkav's fists connected.

The Corpseman landed on one knee. Arkav in front of it.

She stepped up behind her brother and grabbed his arm. 'Jump back.'

As he did so, she swung him round, keeping her own gaze on the floor so as to avoid the patterns that tugged at her eyes. Arkav's momentum combined with her exalted strength and he hit the Corpseman full in the face with both feet.

There was a crack of bone breaking but she didn't dare look up to see the effects.

Arkav was standing now, facing her, his back to the Corpseman. 'We fight together,' he said.

'Always.' She took his hands in hers, and they started to swing each other round, using their armour as a set of mirrors, whirling faster and faster. Erratically, chaotically, they lashed out. Not planning, not thinking, relying on lifecycles of training and trust. Some of their blows went wide, but more made contact, forcing the Corpseman to give ground.

No other Tanzanite fought like Pari and her brother, and certainly no Sapphires did. Neither Rochant's nor Samarku's stolen memories would help the demon here. Her fingers clawed at a leathery wing, the blade of her Sky-leg chipped at its face. She knew Arkav was landing hits too.

But none were enough to put it down. Around her, she became aware of the swarm breaking off its attack on the hunters to encircle them. Meanwhile, the Corpseman began to slap their attacks away, and with increasing confidence.

Are we getting tired or is it getting wise to us?

Pari wasn't sure, but either way, they would need a new approach, and soon.

CHAPTER TWENTY-FOUR

Chandni had needed to see its face with her own eyes. It was a Whispercage, but not *the* Whispercage, the one that had taken her baby. This one was different. It was scared of her.

Though the body was warped almost beyond recognition, the tatters of blue clothing and the eyes gave it away. *Satyendra. The thing that I raised.* She had seen the seeds in the face she'd glimpsed many years ago as she'd carried her baby across the Godroad. Now they had bloomed into a terrible, monstrous thing.

By the time she'd crawled into the chamber, Satyendra had fled up the other tunnel with supernatural speed, leaving her with only the memory of his eyes, wide and haunted. She didn't follow. As she waited for Varg and Glider to join her, she tapped the ground and, after a moment, Crowflies hopped down from her shoulder to await instruction.

She stroked the soft feathers of its head with her hand. 'Find my son,' she said. 'Protect him and bring him to me.'

Crowflies nodded once and took wing, going the same way Satyendra had gone. Varg emerged and was quickly forced against the wall by Glider's bulk as it rushed forward, snarling, to where Rochant lay.

Chandni raised a hand and the Dogkin paused, teeth bared on either side of Rochant's head. She removed her hood prompting Varg to do the same as she shook out her long hair. It was hard to be imperious on all fours but she did her best as she turned her attention to Rochant. 'Where is my son?'

Rochant said nothing and gave away nothing. His face was as unreadable as the empty sky. Given the state of him, it impressed her he was even awake. His body seemed to have undergone horrific changes at the hands of the Scuttling Corpseman, and more recent brutalities at Satyendra's hands. Two legs and one arm were broken, and the other twitched uncontrollably at his side.

'Tell me what the Corpseman has done with my son.'

Again, Rochant was silent. The stillness of his face contrasting with the skittering of his alien arm.

It was tempting to follow Crowflies but they had come here for two reasons, and Sa-at was but one of them. Every second that she was here, the flock were fighting for their lives, as were Lord Gada, Lord Arkav, Lady Pari, and two flights of hunters. She could not simply abandon them all. 'Glider, I want you to search the hill for the Corpseman's brood. Kill everything you find until you hear the fighting stop.'

The Dogkin all barked obediently and vanished back the way she'd come.

She heard a soft tut from Rochant. 'The best you'll do is

get its attention, and believe me when I say you do not want that.'

'The Scuttling Corpseman will think twice when it learns I have you.'

'You think threatening me will allow you to control it? Try it if you want and see what happens. You don't know the Corpseman. Nobody does except me. That's why I'm the only one who can stop it and I'm the only one who can guarantee your son's safety.'

She couldn't tell if he was bluffing or not. 'What is your price?'

'Your help. I want to live but not like this. I need a new body to inhabit.'

'You cannot have my son.'

'I confess that I am very impressed with Sa-at. He shows admirable qualities.'

'If he is such a good vessel, why is he back in the Wild? I'd heard he'd been taken to the castle.'

'Ah,' Rochant replied, 'when he learned what his duties would entail, he fled. But you see, that proves what a good match he is. Sa-at is adaptable, bright, resourceful, and has a strong instinct for self-preservation. I could not ask for better.'

A reply came to her lips that was both hers and not hers. 'He is under my protection and you cannot have him.'

'I too am nothing if not adaptable. Should Sa-at be too much for you to sacrifice I'll accept any of his offspring along with a guarantee that you'll do everything in your power to assist the facilitation of my rebirth.'

She stared hard at the floor, thinking, as Varg shuffled over.

'You can't make a deal with him, Chand. He's worse than the bloody demons.'

'This is bigger than my wants and feelings. It's bigger than us. It's even bigger than Rochant's crimes. I have to weigh up what is best for everyone, not just today, but for the future.'

'But—'

She held up a hand. 'I know. Trust me. Whatever we do here, it won't be done lightly. It's time for us to go. I agree that we don't want to be here when the Corpseman returns. Varg, can you carry Rochant up the tunnel?'

Varg crawled over to it and looked upwards. His face immediately fell. 'Fuck.'

'I'll take that as a yes.'

'So,' said Rochant, still on his back. 'Do we have an accord?'

This time, it was Chandni's turn to give nothing away.

Satyendra moved so quickly he seemed to fly. In moments he was bursting from the top of the hill, driven by the need to escape his mother's gaze and an unearthly strength. A broken amber dome surrounded him. There was a ready-made hole for him to climb through but a single sweep of his arm was enough to blast a new exit.

Out here, the buzz of the swarm was louder, but still muted by the roar of blood and emotion in his ears. He could see fighting going on all around him, in the air, on the ground, between human and demon, and demon and demon.

A familiar form lay in the soft grass. It was rolling back and forth in clear distress. *Sa-at.*

He moved towards it, gliding as much as walking.

Something about the way his legs were working had changed but it felt so natural he couldn't tell what it was without looking, and he found himself unable to tear his eyes away from Sa-at.

A need for a friendly face had brought him here, but now that he could see that face, actually see it, a primal urge rose in him. To destroy. He'd had the same reaction the very first time they'd met, but this was stronger. His body was ready for it now. Needed it on some level.

I don't want to destroy my only friend. Do I?

His hands began to shake, trapped between opposing needs.

Sa-at's pain and fear wafted towards him, enticing, and he carried on, his legs moving independently to his thoughts. He might not know what he wanted, but his limbs did.

Other people's emotions were no longer a taste or smell to him, he could see them like clouds of freshly sprayed perfume dappling the air. And like a well-crafted scent, they spoke to him, made him want to sample them.

His face began to open in four places. His tongue, adapted now for things other than aiding speech, prepared to unfurl.

I do want it. So help me, I do!

Sa-at's name slipped from his mind. His human needs faded too, suppressed at least for the moment. All that mattered was that he do this one thing, and then . . .

And then? A little spurt of fear, also swiftly suppressed. Also forgotten.

He was the hunger now. And he would sate it. He would destroy.

And then? That voice again. He could push it away but not quite ignore it.

What will I do afterwards? What will be left of me: Satyendra?

Somehow, he stopped himself. His body was like a giant Dogkin straining at the leash. He fought it. Himself. There were many ways to sate hunger, but only one Sa-at.

He rooted himself to the spot, quivering with effort, forcing his body to wait, pulling his long tongue back inside and folding his face back into place.

I will go to Sa-at, but as myself.

A few more seconds went by as he tested his will against the lure of Sa-at's suffering and found it adequate, just.

Vasinidra and Mother and all the others used me. I was nothing but a vessel to them, but Sa-at helped me when he didn't have to. He saved me from Rochant's prison. I will save him now.

Resolved, he moved forward again. It was just a few more feet. His arms reached out, eager, and—

Something dark shot past his shoulder, landing between him and Sa-at. A Birdkin with white beak and talons. It spread its wings wide, screeched at him. He raised a hand to knock it aside but found himself unable to attack. In its voice lay the echo of his mother's, and in that the echo of ancient authority.

Whatever control he'd mustered shattered at the sound. Even his hunger wilted before it.

Unable to sate himself and unable to stand before those glaring, compound eyes, Satyendra turned and fled. A gliding shadow fleeing the light. Down the hill, away from the fighting. Away from it all.

When he reached the dark of the trees, they welcomed him with open arms.

* * *

Pari swung on the end of Arkav's arm, aiming a kick for the Corpseman's head. It wasn't easy to do given that she couldn't look directly at the demon. Instead, she was using a combination of its three shadows and the reflection in Arkav's armour. She hoped Chandni would get to Rochant before the Corpseman fully adapted to them, and before the swarm could finish closing them in.

Or maybe we can beat it ourselves. We've hit it so many times. It must be more hurt than it's letting on. Perhaps one more strike – this strike – will be enough to drop it.

Her foot swept through empty air, missing by several inches.

Damn!

She landed, braced herself, and was about to swing Arkav when the Corpseman made its move.

Faster than she would have liked, it grabbed them. One hand on her arm, another on Arkav's, two more on his shoulder. Realizing what it was about to do, she let go of her brother.

It didn't make any difference.

Abruptly, they were moving in different directions, Arkav one way, Pari and her brother's arm in the other.

A shoulder plate shattered.

A bone popped from its joint.

Skin tore.

Blood spurted.

Pari was thrown aside. She quickly adjusted, coming to a skidding stop a few feet away. Arkav's arm hit the ground between them. Many different emotions threatened to overwhelm her, but she ignored her thoughts, letting instinct guide her body. In a blur of motion, she had her whip in hand and was leaping forwards – only to find herself coming to a halt.

The Corpseman held her unconscious brother in three hands. Its fourth was clamped on his head, ready to twist. Slowly the antennae protruding from skull and hands moved to point at her, like an army of curious fingers.

'Please,' she said. 'Don't kill him.'

In her last lifecycle, she had been forced to watch as the Corpseman killed an innocent young man. It had shown no mercy then, why would it now?

Suddenly, the noise of the swarm around her altered, from battle drone to a high-pitched whine of alarm. The Corpseman's antennae flicked away from her towards the hill. When she looked that way, she could see white shapes moving swiftly across the hillside, digging and tearing at the things buried there.

Arkav was dropped, forgotten, as the Corpseman leapt high into the air, and sped in the direction of the Dogkin. Some of the swarm followed though the majority continued to fight.

I hope that's your doing, Chandni.

She took a step towards the hill, bracing herself for another meeting with Rochant and the demon, then she looked at her brother and the blood pouring rapidly from his body.

Arkav would want me leave him here and go after the Corpseman. After all, I'm the only one it won't kill. She shook her head. *But I'm not saving a world that doesn't have him in it, and I'm not confident there's going to be any rebirths for a while.*

She let the Corpseman go and went to her brother's side.

'I'm here,' she said as she began to try to staunch the bleeding. 'Don't even think about dying.'

Sa-at became aware of a song, gentle, soft, the one that Crowflies used to sing to him when he was very small. The more he focused on it, the more the noises of the swarm and the fighting faded away.

The chaotic jumble of his thoughts began to settle, the pain in his ears vanished, and he became aware that he was on his back on top of a hill. Crowflies stood by his head, one wing shielding off the view to his left.

'Sa-aat,' it said.

'Crowflies?' He reached out to touch it and was delighted to find it was really there. 'Oh, Crowflies! You came back for me.'

The Birdkin gave a quick nod, tapped his cheek with the side of its beak, and then pointed to his right. When Sa-at looked that way, he saw figures emerging from the shattered amber dome. A woman dressed in dark feathers with hair like his. A bearded man with a hard face and soft eyes followed her, heaving Rochant after him.

Both of them looked tired and out of breath.

'Cha-aan!' said Crowflies, and the woman's head snapped round in their direction. As soon as she saw Sa-at, she smiled, and despite everything that had just happened to him, he smiled back.

The woman stepped through the gap in the dome and started in their direction. 'You found him. Well done, my friend. Well done!'

Crowflies tilted its head in a coy manner.

'You must be Sa-at,' she continued.

Sa-at just stared at her, still smiling.

'My name is Chandni. I'm your mother. There is so much to say and . . .' she shook her head. 'Right now, we need to go. Will you come with me?'

'Yes,' said Sa-at.

She held out a hand to him and he reached up to take it, but before he could, she was stepping back, her attention now on something else. Something above them.

Chandni was turning away from him. He heard her shout 'Varg!' and then her voice was drowned out by the arrival of the swarm. They came like a swirling storm to surround the hill, and ahead of them, bigger, faster, was the Scuttling Corpseman.

Sa-at turned his head towards the grass. He knew that one glance at those wings would steal this consciousness again. Crowflies nipped at his hand, connecting through his old scar, and he heard singing, in his mind this time, soothing and protecting.

Thank you, Crowflies.

He felt rather than saw the Corpseman land. Long feet dug into the grasses, making the earth tremble. The tips of those feet brushed against his back. Had it come to get him? Had it even noticed him? Sa-at wasn't sure, and so he kept very still, hoping dearly that it would leave them all alone.

The man, Varg, was holding Rochant against the side of the dome. He held a spear to Rochant's neck. He could see that his mother was talking but couldn't hear her words.

But her message was easy enough to understand. *Take any action against us and Rochant will die.*

There was a rustling as the Corpseman's wings wrapped around it like a robe, hiding the sigils. The swarm started to land. Some around the edges of the hill, but most went below, out of sight. Their noise diminished to a low hum, allowing him to hear the end of Chandni's sentence.

'. . . utterly. Do not test me on this.'

He felt the pressure of the Corpseman's presence, like a headache before a storm, as it knelt down beside him. One of its four arms came to rest on the top of his head.

'Let him go,' said Chandni.

The Corpseman gestured towards Rochant.

'I am willing to discuss an exchange,' she said.

There was silence.

No, that isn't what it wants. He thought about what Rochant had taught him. To understand the needs of the other person so that you don't have to give up so much. He dared to look up at the Corpseman. It was vaguely man-shaped but much larger, its upper body plated and broad enough to support those huge wings and four arms. It wore a large jawless skull on its head riddled with cracks, its antennae poking through the eye sockets. In places, its carapace had holes that had been plugged with bone. A few of these plugs had fallen away in the fighting.

If I had a very thin knife, I could hurt it.

The fingers resting on his head flexed, establishing a firm grip.

'The moment you do anything to him is the moment Rochant dies,' said Chandni. Her voice was icy calm.

Sa-at continued to study the Corpseman. A section of the skull had been broken off in the fighting, revealing a patch of old greying skin stretched tight.

That must be Rochant's skin from his story, when he fixed its missing face. And it has replaced its missing arm with

Rochant's arm. But why wait for that arm? It had lots and lots of arms to choose from.

An idea began to form in his mind.

Rochant fixed the Corpseman with bits of himself. What if it needs him to heal?

He remembered that they'd made a pact. The Corpseman could not harm Rochant nor the ones he loved. *What if the only way it can get new body parts for itself is if Rochant gives them?*

Oh.

I know what to do.

'Sa-aat!' Crowflies warned.

'I'm sorry,' he replied, carefully removing his hand from the Birdkin's beak and putting it on top of his head so that he could feel the Corpseman's fingers next to his own. He ran his thumb over the small antennae sprouting from its knuckles.

There was connection, similar to when he shared his thoughts with Crowflies but instead of there being a link, it was like throwing himself into a river. He couldn't stop himself going under, but he could make sure he didn't swallow the water.

The Corpseman didn't speak but it was there, all around him. Watching. Studying. In its own way, it was surprised. Sa-at realized that aside from Rochant, no one had ever sought contact with it before.

Hello, he thought. *I'm Sa-at. I'd like to hear your story.*

CHAPTER TWENTY-FIVE

Sa-at was in darkness. It wasn't like being outside at night. It was a closer, smothering dark. And he was alone.

Utterly alone.

And then, he sensed another. A quivering in the air announced their presence, along with a scent, very different from the larvae he knew, or the hated Dogkin and Birdkin.

Though it would change its shell many times in their relationship, he could always smell and taste the soul beneath. His friend, his saviour, his creator: Rochant.

He remembered Rochant carrying him from a place of death. Of them making a pact together, sealed with blood and skin and bone. As he grew, Rochant tended to him, helped him grow strong. In return, he did as Rochant asked.

And Rochant asked for many things.

The death of other humans to bring down the hunters. The death of small creatures of the Wild that Rochant could claim as his own. Always, Rochant would ask that others die.

He complied. Of course he did. Rochant had bound him via a pact, had taught him everything. Did he not want to restore his people to power? (*I do not know my people. Who were they?*) Did he not want to rule the Wild in Rochant's name? (*I do not want this.*) Surely, after all Rochant had done for him, the least he could do was grant the man's desire?

To make Rochant Deathless, he captured another Deathless named Samarku. Samarku's thoughts were strange. They did not match the truth he knew. No matter how many times he sampled them and prodded them, he could not match them to the shapes already in his mind. But he learned much. Rochant was always keen that he learn.

But what do I want? Sa-at wondered.

The answer was simple: To please Rochant *(to be one with Rochant).*

To restore his people *(to restore myself).*

To have revenge on those that cast him down *(yes, this is true).*

To finish the joining *(to finish the joining).*

Rochant had promised that they would build a new world together, one that combined the sky and the earth and the creatures of suns and shadows just as they were to be combined. For Rochant's blood was in his veins. Rochant's skin was joined to his. But as time went on, that process stopped. Rochant would fix foreign bones to his body instead of his own, ones that sat there, not bonding, inert.

He did not understand why.

Rochant told him that as he grew, the cost of giving parts of himself was becoming too great, but even if Rochant gave up a whole shell, he would soon return with another.

Every time he tried to raise this, Rochant would shower him with words and ideas, leaving him confused.

And soon he was distracted with plans of conquest. Through Rochant and Samarku he learned first of House Sapphire and then of the other houses. Rochant taught him how they worked and what made them powerful. One day they would take that power for themselves.

After Rochant became Deathless, he went away a lot, leaving Sa-at alone. In those times, he would work hard, learning and planning, and testing his strength against others in the Wild. They were strange at first, but soon became predictable. In that way, they were no different from the humans living on the forest's edge. He found ways to catch and crush them all.

The pact allowed him to kill any human he pleased, so long as they were not the ones called Nidra and Pari. Over the years he would meet both and touch their minds. In their ways they both loved Rochant but their pictures of him were wrong and contradictory, and their love for him flawed.

He did not understand what made them special nor why Rochant singled them out.

And Nidra had cut off one of his arms.

He did not like Nidra at all.

But it had meant that when he found Rochant again this last time, he had been able to take one of the man's arms and join it to himself. That was fair. The pact had forced him to lose an arm and the pact demanded it was restored. There was a little essence in the arm just as there had been with Rochant's blood and it had been good to finally mix more with his own.

Rochant did not seem to understand this, which made no

sense as he understood everything, had already promised everything. Sa-at wanted more but the pact forbade him from taking it. Oh, they had come so far together and yet still he was left incomplete and alone.

Why is this? Have I done something wrong?

Though Rochant assured him that he was doing well, it rankled. Yes, he had his children, but they were crafted to be simple-minded and violent, poor substitutes for what he wanted. Yes, he had evolved and become more powerful than ever, but what use was power if it did not grant your desires? Yes, it was a joy to fly, but the sky was even more desolate than the land.

I have been so very patient. Perhaps when the last enemies are defeated and Rochant's power is absolute, we will be together again, and I will be whole.

Despite it all, I am so very lonely.

The fighting around Pari was intensifying. While she tended to her brother's injury, a desperate struggle was unfolding around her as the swarm tried to get to them through the hunters that had formed a human fence.

Kneeling beside Arkav, she'd managed to staunch the worst of the bleeding but worried it was too little, too late. He'd lost a lot of blood in a very short time and was at least as tired as she was.

We need to be in a place he can rest. In our lands, at home, surrounded by comfort and good food. Not languishing in the mud on the borders between House Sapphire and the Wild.

Arkav wasn't saying anything, but his eyes were open, watching with a mix of sadness and love.

'No need for that,' she said firmly. 'You're going to be fine.'

His eyes flicked away suddenly, making her turn. Nidra was running towards them. There was a wild look in her eye and a determined set to her jaw. She took in Arkav's situation at a glance, seemed to dismiss it, and crouched heavily beside Pari, pulling the plugs from her ears. 'Good,' she gasped, catching her breath. 'You're both together.'

Pari tucked away the pain in her heart. 'I'm not sure what's good about this situation, my dear. After all—'

'Not now,' snapped Nidra. 'You talk too much. We're losing. They have the numbers and they're using sound to coordinate. And they've weaponized it. When our hunters plugged their ears for protection, they put themselves at a disadvantage.'

'But if they unplug their ears, they won't be able to fight. The swarm's infernal noise will overwhelm them.'

'Not if we make our own. When I give the signal, strike your brother's armour, make it sing.'

Before Pari could reply, Nidra signalled the ring of hunters and they stepped aside to allow a single Flykin to pass through. It immediately dived towards Arkav, no doubt attracted by his wound. There was no time to intercept it, no time to get clear without abandoning him, so she lunged forward – knees one side of him, her hands on the other – to make her body a protective barrier between her brother and the demon.

'Now!' shouted Nidra.

Arkav raised his other arm across his face, and she struck his bracer with her own, the crystal plates trilling unpleasantly together.

Pari braced for the demon's attack.

It didn't come.

She looked up to find it standing over them, swaying, stunned.

'Again!' said Nidra.

Pari looked at Arkav.

Arkav looked at Pari.

She nodded to him and he reached up and slapped her wing with the crystal knuckles of his gauntlet. Again, there was a ringing, and the demon flinched away.

Before it could recover, Pari jumped up and tore off its head.

She looked back towards Nidra and smiled. 'I think you've just found something brilliant.'

Nidra gave her a tired smile.

One bound took Pari next to the nearest hunters, fighting for their life against a group of the Corpseman's children. 'Attack on my command,' she said and clapped her gauntlets together.

As if struck by invisible hands, the demons all flinched, their delicate antennae recoiling from the sound.

'Now!'

The hunters made short work of their defenceless enemy.

'Protect Lord Arkav with your lives,' she ordered, and set off to find Lord Gada. Between them, they could turn the tide of battle. At least until the Corpseman returned. She still had no answer for it.

Every time we meet it is two steps ahead. It reads my intentions, knows my weaknesses. Arkav's suffering is a tactic to keep me busy while it pursues its goals. None of my tactics work for more than a few moments. It won't kill me and I can't kill it, but everyone around us is dying! I have to do something. But what? She sighed. *One thing at a time, Pari. One thing at a time.*

Another leap and a glide took her to the nearest skirmish, and again her hands came together, resonant, cutting through the drone, turning the tide.

It took Sa-at a few moments to reconnect with his body. *I am so small! And so . . . vulnerable.*

Very little had changed. The Corpseman remained crouched behind him, Crowflies was in front, feathers bristling. Chandni – *my Mother!* – had moved over to Rochant, who was still being threatened by Varg's spear.

Further out, the fighting had stopped between Birdkin and the swarm, though it continued to rage on the other side of the hill.

But around him, everything was incredibly still and quiet.

Chandni raised her head to look directly at the Corpseman and spoke without fear. 'You have what belongs to me. I will take back my son and then we will leave you in peace. In return for his life, I will spare Rochant's life, but he will not be returned to you. Rochant will live with me as insurance. If you or your servants trespass in my domain, if they harm those under my protection, if they plot against me, then Rochant will suffer. You will cease your conquest of my peoples, human and Wild, and you will leave this place.'

She took a step forward and extended her hand. 'Now, release my son and return him to me.'

The Corpseman's grip remained firm on Sa-at's head, and he could see the antennae shifting back and forth between Chandni and Rochant. It reminded Sa-at of a predator studying prey before an attack.

'No,' said Sa-at, and then louder, 'No!' Everyone, every demon, every human, eyes and feelers, they all turned towards him.

His throat went tight.

He knew Chandni's proposal wasn't going to work and that he needed to say something but it was so hard to find the words at times like these.

'I . . .'

Chandni knelt down so that she was closer to his level. She moved slowly, non-threateningly. 'What is it, Sa-at? Are you in pain?'

'No.'

'I ask you a second time, is the Corpseman hurting you?'

'No, it isn't that.' He turned as best he could in the Corpseman's grip so he could look directly at it. 'I know what you want. If you agree to Chandni's terms, I'll give it to you.'

He felt the Corpseman's scrutiny like a finger through the skull. A hundred of his own memories flashed before his eyes, of loneliness, of wanting to be held, of wanting friends, family, and the anger of being denied it for so long.

The Corpseman let go of his head.

Very slowly, he got up and moved towards his mother.

She too, got up, and opened her arms.

They embraced, and he sank into the soft feathers of her cloak. It was both familiar and wonderfully new all at the same time. 'I'm here,' he whispered.

Where their cheeks touched, tears mingled.

'I'm so sorry,' she said.

'Why?'

'Oh Sa-at, too many things. Be patient a while longer and then we will make up for lost time. Tell me, what does the Scuttling Corpseman want?'

'What we want. To be loved.' He paused, then glanced over at Rochant. 'And it wants his face.'

The flock covered the Scuttling Corpseman and Rochant like some great wriggling shroud. Varg couldn't bring himself to look but Chandni kept her eyes on what transpired. Though Rochant's pleas and screams were drowned out by the feathers now, his writhing body was still recognizable beneath the smothering wings.

For better or worse I have allowed this to happen. I will not flinch from it.

Sa-at stood alongside, holding her hand. Ever since their embrace, he'd kept in contact with her. It was almost too much. It was just right.

I should be happy, she told herself, and yet it was hard not to lament the years lost. Her time raising Satyendra had been so tortuous and so . . . meaningless. What had all that sacrifice been for? What had it achieved? If she had run away with Varg as a young woman, she could have had such a different life. Perhaps this reunion with Sa-at would have happened much earlier.

She squeezed her son's hand. 'You have saved many lives. I'm proud of you.'

His face lit up but when he took a breath to speak no words came out.

A strange mix of courageous and shy. I will encourage the former and fix the latter. He will need to be stronger if he is to inherit my mantle.

Crowflies came to land on her shoulder. 'Cha-aan,' it said, and she knew its meaning perfectly. *They have finished their work.*

'Come back to me, my children,' she murmured, and they did, exploding up and out in a spiralling flurry before settling around her in neat rows.

The Corpseman was already stooping to pick up Rochant's body. It no longer wore the skull. Instead, it wore Rochant's face stitched to the shell of its head just below the antennae.

'We have an accord?'

It stretched its new jaw startlingly low and rotated it twice before answering. 'Yes.'

Strange. It doesn't sound like Rochant.

'No,' it replied, the antennae flexing in response to her thoughts. 'I sound like me.'

'Then we are done here.'

It looked at the bundle in its arms. A patch of old grey skin sat where Rochant's face had been. Somehow, he was still alive. Chandni didn't think about how that was possible.

'Yes,' said the Corpseman.

'Let us hold fast to this pact,' said Chandni, 'and when we are gone, let our children hold it.'

'Yes,' said the Corpseman.

She didn't mean to ask but for once her self control slipped. 'What will you do with . . .' she wasn't sure if what remained of Rochant still warranted a name so she pointed at him.

The Corpseman gave a strange wistful smile and unfurled its great wings. 'Farewell.'

It took to the sky and the swarm followed. Very few demons left the side of the field where the hunters were. She waited until the noise of their wings had faded and then moved to the edge of the hill so that the Deathless and their followers would see her.

'Varg,' she said, 'I have another task for you. I need you to take a message to Lady Pari.'

Pari stood amid the carnage. There was no doubt they'd broken the enemy. Once she and Lord Gada had started using their armour to stun the swarm, their hunters made short work of them. But the price had been high.

Too high, really. We should have thought of this much sooner.

Arkav was stable, and in the care of two Sapphire hunters. Mia looked like she wanted to lead the remains of her flight in pursuit of the Corpseman, while Lord Gada Sapphire looked like he'd be happy never to see the swarm again. Incredibly, Nidra had fallen asleep, looking more peaceful than Pari had seen her in years.

'Well,' said Pari. 'That was incredibly unpleasant. Shall we go home? I think I've had enough of chasing the Corpseman for one lifecycle.'

'Yes,' replied Gada. 'Please come and stay with us until your brother is recovered.'

'Thank you.'

'It's the least we can do.'

'I couldn't agree more.'

Mia stepped forward. 'Forgive the interruption, but what about that?' She pointed towards the hill. On the top of it was Chandni, or whatever the Honoured Mother had become. A black silhouette of a figure, both regal and oddly threatening.

'We should purge the hill,' said Gada, 'and anything on it.'

Pari nodded but it was hard to care. *After all this, we've failed. The Corpseman has escaped. Rochant has escaped. It was all for nothing.*

While Mia led her flight towards the hill, Gada oversaw the collection of the bodies. It would be tough, unpleasant work taking them home, but they would bear it gladly, rather than leave their fallen comrades to the mercy of the Wild.

After a while, Pari became aware of a single Birdkin watching her from the trees. *The one with the white beak.*

It signalled for her to follow it.

'Oh, go away,' she muttered. 'Whatever this is, I'm too tired for it.'

It signalled again, impatient.

She told the hunters to take care of Arkav as if their lives depended on it and wearily set off towards the Birdkin. Soon, she found herself in the shadow of the trees opposite a haggard looking Varg.

'This had better be good,' she said.

'I dunno about good,' Varg replied. 'But the Corpseman is gonna leave you alone from now on.'

'That was already the case. It's everyone else I'm worried for.'

'Nah, that's not what I mean. They've done a deal. You're safe. The road-born are safe. Everyone is.'

'What, the Corpseman's just going to live quietly and knit socks?'

Varg shrugged.

'Who did the deal?'

'Don't matter. Point is, it's done.'

'And what about Rochant?'

This time Varg shuddered. 'Oh, he's fucked.'

'Marvellous. There's just one more thing, when are we getting our High Lord Spinel back?'

'What?'

'The Corpseman did something to him to stop him moving between lives. We need him back.'

'Sorry, we didn't know anything about the High Lords. Don't reckon that's going to happen anytime soon.'

'Well, this is . . . unacceptable!'

'Like I said. It's done. I'm just passing on the message.'

'I'd rather have heard it from Chandni herself. Is she too important to talk to me these days, or just scared?'

'Nah, she ain't scared of anything now. It's just she promised you'd never meet again, so you won't. Probably won't see me after this neither.'

'Varg, are you sure you know what you're getting yourself into? I may be difficult at times, eccentric even, but Chandni might be a bit of a stretch, even for you.'

'I'm all right.'

'Well, thank you for your service. Despite how it ended, you gave me many years of loyalty, and you even made me laugh once or twice. A talent I find distressingly rare in people these days.' She smiled at him fondly for a moment, then let it drop. 'I think it is probably for the best that we don't see each other again. Best for your health, I mean.'

'Yeah.' He turned to go.

'Oh, and Varg?'

'Yeah?'

'Good luck. I think you're going to need it.'

'Yeah.'

And with that, she left him there.

Arkav was conscious when she got back. 'What's going on?'

'Later, dear brother. I need to sleep for a day or three. If you're still with us when I wake up, I'll give you the full story.'

CHAPTER TWENTY-SIX

True to her word Pari slept for days.

They had returned to Vasinidra's castle with Mia and the remainder of his hunters, while Lord Gada had taken up duties managing things in his High Lord's absence.

Pari vaguely remembered bathing and waking for a series of meals that blurred blandly together. For most of the time, she had drifted and dreamed, recovering slowly.

The next time she woke, though, it was with the sudden awareness that something had changed. Old instincts became alert, and adrenaline surged through her body. She cracked one eye open just a little and saw that she was surrounded.

Seven figures, blue tinged in the gemslight, all wearing robes that were half black and half white: The Bringers of Endless Order. 'Oh,' she said, closing her eye again. 'It's you.'

One of the Bringers leaned forward over the bed. 'It is time for us to go.'

'Yes, yes, I know. My brother and I discussed it and agreed that we will go when he's ready.'

'But Lord Arkav's armour has been ruined and his body maimed. It will take years to restore him.'

'What's a few years between friends, hmm? Besides, you'll have plenty to keep you busy. There are so many rebirths and new ascensions to oversee that the years will fly by.'

The Bringers paused long enough for her to open her eyes again. She saw the one she'd been talking to exchanging an awkward look with their peers. 'What aren't you telling me?'

'We do not have years,' replied the lead Bringer. 'We have to go now.'

Pari sat up. 'I'm sorry but that simply won't do. We have a society to rebuild! You have a sacred duty!'

Another Bringer said, 'Show her.'

'Show her,' chorused the others.

The lead Bringer sighed and began to unfasten a set of hidden ties.

Pari did her best not to appear eager. She'd always wanted to know what the Bringers were hiding.

Where the black and white fabric parted was a slice of desiccated body, the skin dry and tight on the bones, reminding Pari more of one of the Wild's demons than a person. The stomach was concave, with veins standing proud like purple Wormkin. Organs hung from the Bringer's hips, a heart, a kidney, and others that she didn't recognize, each held in a filmy bag of opaque skin and plumbed in with tubes. Other limbs sprouted from the sides of their body, but Pari could only see the beginnings of them, not the ends and so could not discern their purpose.

Whatever she was looking at was ancient and brittle, and though she was no expert, it was clear that some of the organs were past their best.

They're dying. In fact, from the look of them, they're more than halfway there already.

The Bringer closed the robe. 'Now, do you understand?'

Pari nodded slowly. 'But if I take you now, there might not be anything left for your replacements to save.'

'If they arrive,' said the lead Bringer.

'If,' agreed the others.

'We have lost hope. Perhaps they've forgotten us,' said another.

'Or abandoned us,' finished the lead Bringer. 'You have to help us or all is lost.'

Pari took a deep calming breath. There had been a time, many lifecycles ago, when she had believed in so many things: Her High Lord, the honour of the Crystal Dynasties, the importance of following the rules. That faith had long since crumbled, and now it seemed that beneath their masks even the Bringers were in need of help. *Well, Pari,* she thought, *you're going to have to find a way to fix all this because nobody else is going to.*

She looked at each of the seven figures in turn. 'Given that you're desperate, I take it I can name my price?'

Only the briefest of glances were exchanged before the lead Bringer nodded.

'In that case, here are my conditions: When you go home, I'll be coming with you, and we'll work together to sort out this whole mess.' She waited for their consent before continuing. It was given quickly. 'Good. Next, you are going to tell me everything I want to know about anything I care to ask.' Again, they conceded. 'And before we leave, you are going to help me make sure that the Deathless stay Deathless while I'm gone.'

'But,' said the lead Bringer, 'we do not have time to bring them back or re-attune new ones. There are too many.'

'I know. But I have a solution for that.' She sat up straighter, a gleam in her eye. 'Now listen closely, this is what you're going to do . . .'

As the suns set, the Whispercage moved with increasing speed. It had his essence scent, that unmistakable mix of hopes and fears, and it could not help but follow it.

This part of the forest was dangerous. There were many eyes watching, many trees listening, the hated Dogkin pack ever-vigilant, but the Whispercage knew how to use the lengthening shadows to its advantage. It moved with predatory grace, silent. Plants shivered as it passed but they did not speak nor give it away, and soon it arrived in the deep Wild, a place where its prey would feel safe.

Yes, it was close now.

There was a space between the trees where a fat mossy stone sat. A figure perched on the stone. A human with a Birdkin's posture, he was dressed in a coat of feathers. He was tying leaves to the end of a stick, his tongue poking from between his lips in concentration.

The Whispercage was virtually upon him by the time he noticed something was wrong. He started to look up, but by then it was already reaching out . . .

Sa-at looked up to find himself face to face with the Whispercage.

And he smiled.

'Hello. You're early, but it's okay. I'm nearly done.'

He finished tying his knot and leant the stick against the

rock. Then he took another stone from his pocket and began striking it to make sparks. The Whispercage stood, its arms reaching towards him, quivering with impatience. 'Sorry,' he muttered, 'this bit's hard.'

It took a while, Sa-at was still learning how to do this, but eventually, the dry leaves caught.

'Yes!'

He hopped from the stone, stick in hand, and walked around the Whispercage, a thin plume of smoke following. When he'd made four circuits, he planted the stick into the earth.

That should keep the Dogkin from smelling it.

He sat back on the rock. 'Varg's been teaching me some new words. Do you want to hear them? They're really crunchy and thick.'

The Whispercage's eyes bored into him.

'And you can put them together too. I think my favourite one is . . .'

Sa-at chattered away like the Birdkin in the trees, and as he did so, the Whispercage calmed and became still. Not a hunting stillness, but a peaceful one. It came to him every sunsset now, and he told it about his day, and his worries and his triumphs. And each time it listened, saying nothing. When he was done, it would incline its head once, as if to say thank you or goodbye, Sa-at wasn't sure which. Then it would leave.

He did not know about the Whispercage's incessant hunger, nor the emptiness that could never be filled, but he did know that it needed him. Because it was his friend now, and friends needed each other.

Footsteps approached, and Sa-at glanced round to see

Varg making his way through the trees. He knew that when he looked back, the Whispercage would be gone. He also knew that it would return tomorrow.

'All right?' asked Varg as he joined Sa-at on the rock.

'Yes,' Sa-at replied, giving Varg a hug. *Varg is my friend too. And he's Chandni's special friend. She makes his cheeks change colour.*

'What are you grinning about?' asked Varg.

'Nothing.'

'Bollocks.'

'What's "bollocks" mean?'

Varg looked up towards the sky. 'Oh shit, not this again.'

'What? I like learning new words.'

'Yeah, I know. It's just . . . I'm still getting used to all this.'

'Me too.'

'I thought you grew up here.'

'I did. Me and Crowflies. But now it's me and Crowflies and you and Chandni and all the Birdkin and the Dogkin and the Stranger and those—'

Varg patted his arm. 'I know, I know, it's a bit of a head-fuck. Don't ask what that means. Just came out here to see how you are.' He looked at the stick. 'What's that for?'

'To stop the Dogkin knowing where I am.' He looked up at Varg. 'How did you know where I am?'

'I didn't. I was looking for you though. I think maybe the trees led me here.' He shook his head. 'I'll never get used to that. Anyway, I was wondering if you wanted to do something together?'

Sa-at beamed. 'Yes!'

Varg's beard curled as he smiled. 'Was hoping you would. It's going to be hard work, mind.'

'Yes! I'll do it. What is it?'

Varg put a hand on his shoulder. 'It's time we built a home.'

'But, this is home.'

'Yeah, but we need a roof over our heads and a door we can shut against the cold.'

'Somewhere that's warm?'

Varg nodded. 'Bloody right. It's all right you or me sleeping rough but it ain't right for a baby.'

Sa-at realized that Varg was watching him very closely. 'A baby that you've made or one the Wild had brought as a gift or one you've stolen?'

'The first one. Of course, the fucking first one!'

'That's good.'

'You're going to have a sister or a brother, or maybe two.' His cheeks went rosy. 'Maybe more in time, I dunno.'

'How soon will it be here?'

'Too fucking soon. We should get started.'

'Okay.'

They stood up and set off, Sa-at giving one last wave to the shadows as they went.

Chandni listened as the trees whispered, reassuring her that Varg and Sa-at were safe. It pleased her that they were happy together, and it suited her that they were distracted.

She stood between two elderly birch trees, taking shelter from the rain beneath their thin branches. Their leaves caught the rain and tilted to divert the water away. Not a single drop found her shoulders nor the many feathers in her hair.

The Wild was in her heart now. It loved her and she loved it in return. Not every piece, of course. Some parts of the forest remained aloof or afraid, and many demons lurked on her borders, threatening. But none of them frightened her. With the Scuttling Corpseman and its swarm gone, and many of the old powers destroyed, Chandni was in a unique position to take advantage.

One day, the Deathless will recover. One day, the Corpseman will return. I must begin preparations.

She had already started building alliances with her neighbours. They did not know that her flock was decimated, nor that she was still adjusting to her new role. Life as a Sapphire had taught her to hide her weaknesses, and her time with Varg had taught her a different kind of bravery. When the demons saw her, they saw a figure of iron and darkness, and they were afraid.

Never again would Chandni serve another, she'd rather die than let that happen. Varg would build her a home and she would build a community, part family, part army, all hers.

The trees murmured of a visitor, allowing her a moment to prepare before Kennelgrove emerged from the shadows. It had recovered somewhat from its wounds, but had maintained its odd brand of bitter deference.

'Prince Kennelgrove, welcome. I have something to ask of you.'

'You say "ask", I hear "demand".'

She did not rise to its petulance. 'We agreed upon fair terms, remember? And one of those terms was that you would lift the curse on Fiya, Glider, and the rest of the pack.'

It mumbled something incoherent.

'You gave your word as a Prince of the Wild.' The trees rumbled agreement.

'A prince, bah! What use is being a prince when I am standing before a queen?'

'When the pack's year of servitude is at an end, you will return them to their original forms, hale and hearty. That is my decree.'

'But then who will serve poor Kennelgrove?'

'That is my decree,' she repeated, this time with a stronger note of finality.

The demon bowed and slunk away, bemoaning its fate.

After it had left, Crowflies swooped low through the branches to land on her outstretched arm. She stroked its head lovingly. The two of them had a bond: Both loved Sa-at and both had been beloved of Murderkind. And both of them wanted revenge.

'Have you found it?'

Crowflies nodded. There was a smugness to the puff of its chest that suggested more.

'Have you caught it?'

This time when Crowflies nodded it left its head down, inviting her to scratch.

Chandni complied. 'Well done. Bring it to me.'

Crowflies shrieked a command. Not long afterwards Glider and Rayen arrived, along with a cluster of Birdkin. Between them all, they dragged a ragged, spindly demon. A Whispercage, but not just any Whispercage.

My Whispercage. The one that took Satyendra from me all those years ago.

She could still remember the first time she saw it, the way it had glided across the long grass towards her. The Chandni then had been terrified and a part of her had carried that fear ever since, like a splinter in her heart.

Beaks and paws pinned the Whispercage down, allowing her to study it.

Away from the shadows it was a strange and miserable thing. Strung out and hollow. It hissed piteously, unable to move nor free itself. Chandni took in every detail of the demon. From the elongated bones, to the split face and tongue that extended, too long, too far, slashing wildly back and forth.

I will remember this moment, she thought. *I will make this the memory that comes when I think of you.*

She took a deep breath and made herself stare at it. Stare directly at her fear. And then, with a simple gesture, she ordered her followers to destroy it.

There was a flash of movement, a flurry of biting, and pecking, and stabbing, and rending.

And it was done.

The Whispercage was no more.

Chandni's fear was no more.

She swept out into the rain without a backwards glance, her pack and flock falling in behind, a living train of white and black, of fur and feather.

The trees bowed as she passed.

Not a single rain drop touched her.

EPILOGUE

Vasinidra woke up.

He had been drifting, dreaming. Oblivious. But there was something that felt like it was important. Someone had said something to him while he was between lives. He'd had similar experiences before but this time the words he'd heard had been clearer and delivered by a familiar, and fairly blunt voice.

He found himself picturing Lady Pari, diving past him in her armour. A bright light among many stranger, smaller ones. With the memory came her message:

'This is all on you again until I come back. Don't fuck it up.'

He opened his eyes to be presented with the well-worn sight of the Rebirthing Chamber. Straps bound him fast to a cold stone slab and two Bringers loomed over him, masked, dressed in their robes.

'One man is welcome here,' said the first. 'Are you that man?'

Vasinidra frowned. *Something isn't right.* He still felt groggy from his time between lives and his brain was struggling to keep up. Experience told him that he'd better recover quickly if he was to convince the Bringers of Endless Order that he wasn't an abomination.

'I am Vasinidra, High Lord of House Sapphire.'

'High Lord Vasinidra is welcome,' said the first Bringer. 'If you are he.'

Wait. I know that voice. But it can't be . . .

'If,' echoed the second.

He turned to look at the other Bringer and noticed they only had one arm. *I think I know that voice too. And why are there only two of them? What is going on?*

'If you are he,' continued the first Bringer, you will prove your humanity.'

'Gada?'

There was a pause, then the Bringer added. 'E-examine yourself, and tell us what you find.'

Vasinidra tried to sit up but the straps held him firmly. 'Gada, I know it's you. Take off that mask and tell me what's going on.'

The two figures looked at each other, and then the first, the one that sounded like Gada, said again, 'Examine yourself, and tell us what you find.'

He looked down at his body and saw a slender, adolescent frame. *One of mine and Mia's sons. The body is still young, so I can't have been away for more than a year or two*. The usual marks were there, golden tattoos that still glistened in their newness. Now that he attended to it, he felt another mark on his forehead that had not been there in previous lifecycles. *But that makes no sense. Only the High Lord of a house could add to the legend of a Deathless, and I am High Lord!*

'I find my body as expected. You, however, do not hold up to scrutiny. Your robes hang in the wrong fashion. Your demeanour is off for a Bringer. There should be seven, one for each of the houses. There are always seven and none of them has ever sounded like my brother!'

The second Bringer chuckled in a most unlikely way. 'I don't know about you, Lord Gada, but I'm convinced it's him.' They pulled back their mask and hood to reveal the face of Lord Arkav Tanzanite. 'How about we release you, High Lord Sapphire, and then we explain everything?'

'And the Bringers agreed to that?' asked Vasinidra, reclining in his throne.

Gada nodded like he still couldn't believe it either.

'They did,' agreed Arkav. 'It was that or rot here with the rest of us.'

Vasinidra looked through the glazed windows at the familiar view of the sky. Despite the skittering clouds, it remained, unchanging. 'Lady Pari made all of this happen?'

Arkav's eyes sparkled. 'She did.'

'And the Bringers themselves . . . are gone?'

'Yes. They taught Lord Gada and me the secrets of their rituals and left. Now that you're back we need to travel to the other houses and bring back those Deathless that have fallen. High Lord Spinel is trapped between lives by the Scuttling Corpseman. We don't know where he is or if we'll ever get him back. But we can restore High Lords Ruby, Jet, Peridot, Opal, and Tanzanite.'

Vasinidra shook his head in amazement. 'I hope your

second rebirth ceremony is more convincing than mine was.'

'Actually,' said Gada, 'you were our second ceremony.'

His eyes widened. 'Do you mean?'

'Yes.' For once, Gada's smile was full of vigour. Behind him, a woman's voice sang for entrance.

Mother!

As Vasinidra stood up, he saw her. Paint gave her an ageless look, but she was in a body in its middle years, lean and strong. He'd met the vessel before many times. Her name had been Yi, and she was Nidra's agent and messenger.

He rushed forward to embrace her, but she bowed low, forcing him to pause.

'I welcome you back to our world, High Lord Sapphire, and recognize your authority in all things.'

She's making a statement to my brother and Lord Arkav Tanzanite. I should make one too.

He straightened, nodded. 'And I welcome you home, Lady Nidra, returned child of the Sapphire Everlasting. You come back to us at a time of difficulty and we welcome your strength and counsel.'

She came forward then and clasped his wrists. He felt small next to her, and it had little to do with his half-grown body. 'My High Lord, my son. Your new legend suits you well.'

My what? He suddenly recalled the new tattoo on his forehead. In all the excitement he'd not yet examined it. 'Please, Mother, describe it to me.'

'You bear the golden disc of Fortune's Eye, greatest of our three suns. Like it, you have protected those beneath you, and lead us from dark places. Like it, you will continue to do so, day after day, cycle after cycle.'

He felt the burden land in his chest with a thump.

'But, like Fortune's Eye, you will not be alone in the sky.'

Vasinidra gave a half smile. He had his family around him and good friends in the other houses. He had Mia and a land full of the best people he could hope for. They were wounded, but they would recover, and perhaps salvage some good from the senseless horrors caused by Rochant Un-Sapphire.

But Lady Pari was right, in the end it was all on him.

He vowed not to fuck it up before she returned.

Acknowledgements

I've had the pleasure of not one but two editors working on the Boundless, Natasha and Jack, who have aided the process in many unseen ways. Special thanks to Jack who endured several calls with me and helped bring the book more tightly into focus.

They are not alone, and as ever a big thanks to the team at Harper*Voyager* who work so hard to make our books the best that they can be. And a special thanks to Chris Tulloch McCabe for yet another fab cover.

Of course, a massive thanks has to go to Juliet, my superhero agent who has been there for me in the bad times as well as the good. You are the best!

And lastly, thank you for reading. It means the world that you do. See you in the next lifecycle!